MW01674714

A DISTANT MAGIC

THE GUARDIAN TRILOGY: BOOK 3

M.J. PUTNEY

PANDAMAX PRESS

COPYRIGHT

A Distant Magic: The Guardians Trilogy, Book 3

ISBN: 978-1-948880-53-4

Published by Pandamax Press, a division of Mary Jo Putney, Inc.

Cover by Kimberly Killion of The Killion Group.

Pandamax logo by Elizabeth Person.

THE GUARDIAN TRILOGY

A Kiss of Fate

Stolen Magic

A Distant Magic

PANDAMAX
PRESS

Praise for
The Guardian Trilogy

"Magic and traditions of all kinds, an abundance of well-delineated characters, and fascinating historical and political detail make [*A Distant Magic*] the most complex and unusual [Guardian novel] to date."

—*Library Journal*

"[*Stolen Magic* is] a wondrously original tale that mixes the dark vision of the film *Underworld* with the beauty of the unicorn tapestries... a haunting evening's read."

—*Romantic Times*

"Putney's fully imagined magical system, combined with Georgian detail, is a terrific setting for a tale of intrigue and danger... The sexual tension is high in this enchanting blend of fantasy and romance."

—*Booklist* (starred review)

"Enchanting... Putney does a fine job of weaving magical elements together with actual historical events to create a rich, romantic tapestry."

—*Publishers Weekly*

To all who have fought for our freedoms,
both the famous and the unknown.
And especially for those who have
paid a high price for doing so.

ACKNOWLEDGMENTS

A special thanks to Patricia Rice and Susan King, who have had to endure my pleas that if I ever again express an interest in writing a book based on a social movement, they should haul out the Salmon of Correction and *hit* me.

Even more thanks to John, who cheerfully accepts my crankiness when The Book isn't going well.

Thanks also to my most excellent editor, Betsy Mitchell, and my two agents, Ruth Cohen and Robin Rue, for supporting the concept of this story.

I am amazingly lucky in my writing career to work with such fine people.

Never doubt that a small group of committed citizens can change the world. In fact, it is the only thing that ever has.

—*Margaret Mead*

BOOK ONE

STRIKING A SPARK

1733

CHAPTER ONE

Valletta, Island of Malta
Autumn 1733

THE TWO FOREIGN gentlemen strolling through Valletta's market square looked like they had pockets worth picking. Nikolai quietly shadowed them through the crowds, knowing they would never notice a boy his size in the noisy throng. A dozen or more languages babbled above his head. He recognized all of them, and could make himself understood in most. Valletta was the crossroads of the Mediterranean, a place where Europe, Africa, and Asia met and exchanged their goods.

The men had the pale coloring of northern Europeans. When Nikolai got close enough to hear their conversation, he found that they spoke in English. That was one of his better languages, since his mother had had a taste for English sailors.

Other foreigners roamed the market, but these two had the air and garments of wealth—and they were fool enough to walk alone, with no guards. They'd be lucky to get back to their ship with the clothes still on their backs.

Nikolai followed the men, slipping behind a tethered donkey cart to get closer to his quarry. His talent for going unnoticed had enabled him to keep from starving in the years since his grandmother's death, though he seldom managed to be well fed.

The taller Englishman, a powerfully built fellow whose dark red hair was heavily streaked with gray, stopped to admire the silver trinkets of a local peddler. He lifted a pair of lacy filigree earrings. "My wife will like these, I think."

"We saw better in Greece, Macrae," his companion observed. He was shorter and younger, with a wiry build and a dandy's taste in clothing. "Tell me again why you were so keen to stop in Malta."

"Worth it to walk on land again for a day or two." Having reached an agreement with the peddler, Macrae paid for two pairs of silver earrings. "Besides, I felt there was something, or someone, worth meeting here."

"Unlikely!" the other man snorted.

Nikolai paid little heed to the conversation, apart from gratitude that it engaged his quarry's attention. As the taller man turned to his companion, Nikolai's fingers reached into the fellow's right pocket, light as a butterfly's wings. Yes, there were coins there...

Suddenly Nikolai's wrist was caught, and he found

himself skewered by piercing gray eyes. Eyes that saw him as no one had since his grandmother died.

He fought to escape, biting Macrae's hand and jerking free as the man released his grip with an oath. He darted toward a nearby alley. In the rank, twisting backstreets of Valletta, he could lose these great clumsy oafs in no time.

The short man snapped several unintelligible words. The air tingled oddly, and suddenly Nikolai's limbs didn't work. Though he wanted to run, he could barely manage to hold himself upright. He fell against the bricks of the alley wall, his breathing rough. He hadn't felt so weak since he'd almost died of the fever that killed his mother.

Macrae entered the alley and placed his hands on Nikolai's shoulders, then knelt so their eyes were on the same level. "We mean you no harm," he said in fair Italian.

Nikolai spat at him, but somehow missed his mark. Macrae frowned. "He doesn't seem to understand Italian," he said in English. "I wish I knew that dog Arabic the locals speak."

Nikolai didn't bother spitting again, since it had done no good, but he growled like a mongrel. Dog Arabic indeed! *Malti* was the ancient tongue of the Phoenicians. Since it had never been trapped in an alphabet, it was the private speech of Malta, a mystery to stupid foreigners like this one.

The short man, who stood behind Redhead, said drily, "Are you sure you want to converse with a rabid pup like this?"

Macrae stood, releasing his grip on Nikolai's shoulders. "Look at him with the sight, then ask me that again."

The short man's eyes narrowed for a moment, then opened wide. "Good God, the boy blazes with power! When he comes of age, he'll be a formidable mage."

"If he lives long enough and receives the proper training," Macrae said grimly. "From the looks of him, he's halfway to starvation."

"Don' talk 'bout me as if I'm no' here!" Nikolai blurted out. "Rude!"

"The creature speaks English," the short man said with amazement. "His accent is abominable, but he's fluent enough."

"He's not a 'creature,' " Macrae said irritably. "He's a boy, probably younger than my Duncan. He's one of *us,* Jasper. His power has a different flavor from any I've known, but it's real and has great potential."

"African blood, perhaps," Jasper murmured. "There is some of that in his face and coloring as well as in the flavor of his magic."

Nikolai's strength was returning, but he was still trapped between the two men. Why was no one noticing this scene? People walked by in the square just a few feet away and didn't even glance in the alley.

Mage. One of them had used the word. His grandmother had said it meant wizard or witch doctor. They'd used magic to trap him, then to ensure that no one looked their way. He scrunched his mind up like Nona had showed him and dived under Macrae's arm in another bid for freedom.

A hard hand caught him again. "Look at that, Jasper! The boy has shields strong enough to make him disappear from mage sight!"

"Either he's had training, or he learned that to survive," Jasper said thoughtfully. "I begin to share your interest. But what's to be done with a wild lad like this one?"

"Let's start by feeding him." The tall man caught Nikolai's gaze. "I'm Macrae of Dunrath and this is Jasper Polmarric. You have always known you were different, haven't you?"

Nikolai debated lying before giving a reluctant nod. Macrae continued, "We are also different in the same way you are. Or similar, anyhow. Among our duties is to help others of our sort when there is need. At the least, you stand in need of a good meal. Will you join us? If you look at me with your mind, you'll know I mean no harm."

Nikolai had always been good at reading intentions, and he sensed no desire to hurt, but there was more than one kind of assault. "Won' be your whore!"

Instead of anger, Macrae smiled. "I have no interest in dirty little boys. Except when they have the potential you do. Is there a tavern where we can get a good meal and talk in privacy?"

Nikolai nodded and led the two men through the alleys, emerging by the best tavern on the waterfront. It looked over the Grand Harbor and was a favored place for ship's officers and merchants. Of course he'd not eaten there himself, but he sometimes scavenged leavings at the back door.

The landlord scowled when he saw Nikolai enter, but the obvious wealth of the Englishmen saved him from being thrown out. Jasper paused to order food and drink while Macrae escorted Nikolai to a quiet booth in the far corner of the taproom. Nikolai didn't like being herded, but tantalizing scents made him willing to tolerate it. He would endure a great deal to feast on the tavern's best.

Besides, he was curious what these men wanted of him.

Macrae sat on Nikolai's right, Jasper Polmarric on his left. Though they didn't crowd him, it was clear they could stop him from running if he tried. Yet he still felt no danger from them. Only a deep, intense interest.

"What is your name?" Macrae asked. "You can lie if you wish, but I'd like to have something to call you."

Lying was no fun when put like that. "Nikolai Gregorio."

"Russian and Italian?" Polmarric asked. "Any African blood?"

"Some." A quarter at least. Nikolai's grandmother had been pure African, but he didn't know all his relations. His grandfather had been Malti, and his mother wasn't sure who his father was. Perhaps an Italian, maybe a Greek, even an Englishman. Hard to say. The fact that his mother had liked the name Nikolai didn't make him Russian.

Conversation ended when a barmaid sauntered over with a jug of wine and three crude goblets. The tray also held a loaf of sourdough bread, a wedge of cheese, and a dish of pickled fish.

His hunger almost uncontrollable, Nikolai grabbed a piece of fish and gobbled it down while he ripped off a chunk of the cottage loaf. There was a knife on the board, so he hacked a sizable piece of the cheese and crammed it into his mouth, followed by a bite of bread. The sharp flavor of the goat cheese exploded gloriously on his tongue.

"Not very civilized," Polmarric said in French, his expression a study in fascinated horror.

"Give thanks you have never been so hungry." Macrae poured the red wine into the goblets and swallowed a mouthful. Though he'd answered Polmarric in French, he switched back to English to speak to Nikolai. "Eat as much as you want, but it might be wise to slow down. If you make yourself sick, you'll have an empty stomach again."

There was sense to that. Nikolai swallowed another mouthful of bread and cheese and reached for his wine to wash it down. The wine was a light table vintage, pleasant and probably chosen so it wouldn't go to a boy's head. That was another sign of their good intentions, for this wasn't the wine they'd use if they wanted him drunk.

The barmaid returned with three plates of *fenek*. Nikolai dug in greedily. He hadn't had good *fenek* since his grandmother died. Less hurriedly, the foreigners tasted theirs. "This rabbit is rather good," Polmarric said.

"Stew a boot in this much wine and it would be good," Macrae replied, but he dug in with enthusiasm.

Nikolai finished two pieces of stewed rabbit, then sat

back on the wooden bench. With the edge off his hunger, curiosity returned. "You say you are different. How?"

Macrae's gaze flicked to the taproom, checking that no one was in a position to look into their shadowy booth. When he was sure of their privacy, he raised one hand and sparkles of light danced around it like sprays of golden fireworks.

He scooped up the dancing lights and poured them in front of Nikolai. Enchanted, Nikolai tried to catch the golden sparks. They faded in his grasp, a cool tingle against his palm. "Magic," he whispered. He thought all the magic had gone from the world when his grandmother died.

"We usually say power," Macrae said in a low voice. "It's a less-alarming term than magic. Polmarric and I are both Guardians—members of families where power runs strong. Guardians exist in all nations of Europe, and we are sworn to use our abilities to help others rather than for personal gain."

"What kind of magic—power—do you have?" Nikolai tried not to show how hungry he was for the information.

Polmarric gave his companion a warning glance. "Are you sure you want to say so much about us?"

"He has to know." Macrae concentrated on Nikolai. "There are certain things that all Guardian mages can do to some extent. Healing, reading the energies of other people, concealing, creating mage light. Most Guardians are also gifted in some particular area. I am a weather mage, able to shape the winds and storms. It is a common talent in my family. Polmarric here has a great talent for communication."

"You say you swore to help people. What keeps you from becoming kings? Though you seem to live well enough." Nikolai glanced pointedly at the men's rich garments.

"It is harder to become a king than one might think," Macrae said drily. "Over the centuries, we have learned that it is best not to interfere often with mundane society because the consequences are unpredictable, and usually worse than one expects. Among ourselves, we maintain order by national councils of Guardians. Polmarric will likely become a council member the next time there is an opening, because of his communication abilities. If any of our number turns rogue and injures others—Well, we have mages who are gifted in detecting evil and enforcing order."

Nikolai ripped off a piece of bread and soaked it in the *fenek* gravy. The Guardians sounded like a great, secret family that had both power and wisdom. Thinking of his grandmother, he asked, "Mages are all men?"

"Not at all. Women can be as strong or stronger than male mages. My wife is a very gifted healer. Polmarric's wife is the best finder in England, I think." Macrae paused as if deciding what needed to be said. "Usually full power comes when one is reaching adulthood, but it's not uncommon for those who are unusually talented to show magical ability in childhood. My son, Duncan, has, and so have you."

Nikolai stared at his empty plate, trying to grasp what he was being told. "Why you tellin' me this?"

"Because you seem to need help." Macrae looked tired, and Nikolai realized the man was older than he'd guessed. "There are too many homeless children in the world for us to save them all. But you are of our kind, so I am obligated to try to help you."

"How?"

"One possibility would be to find you a place in a Valletta school so you would be fed and clothed and could learn to read and write."

"I know how to read and write," Nikolai said pugnaciously.

Macrae's brows arched. "Impressive. How did you learn?"

Nikolai shrugged. "My grandmother ran a waterfront boardinghouse. She cared for a dyin' English ship's mate in return for him teachin' me. Old Smithy took a long time to die." Long enough that Nikolai had studied numbers and some history as well as reading and writing.

"You learn quickly," Polmarric observed. "Your English accent has improved as we speak. Almost as if you can take the language from our minds. Do you read minds?"

Nikolai scrunched down warily, wondering how the Englishman had figured that out. He didn't exactly read minds, but sometimes he would sense answers that people around him knew. Being with these men who spoke English did improve his own speech. "Smithy said I was clever."

"A clever lad with power might not be safe in a local school, not with the Knights of St. John ruling Malta," Polmarric remarked. "The Knights have a history of turning mages over to the Inquisition."

"I know," Macrae said. "What you really need is a family, Nikolai. People who care about you, and for you to care about."

A *family.* Nikolai looked down so the foreigners wouldn't see the humiliating sting of tears in his eyes. His family had been small but real. With his mother and grandmother dead, he had thought himself alone forever. Thinking of what he'd lost made it hard for him to swallow his stewed rabbit.

"We could find a Guardian family in Italy or France to foster you, if you prefer staying closer to your home. But if you are willing to travel to the North, I will take you to my home and raise you with my own children," Macrae said quietly.

Nikolai raised his head, staring. "You would do such a thing?"

Polmarric gasped when he heard his friend's words. In French, he said, "You're really willing to take this little savage into your own home?"

In the same language, Macrae said, "I'm a Scot and not so very civilized myself." Switching to English, he caught Nikolai's gaze. "You need a home, and it would do my son, Duncan, good to have another lad with power in the household. My daughter is so much younger that she's not much of a companion to him." Nikolai turned the idea over in his mind, reluctant to leave his home, but also excited almost beyond bearing. "You would make me a gentleman?"

Macrae nodded. "You'll have the same food and clothing and education my son receives. Most of all, you'll have the training you will need as your talent manifests. You have some use of power now, but your abilities will explode when you reach manhood. Without training, you risk damaging yourself and others. You would not be the heir to my estate of Dunrath, of course, but the Guardians have funds to help establish young men and women in your circumstances. So, yes, you'll be my foster son and a gentleman. My wife will receive you gladly."

Polmarric said in French, "Your lady is always bringing in stray puppies, so she probably won't mind one more. Though this lad will be much more work than a puppy."

"And more reward as well," Macrae said imperturbably. "This is the right thing to do, Jasper. I know it."

Nikolai's nervous fingers shredded a piece of the sourdough bread. His grandmother had once foretold that he would become a gentleman. He'd laughed, of course, unable to imagine a position in life beyond that of common sailor.

He should have known that his grandmother did not make such mistakes. He thought of her dark, ageless face wistfully. Leaving the graves of her and his mother would hurt, but both of them would have urged him to seize this opportunity. Macrae meant him no harm, of that Nikolai was sure.

His hand tightened convulsively over the bread,

squeezing it into a shapeless mass. "I will go with you and be your son," he told Macrae.

The Scot grinned. "I'm glad of that, Nikolai. I'm sure you will be, too."

Nikolai glanced at Polmarric with wicked mischief and said in French, "And you need another language if you want to speak privately in front of me."

To his credit, Polmarric joined Macrae's laughter.

Men who could laugh and all the food he could eat. The ancestors were looking out for him. Nikolai sliced another chunk of cheese, and wondered happily how he would look in the clothing of a gentleman.

CHAPTER TWO

NIKOLAI WOKE BEFORE DAWN, enjoying the gentle rocking of the schooner *Hermes.* The ship had become his home in the month since Macrae had casually, completely, changed his life. Polmarric owned the ship, so they were all treated very well.

After a week's stop in Sicily, the *Hermes* was heading back to London, her homeport. The weather had been good, with steady winds filling the sails and driving the ship at a brisk pace. They were in the western Mediterranean now. In a day or two they would pass Gibraltar and enter the stormy Atlantic for the final leg of the journey.

He closed his eyes, lulled back toward sleep by the soft splashing of waves against the schooner's hull. Though he'd been raised on an island with the sea ever present, he hadn't guessed just how much he would enjoy sailing. There was freedom and purity in the winds and waves. This could be a good life for a man.

He'd also learned that life as a gentleman's son was far sweeter than scratching for survival like an alley rat. He'd had a month of fine clothes, safety, and, most of all, food. All the food he could eat. So much that he no longer felt the need to gobble whatever was set on the table before it could be taken away.

He even had privacy. This tiny cabin was scarcely more than a sail locker, but it was his. Macrae and Polmarric shared a larger cabin at the back of the vessel, but Nikolai enjoyed his cubbyhole near the bow, which felt very close to the sea.

He reached under the bunk and touched his small, brass-studded trunk, which contained the clothing of a gentleman's son. After Nikolai had agreed to go with Macrae, he'd been taken to the *Hermes* and scrubbed so hard his skin had lightened several shades. Then Macrae took him to the best tailor in Valletta.

The tailor had made a coat and breeches of blue silk brocade and shirts of the best muslin. Wise in the ways of boys, Macrae had also ordered several sets of garments made of rugged linen and wool. Though Nikolai loved his fashionable costume, he felt more comfortable in the plain, everyday garments. Even they were far superior to anything he'd ever owned before.

But he refused to give up his coarse linen trousers and shirt, ragged though they were. His grandmother had sewn them herself, and he could not bear to let them go.

Macrae hadn't argued, merely insisted that the garments be washed. Nikolai's old clothes proved perfect for scrambling up the masts and lines of the *Hermes.* The sailors were a rough but friendly lot, and they taught him the ways of sailing.

Every waking moment was devoted to lessons of one sort or another. Macrae and Polmarric taught him the history of Guardians and how magic could be used. He was also instructed in basic techniques of control. Though his power was modest now, that would change when he reached manhood. The more he knew of control now, the better off he would be later.

Some techniques Nikolai had puzzled out on his own. Others made him catch his breath with a sense of recognition, of learning what seemed utterly right.

He'd been given lessons in manners and society, too. Becoming a gentleman was hard work.

Sometimes Nikolai wondered about the mysterious

Duncan, who would be his brother. Did Duncan know how lucky he was to have a father, especially one like this? No, a boy who had been raised to take food and clothing and the protection of a father for granted couldn't appreciate how incredibly fortunate he was. Sight unseen, Nikolai was inclined to despise Duncan for being soft, but, for Macrae's sake, he'd strive for courtesy.

Macrae had emphasized that he must observe with all his senses, both inner and outer. One of these had awakened him this early, he realized. The predawn darkness was quiet except for the sounds of water, the creaking of the ship's planking, and the distant cry of a lone gull. Yet something was... wrong.

More curious than worried, Nikolai rose and pulled

on his old clothes. Soon they'd be too small since he'd put on weight and grown an inch taller this last month.

Barefoot, he left his tiny cabin and climbed the ladder to the main deck. Dense fog lay over the *Hermes* and the surrounding sea. A mate stood watch aft, his dark figure at the wheel almost invisible except for the faint glow from his pipe when he drew on it. The ship was moving very slowly, making just enough way to stay stable.

Curious what might have awakened him, Nikolai moved forward to stand in the bow, his hands braced on the railings as the ship rose and fell. With the fog and darkness, he couldn't see more than a few feet into the night.

Did they risk running into rocks or an island? Not likely when the mate knew these waters, and their slow speed reduced the chances of serious harm even if there was an error of navigation.

He sighed with frustration. Perhaps in two or three years, his magical abilities would blossom and he would be able to define what bothered him. Or maybe not. As Polmarric pointed out regularly, magic was a tool for dealing with the world, it wasn't a reliable source of miracles.

Splashing sounded from somewhere ahead. A school of fish jumping? It was hard to judge direction in the fog.

He was about to turn away and return to his bed when a low, dark shape leaped from the fog with amazing speed. It was a vessel—a galley, the long sweep of dozens of oars driving it furiously toward the schooner. *Corsairs.*

Nikolai froze in horror. For centuries, the Barbary

pirates had attacked not only ships but sea coasts to capture slaves, and Malta had suffered more than its share of raids. Recovering, he shouted at the top of his lungs, "Pirates!"

All hell broke loose after he raised the alarm. Now that they'd been seen, the pirates cut loose with a ragged volley of musket shots. Nikolai ducked as balls slammed into the wood around him. Aft, the mate on watch swore furiously as he yanked on the bell rope to boom out a warning. Half-naked men began boiling up from belowdecks, weapons in hand.

As Nikolai straightened, the armored prow of the galley rammed the *Hermes,* smashing into the hull only a few feet below his position. The shattering impact knocked him from his feet. His head banged into the railing, and he briefly lost consciousness.

When he regained awareness, a pitched battle was being fought around him. Sharp wind shredded the fog, and the sky had lightened, revealing that the two ships were locked together with grappling hooks. Twenty or more turbaned soldiers had swarmed aboard the *Hermes.* The schooner's crew and passengers fought back with swords, pistols, and anything else that might be used as a weapon. Clouds of black smoke stung the eyes and burned the lungs.

Wearing only loose shirts and smallclothes, Macrae and Polmarric were in the thick of the fight, the Scot slashing about him with a broadsword and Polmarric armed with a pair of pistols. Nikolai wanted to run to Macrae, but he was too weak to move. Crunched into the angle of the bow, he watched the battle with horror and wondered why the Guardians weren't using magic to end this. Surely they could do something! Or was that sharp wind Macrae's work?

Nikolai gasped when a corsair slashed Macrae's arm with his curved sword. Blood splashed darkly across the Scot's white shirt as he ran his assailant through. Coolly Polmarric aimed and took down one pirate with the pistol in his right hand, then a second with the left-hand pistol. As the pirates looked for less dangerous game, Polmarric reloaded and Macrae stood guard over his friend.

Nikolai tried to stand, and almost blacked out again as vicious pain stabbed through his ribs. He must have cracked one when he fell. Since he couldn't fight, he made himself observe, using all his senses.

The *Hermes* was winning the battle. Several crewmen were wounded, but most of the bodies on the blood-stained deck were pirates. He guessed that the attackers hadn't expected such a fierce defense, and that they were wondering if it was worth it. Corsairs preferred to assault people who hadn't much ability to protect themselves.

As the last of the fog and smoke dissolved, a grappling hook banged to the deck near Nikolai's feet. The line that held the schooner to the galley snapped. One by one, the other lines broke and the galley began drifting away.

Another gust of wind caught the galley's sails, and it heeled over to starboard, the port oars thrashing in the air like the legs of a spider. A commanding voice on the galley shouted out in Arabic, "Fall back!"

A cursing pirate retreated along the deck of the *Hermes,* most of his attention on the schooner's crew in case one came after him. He tripped over Nikolai, sending jangles of agony through Nikolai's ribs. The pirate glanced down, then scooped Nikolai up with one powerful hand. "Here's one at least." He spoke a crude form of North African Arabic that Nikolai had heard on the Valletta waterfront.

Nikolai struggled against the pirate, but he dangled helpless as a puppy in the giant's grip. "Macrae! *Macrae!*" he screamed.

The Scot started to turn toward him, but another volley of musket shots came from the galley, and Polmarric collapsed. Macrae whipped around and knelt by his friend, no longer in Nikolai's view.

The galley had righted itself, and floated only a few feet from the *Hermes.* Nikolai's captor called to one of the pirates on the galley, "Catch this brat!"

He threw Nikolai down to the galley. After a few dizzying seconds of flight, Nikolai was caught roughly and deposited on the slanting deck. He slid across the galley, fetching up in the starboard gunwales. Water sloshed around him, and he gasped from the agony of his cracked ribs, fearing he would drown.

He must fight the pain. Macrae had spoken of that. The trick was to detach, to think of the pain as distant, belonging to someone else.

Nikolai concentrated on detachment, and the pain

diminished a little. He staggered to his feet, desperate to return to the *Hermes* before the ships separated.

Macrae was standing amidships the schooner and looking toward the galley, his brows drawn into a frown. As he ran across the galley, Nikolai waved his arms frantically to get the Scotsman's attention. Surely Macrae had some magic that would rescue Nikolai! He was Macrae's foster son, a great mage in the making!

Macrae looked right at him. Then he turned away, his face like granite.

Nikolai watched in disbelief as the man who had promised protection and family abandoned him to his fate. Panicked, he started to scramble over the railing. Better to risk the sea than slavery.

Hard hands caught him again. This time he was in the grip of the galley's captain, the *reis,* a burly man with gold chains around his neck and eyes cold as death. "So all we have to show for this attack is one miserable little piglet!"

"I am a rich man's son," Nikolai said desperately. "My father will ransom me!"

The *reis's* contemptuous gaze went over his ragged garments. "You? Ha!"

"I am English. Scottish. My father, Macrae of Dunrath, will pay to have me back." Yet he wondered if that was true. Macrae had seen him in the hands of the corsairs, then turned away. Would he pay a ransom?

"You're no Englishman." The heavy hand of the *reis* smashed into the side of Nikolai's head, knocking him to his knees. "You look like a mulatto wharf rat to me." The *reis* gestured to summon the overseer of the galley slaves, a pockmarked man who carried a whip. "This brat is too small to row, but he can bail. Take him."

The overseer lashed the whip across Nikolai's back, shredding the linen. Nikolai screamed, the fire of the whip triggering the agony of his cracked rib.

"This is what disobedient slaves get, boy," the overseer growled. "Follow orders, and you may live to grow up. Bail!"

Numbly Nikolai lurched to his feet, barely able to breathe. The overseer shoved a bucket in his hands and pointed to the starboard side of the ship, where water sloshed around the ankles of the galley slaves. Bruised and disoriented, Nikolai obeyed, bitterly ashamed of the tears pouring down his cheeks.

As he scooped water and poured it over the side, Nikolai saw the *Hermes* sailing away to the west. Macrae and Polmarric were safe, and they had abandoned Nikolai to his fate without so much as a second glance. If this is what it meant to be a Guardian, sworn to protect, then he wanted nothing to do with the swine.

The overseer of the galley slaves slashed the whip across his back again. "Faster, or I'll throw you over the side for the fish to eat!"

Nikolai bit his lips and obeyed, but inside, fury began to grow. He had been promised paradise by Macrae, and then betrayed. *Betrayed!*

As he filled and emptied the bucket, his rage grew until it saturated every fiber of his being. When he felt he could bail no longer, he kept himself going by swearing an oath on his blood and bones and dead grandmother that he would survive slavery, and someday he would escape.

Then, when he was ready, he would avenge himself on Macrae and his family. The lying man, the beautiful wife, the handsome son, the pampered little daughter.

All would be his prey.

BOOK TWO

LIGHTING THE TINDER

1752

CHAPTER THREE

London, 1752

Jean Macrae surveyed the dockside crowd with amazement. "Did everyone in London come to see me off?"

"Very likely," Lady Bethany Fox said placidly. "The sun is shining, and saying bon voyage is a good excuse for amusement. After you've sailed away on the tide, I expect that most of this lot will end up at someone's house, eating and drinking like there's no tomorrow and having a gay time of it." The silver-haired woman gave Jean a hug. "Give my love to the children. If I weren't so old and frail, I'd come myself."

"Not children, Lady Beth. They're getting married, after all!" Jean said, laughing, as she returned the hug. "Why not come? The *Mercury* is one of Sir Jasper's ships, so you'd be treated as a queen the whole way." Lady Bethany looked briefly tempted, but shook her head.

"No, my dear, this is your adventure, not mine." Jean eyed her with misgivings. Lady Beth might look like an innocent grandmother, but she was one of the finest sorceresses in Europe and the leader of the British Guardian Council. "Is this an adventure? I thought I was making a genteel trip to see friends marry."

The older woman's eyes glinted. "Adventure may strike at any time."

"I hope it doesn't strike Jean," said her big brother, Duncan. "You look so undersized that it makes me nervous to think of you going such a distance alone."

"I have Annie, I'm traveling on a Polmarric ship, I'll be met at the dock in Marseilles—and you know perfectly well that I'm not the least bit fragile!" she retorted.

"Granted that these days you dress as primly as a nun, but you can't fool me," he said dourly. "Knowing your past exploits can't help but make a brother anxious." She smiled. Ten years her senior, Duncan often acted more like a father than a brother. "My wild days are behind me. I'm now a proper spinster aunt."

"Maybe the wedding will be a good example to you," her brother said hopefully. "Make you more marriage-minded. Three honorable, prosperous, highly eligible men have asked me for your hand, and you didn't want any of them."

And that wasn't counting the two men who had asked Jean directly. Those she hadn't mentioned to her brother. There was no sense in frustrating him even further.

Duncan's wife, Gwynne, said firmly, "Leave Jean

alone, Duncan. Better to. be a happy spinster than a miserable wife."

Jean grinned at her beautiful sister-in-law. "And as a spinster, I'm useful as a nursery maid with those handsome children of yours."

Gwynne grinned back. "Precisely." She hugged Jean. "Have a marvelous time, Jean. And think of us in cold, drafty Dunrath while you are wintering in the Mediterranean sunshine."

Since Duncan was the best weather mage in Britain, Dunrath was quite comfortable, but it wouldn't be the same as Marseilles. Jean dreamed of warmth and Roman ruins.

"Pm glad we got here in time!" Megan, the petite Countess of Falconer, slid through the crowd and caught Jean's hands. "We have wedding gifts for you to take. I wish I could be there." She patted her midriff. "But it's not a good time for me to travel."

"I shall write you every detail," Jean promised. After hugging Meg, she turned to Simon, the Earl of Falconer. The chief enforcer of the Guardians, he'd always seemed rather alarming when Jean was younger. Marriage to Meg had relaxed him considerably.

Simon hugged her with one arm since he was carrying a large basket on the other. "I'll take the gifts aboard ship so they can be stowed properly. Give my best wishes to Moses and Lily and Jemmy and Breeda."

"I will, and I promise that I'll encourage them to visit England soon." Simon and Meg had rescued the four young people from an appalling captivity, where they had been mentally enslaved, "enthralled," by a rogue mage. Jean had helped the four thralls recover from that captivity, and she'd become something of an honorary aunt in the process. She looked forward to seeing them again after four long years. Letters weren't the same.

Jean finished her farewells, needing to conceal a few tears. She had never traveled outside of Britain before, nor been away from family for months at a time.

Yet when she stood on the afterdeck and waved goodbye while the *Mercury* eased down the Thames, excitement triumphed over regrets. Except for the Rising seven years earlier, when Bonnie Prince Charlie had upended the lives of her and much of Scotland, she had lived a quiet life. She was ready to taste a wider world.

Her companion and maid, Annie Macrae, was weeping copiously beside her. A little concerned, Jean asked, "Are you regretting this trip to Marseilles? You can be put off at Greenwich if you'd really rather stay."

Annie shook her head vigorously. She was a distant cousin of Jean's; there was a family resemblance, but she was taller, more roundly built, and her hair was more auburn than red. In the valley of Dunrath, she was known

as a braw fine lassie. "Oh, no, Miss Jean, it's glad I am to be going! Every lass in Dunrath envies me. But a leave-taking for such a grand journey deserves a good cry."

"No doubt you're right," Jean said as she passed her handkerchief to Annie. "I simply haven't a proper sensibility."

"That's because you're a heroine, Miss Jean. Heroines don't have sensibility."

Jean blushed and turned her gaze back to the river, watching London slip away. Ever since the Rising, the people of Dunrath had regarded her with ridiculous awe. She was no heroine. She'd been wrongheaded and terrified and desperate, and it had taken Gwynne and Duncan to save them all from disaster.

Annie's remark was a good reminder that adventures were not only frightening but devilishly uncomfortable. She would leave them for the young and foolhardy.

THE VOYAGE WAS peaceful and a little boring, though it was pleasant to sail into warmer weather. Jean could hardly contain her excitement when they passed Gibraltar and entered the Mediterranean. The Middle Sea, the center of the world. Even the light was different from Britain, warmer and more luminous.

Jean read and chatted with the handful of other passengers and slept well, until the night she was shocked awake by the numbing clamor of an alarm bell. In these waters, it could only mean one thing. "Pirates!"

She swung out of her bunk bed, grabbed the cloak hanging on the back of the door, then scooped her pistols from her small trunk. She spent a few moments loading while Annie rolled over and peered down from the upper berth, her face pale in the moonlight that came through the porthole. "What's happening, Miss Jean?"

"There's a chance Barbary pirates have been sighted. Probably it's a false alarm, but you stay here while I find out." As Annie gasped and ducked under her covers, Jean raced from the small cabin and up the stairs. Armed crew members were taking stations, and the two swivel-mounted cannon were now manned.

Pistol in hand, Jean found a quiet spot by the wheel-house where she wouldn't be in the way. For a tense quarter hour, she waited along with the crew.

Then the lookout high on the forward mast called out, " 'Tis a Venetian trading ship, not a corsair!"

"Are you sure?" Captain Gordon called back. His spyglass was sweeping the horizon.

"Aye, sir, 'tis no pirate galley."

After more long moments, the craggy captain lowered his spyglass. "Very well. Off-watch crew can return to your berths."

With chatter and sighs of relief, most of the crew members headed below. Captain Gordon was walking toward the stern of the ship when he saw Jean in the wheelhouse shadows. "Good God, Miss Macrae! What are you doing up here?"

Jean gestured with her downward-pointing pistol. "I was preparing to defend my virtue if necessary." Gordon looked startled. "Do you know how to use that?"

"I'd demonstrate, but a shot would just alarm everyone again."

He nodded approval. "You were in the Highlands during the Rising, weren't you? That would encourage alertness and knowledge of weapons."

"So it did." She lowered the pistol to her side, her fingers trembling in reaction now that the danger was past. "Also, my father was on a ship attacked in these waters. He and Sir Jasper Polmarric were traveling together."

"Your father was on that voyage? That attack is why Sir Jasper takes such precautions on all his ships. All Polmarric vessels have extra cannon, and we're required

to train our crews how to react in an emergency. We'll have more drills now that we've entered into the Mediterranean. In fact, I planned on holding one tomorrow, but then I'd have warned you and the other passengers not to worry."

"That would have been pleasant," she said wryly. "After waking up to the alarm bell, I'll not get to sleep again soon."

"Walk with me," he suggested. "After any alarm, I like to check that all is well." As she fell into step beside him, he added, "Mind you, only a nervous young lookout would mistake a Venetian galley for a corsair, but the men are extra careful now that we're in the Mediterranean. I'd rather have false alarms than miss a real pirate."

"Have you ever been on a ship attacked by corsairs, Captain?"

"Once, when I was a lad." He frowned. "It's a bad business, and worse if Englishmen are captured. The Catholic countries have religious orders like the Trinitarians, who devote themselves to ransoming slaves, but the Protestant countries are not so well organized."

"I didn't know that." She remembered back to her father's tale of the attack on the *Hermes.* "Even if one is ransomed, there would be unpleasant years in slavery." Unpleasant, and quite possibly fatal.

"And worse for a woman." He glanced at her. "A pretty young lass like you, with that red hair, would bring a high price in the Barbary slave markets."

She laughed and brushed back her windswept hair. She hadn't powdered it or worn a wig since leaving London. Much easier to leave it natural and simply tie it back. The sailors and other passengers had become used to the blazing color by now. "It's nice to know that red hair is good for something."

"You'd be purchased for a sultan's harem for sure," he said with a chuckle. "Rarity value, you know."

"I shall take that as a compliment." They had reached the bow of the *Mercury,* so she continued, "I think I'll stay here for a while, if you don't mind. I love the feel of the wind in my face."

"We'll make a sailor of you yet, Miss Macrae." Captain Gordon continued on his inspection of the schooner. Jean had enjoyed the captain's company, but now she was ready to be alone. The best thing about this voyage had been long hours with nothing to do but observe the weather. The Macrae family produced the best weather mages in Britain—her brother was merely the latest of a long, distinguished line.

But controlling the weather was almost exclusively a masculine talent. A Macrae female might have a modest talent for managing the elements, but the great weather mages were always men. It was most unfair.

Not that Jean had ever been a magical prodigy. Plenty of established mages had told her that she had substantial power, but she'd never learned how to use it fully. Except in really desperate circumstances, which was an alarming and uncertain business.

As a girl coming into womanhood, she had believed that she would get past her problems and learn to use power as easily as most Guardians did. But that had never happened, and she'd largely stopped trying. In a family of mages, someone needed to be practical, and at Dunrath, that person had been Jean. She'd become a capable estate manager during her brother's years of traveling. After Duncan's marriage, his wife, Gwynne, had encouraged Jean to study magic more deeply, and that had been useful for scrying and small spells. But a great sorceress she'd never be.

She'd never be a wife, either. She had always sensed that she wouldn't marry a Guardian. She had pledged herself to her childhood sweetheart, Robbie Mackenzie, and had even followed him to war.

Ah, he'd been a bonnie lad, the only man she'd ever loved. Robbie had been a mundane, and she'd never told him about the Guardians, thinking her own power wasn't great enough for it to matter to their marriage. But he'd died at Culloden, and, despite the best efforts of her family and friends, she'd met no one yet to take his place.

No matter. She was a good teacher and an excellent shot, and too much a Macrae not to enjoy weather. To her great satisfaction, on this voyage she had discovered that she had a dash of the family magic. She could reach beyond the visible sky to sense distant winds and storms. She had influenced weather patterns a little as well. It was not entirely luck that had granted the *Mercury* such a smooth voyage.

Closing her eyes, she absorbed the south wind and imagined the dry, mysterious African deserts from whence it came. Strange places with strange names...

She really should have started traveling sooner.

CHAPTER FOUR

Adia, West Africa
1752

ADIA STRAIGHTENED up front hoeing yams, her back aching. Her family grew the best yams in the village, but much work was required. "I'll be glad when Abeje finishes her initiation and is back here doing her share!"

Her mother laughed. "You'll be even more glad when you are initiated yourself, little one, but you must wait a few years for that." She glanced up at the sun. "Why don't you and Chike play while I feed the baby?"

The fatigue of hoeing vanished instantly. While her mother took the baby to the side of the field, Adia and Chike began a game of tag among the yam plants, running for the pure fun of it. Sometimes Adia let her little brother catch her even though he was only four and had short legs.

In later years, Adia would wonder if their squeals of delight were what brought the slavers to them, but probably not. Slavers were very good at finding victims.

The first warning came when she glanced up to see a party of large, menacing men emerge from the forest, spears ready and mouths silent. They were not Iske like her, but some other tribe she didn't recognize. As *she stared, frightened, her mother cried out, "Run, Adia! Help your brother!"*

Her mother gestured with both hands and sent a blast of magic across the field, raising a cloud of thick, eye-stinging dust between Adia and Chike and the men. Then she scooped up the baby and raced into the forest, unable to do more for her children.

Slavers! *Adia heard them swearing and coughing from the dust. Her mother had given her children a little time. Adia ran to her brother and grabbed his hand. "Come!" she gasped. "The bad men will steal us!"*

Chike ran as fast as he could, aided by Adia's tugging hand. If only she had been initiated! She came from a family of priests and priestesses, and someday she would have power enough to fight evil men, but all she had now was her speed and her stubbornness.

They were not enough. With a shout of satisfaction, the slavers burst through the dust cloud and caught Adia and Chike before they could escape into the forest. Brutal hands knocked Adia to the ground and tied her wrists behind her. The same was done to Chike, who was crying frantically.

One of the slavers said, "These brats won't be worth much." The language he spoke was not Iske, but it was similar enough to the dialect of a neighboring tribe that Adia could understand.

Another said, "They're worth a bar or two of iron if they survive, so we might as well take them."

He yanked Chike to his feet while the first slaver did the same to Adia. Her knees and arms were bleeding from her fall. For as long as anyone could remember, slavers had preyed on the Iske and other tribes. No one who was taken ever returned. Her favorite cousin and his best friend had vanished one day, taken by slavers.

As the raiders dragged Adia and Chike away, she thought of her father's slaves, warriors who had been taken in tribal warfare, but that was different from kidnapping children. Help me, Grandmother, *she prayed silently. She had been close to her mother's mother, Monifa, who had died only a year ago.* As *she prayed, she felt the spirit touch of her grandmother's hands.* Survive, little one. There is hope for the future.

Adia closed her eyes, thanking the ancestors for helping her mother and the baby escape. Then she prayed that her father and the other hunters would come after the slavers and rescue Adia and Chike.

Hope faded as they joined with a larger band of slavers and were marched out of the fruitful valley of the Iske. The group headed west, toward the great sea. There were dozens of other captives manacled together in long lines that made it impossible for anyone to escape. The first time Adia saw a skeleton lying forgotten in the bush, she shuddered at the knowledge that some poor captive had died on a march like this one.

Soon she had seen enough skeletons to barely notice them. As *more weeks passed, she began to envy those who had died and no longer had to walk or drink stagnant water or try to survive on a handful of cooked grain a day.*

There were a few brighter moments. A tall, strongly built youth named Mazi was shackled behind Chike, and he carried the child for long hours every day. He and Adia spoke different languages, but he made it clear that he considered her brother no burden. Then the slavers met with another group. Sales were made, captives were swapped, and Mazi was taken off by the others. Adia missed him. Only a few years older than she, he had been nearly a man, not a child, and she had felt safer with him near.

Chike died a week before they reached the coast. Adia prayed over his thin body, asking the ancestors to take special care of his spirit because he was only small. Then a slaver jerked her to her feet, and she had to start marching again.

But she would not die, no, not her. Adia of the Iske would survive, and someday she would find a way to make the slavers pay.

CHAPTER FIVE

THE *MERCURY'S* leisurely progress through the crowded harbor at Marseilles gave Jean ample time to go mad with excitement. She managed to control herself enough that she didn't jump up and down, but she and Annie hung over the railing by the bow, drinking in the sights and smells of France.

"They'll never believe this back in Dunrath," Annie said happily. "I'll be telling tales to my grandchildren about my trip to Marseilles."

"So will I," Jean said, though she was less certain about grandchildren in her case.

The sun reflected brilliantly from the sea, and even with her broad-brimmed hat, she had to use her hand to shade her eyes as she studied the people waiting on the shore. Had the schooner been identified early enough so that her friends would be waiting?

"Try this, Miss Macrae." Captain Gordon appeared

and handed her his spyglass. “Perhaps you’ll be able to see your friends.”

“Thank you.” Jean put the spyglass to her right eye and slowly scanned the waterfront. “There they are!” The thralls had changed so much that she might have missed the group if not for the tall, dark presence of Moses Fontaine. With skin like ebony and a gentleman’s elegance, his presence and his African heritage made him unmistakable.

Holding his arm was his blond bride-to-be, Lily

Winters. She had been frail to the point of collapse when she and her friends had been freed from thralldom. Now she was graceful and healthy, with an elegance to match that of Moses. Born the daughter of a village apothecary, now she was every inch a lady.

Moving about more restlessly were Jemmy and Breeda, the other betrothed couple. Of the four thralls, Jemmy had been in the direst straits. He had been a chimney sweep, a starved and pallid boy who looked unlikely to survive to adulthood. Now he was fit and strong and tanned. Never having had a surname, he’d decided to call himself James King once he gained his freedom. “Jemmy” to his friends.

Last was Bridget O’Malley, the Irish serving girl whose carrot-red hair rivaled Jean’s bright locks. After being freed, Breeda’s greatest ambition had been to learn how to read and write. Jean had taught her and Jemmy, and the letters they’d written over the years were a testament to how well the two had learned. Jean thought the pair were living proof that breeding meant much less than opportunity. Breeda and Jemmy had always had intelligence. Once they were freed and given the chance to grow, that potential had blossomed.

"Would you like to look?" She passed the spyglass to Annie.

"I never knew there were so many kinds of people in the world!" her companion exclaimed as she examined the port. "Black skin, white, brown, and every shade between. And the way they dress! It's not like Dunrath, Miss Jean."

"Indeed, it's not." Jean studied the buildings and hills around the harbor hungrily, thinking that an advantage of being a maiden aunt was the freedom to travel. She took off her bonnet and waved, at the same time trying to send a mental message to her friends. Either the hat or the mind touch worked, because Breeda saw her and waved excitedly, quickly followed by the others.

Docking seemed to take forever, but soon enough Jean was able to skip down the gangplank to the shore while Annie stayed behind to supervise removal of their baggage. Breeda reached Jean first and they hugged, laughing and crying at once. The circumstances under which they'd met had created a bond that went deep. As she embraced Lily, Jean said, "You all look wonderful! Marseilles has been good to you."

"Marseilles and Moses's family." An orphan when she was enthralled, Lily had gone gladly to her betrothed's warm, accepting household.

"You've become smaller, Miss Jean," Jemmy said with a mischievous twinkle in his eyes. "You're just a little bit of a thing."

"You're not so very tall yourself, Mr. King," she retorted. "But Breeda wrote that you're the most sought-after jockey in the south of France."

"I am that," he said with great satisfaction. "And turning into a fair trainer, too."

Moses, always the leader of the quartet, gestured toward the two carriages waiting behind them. "Come, Miss Jean, we will take you home."

His lanky frame had filled out into the solid muscles of a man. Moses had been born in Zanzibar as the eldest son of a shrewd merchant who had moved his family and the headquarters of his trading empire to France when Moses was six.

As acknowledged heir to the business, Moses had been given a first-class education and spoke several languages. Then he had been kidnapped into thralldom. After Moses's release, he and his family had taken in the other thralls, who had nowhere else to go. The four young people had flourished, recovering from their enslavement as they matured to full adulthood.

The rest of the day passed quickly as they traveled to Moses's family compound and settled in. The sprawling

Fontaine household had multiple courtyards that contained fountains and gardens. Moses said it was modeled after the family compound in Zanzibar. Jean was entranced by the way inside and outside flowed together.

Not like Scotland, where a house's main purpose was to keep the weather safely outside.

Moses's parents greeted Jean as if she had personally saved their son's life instead of merely being his tutor. The Falconers were the true rescuers; if Meg and Simon ever came to Marseilles, they would be treated like royalty. In the meantime, the Fontaines lavished their gratitude on Jean.

After a sumptuous dinner that combined the best of French cooking with some African dishes spiced differently from anything Jean had ever tasted, the elders tactfully withdrew so that Jean and her four friends could talk in private. The salon where they gathered had a balcony open to the mild night air. As Jean sipped excellent sherry, she thought she could become very fond of Mediterranean living.

The weddings were still weeks away, but the three women discussed the details until Jemmy and Moses looked ready to flee. Taking pity on the men, Jean turned the topic to magic. "I see a shimmer of energy connecting you. Do you still feel as closely linked as when you were in England?"

The four exchanged glances. "Yes, though it's different from when Lord Drayton had us enthralled," Lily said.

"And God be thanked for that!" Breeda added.

"We are always aware of one another's feeling and presence," Moses said, "but we've had no need to meld our powers."

"So we've not killed anyone lately," Jemmy finished with acid humor.

"I'm glad to hear that." Jean took another sip of sherry, knowing that wasn't a joke. "But you've become most adept at finishing one another's sentences."

Moses shrugged. "We are part of one another, Miss Jean. Marriage is the logical next step." His warm gaze went to Lily.

Breeda reached out to take Jemmy's hand. "We would wither if separated."

Power made it possible for mates to join with special intensity. Jean had seen that among the Guardian families, most closely with her parents and now her brother and his wife. She had loved Robbie, and his death had left a hole in her heart that no other man had ever filled. Losing him had devastated her, so perhaps it was just as well that marriage to a Guardian wasn't in her future. If the closeness was greater than she'd known with him, loss would be beyond bearing.

"Have you studied magic since coming here?" Though individually none of them but Moses had unusual power, when they worked together they were rather terrifying. "I've wondered, but, of course, it's not the sort of thing one can ask in a letter."

"Several French Guardians worked with us, teaching shielding and control." Lily turned her glass goblet in her hand, her expression troubled. "Those lessons were welcome, but I haven't wanted to go further. My experiences with serious magic have not been pleasant. I enjoy helping others with my potions and lotions. That is enough." The others silently nodded. "We're not really Guardians, Miss Jean," Breeda said. "I hope Lord and Lady Falconer won't be too disappointed to hear how we haven't pursued our studies."

Jean smiled ruefully. "I'm not much of a Guardian myself, so I'm in no position to chastise you. I sometimes think magic is more trouble than it's worth." Though it could be most useful when one was in trouble. Conversation drifted to other topics until Breeda rose, smothering a yawn. "I'm for bed now. Tomorrow we can show you more of the city, Miss Jean. Is there anything in particular you would like to see? The chapel of Notre Dame de la Garde is splendid, and it has the most magnificent views of the city."

"I should love to see the chapel, and any other sights you deem worthy." Jean debated before adding, "It's very low of me, but I also wish to buy gifts for friends and family. There's no rush on that, though, since I'll be here for months."

Lily chuckled. "Breeda and I will be happy to help you spend your money. One of the best places in the city is actually the Fontaine showroom. Though the family business is primarily importing, several years ago Moses thought to open an emporium to sell directly to the public. It has been a great success."

"And you will get very special prices," Moses added. "I will pay the usual price," Jean said firmly. "I am already benefiting by your generosity."

"We shall see," Lily said mischievously as she rose and

said good night. Breeda and Jemmy followed her from the room, their hands linked.

Not yet ready to retire, Jean took her remaining sherry out to the balcony. Moses joined her. "Will you need a guide back to your chambers, Miss Jean?"

She laughed. "I might. Maison Fontaine is the next thing to a labyrinth."

"I shall escort you back when you're ready." He smiled, his teeth a white flash against his dark skin. "And provide you with a spool of thread so you can mark your way in the future."

"I may take you up on that." She gazed out at the scattered lights of the city and the dark curve of the sea beyond. "It's beautiful here, but do you miss Africa?" He leaned on the railing, his dark face limned by moonlight. "Sometimes. I was only a child when we left

Zanzibar, but twice I accompanied my father back for long visits. Though he took the family name Fontaine and lives as a French gentleman, he does not want us to forget our roots."

"You won't. But if your children are born here, they will."

He sighed. "I know. And they will be half European, caught between two worlds even more than I."

"We are all outsiders in some way. Those who have magic stand apart from those who don't." She finished her sherry in one swallow. "Guardians with little power are apart from those who are great mages. And men and women seem to be entirely different breeds much of the time."

He laughed. "You're right. My true home is in Lily, Jemmy, and Breeda. All of us outsiders, yet together whole."

"It's something of a miracle that the flower of love and friendship has grown out of the despair of your experiences." Would she have been willing to endure the enslavement of her selfhood and will if the reward was a deep and lasting love like that which joined her friends? Probably not—the thought of losing her soul to an evil man like Drayton was too horrifying.

"The others have put aside magic," Moses said hesitantly. "That has not been entirely true of me."

She wasn't surprised by his admission. "You always seemed the most interested in the subject. What have you learned?"

"I asked a ship captain who carries much merchandise for my father to find me an African shaman, and he did. Sekou stayed in Marseilles and tutored me for a year and a day. He said there were things he must teach me that would be essential later."

When he fell silent, Jean asked, "What did you learn? Are European and African forms of magic different?"

"In some ways they are alike, in others unlike. The ancestors are very powerful in African magic." His voice gathered intensity. "I learned so much, Miss Jean! Sekou guided me in an initiation where I walked on other worlds. Not physically, of course, but in my mind. Yet so clear, so vivid, that if I touched fire, I was burned. I learned from Sekou that some African shamans have special abilities to work with time and place that I've not heard of in European magic. I don't know if I have those abilities, but he taught me the techniques, and I practice daily. A lifetime would not be enough to learn it all." He caught himself. "Forgive my enthusiasm. I have wanted to speak of this, but the others have not been keen on hearing."

"I'd like to learn more, if you have the time to tell me," Jean said, fascinated. "My brother's wife is a scholar of magic, and she won't forgive me if I waste such an opportunity to acquire more knowledge."

"I will share willingly." His expression turned grim. "One reason I decided to study more was the need to wield magic to protect myself. There are those who see a black man in the streets and think him a slave for the stealing. Twice I have been attacked by gangs who wanted to capture and enslave me. Once I was able to fight my way free with my fists. The other time..." He shook his head. "Without magic, I might now be working in the sugar plantations of the Indies. But I do not like having blood on my hands."

She winced at his flat recitation. "I've heard that happens in England as well. It didn't occur to me that a man who is clearly a gentleman like you would be at risk."

"Black is black," he said drily. "The rest is mere clothing. I've not told the others this, though perhaps Jemmy suspects that I have had trouble. I don't want Lily to know that... that I had to kill a man to preserve my freedom."

"I won't tell her." Jean's eyes narrowed. "If you want

absolution for killing to save yourself, you have mine, for what it's worth."

He exhaled softly. "I think that is what I wanted. Thank you, Miss Jean." He offered her his arm. "Shall I escort you back to your chambers?"

"Please do, Monsieur Fontaine." She took his arm. "And don't forget the spool of thread for future travels!"

CHAPTER SIX

THOUGH JEAN WOULD HAVE LIKED to spend more time learning about African magic from Moses, the following weeks were a flurry of sightseeing, picnics and balls, and preparing for the weddings. Annie was the ideal companion because she also wanted to see everything and was eager to visit any church or hike any hill. Lily and Breeda would join their excursions, and Moses and Jemmy came when they weren't working.

Occasionally, as they enjoyed the mild, sunny days, Jean and Annie would speculate on what dreadful storms were battering the hills of Scotland. Jean had a tingly, magical feeling that she actually did know what the weather was like in Dunrath, but there was no way to be sure she was right. Maybe she just had a good imagination.

The weddings, when they finally took place, were beautiful. Breeda had laughingly insisted on a separate ceremony, saying that she didn't want to be overshadowed by Lily on her own wedding day. She needn't have worried— she was beautiful, her bright hair blazing under a lace veil, and Jemmy gazed at her as if she were the only woman in the world. A glow of light surrounded them, their love made visible to those with the power to see it.

That afternoon, Lily and Moses were joined in an equally moving ceremony. Jean wept unashamedly, as she had that morning. As she blotted her eyes, she had the ironic thought that both couples owed something to the despicable Lord Drayton. His wicked enthrallment had brought four strangers together and created deep, lasting bonds. These marriages had been forged in fire.

After the lavish wedding feast presided over by Moses's beaming parents, the newlyweds traveled to a private estate in the country for a fortnight's honeymoon. There each couple would have the privacy to explore their new relationship, but they also had the company of their dearest friends.

The Fontaine household was very quiet the next day as everyone recovered from the festivities, but Jean woke on Monday full of energy and determination. As she sipped her morning chocolate in bed, Annie entered the room, already dressed. "I look forward to another peaceful day, Miss Jean."

"One day of quiet was enough. It's time I visited the Fontaine emporium. I haven't done a lick of shopping yet, and I have dozens of people to buy presents for." Invigorated by the prospect, Jean finished her hot chocolate. "Will you join me?"

"Not today, miss. I need to mend clothes and write letters home." Annie moved to the wardrobe that held Jean's clothing and began to look for garments in need of work. "I'll go there another day, if you tell me there are pretty things I can afford."

"Very well." Jean rose and rescued her favorite green calico gown from Annie's growing collection. "This can wait for mending. The tie that's broken isn't visible." Annie sniffed but allowed it, and soon Jean was sharing a carriage to the waterfront with Monsieur Fontaine, Moses's father. A large man with a powerful presence, he was a gray-haired version of his son. In the previous weeks, as Jean had questioned Moses about African magic in odd moments, she'd learned that his father and mother both had some power. With that dual inheritance, Moses had surpassed both parents in his abilities.

As Monsieur Fontaine helped Jean from the carriage, he said, "You will have a peaceful time this morning. Most days the showroom is open to the public, but on Mondays only other merchants and very special private customers are allowed in." His African accent was heavy, but his French was fluent, and he spoke some English as well. As he ushered her into the building, he added, "And you are a very special customer."

The showroom was part of the sprawling stone Fontaine warehouse that covered a whole block on the Marseilles waterfront. The working part of the warehouse faced the harbor. On the street that ran past the back, a modest but attractive entrance had been created. Lemon trees in tubs flanked the doorway, and a small brass plaque said simply FONTAINE. Lily had said that on busy days, the street was jammed with the carriages of those who came to find rare and special goods.

Inside, Jean surveyed her surroundings with interest. The large room was divided into cubicles, each containing one type of merchandise. On a public day, each area would contain a salesman to help and guard, but today the emporium was almost empty. "The windows you put up by the ceiling light the space very well."

"And make thievery more difficult than lower windows. Moses suggested putting the clerestories in when we decided to open the public showroom." Monsieur Fontaine took a wicker basket from a stack by the door and gave it to her to carry her selections. "Though we specialize in African goods, there is much that comes from other lands as well. Choose whatever interests you, then we can discuss the prices."

"You must promise to give yourself a profit," she said firmly. "The Fontaine family is large and needs to make money."

He smiled. "I promise that I will charge you more than the cost, but not full price. We owe you too much."

"Lord and Lady Falconer rescued your son, not me."

"But they are not here." His voice softened. "Moses has told me what it meant for four battered souls to come under your protection. He said that you and Lady Bethany Fox were their sanctuary. You made them human again."

There was truth to that, though Jean was still embarrassed to be the recipient of such gratitude. "It's the most rewarding work I've ever done."

He inclined his head. "I shall be in the offices if you need me. The doors are locked to the public, so you will not be disturbed." He turned and headed for the emporium offices.

Jean decided to start with a quick swing around the showroom to get an idea of what was available before she began shopping in earnest. Her resolve was continually tested as she found treasure after treasure. There were textiles, beads, and brasswork from Africa, silks and porcelain and lacquerwork from China, spices from the East, jewels from India, and much more. She would be able to buy a lifetime's worth of gifts here. Peeling off her gloves so she could feel the textures, she moved through the labyrinth of display rooms.

In the far-left corner she found an alcove devoted to buttons. Since two women were there, she started to withdraw. The taller woman made a beckoning motion with her hand. "M'selle, if you visited a *modiste,* would you be willing to buy such buttons?"

On her palm lay several buttons of different materials. One was carved green jade, another red cinnabar, others enameled with Chinese designs. "These are wonderful!" Jean replied. "I would certainly be interested if I were your customer."

The woman indicated the signs showing price and origin, which sat neatly beside each dish of buttons. "My sister says they are too dear."

Jean saw the prices and blinked. "Dear indeed, but very attractive. They would add distinction to any gown."

"We have an *atelier* in Paris," the shorter sister explained. "We come here every year to find rare goods, but our customers are of the middling sort, not wealthy. I do not wish to sink a fortune into Asian buttons." The words were clearly aimed at her sister.

"Perhaps you could buy a sampling of different styles and your customers can order more if they wish?" Jean suggested. "With the understanding that the set might not be precisely like your sample, but would be the same material and general look. If you talked to Monsieur Fontaine, I'm sure he'd be happy to supply buttons on that basis."

The taller woman looked thoughtful. "That should work. Thank you, m'selle."

As the sisters debated which samples to select, Jean headed to the first quadrant of the showroom to begin serious shopping. The Parisiennes seemed to think that she was French, which pleased her. The weeks in Marseilles had improved her accent.

In a room filled with shining brasswork from Africa and Asia, she chose a large Chinese teapot with engraved patterns as a gift for her sister-in-law. For Lady Bethany, her honorary grandmother and friend, she picked a lovely ivory carving of a rhinoceros. Lady Beth had said once that the rhinoceros was the African version of a unicorn, and she had a fondness for unicorns.

After the sisters left with their bulging baskets, Jean had the showroom to herself. She filled one basket, set it by the door into the offices, and began to fill another basket. She was examining the area that displayed African beadwork when a man entered the showroom from the warehouse side.

Forgetting her manners, she stared in frank appreciation at one of the handsomest men she'd ever seen. The

newcomer was dressed with expensive European elegance, but his strong features and dark coloring surely came from some more exotic land. Lean and a little above average height, he moved like a man who walked in dangerous places. And wherever he walked, women would notice.

The newcomer was so compelling that it took Jean several moments to realize that he was followed by a servant, or perhaps a slave, a black African who carried a basket for his master. The elegant gentleman examined several lengths of fabric before placing two in the basket, then moving to the next area.

Since he was coming toward her, Jean returned her attention to the bead necklaces she had been examining. They were so lovely and varied that she wanted to buy them all. Not all women would enjoy jewelry of such barbaric splendor, but Meg, the Countess of Falconer, would love this broad collar of brilliant red beads and tiny shells, while this delicate necklace of silver links and sparkling gemstones would be perfect for Duncan's small daughter.

She became so engrossed in her selections that she forgot the handsome stranger until she turned to leave the beadwork area and bumped into him when she stepped into the passage. She was knocked backward, but he caught her arm quickly. "My apologies, mademoiselle," he said in flawless French as he released her.

Intensely aware of where he'd touched her arm, she said, "The fault is mine, monsieur. I am so dazzled by the Fontaine treasures that I didn't take proper care."

It was all she could do not to stammer since the man was even more compelling this close. The wavy black hair pulled into a queue was his own, not a wig, and his dark eyes had mysteries in their depths. She tried to read his energy, but it was tightly closed.

Switching to English with only the faintest trace of an accent, he said, "Forgive my forwardness, but you are English, I think?"

So much for the quality of her French. "Scottish, actually, but close enough."

"Scottish?" Hot, indefinable emotion flickered in those dark eyes. "I knew a gentleman of Scotland once. Macrae of Dunrath."

"My father or brother," Jean exclaimed, pleased to have a reason to continue the conversation.

"Your father, I think," he said, his gaze intense. "It has been many years since we met in Malta. You would have been hardly more than a babe. He said that he had a son, Duncan, and a bonnie wee daughter, but I don't remember the name. Would that be you, or an older sister?"

"I have no sisters and only one brother." She smiled at him. "I'm Jean Macrae."

"I am called Nicholas Gregorio." His eyes narrowed. "Does your father yet live?"

"He died ten years ago."

"So James Macrae is dead," Gregorio said softly. "A pity. I had dreamed of meeting him again. I trust your brother is well?"

"Yes, and with two bonnie bairns of his own."

"So the Macrae line continues." Gregorio's gaze became abstracted, as if seeing the past, before his focus sharpened on her again. "May I shake the hand of James Macrae's only daughter?"

His intensity was beginning to unnerve her, but he still fascinated her. "Of course." She extended her right hand, thinking it might have been better if she'd not removed her glove. His hand was also bare, and the touch of skin to skin seemed dangerously intimate. But he had known her father, so he was not really a stranger.

He clasped her hand with a powerful grip and energy blazed through her. Darkness, fury—

—and the world shattered.

NIKOLAI'S HAND still held the girl's, which slowed her collapse enough for him to catch her before she folded onto the floor. Dear God, but she was light, scarcely heavier than a child! He stared down into the small, pale face. She must be in her middle twenties, but she looked much younger, a prim, sheltered child of the British aristocracy.

He felt an uneasy qualm. This girl was not the one who had betrayed him into slavery. But the sins of the father were visited on their sons, and on their daughters. For too many years, during burning days and bleeding nights, he had planned the revenge He would take against Macrae. He had reveled in it, and sometimes that lust for vengeance was all that had kept him alive.

Though he was bitterly disappointed to know that his enemy was dead, he was not really surprised, not after so many years. But until now the time hadn't been right for Nikolai to seek justice. He had needed to obtain freedom and power to put himself in a position to pursue Macrae and his family.

Ironically, he was in the Fontaine warehouse to purchase goods for his first voyage to London. He had planned this journey for years, for he was finally prepared to seek out his enemy. Now that enemy's daughter had fallen into his hands. Perhaps the force of his obsession had drawn her to him.

With Macrae gone, vengeance must be wreaked on the son who was now Macrae of Dunrath. And this pallid girl, who had become his by the merest chance, would be his weapon. He studied her with avid curiosity, thinking that her slight body had never known adversity or hard labor. Her coloring was delicate, and her hair so heavily powdered that the color was disguised. He hadn't really noticed her eyes. They might have been a light hazel.

But she was a pretty thing, in a fragile, high-bred fashion. He had a sudden violent vision of himself assaulting her, ripping off that expensive gown and hammering into her soft, pampered body.

The fierce desire that accompanied his vision left him trembling. He took a deep breath and laid her on the floor. He would not rape, not even Macrae's daughter.

Tano returned and halted to stare at the girl. "Captain?"

"She is the daughter of my enemy." Nikolai's resolve hardened. Fate had brought this Macrae to him, and he would not waste the gift. Later he could decide the best way to use her. For now, he must get her to his ship without being noticed. "She's small enough to fit into one of the merchandise hampers. Bring one from the warehouse and don't let yourself be seen."

Tano frowned at the girl before turning to obey. Nikolai studied her again, wondering how long she would be unconscious. He'd used a huge amount of power on her—thinking of Macrae had made him burn with a red rage. It was fortunate he hadn't killed her by mistake. In fact, he probably would have if she hadn't been shielded. She was a Guardian, after all. His own power was undeveloped and rigidly suppressed—except for occasions like this.

He wondered how great her power was—the shield had been quite competent. But perhaps she'd had help with it. When Macrae talked of his children, he had shown pride in his son's great talent, but had not mentioned the daughter's. Likely Jean Macrae did not have unusual magical ability, but he mustn't take that for granted. A captive Guardian mage would be dangerous.

Tano returned with one of the large wicker hampers used for packing fragile valuables. Nikolai removed the lid, then lifted Jean Macrae and folded her into the basket. She barely fit, her knees drawn up and her arms crossed on her chest like a child. Once more he felt a twinge of discomfort at what he was doing. She'd looked so sweet and innocent when she had smiled up at him, pleased to find a man who knew her father.

But all who lived were the products of their ancestors. She should have chosen hers more carefully. He dropped her fallen bonnet on top of her.

"Will she stay asleep?" Tano asked.

Nikolai touched the smooth, pale ivory of her forehead. Her consciousness was still buried deeply, but he sent more energy just in case. "Long enough." He closed the hamper.

The next step was getting her to the ship. Nikolai would have to take her himself because of his ability to make people overlook his presence. Though he didn't become invisible, people tended to look past him. "I'll carry her out through the public door. Stay here to let me back in. Then we'll complete our business and leave from the warehouse side, so no one will know that I left and returned."

Tano nodded and lifted the handle at one end of the hamper. Together they carried it to the public door, then Nikolai took over. Though the Macrae chit wasn't heavy, the hamper was awkward. Luckily, the *Justice* was moored nearby. After his prisoner was locked in the mate's cabin, he returned to the Fontaine emporium and finished his purchases, his face impassive.

As soon as the last container was stowed, the ship sailed, blessed by a timely tide. The gods favored his quest, it seemed.

JEAN'S DISAPPEARANCE was noted at midday, when Monsieur Fontaine sought her out so they could return home for a luncheon. Her baskets of goods were found, but no trace of her remained. The warehouse and showroom were searched, residents of the waterfront neighborhood questioned with increasing desperation, but to no avail. Miss Jean Macrae, a gently bred young lady of Scotland, had vanished without a trace.

CHAPTER SEVEN

Adia on the Middle Passage

The Slave Coast fortress that held the captives was the largest, most impressive building Adia had ever seen, but it was the gateway to hell. A narrow door, just wide enough to accommodate one person at a time, allowed chained lines of slaves to pass through to the ship. As *she shuffled through the door, Adia knew in her bones that she would never see her homeland again.* Please don't leave me, Grandmother, even though I'm leaving Africa.

As *always when she asked her grandmother for help, she felt a gentle touch in her heart. Though that response was wordless, Adia's mind turned the feeling into words in her grandmother's dearly remembered voice.* I won't, child. I will always be with you.

Her grandmother's spirit gave her the dogged determination needed to survive. The voyage was an endless horror beyond anything she had ever imagined. Perhaps one in five of the slaves died during the passage. Once three men broke free and jumped overboard, seeking escape in the only way available to them.

Two succeeded. The third was dragged back to life by sailors who pursued him in a boat. Once the slave was back on board, he was whipped half to death because of his attempt to escape. Kondo, the vicious, snakelike man wielding the whip, was an African and a special aide to the captain. The fact that he was as black as she made him particularly easy to hate.

Yet even in the midst of hunger and despair, there were blessed touches of kindness. One woman in particular, a Yoruba called Fola, looked out for Adia, sleeping beside her at night and making sure that she got her share of the rancid food. Without a word being said, Adia knew that Fola's daughter had been captured and not survived the march to the coast.

Slaves were taken to the deck in small, chained groups to get fresh air. Adia thought this was wise of the captain since without these respites from the stench and disease of the slave decks, few would have survived the passage. Once she saw a crewman looking through a peculiar device made of metal. Seeing her interest, the sailor said, "This is a quadrant, girl. It tells us where we are. Want to look through?"

"Quad-rant," she said carefully, as she accepted the instrument. She listened to the speech of the sailors whenever she could, trying to learn the language. Grandmother assured her that doing so would be of advantage later. She looked through the metal tube, startled to see the horizon and the sun set next to each other. "Thank-you," she said as she handed back the device. Grandmother also encouraged her to be polite, because that would make people more willing to help her.

Deck outings taught her that the white sailors could be

treated as badly as the black slaves. Once Adia saw the captain beat one of his sailors unconscious, wielding the whip himself. Captain Trent had blue eyes, the coldest color Adia had ever seen. The sailor was left bleeding on the deck while other crewmen brought up the bodies of slaves who had died during the night.

As *the first body was thrown overboard, splashing broke out in the water. Adia saw that great finned fish were fighting for the corpse. Fola said emotionlessly, "Sharks follow the slave ships," and put her arm around Adia's trembling shoulders.*

Adia's only escape was in her dreams. Sometimes she was back in the valley with her family, laughing and happy and well fed. Other times she saw herself grown and in a distant land, happy again, though the future was so unclear that she saw no detail of what might produce happiness. Yet the dreams gave her hope, and hope gave her strength.

The moon had gone through one full cycle and half of another before they made landfall. Adia woke, thinking something had changed. The ship rolled as it hadn't since they'd set sail. They must be anchored.

Other slaves in the hold were waking and noticing the same thing. A ripple of excitement went through the group. No matter what horrors waited on land, life would have to be better in the open air than this stinking ship.

When two sailors came down with the pots of stewed rice used to feed the captives, someone called, "Where are we?"

The younger sailor, who seemed less hardened than his crewmates, said, "Jamaica. It's a fine sugar island. Later today you'll be divided into parcels and taken to the market."

Adia ate a bite of her rice, which today had bits of fish in it. She swallowed it slowly, though she wanted to gulp down the whole bowl. For the last half moon she had been giving most of her rice to Fola. Her friend was a tall, strong woman who needed more food, and during the voyage she had become gaunt with hunger.

"You must eat, child," Fola murmured when Adia offered the bowl.

"Now that we are arrived, there will be more food," Adia said. "I have had enough."

Fola's hunger made her easily persuaded. She finished her rice, then Adia's. Then they waited in the dark and stink of the hold. Finally the hatch opened and slaves were conducted up in groups. The sailors watched like jackals to prevent any escapes, since this close to land a slave would be tempted.

Adia squinted in the dazzling light when her group was ordered out. This Jamaica was beautiful, with turquoise water and jagged green mountains surrounding a bay. Fat clouds grazed across the sky. A blast of rain hit her boat as they were being transported to shore. She welcomed the squall, which cooled the heat and washed away some of the smell.

On shore, the captives were kept under armed guard as they were divided into groups equal to two hands' worth of fingers. Adia noticed that the parcels were mixed between men and women, weak and strong, with a child or two per group. There was a single hand of slaves left over at the end, including Adia.

They were herded into a merchant's yard with high fences, each parcel chained together. After a long wait standing in the noonday sun, a gate opened and a group of white men rushed in, eager to find parcels that pleased them. Adia's English wasn't good enough to follow most of the bargaining, but the yard soon cleared as parcels were bought and the groups herded out by the new owners. Tier straggly group of five was the last left. Fola was in one of the first parcels to be sold. They exchanged a last glance before Fola vanished from the yard. It was yet another loss, leaving Adia alone again. Her jaw clenched. She would not cry.

One of the white men was brought over by the merchant. "Your last chance, Harris," the merchant said. "You know you need more slaves, and who knows when the next ship will arrive?"

Harris frowned. "This is a weakly lot—they'll all die before I get my money's worth out of 'em." His gaze fell on Adia, and he stepped close, taking her chin in his hands and forcing her face up. "This one has some spirit, but she's just a little scrap who won't be useful for years."

"I'll give you a good price on this parcel."

"Not interested in any but the girl." Harris started to walk away.

"I'll sell her to you at three pence a pound," the merchant offered.

"Two pence a pound. I'll have to spend a fortune in rice and salt pork to fatten her up."

The merchant shrugged and unlocked Adia's shackles, then led her into a small room that opened off the yard. Adia was prodded up onto a scale and weighed. Thus, rigid with fury, she was sold like a basket of vegetables. Her new life had begun.

The only thing that kept her sane was Grandmother's reassurance. "You will die free."

CHAPTER EIGHT

JEAN AWOKE FEELING VERTIGO, as if she was rocking back and forth. Gradually she realized that she really was moving, her body rising and falling from the familiar motions of a ship. But what ship, and why?

She opened her eyes and found that she was lying on a narrow bunk in a small cabin. A porthole admitted enough light to illuminate her stark surroundings. She was rumpled, bruised, and her mouth was dust-dry.

She swung from the bunk and lurched to the porthole. A distant dark line marked the coast. The ship was well out to sea—too far to swim even if the window were large enough for her to escape. From the angle of the sun, she guessed it was late afternoon.

The cabin was so small that she could stand in the middle and touch all four walls. The bunk was built in, along with several storage cabinets and a tiny washbasin that was set into a counter. Next to it, a pitcher was set into a well to protect it during rough weather. Mercifully it was filled with water. She drank greedily and felt better.

The cabinets were mostly empty, probably cleaned out in haste by the prior inhabitant. The cabinet under the bunk contained several worn but neatly folded male garments with her battered bonnet stuffed in on top. The area under the washbasin contained two threadbare towels and an irregularly shaped bar of soap. There was also a chamber pot tucked into another cabinet. No weapons or other interesting items had been left behind. Nothing to tell her more about the ship or its crew.

The lock on the door was solid but simple. She could probably open it with a hairpin and a touch of magic, but there was no point in doing that now, when she had no place to run. Even if she crept out and stole a ship's dinghy, she'd be recaptured in no time. Either that, or used as target practice.

The slim knife that she wore sheathed on her inner thigh was still in place, so apparently she hadn't been searched carefully. It probably hadn't occurred to her captor that such a demure and useless maiden might be armed.

She took the two steps back to the bunk and sat down. The last thing she remembered was the man who called himself Nicholas Gregorio. He had taken her hand, there had been a rush of energy, and everything had gone black. She ran a palm over her head. No bumps or pains. She had been knocked out by magic.

Gregorio must be a mage. But why the devil had he kidnapped her?

Her stomach lurched again, so she stood and opened the porthole, breathing deeply of the fresh air. Ordinarily Guardians didn't talk about themselves to mundanes, and Gregorio would have been only a boy twenty years ago.

But he had power, so he was probably a Guardian himself. If he had Guardian parents, her father might have visited the household of the young Gregorio. Her father and Sir Jasper Polmarric had toured the Mediterranean about twenty years ago, calling on Guardians everywhere they visited. Such tours were a way of maintaining bonds among Guardians of different nations.

If Gregorio was a Guardian, why would he kidnap her? Guardians almost never injured other Guardians, except for the rare rogue mages. Perhaps Gregorio was a rogue. That was more likely than that he was a white slaver—she wasn't so dazzlingly beautiful that he would instantly feel a need to steal her away to be sold in Barbary. Though Captain Gordon had commented on the rarity of her red hair, today it was heavily powdered and she looked thoroughly bland.

More likely the kidnapping had to be related to Gregorio's knowing her father. Anger had blazed from him when he took her hand. But why on earth would he be angry at her father after twenty years? James Macrae had been a calm man, well liked by everyone. Jean and Duncan had inherited their tempers from their mother.

She relaxed and tried to scan the ship, but the cabin must have been shielded. She could detect only the faintest traces of the crew. For the thousandth time, she wished she was a more powerful mage.

Did she still have her scrying glass? She always carried it in a hidden pocket sewed into her gowns. She patted a seam on the left side of her gown. Yes, like the knife, the glass had been overlooked. She retrieved the quilted pouch and removed the polished disk of obsidian. She and her sister-in-law had studied scrying together. She couldn't match Gwynne's ability with the glass, but she'd become moderately competent.

After warming the glass between her palms, she asked a mental question about her situation. A wave of anxiety shivered through the obsidian, and she saw vague images of people searching for her. She sensed that Monsieur Fontaine had sent a message to the newlyweds reporting Jean's disappearance. She frowned, hating the idea that their honeymoons would be ruined.

Even if her friends discovered what had happened to her, there was little they could do. A ship at sea was a very small needle in a very large haystack. Perhaps a Guardian who was an exceptionally gifted hunter, like Simon, might be able to locate her, but even that was doubtful. She suspected that Gregorio was adept at covering his tracks.

What about Gregorio himself? She tried to bring up his image in the scrying glass, but he remained frustratingly out of focus. Though she sensed that he was a man who burned with anger and determination, she couldn't tell what his goals were, or what had made him what he was.

As always, serious attempts to use magic gave her a headache, so she hid the scrying glass away and lay back on the bunk. She cleared her mind and tried to reach Breeda. The two of them were alike in ways that went beyond red hair, so Breeda was the best chance for communicating.

After long minutes of striving, she felt that she touched Breeda, who was tense with anxiety. Jean tried to send the message that she was alive and unharmed, but she wasn't sure if she'd succeeded. Then she tried to reach the other thralls, with even less sense of success.

With nothing useful left to do, she rolled on her side and went back to sleep.

JEAN THOUGHT that Gregorio would appear soon to threaten, explain, or taunt, but she was left alone. As the hours passed, she realized that boredom was going to be a major problem in captivity. She'd never been good at sitting still and doing nothing.

After a few hours of inactivity, she was ready to leap out of her skin. Since pacing the tiny cabin did no good, she forced herself to relax and review all the kinds of magic that might be useful.

Her heart jerked as dusk approached and the door opened, but it was only a pair of sailors delivering a meal. The tray was carried by a hard-faced man of uncertain ancestry. He was accompanied by an armed African who kept his pistol aimed at her. She'd had no idea what an alarming female she was.

She tried to coax them to speak using English,

French, and Latin, with no success. Perhaps the damned men were mute. Being ignored was simultaneously soothing and anxiety provoking. What did Gregorio have in mind for her?

After they left, she clamped down on her anxiety and turned her attention to the food. The tray contained a wooden bowl holding a sticky, rice-based dish. Bits of fish and onion were mixed in, and it was surprisingly tasty. There was also a piece of good bread and a heavy glass tumbler of white table wine. She'd dined on worse in the homes of British gentry.

The only utensil was a spoon made of soft metal. She supposed her captors were being cautious, but they lacked imagination if they didn't realize that a glass tumbler or a china washing pitcher could be broken and turned into a weapon. Or maybe they merely recognized that such heroics on her part would do no good under the present circumstances.

With no candle nor any reason to stay awake, she retired when the sun went down. Since she didn't want to sleep in her gown and stays, she retrieved the worn garments she'd found in the cabinet. A pair of loose sailor's trousers in faded navy blue and a white shirt stained by dubious substances would make decent sleepwear.

She hacked the trousers to ankle length so she wouldn't trip over folds of extra cloth. The waist was huge, but it was secured by a length of cord so she could tie the trousers tightly enough to stay on. The sleeves she rolled up to free her hands. Though she looked like a ragpicker, it was a relief to be out of her regular garments. She kept her knife and scrying glass on her, just in case she had a chance to escape.

For someone who had slept on stones and piles of bracken or heather, the hard bunk was comfortable enough. She pulled the blanket close against the chilly night air. Perhaps because she had slept earlier, she found it difficult to doze off.

A sailing ship was a living entity, a symphony of creaks and thumps as well as the steady splashing of water against the hull. She'd grown accustomed to sailing sounds on the voyage to Marseilles, had even found them friendly. Now she was intensely aware that this ship was taking her away from everything and everyone she knew.

Lady Bethany had said Jean would have an adventure. Surely she would have been more concerned if she'd sensed that Jean was going to be murdered out of hand by a vengeful pirate? If this was merely an "adventure," the implication was that Jean would survive. On that hopeful note, she finally dozed off.

FOR TWO DAYS, she was alone except for the brief visits of the food sailors. The morning meal was some kind of stewed grain paste, probably wheat, with bits of dried fruit mixed in. Served with hot mint tea, it wasn't bad.

When she tired of cataloging her store of spells, she tried to remember poetry she'd memorized. She was definitely not cut out for long-term imprisonment.

Boredom ended on the third day when the door opened at midday, not a time when a meal was expected. She glanced up, her senses on high alert. Nicholas Gregorio filled the doorway, dark and threatening. Though he still wore impeccably tailored clothing and admirable boots, his garments were not those of a gentleman. With his head bare and a cutlass hanging at his side, he looked like a pirate. A disturbingly powerful and attractive pirate.

"So my kidnapper deigns to visit." She slid from the bed and stood with her back to the outside wall as she tried to read his energy. No luck—he was tightly shielded. He burned with leashed fury, and he was clearly the captain of this vessel, but those facts could be read in his face and bearing with no need for magic. "Why am I here?"

His dark eyes glinted maliciously. "Letting you wonder suits my purpose."

"Rubbish," she said impatiently. "You've kidnapped me, a woman you've never met, and seem intent on destroying my life. At the least, you owe me an explanation."

"Since you wish to know..." He closed the cabin door behind him with an ominous click. "You are here because your father betrayed me in the vilest possible way. I swore I would avenge myself against him and the house of Macrae. Since he is dead, that means you and your brother must pay for your father's crimes."

Her jaw dropped with shock. "That's utter nonsense!

My father was the last man on earth to betray anyone. You must be mistaken."

"James Macrae of Dunrath, yes? Also known as Lord Ballister, with a son and heir named Duncan. You confirmed that yourself. Or does Dunrath have another Macrae claiming chieftainship?"

"No," she admitted. "But perhaps someone used his name falsely."

He snorted. "And this mysterious person had Guardian powers? You are grasping at straws, madam."

She had to agree that such a deception was unlikely. "What is the crime you accuse him of?"

A muscle jerked in the captain's cheek. "Your precious father betrayed me into slavery. There is no punishment great enough for that."

Shock piled on shock. "No! My father would never do such a thing!"

"No?" His smile was bitter. "I was there, madam. You were not."

"Tell me what happened." When he didn't reply, she added, "I'll need a great deal of convincing to believe such slander. At the moment, I believe you're deranged."

"It doesn't matter whether or not you believe." He moved forward a step, close enough to touch her if he chose. A thin, almost invisible scar curved from his left jaw into his black hair. "I told you the truth only because you asked."

If he was deliberately trying to intimidate her, he was doing a good job of it. Hands clenched, she tried to shield herself, but she wasn't sure that her spell would work against a man like this. "I do wish to know the truth, Captain," she said with an attempt at calm. "Even if it turns my world upside down. Where did you meet my father? What was the act of betrayal?"

"I was born in Malta and orphaned young," he replied, voice clipped. "Twenty years ago, on the worst day of my life, your father and his friend, Sir Jasper Polmarric, found me in Valletta and said I had magical power. They told me of the Guardians and said they would protect and educate me." Gregorio's mouth twisted. "Your father claimed he would take me to Scotland and foster me with his own children."

"That sounds like him." Jean's parents had often fostered Guardian children in need of a temporary home. Simon, Earl of Falconer, had been one such child after his parents died. But while Simon had been a slightly unnerving older brother to her, it was impossible to imagine this pirate in that role. "What happened to prevent you from coming to Dunrath?"

"On the way to Britain, our ship was attacked by Barbary pirates." His dark eyes blazed with remembered fury. "I was taken captive. When I called for help, your father saw me in the hands of pirates, and he turned away. He bloody well turned his back!"

Jean had a vivid, deeply disturbing image of a child crying out while the adult he trusted abandoned him.

The image was so sharp that she wondered if it came right from Gregorio's mind. But her father would not have behaved in such a way. He *wouldn't.* "Battle is chaos. He must not have seen you."

"He looked right into my eyes and turned away," the captain said coldly. "Besides, was he not a mage? In the weeks I knew him, he proved often that he could detect my presence when I was near. He saw me taken, and decided it was not worth risking himself for a gutter rat, despite the promises he'd made." Anger throbbed through his voice, white hot despite all the years that had passed.

The anger and rage were real, no matter what the actual facts of what happened. Trying to get a clearer picture, she asked, "Why is all your anger for my father? Did Jasper Polmarric try to help you?"

"It was not Polmarric who made the promises." His expression was brooding. "I think Polmarric died that day, but if he survived and lives still, I shall find him when I sail to London."

"You saw Sir Jasper shot?" Jean asked, startled.

"Yes. You seem to know him. Did he survive?"

"Yes, but he took a musket ball in his back that day. Though my father managed to save his life, Sir Jasper never walked again. He is confined to a wheelchair." There was satisfaction in seeing Gregorio's shock, but Jean realized uneasily that this might be the answer. She had heard the story of how Sir Jasper was shot during a pirate attack, literally falling at her father's feet. "Perhaps my father was forced to choose between you and the life of one of his oldest friends," she said slowly. "The safety of the whole ship might have been on his shoulders—he was a natural leader and a fine swordsman as well as a mage."

Gregorio moved forward another half step. "Do you think that knowing he made such a choice would make me feel better about it?"

She refused to drop her gaze. "No. But I also know that in battle, events happen with shattering swiftness. Life-or-death decisions must be made with no time to think. Regret is a luxury that comes later, if you survive." And it haunted dreams forever.

"For a pampered girl, you speak of war with great authority," he said drily.

Though she knew it was best if he underestimated her, she could not let his comment pass. "Am I wrong?"

"No," he admitted. "In the heat of battle, strange things happen. Small details can be magnified; great events can take place a glance away and be missed entirely. You have listened to soldiers, I think."

"Scotland suffered a bloody civil war a few years ago. I knew many men who participated in it." Changing the subject, she continued, "Even if my father deliberately abandoned you, which is still hard to believe, you have not done badly." Her gesture included the ship. "How did you escape slavery and become a pirate captain?"

"I led a slave rising on a galley," he said coolly. "We killed the officers and crew, and the ship was ours."

She thought of the chains that locked galley slaves to their benches and shuddered. "That was surely more difficult than it sounds."

His eyes narrowed. "I didn't say it was easy."

She had another vision, this time of blood and steel as unarmed men tackled their captors in a desperate bid for freedom. That they succeeded, she guessed, was because of the man before her. With his intelligence, ruthlessness, and power, he was a born leader. "Once more I ask your intentions toward me. I don't suppose you want to kill me, or I would be dead already."

"You are correct. Death is far too easy." There was a flash of teeth that could never be called a smile. "I have not yet decided. Ransom, perhaps?"

She shrugged. "You may try, but my family is not wealthy by the standards of the aristocracy. Scotland is a poor country, and whatever the chieftain of the Macraes possesses is at the service of his people."

He moved closer still, his energy pressing against hers with the force of a physical shove. "Perhaps, but taken together, the Guardians control great wealth. Would they allow one of their own to languish in vile captivity?"

She shrugged again. "A spinster of no great magic has little value to the community. My own family will care, but they cannot afford to beggar themselves to bring me home. You will not be able to extract a ransom large enough to satisfy your anger." Her statement was less than the whole truth, for the Guardians took care of their own, and as a group they had great resources. "However, the council might send searchers to find me, and they are not people you would wish to meet unless you have a dozen powerful mages standing beside you."

"Ransom was never my first choice." He reached out and trailed a fingernail around her throat. "Selling you into slavery is better justice."

She shivered at his touch, which held both threat and

dark promise. This was a man who could destroy her, body and soul, without drawing a deep breath. But his touch made it easier to read him. "You will sell no one into slavery," she said flatly. "You hate slavery so much that you would not condemn even your worst enemy to that."

His hand clamped around her throat so tightly she could scarcely breathe. "Perhaps you are right," he breathed. "Perhaps it would be better to keep you as my prisoner here on the *Justice* so I can rape you whenever I wish."

He wanted to do exactly that; she could feel his desire and the rage that demanded vengeance for what he'd suffered. But he prided himself on being a strong man, one who would not yield to raw emotion. "You will not ravish me, I think. Not today."

She felt a flicker of surprise, though his expression didn't change. "What an innocent you are," he snapped. "Why should I not take you right now? If I'm not going to sell you in Tangier, lost virginity won't affect your value, and I would find great satisfaction in ruining James Macrae's daughter."

The same mental link that had told her how he felt about slavery produced more information. "Because of Ulindi, ravishing helpless women is not to your taste." As she said the name, horrific images surged through her mind. A lithe young woman with cinnamon skin attacked by a hoard of drunken men. The brutal, repeated assaults as she screamed desperately. The kicks and blows that ended the girl's life.

Gregorio jerked away as if she was poisonous. "You bloody witch!" he snarled. "You are your father's daughter—innocence disguising evil. Be damned to you, Jean Macrae!" He whirled and slammed his way out of the cabin.

So Jean was a prisoner on a ship named *Justice,* and the captain wanted her to pay for the perceived sins of her father. She folded, shaking, onto her bunk.

May God have mercy on her soul.

CHAPTER NINE

NIKOLAI'S HEART pounded as he locked the cabin door and stalked away. The damned female had the ability to drive him mad. He should have realized that a Guardian would not be an ordinary British girl, no matter how prim she looked. Perhaps he should have confronted her the day of her capture, before she'd had a chance to gather that intimidating cloak of self-possession around her. And before she'd had time to rummage through his mind and memories.

He climbed the ladder to the main deck, hoping the stiff breeze would clear his thoughts. What was he to do with her? As she had recognized, he wouldn't sell her into slavery even though that would be perfect justice. Perhaps he could have condemned James Macrae to such a fate, but the daughter had not harmed him directly, even though she carried her family's blood guilt.

How much had the Scottish witch known about

Ulindi? Too much, since she'd realized that because of Ulindi, he could not assault a defenseless woman.

Swearing again, he raised his spyglass and scanned the horizon. Instinct said that somewhere out there was a ship ripe for his taking, and by God, he would find it.

AFTER THE CAPTAIN STORMED OUT, Jean locked her arms around herself and rocked back and forth, shaking. She was in the hands of the most dangerous and unpredictable man she'd ever met, and he despised her. Today, at least, he hadn't released his violence, but there were no guarantees for tomorrow. Anger might overcome his distaste for rape.

Given time, the Guardians could find her, but she didn't have time and her family was a thousand miles away. If she was to survive and return home, it must be through her own wits and resourcefulness.

She jumped like a nervous hare when a key grated in the lock, but this time it was only the crewman carrying her supper, along with his usual guard. Since she'd had no luck getting information on previous days, today she asked for hot water to wash herself. She asked in French and repeated the request in English, but again, the sailors ignored her. They withdrew, locking the door firmly behind them.

As she finished eating, the door opened again and a sailor she hadn't seen before delivered a large bucket of water. He was carefully guarded, of course.

"Merci," she said politely as she handed over the tray with her empty bowl and spoon. She hadn't finished the wine, so she kept that. She added the smile that had been called charming in some of London's best ballrooms.

At her thanks, the sailor dropped his eyes bashfully as he left. He was just a boy, probably under twenty. Young enough to be embarrassed by the mere presence of a woman. Possibly he might become an ally.

Under the circumstances, she was reluctant to disrobe for a really thorough bath, but with a corner of one of the towels she'd found below the washbasin, she could clean herself well enough. Then she washed her hair, getting as much powder out as possible. If she was to face the unknown, she'd do it looking like herself.

Like a damned redheaded Scot.

SHE WOKE from a sound sleep when an almighty boom shuddered through the ship, knocking her from her bunk. Swearing, she scrambled to her feet. Had the ship struck a reef or rock? No, she heard shouts, then another ragged volley of explosions that rocked the vessel. They were being fired on by cannon.

More cannon shots, this time deafeningly close as the *Justice* fired back. Her blood ran cold. If the ship was damaged badly enough to sink, she could die here, trapped like a rat in a cage.

Hell, no! She slid into her lightweight shoes, then set to work on the door lock with a hairpin, creating a small mage light so she could see what she was doing. She hadn't the magical ability to move the tumblers by pure thought, but she did have a knack for puzzles and locks, and this one took only moments to pick.

Knife in hand, she dowsed the mage light and opened the door. The narrow corridor was dark and silent, though overhead cacophony ruled. There had been no more cannon volleys. Shouts and pistol shots suggested that one ship had tried to board the other, and the crews were fighting hand to hand. In the confusion, there might be an opportunity to escape.

Invoking a don't-look spell, she ran down the corridor and climbed the ladder, emerging onto the deck warily. Dawn was a slash of orange along the eastern horizon, and there was just enough light to outline the men fighting with swords and sometimes pistols. She took shelter in the shadow of the wheelhouse and tried to make sense of the action. To her surprise, Gregorio's ship was a European trading vessel not dissimilar to the *Mercury*. She'd expected a pirate ship to look different.

But the slim, narrow vessel lying alongside was unquestionably a corsair galley. Low and sleek, it had dozens of slaves chained to oars. Sections of the oars that extended beyond the ship were broken where the hulls banged together. So which ship was the attacker and which the victim? Had one pirate accidentally attacked another?

The battle spilled across both ships, with the corsairs wearing light-colored turbans. They outnumbered the crew of the *Justice*, but Gregorio's men, a very mixed lot, fought very, very well. In fact, they were gradually prevailing, killing some of the corsairs and pushing the others back onto the galley. Gregorio was right in the middle of the action, moving with lithe ruthlessness as he struck down pirate after pirate.

She had considered crossing to the other ship until she saw that it was a corsair. Joining them was unlikely to be an improvement. Perhaps she could escape from the *Justice* when its crew was looking the other way.

She slipped around the wheelhouse and studied the starboard side of the ship, opposite the fighting. The *Justice* carried several dinghies, with the smallest secured a little forward of her position. She moved closer. After a quick survey, she decided she could cut the vessel loose with her knife. It was small enough that she could push it over the railing into the water. The sea was fairly calm, and if the boat stayed upright she could dive in next to it, then board and row away.

But would such an escape improve her situation? When the *Justice* won its current battle, she'd be missed. Once they realized she wasn't aboard the ship, it probably wouldn't take them long to spot her, and rowing wasn't a fast way to travel. Even if she managed to escape, she might well be sentencing herself to death from thirst or starvation.

She consulted her intuition. She didn't have the sense that she was likely to die escaping on a dinghy, so it was worth the risk. Of course, intuition might just be saying that she wouldn't manage to get away, but she was willing to try.

She was sawing on a line that secured the bow of the dinghy when she heard Gregorio bellow with a fury that curdled the air. Curious, she moved back to the wheelhouse and saw that he and his men had advanced onto the galley.

Gregorio was engaged in a shouting match with the corsair captain in a language she didn't recognize. The sky had lightened enough to reveal Gregorio's expression, and the blood on his curved sword. Most of the corsairs were wounded or captive. Very soon the fighting would be over.

Sneering, the corsair captain—a *reis,* that's what they were called—jumped to the raised aisle that ran between the seats where the rowers were chained. He raised his sword to chop at the nearest slave. The slave screamed and cowered away, desperately trying to avoid the blow.

With a roar, Gregorio leaped after the *reis* and smashed the other man's blade aside with his sword. Jean stared. It looked as if he was defending the slaves! Probably because they were valuable. She was about to return to the dinghy when three of the remaining corsair fighters joined their captain, all of them hacking at Gregorio.

Damnation, the *reis* was pulling a pistol out from under his flowing robe and aiming it point-blank at Gregorio! She shouldn't care, but every fiber of her being screamed that she couldn't let him die.

She darted to the railing, knife in hand. The action of the battle seemed to slow, giving her all the time she needed to skid to a halt, take aim, and hurl her knife into the *reis*'s throat.

The *reis* crumbled, his pistol discharging harmlessly into the air. By the time his body hit the deck, three of Gregorio's sailors had reached their captain's side. Fighting in the narrow aisle between the rows of oars, they cut down the remaining corsairs.

With his back protected, Gregorio spun around to look at the source of the knife. His gaze moved right to her, but that didn't mean he'd recognized her. She strengthened her don't-see spell and dropped to the deck of the *Justice,* out of the captain's sight. If she was to have any chance of escaping, she would have to move fast.

With her knife gone, she would need some sort of a weapon. She passed a dead pirate and appropriated his sword. Slim and curving, it was light enough for her to handle. Not as good as her throwing knife, but a great deal better than nothing.

Grimly she began hacking at the ropes that secured the dinghy.

CHAPTER TEN

WHO THE DEVIL? Nikolai's crew contained no one like the boy who had thrown the knife. Might the child have crossed over from the corsair?

Then the small figure turned and vanished, and Nikolai realized that was no boy. "Tano, take charge here!"

The death of the corsair captain had ended the battle. Moulay Reis was an old enemy of Nikolai's, and he had wanted to take the man's life himself. Of course, their fight had almost gone the other way. Leave it to Moulay to cheat with a pistol.

But why had the little witch saved him? Assuming the scruffy little urchin who had hurled that knife was her. The idea was incredible, but he'd seen her face, and the outlines of a slight but distinctly female form under her shapeless sailor's garments.

Nikolai leaped back aboard his ship to find the Scottish witch. He found her at the dinghy, slashing at the lines that secured it to the deck. A thick red braid fell over her shoulder, and her small white hands wielded a corsair blade with unnerving expertise.

"Don't waste your strength," he barked. "You're not leaving this ship."

She pivoted, sword in hand. It was a lovely *nimcha,* one he wouldn't mind owning. She hissed, "Don't come near me!"

He paused out of her reach, realizing that he was disinclined to move closer. She was using some kind of magical shield. He could overcome it, but he would have to use his own magic to do so.

Reluctantly amused by the blazing red-haired hellion who confronted him with lethal menace, he asked, "Where is that well-bred young lady I kidnapped in Marseilles?"

"She existed mostly in your mind." Her crisp voice was as different as her demeanor and her garb. "I'm no meek English virgin, Captain. I rode to battle against the king's army in the Rising of Forty-five. When my lover died, I led our men myself. After Culloden, I guided them home safely across country filled with pillaging English soldiers. You underestimated me, as most men do." Her eyes narrowed. "I could have killed you. Instead, I saved your life. Surely that is worth my freedom."

"Why should I be fair when I hold all the power?" Thinking she was unlikely to attack him, he concentrated his power and reached out slowly to take the sword.

She sliced the blade across his wrist with just enough pressure to draw blood, then danced back a step. "Not all the power. There's a good chance that I can kill you before any of your men observe this little scene." She showed her teeth. "We shall learn if your power of attack is greater than my ability to shield."

"I doubt you have enough power to fight off me and my whole crew!"

"It would be interesting to find out." She lowered the point of her sword. "Promise me my life and freedom, and in return I shall spare your life and not send any Guardian enforcers after you."

"I have no intention of killing you, but your freedom is another matter." He muttered an oath as he wiped blood from his wrist. The wound wasn't dangerous, but it stung like Hades. "What makes you think I would keep a promise made under duress?"

She laughed wickedly. "Because you are a man of principles, even though you are a kidnapping, bloodthirsty pirate."

He swore again. This woman could read him like no one he'd ever known. Except, perhaps, his grandmother. "You have little bargaining power. Kill me and my men will kill you."

"A man who seeks vengeance with such passion surely has a sense of justice," she said flatly. "Do you owe me nothing for saving your life?"

He frowned, hating the fact that she was right. Moulay Reis had guessed that threatening a helpless slave would enrage Nikolai to the point where he would cast caution to the winds. "I might have avoided Moulay Reis's musket ball, for I have survived many battles such as this. But it's possible that he would have killed me, so I do owe you something. Not your freedom, though. My life is too paltry a price for that."

Her mouth tightened. "At the least, you should release me from that cabin before I go mad with boredom."

So the Scottish witch was impatient. With that red hair, he wasn't surprised. "If you give me your word that you will not injure anyone, you may have the key to your cabin and the freedom of the ship."

"You aren't asking me to promise not to escape?"

"The ship will not call anywhere that will offer you freedom," he said bluntly.

"Very well," she said, after considering. "But if saving your life is worth so little, what would it take to win my freedom?"

He guessed that the question was rhetorical, but he chose to answer it. "Saving the entire ship and crew would do, I believe. Now give me that sword."

She refused to hand it over, though he felt her relax her protective shield. "Only if I get my own knife back. It was made for my hand."

"Very well. Come and take it from Moulay Reis's throat."

He was deliberately harsh in his words, but she didn't blink. As she started across the deck, she said, "You knew the captain of the other ship?"

"Oh, yes," he said softly. "I knew him well."

She slanted a glance upward. "Sorry to have denied you the pleasure of killing him," she said with uncomfortable perception. "Who was the attacker in this battle?"

"He was. Exactly what I had wished for." They reached the railing. Though the two ships lay side by side, hulls grinding, it still took great care to jump to the deck of the galley. He timed the rise and fall of the ships before leaping down.

He turned and saw Jean hesitating as she studied the shifting gap between the ships. For a petite woman, the risk was greater. He extended his hand to her. "Come."

"No need." Her muscles tensed as she prepared to jump.

He said impatiently, "If you slip and fall, you'll be ground to pieces between the hulls. Take my hand." Reluctantly she obeyed. When their hands clasped, there was a snap of energy, and he realized that the current between them ran both ways. She was much less cool than she appeared. Though she had experienced battle, she was no hardened warrior. Her determination to look fierce was curiously endearing.

She leaped down to the deck of the galley and almost fell when the ship pitched. His grip held her steady until she regained her balance.

"Thank you." She yanked her hand away. He stepped back, unnerved by their interaction. Maybe he should free her for his own peace of mind. Either that or feed her to the sharks. Though the sharks might not thank him for such a sharp-edged morsel.

Nikolai's experienced crew was already cleaning up the debris of battle. The dead were stacked to one side.

Most were Muslim, and they would have the rites of their religion said before being consigned to the sea. The captives were huddled under guard in the stern of the ship. Their unhappy expressions suggested that they had heard of Nikolai and the *Justice.*

The banging of hammer and chisel on iron marked the blows of the ship's blacksmith as he struck the irons from the galley slaves. Other crewmen distributed modest portions of bread, cheese, and ale. The freed slaves fell on the food ravenously. Rowers were seldom fed more than the bare essentials necessary to keep them working. Later they would be given better food, but Nikolai knew from experience that feeding them too much now would make them ill.

Most of the rowers were European, though a few Africans were scattered in. One of the first freed rose shakily from his bench and stretched to his full height, extending his arms as he embraced the ability to move freely. He wore only a loincloth and his sunburned skin covered hard, ropy muscles. His face was luminescent with joy. "God bless you, Captain," he said in French. "What will you do with us?"—

"Sell them for a good profit," Jean muttered under her breath. "The poor devils."

Nikolai's eyes narrowed. "Watch and learn." He took the sword from her. "But first, retrieve your knife." Feeling that she had fallen into another world, Jean picked her way between the rowers to the crumpled body of Moulay Reis. Some of the freed slaves openly gaped when they realized she was a woman, but they said nothing. Food and freedom were more important now.

The splendid red-and-gold brocade robe the *reis* wore was saturated with blood, and Jean's knife still rested in his slashed throat. His dark eyes stared sightlessly at his killer when Jean bent over to retrieve the weapon. Forcing herself to be impassive, she pulled out the dagger and wiped the blood off on the robe's ermine trim.

She stood and turned back, wanting to escape this charnel house. The small, quiet cabin that had been her prison was appealing now that she wouldn't be locked in.

As she made her way along the aisle between the rowing stations, another freed slave called to Gregorio, his face desperate with hope, "Will you take us home?" He spoke French, but his accent was Italian, Jean thought.

Though she had been ready to retreat to her cabin, now curiosity held her. She took a spot on the railing below the *justice* so she could retreat quickly if necessary, then turned to watch how the captain would handle the situation.

Gregorio moved to the end of the rowing area and raised his arms commandingly, Jean's sword in his hand. Using French, the most widely spoken language in Europe, he said, "We will deliver you to the Mediterranean port that is convenient for the greatest number of you. Those still far from home will receive funds to travel the rest of the way." His gaze swept the bony, wild-eyed men before him. A few were translating quietly to comrades who didn't understand French.

It was shocking to look at Gregorio and realize that he had been a galley slave just like these men. Shocking, and disturbing to think of him chained and naked, only a loincloth on his gaunt, sunburned body.

A grizzled man stared at his scarred wrists, deeply grooved by years of manacles. "What about those of us who have no home?" he said in a hoarse voice.

He might not have expected an answer, but Gregorio said, "There is an alternative. I can take you to the island of Santola. It is inhabited almost entirely by freed slaves, both men and women. All are welcome on Santola no matter what your past. In return for a home, you must accept others as they accept you. You must also work, but as free men, not slaves. You may stay as long as you wish. If you ever decide to leave, you will have passage to the mainland on the next available ship."

His words produced a rustle of interest among the galley slaves, with the word Santola being repeated in hushed voices. Jean studied the men's faces and auras and had the sense that a fair number of them, perhaps a third, were excited by the idea of a new home where the shame of slavery wouldn't matter. But where was Santola? She had never heard of it.

One of the slaves rose and stalked toward the sullen group of prisoners. His back was a hideous snarl of scars. "You speak of life. Now that I am free, I am interested only in death. *His* death!"

Eyes wild, he lunged at the most richly dressed of the captives, locking his hands around the man's throat and wrestling him to the deck. The guards pried the galley slave off the struggling corsair.

"Contain yourself. I assure you that justice will be done." Gregorio's gaze passed over the freed slaves, touching each man. "You who were their victims will choose which among the corsairs were truly evil, which merely did as they were told, and if some few might have been merciful." He pointed at that man who had been attacked. "We begin with him."

"Hassan was the slave overseer," a man growled. "He enjoyed the lash."

"He killed that Greek boy for no reason," another snarled..

"Give him to us for punishment!"

Voice calming, Gregorio asked, "Can anyone speak any good of Hassan?"

There was muttering, but no one volunteered a reply. Gregorio gestured with the sword, and his men took the overseer to a spot by the far railing. "Now, what about this one?" He pointed the sword at another corsair, a thin man with haunted eyes.

One of the *Justice* sailors pulled the man forward to be judged. At first there was silence. Then one of the rowers said reluctantly, "Nazeer used to give me extra water when Hassan wasn't looking."

Several of the others nodded. Another said, "Once Hassan told him to whip me, but Nazeer didn't hit very hard."

"He didn't enjoy hurting us," another agreed. "Once I collapsed and Hassan would have thrown me over the side, but Nazeer said I still had some good years in me. He gave me bread and a piece of his own fish and allowed me time to recover."

"So he is not evil." Gregorio gestured toward a different spot by the railing and Nazeer was taken there under guard.

Jean watched in fascination while each corsair was presented to the freed slaves. Some of the rowers wanted as much blood as possible, but Gregorio kept asking questions until there was general agreement about the behavior of each of the surviving corsairs. A handful joined Nazeer as men who had showed kindness when possible. A larger number were judged as neutral—not kind but not cruel, either.

The remaining corsairs, about a third of the captives, stood accused of violence and brutality. In all cases, there were multiple claims of vicious behavior and no redeeming acts. Those slaves who survived spoke for the dead who had been victims.

When the last corsair had been judged, Gregorio said to the captives, "You who have been judged decent will be returned to a Barbary port. I would suggest you consider another line of work. If I find you on another slave ship, I shall not be so merciful. As for the rest..." His remorseless gaze moved to the corsairs who had been judged vicious. "Give them to the freed slaves, one at a time."

Hassan, the overseer, was shoved down the aisle that ran between the rowing stations. He screamed and tried to run away, but within seconds he disappeared under a mass of howling, furious slaves.

His screaming stopped abruptly.

Stomach roiling, Jean spun around and scrambled up onto the *Justice,* not caring about the risk of falling between the ships. She was at the ladder that descended to the cabins when Gregorio caught up with her.

"Do you disapprove of my justice?" he asked mildly. Jean halted above the ladder and forced herself to think calmly rather than of gouging hands and furious kicks. "I... I don't know. The overseer and many of his underlings committed appalling acts. I suppose it is justice to let their victims execute the punishment. But my stomach isn't strong enough to watch it. It seems wrong that they weren't tried in a court of law."

"How very British of you. No court would produce a truer verdict than the one rendered by their victims, and immediate execution saves food." There was malicious amusement in his dark eyes. He enjoyed outraging her. He continued, "They will die quickly. That is more mercy than most of them granted."

"Why not hang or shoot them? That would be quicker yet."

He shook his head. "The galley slaves have been powerless since their capture. Today, they have power again."

She heard the cries of the rowers as another condemned corsair was turned over to them. "I think I can understand that, but this is so... so barbaric."

His face twisted into a sneer. "Slavery is the true

barbarism. For one man to claim he has the right to own another would be an affront to a benevolent God, if such a being existed."

Given his past, she couldn't blame him for his heretical comments. Since he seemed inclined to talk, she asked, "Where is Santola?"

Instead of telling her, he said, "Dine with me tonight in my cabin. I shall answer some of your questions. But now, I must go and watch men be torn apart."

He pivoted and returned to the galley. He obviously liked having the last word. Heaven knew she couldn't think of a response to what he just said.

She descended to the cabin deck, feeling exhausted. So she must dine with her captor. At least with only one dress, she needn't worry about what to wear.

CHAPTER ELEVEN

Adia
Plantation Life in Jamaica

The strangest thing about life as a slave was that, in some ways, it was simply life. The slaves at Harris Hall came from many lands, but together they made a new tribe, and men who would have been sworn enemies in Africa here became friends. Despite the brutally hard work, there were moments of joy and fellowship. Children labored with small hoes, but in slack times they laughed and played games, no different from the free children of the Iske.

Yet there were also horrors beyond what Adia could have imagined before her capture. Most of the fieldwork was done by women, and they were worked so hard that few ever bore children. The millwork of crushing cane and boiling sugar was done mostly by men, and burns and lethal accidents were not uncommon. Even healthy bodies wore out in pitifully few years.

Having a quick, curious mind, Adia learned all she could

from the other slaves, including tales of their gods and magical traditions. She also learned that life was easier for house slaves, so she determined to strive for that.

Usually new slaves were given lighter duties for two or three years to harden them for life in the Indies. Adia was nearing the end of that period when the cook at the big house came looking for a scullery maid. Her ability to learn and cooperative nature paid off when she was selected.

Work in the kitchens was hard, but she ate well and learned to cook European food as she graduated from scullery maid to junior cook. During her kitchen years, she came to womanhood and began to attract the attention of men. The heat of young blood made her tempted by some of those who made advances, but she would not allow herself to succumb.

Grandmother made it clear that she must be cautious for she had a destiny. Adia knew that having children would bind her even more tightly into slavery, but following Grandmother's guidance left her with hot, restless nights.

Her greatest regret was that she became a woman without being initiated. She could feel the magic beating through her blood, but her power remained untrained and undeveloped. All she could manage were a few small spells and charms. Though some of the Harris Hill slaves had modest magical talents, there were no priests or priestesses to take her to the realms of spirit.

One valuable lesson she did learn was how to conceal worship behind the ways of the Christian gods. Mrs. Harris, the mistress of the plantation, believed it was her duty to teach her slaves to be good Christians. Though she attended the Anglican church like her husband, she had been raised a Catholic, so she quietly invited a Catholic priest to teach her slaves religion.

While the official slave baptisms were by Anglican priests, Mrs. Harris did not object when the slaves built altars to the Blessed Virgin Mary. Like the slaves, she had beliefs she kept private.

One of the older women who was like an aunt to Adia explained, "This altar has the image of the Christian mother goddess, but it is really an altar to Oshun, the great woman spirit of my people." She gently laid flowers around the statue of Mary. "While we worship our gods, the masters look on us and smile for they think they have won our hearts and souls as well as stolen our bodies. Fools."

As *the years turned, Adia worked and learned. The chief lesson was that slavery was wrong, always. Ruefully she remembered her own belief that the slavery practiced by her people on captives taken in battle was not so bad as being stolen from her home and sent to a new land. Now she knew better. Slavery was evil, always—a product of the darkest demons.*

Tier hatred of her enslavement was a simmering flame that she buried deep. If she gave in to anger, she would explode into a violence that would get her killed. Jamaica had known slave revolts in the past, and there would be more in the future. After the day's work, when people gathered to talk and tell tales, they spoke of Tacky's Rebellion, which had taken place several years earlier. With few British troops on the island, Mr. Harris armed twenty of his most trusted slaves so they could fight the rebels. The small troop thanked their master, raised their hats to him—and promptly joined the uprising.

The revolt was put down at the cost of hundreds of lives. After, many of the runaways returned, claiming they had run to avoid being forced to join the rebels. Others hanged themselves in the forest rather than return to slavery. Adia could understand why they did that, but she would choose life and hope.

Her situation improved again when Mrs. Harris needed a new maid for her daughter, Sophie. The previous maid had thoughtlessly died of a fever just as Sophie reached marriageable age, so a replacement was required quickly. To the cook's irritation, Adia was chosen, being young, quick, and presentable. She was given the house name of Addie, which was at least close to her own name, and trained by Mrs. Harris's own maid.

Sophie was the only Harris daughter, but there were three sons. The oldest, Master Charlie, was a high-spirited fellow who often invited parties of young people to the house. Once he kissed Adia in the back hall, murmuring how pretty Addie was and how much he'd like to lie with her, but he accepted her firm "No!" and never troubled her again.

It was not Mr. Charlie who raped her, but one of his drunken young friends. He was too strong to fight off, but later she made an image daubed with his seed and laid a curse on him. Perhaps that was why the young devil had a serious riding accident not long after. It was whispered among the slaves that, after, he was incapable of having a woman. She hoped so.

She also made herself a beaded bracelet spelled to reduce her attractiveness to men. She knew there was no point in complaining to the masters, but with the protection spell and her own precautions, at least she was not assaulted again.

She rather missed Master Charlie when he sailed for England to study at Cambridge, but there were still two young masters in the household. She was particularly fond of the youngest, Tommy, who reminded her of Chike.

Working in the house was significant in many ways, not least because Adia met many more white people. She came to realize that whites were not all that different from blacks. Having power over slaves brought out the worst in some people, and most whites accepted slavery as natural and right, but the majority were not evil. The elite among the Iske who owned slaves had behaved much the same as white slave owners.

Mr. Harris didn't really see slaves as people like himself, but he valued them as much as he would a good horse.

He discharged a white overseer who'd beaten a mill slave to death. The overseer was promptly hired by another plantation owner who liked the man's "firm way of dealing with niggers." A year later the overseer was killed by two slaves who then escaped into the hills and joined a community of free Maroons. Every slave on Jamaica silently applauded the deed.

In time Adia realized she should aim her hatred at slavery itself, for it created evil by its existence. Individual slave owners and overseers she would judge on their own sins and virtues. And she listened to every white who came near her to improve her English.

Miss Sophie was a shy girl close to Adia's age. It would never occur to her to put away her own clothing, and she was particular in her requirements, but generally she was a good-natured girl who didn't make a game out of being difficult. Adia heard stories from other lady's maids when there was visiting between the big houses, and she was grateful that Miss Sophie was so pleasant.

She became even more grateful when Miss Sophie gave Adia the greatest gift Adia had ever received. It started when Miss Sophie was sitting by her bedroom window, reading a London newspaper and enjoying the cool breeze from the sea. When she finished, she folded the paper and set it aside. "I wonder what it would be like to read the news when it's new rather than when it's two months' old."

"Not too different, miss. Just pretend this is April, not June." Suppressing her envy, Adia glanced up from the stocking she was darning. "It must be like magic to look at black marks on paper and learn so much from them."

Miss Sophie looked thoughtful. "I suppose it is a kind of magic because reading the newspapers brings England alive for me even though I've never set foot there." Her expression brightened. "Would you like to

learn how to read, Addie? It would be interesting to see if you can do it."

Adia's rush of excitement blocked her irritation at her mistress's assumption that a slave might not be capable of learning. She wanted desperately to read and write, for education was a path to power. "I should like that more than anything, Miss Sophie, but I don't want you to get into trouble for teaching reading to a slave."

Miss Sophie shrugged. "Then we won't tell anyone. Bring me my writing slate and chalk, and we'll start with the alphabet."

Luckily Adia proved an apt student so that Miss Sophie didn't become bored. In fact, she was so apt that during the third lesson, when Adia was learning to read short sentences, her mistress said with a frown, "You're learning so quickly, Addie. Faster than I did."

Gods forbid that a slave be more intelligent than a master. "I'm older," Adia said meekly. "A small child is not so ready to learn."

Mollified, Miss Sophie returned to the lesson. In the future,

Adia made sure she was less quick. And she told no one, not even her closest friends, what she was learning. Miss Sophie would be scolded for teaching a slave, but Adia might be killed if the lessons became known.

Books were rare and expensive, so Adia couldn't risk borrowing any except for the few that belonged to Miss Sophie. But the Harrises received bundles of newspapers when ships arrived from England. After the papers were read by family members, they were piled on a table in the morning room and eventually given to an elderly English friend of Mr. Harris's. This meant that there were usually newspapers in a public room, and no one bothered to keep track of them.

Adia took full advantage of the papers and in the process learned a great deal about England and London. It seemed an interesting place, though cold. Perhaps if

Miss *Sophie visited her British relatives someday, Adia would have a chance to see the country that enslaved more Africans than any other, yet had free blacks living in its capital city.*

She had been Miss Sophie's maid for three years the night she was almost caught borrowing a newspaper. She never went to the morning room until the household was sleeping, but on this night the Harrises had attended a ball at a neighboring plantation. They returned earlier than Adia had expected, when she was in the morning room. The room opened from the front hall, so as soon as she heard the door open, she hid behind a sofa set close to the wall. Though her heart pounded with nerves, rationally she knew she was unlikely to be noticed.

Instead of climbing the stairs, Mr. and Mrs. Harris entered the morning room. The master lit several lamps, then unlocked the cabinet that held his spirits. The clinking of glassware made it clear he was pouring drinks for both of them. Adia settled down as comfortably as possible, resigned to a long wait.

"Thank you, my dear," Mrs. Harris said. There was a brief silence that ended with the clink of a glass being set down. "What did you wish to speak to me about?"

"Tonight Joseph Watson asked for Sophie's hand in marriage."

Mrs. Harris gasped. "But he comes from the Carolina colonies!"

"You can't be surprised," her husband said. "He and Sophie have been cooing at each other like turtledoves since he arrived in Kingstown to visit his uncle. Do you object to his marrying her?"

Mrs. Harris might have been surprised, but Adia wasn't. Miss Sophie had been chattering about handsome Mr. Watson since the two had met.

"He seems a fine young man, and he's heir to a considerable fortune." Mrs. Harris sighed. "I'm not surprised, but I rather hoped it was a mere flirtation. I hate the thought of Sophie going so far from us."

"I'll miss her, too," Mr. Harris said quietly. "But I'll be relieved to see her established away from the islands. You know we live on the edge of an inferno, Anna. The slaves outnumber the whites ten to one. It's only a matter of time until there is another rebellion. I'll feel better knowing my little girl is safe in another land."

Mrs. Harris made a choked sound, and Adia sensed that her husband was putting a comforting arm around her. At length, the older woman said, "I know you're right, and I'm sure she'll accept his proposal if we approve. But sometimes I wonder if we would be better off moving back to England."

"To live in a cramped little house, trying to survive on the salary of some minor government post? Few opportunities for the boys, no rich suitors for Sophie?" Mr. Harris sounded angry. "There is danger here, but danger is everywhere. In Jamaica, at least the rewards are great."

Adia didn't know whether to laugh or sympathize. The English life Mr. Harris sneered at would be heaven to any of the slaves of Harris Hill. Their labor and suffering created the wealth that gave the Harrises "opportunities." Yet in another sense, the Harrises were like anyone else, concerned for their families and worrying about the compromises that life required. She decided she sympathized with them. But only a little.

MISS SOPHIE'S wedding consumed the energy of all the house slaves for weeks, Adia most of all. Naturally she would accompany the bride to the Carolina colony. Leaving her friends, the "tribe" of Harris Hill, was like a knife in Adia's heart, but she also looked forward to seeing the American colonies. Rumor said they were different from the Indies.

They were. There were more whites, and more people in general. The newly married young couple adopted the Watson family pattern of wintering in Charleston, then moving to the family's vast plantation, Magnolia Manor, during the growing season. Miss Sophie was happy in her marriage, and soon she was increasing.

Life in the Watson household was less relaxed than the

Harris home in Jamaica, but as maid to the young mistress, Adia had some status and a tiny room in the attic in whichever house the family occupied. Her position was a comfortable one, and she liked the bustle and variety of Charleston. Though Miss Sophie would never claim a slave as a friend, in the early months she spent a good deal of time in her room with Adia, the only familiar face.

When the family moved to the plantation, Adia found that Magnolia Manor was much the same as Harris Hill, but the working conditions were not quite so bad as Jamaica. The crops were less demanding than sugarcane, and slaves did not die so young. Soon she made new friends. And very quietly, in the slave quarters, she began to teach reading and writing to a few people who could be trusted to stay silent.

Life settled into a comfortable rhythm of city and country. Sophie bore a healthy son, named Joseph for his father and called Joey. Two years later, she had another son. Adia enjoyed the children and spent a fair amount of time with them, but, in quiet times, she grew restless. Was this all that her life held?

Patience, child. Patience.

Her fifth year in America brought change. When the household moved to the plantation, Adia found rot in one of Miss Sophie's windowsills, so she asked that the plantation carpenter be called. There was a delay because the old carpenter had died, and it took time to find a new carpenter who had an owner willing to sell.

The summer was half over when the new carpenter arrived to repair the window frame. He was a tall, handsome young fellow called Daniel, with broad shoulders and a ready smile.

Adia showed him the rotted sill. "You see how the water came in."

"Water, then insects," the carpenter murmured. "Before I be done, I will have replaced every window in this house twice." While he prodded at the sill to see how deep the rot extended, Adia studied him, nagged by a sense of familiarity.

"Mazi!" she exclaimed. "Aren't you the man called Mazi who helped me with my little brother during the march through the jungle after we were captured by slavers?"

He looked startled. Then a smile like sunrise lit up his face. "Adia! You were such a little thing then. Chike was even smaller. Did he..."

She shook her head so he wouldn't have to complete the question. "He joined the ancestors. But I was grateful for your kindness. It helped me carry on."

"You've grown into a fine young lady," he said. Wanting to see more than friendliness in his face, Adia tugged off the charmed bracelet she wore to deter male interest. No matter what Grandmother said, this was a man whose admiration she craved. She thought she heard her grandmother chuckle as the bracelet was set aside, and the carpenter's expression changed from friendly to rapt.

The windowsill was ignored while they exchanged the stories of their lives. His group of slaves had ended up on a different ship that took its cargo to Charleston. He had started as a field hand on one plantation, then learned carpentry on another. Mazi had been baptized Daniel when he became a Christian, and he liked the name.

Adia had thought him a grown man when they had marched together in chains, but he must have been only fourteen or fifteen, she realized. Only a few years older than she. He had grown up well. She found herself laughing as she hadn't since childhood. Grandmother, must I refuse Daniel entry to my heart?

Not this one, child. Daniel is part of your destiny.

A carpenter might be wary of making an advance to one of the family's personal servants, so it was up to Adia to let him know she was willing. After he had taken window measurements and was preparing to leave, she took his hand. "I am so happy to see you again, Daniel."

His gaze holding hers, he raised her hand and kissed it. As quickly as that, she fell in love.

BY THE END of the summer, they had jumped the broomstick. Watson slaves were not allowed to marry in the Christian church, but no matter. Adia and Daniel were wed as truly as man and woman could be.

As she packed Miss Sophie's belongings for the return to Charleston, Adia rehearsed her request. When her mistress came into the room, she looked up from the trunkful of garments and said, "Miss Sophie, the carpenter, Daniel, and I have taken each other as husband and wife. Is it possible... could you ask Mr. Watson if Daniel can work in Charleston during the winter so we can be together?"

Miss Sophie bit her lip. She had never become comfortable with her formidable father-in-law, but she promised to try. That night, after dinner, she said, "I'm sorry, Addie. I asked Mr. Watson, and he said that Daniel is needed on the plantation. He can't come to Charleston." Adia bowed her head, crushed by disappointment. She was barely wed, and now she must leave her husband for months. Her banked hatred of slavery flared into fierce fire. It was a dozen heartbeats before she managed to say, "Thank you for asking, Miss Sophie."

Promise me I will die free, Grandmother!

I promise that, child. But there is still a long road ahead of you.

"*For now, the hope of future freedom must be enough.*

CHAPTER TWELVE

As Nikolai dressed for dinner, he wondered why he had impulsively asked Jean Macrae to join him. Probably because he liked disturbing her. Despite her best efforts to appear calm, she had been upset by the events of the day. But he had to admit that she was coping better than most women of her class. The average well-bred female who bought gifts at the Fontaine emporium would be gibbering hysterically in her cabin after a day like this one.

The average well-bred female had not been to war, nor carried a sword in battle. The little wench was... intriguing.

The door opened, and the wench walked in. She was wearing her green calico dress, and her hair was swept up in a formal style. He studied her critically, as he hadn't really done in their previous encounters. She was slender and delicate, though her shape was most excellently female. Her simple gown was tailored by a master hand to make her appear demure and ladylike.

Reminding himself that this porcelain princess was forged from pure steel, he asked, "Did you use magic to make your gown look like new?"

She nodded. "I have a knack for domestic spells like cleaning fabric and removing wrinkles." Her gaze swept over the room and halted at the wide bookcase, where volumes were held in place by bars to protect them from tumultuous seas.

Drawn by the books, she stepped around the cannon that shared Nikolai's quarters. Her sleekly styled hair blazed like raw fire when she moved through a shaft of sunlight. No wonder her hair had been powdered when he met her in Marseilles. No one with that shade of red hair could ever look convincingly demure.

"Your library is impressive." Her fingertips skimmed the bindings reverently. "I've never seen so many languages in one place. How many do you know?"

"Many." He'd found he had a gift for learning languages, and that skill had proved invaluable. "Would you care for a glass of wine?"

She turned from the books. "Yes, please. What is the purpose of this meeting? Are you going to reveal my fate?" She shivered slightly. "I hope it's different from that of the corsairs whom you tried and condemned today."

"Unless you have tormented people to the point that they wish to tear you limb from limb, you should be spared that." He poured two goblets of claret and handed her one. "As to your fate—I have not yet decided."

She turned the glass in her hand, her gaze on the ruby depths. "I'm grateful that you eschew rape, but that still leaves slavery, murder, or ransom."

"You will not be enslaved," he said sharply. "But I may set you to scrubbing decks to earn your keep."

Her brows arched. They were thick and a darker red than her hair. "If I am held prisoner and forced to work, how is that not slavery?"

Her question caused fury to flash through him. How *dare* she accuse him of enslaving her! The notion was obscene.

But—what was the difference? He drew a slow breath. "You are not a slave, but a prisoner being punished for your crimes."

"My crimes." She sipped delicately at her wine. "I did cut you a bit with that sword, but I was already a prisoner and was careful to do no real damage. Explain to me what my crimes are. Since I don't believe that the sins of the fathers should be visited on the daughters, I can't help but feel like a slave rather than a justly punished criminal."

"Our ancestors are part of us. We are spun of their lives, and their crimes weigh us down," he said harshly. "Now sit."

"How convenient to have a philosophy that allows you to do what you cannot justify by logic." She settled gracefully in the chair on the opposite side of the small dining table, her eyes glittering. "Tell me about Santola, Captain. The rowers seemed to recognize the name."

"Santola is an island not far from here. My island. I'm told that it has become something of a legend among Barbary slaves," he replied. "It is a place of sanctuary where slaves can live free, safe from slave catchers. We hunt and fish and trade, and all who have escaped slavery are welcome."

She frowned. "I studied the maps on the *Mercury* but don't recall seeing Santola in the Mediterranean. Does it have another name?"

"I doubt it. Santola is invisible. If it appears on anyone's map, it would only be as a rock or shoal to be avoided."

Not at all confused by his cryptic comment, she said, "You conceal it by magic?"

"Among other things."

"The ability to hide your lair is most useful to a pirate," she said thoughtfully.

Thinking she had a unique ability to get under his skin, he snapped, "I am no pirate. I do not attack other ships for plunder."

Her gaze was direct as a rapier. "Then what are you, Captain Gregorio?"

"A man who has dedicated his life to ending slavery," he said flatly.

She sucked in her breath. "That's absurd! Slavery is too huge, too integral a part of the world, for one man to bring it down. The West Indies sugar trade alone is a vital part of the world's commerce, and it uses countless slaves. There are galley slaves, slaves in the Americas, in Asia, in Africa. *Everywhere.* Where would you begin to end an institution that involves so many people?"

His eyes narrowed. "Do you believe that slavery is the natural order of life?"

Her eyes narrowed to match. "I'm a Scot—I don't believe that any man has the right to own another. Or to own any woman. But slavery has been with us for as long as history has been recorded, and surely before that. A thousand men couldn't make a difference. Is it worthwhile to devote your life to such an impossible goal?"

"I didn't say I would succeed. Does that mean I shouldn't try?"

"From the point of view of morality, of course it is noble to fight such a great evil," she said slowly. "But even if you spend a long life freeing galley slaves, you will affect only a relative handful of people. You will not make any real difference."

"You saw the men freed today. Did I make a difference to them?"

She bit her lip. "You made a great difference."

He made a gesture encompassing the ship. "All of my crew were slaves. Though they are free to go anywhere, they choose to sail with me to rescue others. This is dangerous work, but satisfying." He didn't try to keep contempt from his voice. "Are your balls and picnics satisfying, Jean Macrae? You don't even have a husband, much less children. Tell me how your life has more meaning than mine."

She jerked as if she'd been slapped. After a long

silence, she said, "You're right. Though you can't eliminate slavery as an institution, what you do has meaning."

"Don't be too sure that there is no way to eliminate slavery. It wouldn't be quick, and certainly not easy, but if there is a way, I shall find it," he said, his voice burning. "I pray to the ancestors to help me."

"You pray to your ancestors?" she said thoughtfully. "So you are not entirely free of religion."

"The ancestors are not gods. They are ancestors." In the corner was a small altar modeled after his grandmother's. He wished he'd learned more of her magic before she died. Sometimes when he tried to invoke the ancestral spirits, he had a fleeting sense that there was more he could do to fight slavery, but he couldn't grasp what it might be.

His frustration was familiar. He had learned a little about magic from Macrae and Polmarric, and discovered more on his own. Then he entered manhood, and self-preservation forced him to suppress most of his power. The warning he'd received from the Guardians was that, if left unchecked, his magic might tear him apart. He'd done such a good job suppressing his power that it barely existed anymore. Likely most of his magic had withered away from lack of use.

As a result, he had a little power, enough to help in some difficult situations. Enough to conceal Santola from passing ships. But he was a crude amateur, not a true mage. Among Macrae's chief sins had been to show young Nikolai breathtaking possibilities that would never be realized.

The Scottish witch had surely had the best magical training available, yet she had nothing like her father's power. What a waste of tutoring. He would have sucked up training like the desert sucked up water.

The conversation was interrupted by his steward, who entered carrying a large tray with their dinner. Nikolai took the chair opposite his guest. The cabin was small and the table smaller yet, which put him much too close to his disturbing guest. He despised her, he wanted her, he couldn't take her. Such circumstances were not conducive to a pleasant dinner.

As the steward set platters on the sideboard, the Scottish witch smiled with appreciation. "Dinner smells delicious. Sea battles work up one's appetite."

He almost laughed at the incongruity of her words. "They do, indeed."

The steward served them—chicken stewed in red wine was the main course—and left. When they were in private again, he asked, "Why were you in Marseilles? I'm grateful that the ancestors put you into my hands, but it was most unexpected."

"I was attending two weddings." She tasted the chicken. "Lovely! Do you have a French chef?"

"Yes. Pierre spent eight years as a kitchen slave of the Dey of Algiers. The dey had him castrated, thinking that would make Pierre content to stay a slave. It didn't." She put down her fork, unnerved. "No doubt every man on this ship has a tale equally horrific."

"Some not quite so bad, some worse." He swallowed a

bite of rice pilaf. "You've never really thought much about slavery, have you?"

"No, I haven't," she admitted. "I've seen a few black slaves in London, but in the distance, dressed in their master's livery. Not so very different from an English footman apart from the color of their skin." She began to eat again.

"You never thought about how the sugar in your tea comes at the price of women working in the sugar fields until they drop, or men scalded to death in the refining sheds." He finished his claret with one gulp and poured more. "The sugar plantations need endless supplies of slaves because so many die there. Even more die before they reach the sugar islands.

"The most dangerous part of the journey into slavery is the march through African jungles, prey to disease and hunger and the lash. When the captives reach the slave ports, they are sold to captains who pack them into ships as tight as herring in a barrel. The slave traders assume a certain number will die and figure that into their profits."

"You are determined to tell me of the horrors." She carefully set her fork down on her plate. "You are right that I have not thought deeply about slavery. So tell me now, so I can never claim ignorance again."

He did exactly as she requested, spitting the words out like a curse as he gave her the ugliest tales of slavery he knew. He spared nothing in telling of the brutality of life on the Indies plantations that produced the sugar Europeans loved so much. Though he'd not seen that himself, he'd spoken to those who had. He spoke of the Barbary slavers whose viciousness was written on his flesh. He told stories of children being wrenched from their mothers' arms, of husbands and wives being torn apart, of sadistic slave masters who raped female slaves, and worse.

Throughout his raging dissertation, Jean Macrae simply watched him, her eyes huge and her face pale as chalk. He'd never seen anyone listen with such intensity. When he ran out of words, she said quietly, "Enough. You have convinced me that slavery is one of the greatest evils that humankind has ever inflicted on itself. Now if you will excuse me..."

She pushed away from the table and stood, took two steps toward the door—then fell to her knees and became violently ill. She had so little in her stomach that she couldn't vomit much, but her outraged body continued its wrenching convulsions.

Swearing, he pulled two towels from under his wash-stand. One he tossed to her. The other he moistened in the water pitcher first. She gasped her thanks before blotting her face and mouth with the damp towel.

He knelt beside her, torn between satisfaction and self-disgust. He'd wanted to shock her into thinking about the unthinkable, but he hadn't expected the violence of her reaction. Even though she was a Macrae, he found he couldn't enjoy her wretchedness.

She pushed herself up and sat back on her heels, then mopped up the mess on the floor with the dry towel. "You have a talent for swearing."

Diverted, he asked, "I was speaking Malti. How did you know I was cursing?"

"Your voice. Even if you were saying 'sweet white lilacs' in Persian, it came out as profanity because of what you felt."

He frowned. "I do not like you to read my mind."

"Then you should be less easy to read." Using the water-dampened towel, she wiped her face again. "You can't blame me for being ill. You wanted me to be shocked and appalled. I am. You spoke most eloquently. I congratulate you on your success."

The ship rolled as she tried to get to her feet. He caught her wrist to steady her. For an instant they were connected by a jolt of scathing awareness.

She yanked her arm away and scrambled up. As she reached for the doorknob, he said, "I'll tell the steward to prepare broth and bread for you. You need something in your stomach or you'll be ill."

"I must be grateful that you treat your slaves better than most owners do." There was a glint of malicious humor in her eyes as she left the cabin.

He scowled at the closed door, exasperated at how effortlessly she angered him with her remarks about him enslaving her. But her comments wouldn't sting so if there wasn't some truth in what she said.

What the devil was he going to do with the damned woman? He would have been better off kidnapping a tiger.

BACK IN HER CABIN, Jean locked the door behind her with the key that had been delivered to her room earlier. Then she folded onto the bed and wrapped her arms around her stomach as she shivered with reaction to the horrors she had just been forced to face.

Gradually she recognized that she was feeling not only the effect of his stories, brought to chilling life by her imagination, but she was also experiencing *his* emotions as well. His outrage was a living flame within him, and he had used it to kindle her. This strange link between them was... not convenient.

Nikolai Gregorio might have the soul and fighting skills of a pirate, but he lived up to his ideals in ways that would do credit to a Presbyterian minister. She remembered the stunned joy of the galley slaves who had been freed. Gregorio had given them the greatest gift imaginable, and at no small risk to himself and his crew.

She envied him that passionate yet practical idealism. When she had ridden off to join the army of Bonnie Prince Charlie, she had felt equally passionate. The dream of freeing Scotland from English oppression had been a prize worth any risk.

Freedom was still precious, but by the time she returned to Dunrath, she would have slit the Young Pretender's throat if she'd been given the chance. Her idealism had died in fury and ashes with Robbie's death and the prince's stubborn stupidity. After Culloden, he'd slipped away and left his Scottish followers to the devastation triggered by their loyalty to the Stuart cause. They'd fought for freedom and been betrayed.

The fight against slavery was also about freedom. It shamed her how little she had thought about the subject. The evil of men claiming ownership over others was as far from her experience as the wild beasts that roamed the plains of Africa.

In her ignorance, she'd enjoyed the fruits of slavery. She thought of the loaves of sugar she'd ground up when baking cakes and tarts. She was reckoned to be a fine baker. How many men and women had suffered to produce the sugar that sweetened those tarts?

Ironic how that sweetness was the product of unspeakable evil. Gregorio might not be able to change the world, but he was doing as much as one man could, and far more than most men dreamed of. Over the course of his lifetime, hundreds, perhaps thousands, of slaves would be freed.

She wished that she could say that her own life had as much meaning.

CHAPTER THIRTEEN

JEAN HAD CHANGED into her loose sailor tunic and trousers and was preparing to sleep when the door to her cabin opened and Gregorio entered. He took up so much *space.* He moved in a cloud of energy that was a blend of natural authority and intimidating magical power. She scowled. "I thought you had granted me privacy."

"I gave you the freedom of the ship. I didn't say that your key to this cabin was the only one. As captain, I must be able to go anywhere. No one else will trouble you."

"You're quite enough trouble all by yourself," she said drily.

"You need to eat something." He handed her a mug of steaming broth and a chunk of bread. "I was... concerned for you."

Since he didn't leave, she perched on the bunk and kept a wary eye on him as she sipped at the broth. The hot chicken stock soothed and strengthened. "Be careful,

Captain, you're showing signs of softness. Or are you fattening me up for sale? I've heard that in the Barbary states, they prefer women with more meat on their bones."

"Stay as scrawny as you want." He leaned against the closed door, arms crossed on his chest and his expression severe. "The main reason I came here was to discuss magic."

"Always an interesting topic." She sipped more broth, guessing that he wanted to learn about Guardian powers while she wanted to learn about his abilities. "Your magic has a different quality than what I'm used to. The only other person I've known who could knock people out as well as you was an African."

He looked intrigued. "My grandmother was African. Perhaps that's where that particular ability comes from."

"Could you teach someone else to do that?"

"I doubt it." He frowned. "Even if I could, I certainly wouldn't teach you."

She grinned, enjoying her ability to irritate him. "You needn't worry. I don't have enough power to lay out a great ox like you, or I would have done so by now."

"I presume you have power in other areas, and not only the ability to keep your clothing clean. Surely you inherited some of the famous Macrae weather magic."

"The great weather mages are invariably male. There have been a few Macrae wives who worked with their husbands and together they were more powerful than the man alone, but very rarely do women become strong weather workers in their own right." And she was not one of the chosen few.

She dipped a corner of the bread in her broth and chewed it slowly. Her stomach seemed willing to accept solid food. "I can sense weather patterns a little better than the average Guardian, but that's all. A really powerful Macrae weather mage can feel a storm over Russia or gather the winds of the western seas."

He cocked his head to one side. "What do you sense now?"

"If you really want to know..." She placed the mug in the washbasin and closed her eyes. The weather had been pleasant and sunny today, but that was about to change. "There's a storm coming. A considerable storm, actually. It will arrive before morning."

"The weather is changing," he agreed. "Most sailors develop a feel for that. But I would have guessed only a bit of rain rather than a major storm."

She shrugged and retrieved her mug. "I could be wrong. I'm no great credit to the Macrae family. But if I'm right, you should think about doing whatever it is that sea captains do when hit by a storm."

"I'll bear that in mind." He studied her intently. "Forecasting weather would be a great benefit at sea if you're any good."

"I never claimed to be good." Her many magical shortcomings had spared her from vanity. "I was trained well, so I have a basic competence in wielding power, but my aptitude wasn't great. My brother was the prodigy."

When she saw Gregorio's expression change, she

wished she hadn't mentioned Duncan. The captain seemed ambivalent about wreaking vengeance on a female, but he would have no such qualms about Duncan. Her brother could handle himself well under any circumstances, but Gregorio would be a formidable opponent.

Maybe it would help if Gregorio started thinking of Duncan as a real person, not a faceless target for revenge. "When Duncan first met his wife, he was so captivated that he attracted thunderstorms. On their wedding night, he almost destroyed a small village by accident. Magic is dangerous when uncontrolled. What kind of training did you receive?"

Another frown. "None, after your father's betrayal. Anything I've learned since I've had to puzzle out on my own."

Her interest quickened. It was difficult to learn to use power well without guidance. "Did you have problems teaching yourself?"

"There were... awkward moments. Luckily, I didn't do any serious damage." He hesitated before continuing. "To be honest, I had to suppress my power for safety's sake. I may have destroyed much of my potential that way."

"To the best of my knowledge, it is impossible to destroy magical potential, at least among the Guardians," she said. "My guess is that you still have all your magical ability, even if you've locked it away."

Painful yearning flashed briefly across his face before he regained his control. "Can you teach me more, Jean Macrae?"

"You've discovered my weakness. I enjoy teaching."

Teaching had led to her closeness with the former thralls, and she had established schools in every area of her brother's property, even the most remote. If she could help Gregorio, it should help her in dealing with him. "Would tutoring help pay the debt you feel my family owes you?"

"Nothing can pay off that debt." He pivoted and slammed from the cabin.

What a moody lad he was. She locked the door, for what good that would do if he wanted to come back.

What would she do if he decided he wished to seduce her? The cabin had been swirling with lust, and it had been mutual. They might be antagonists, but there was also intense attraction. Troubled, she slid into her bunk. Might he drop his vendetta against her family if she became his mistress? Possibly, but she had a dark feeling that saving her family in such a way would cost her her soul.

Nikolai made his way up to the deck, needing to cool off. Talking with the Scottish witch always scrambled his wits. They would be having a reasonably pleasant conversation until he was reminded that she was a Macrae, his sworn enemy. He craved the teaching she might be able to give him, yet becoming her student would give her a kind of power over him, and that was unacceptable.

From what she said about her limited power, she probably wouldn't be much of a teacher. He braced his hands on the railing and inhaled the sea air. But she was right that cooler, wetter weather was moving in. He could feel the change in the moist, silky texture of the air.

Would it be a major storm? The Middle Sea didn't suffer the furious tempests of the Atlantic, but its storms were deadly enough. Was this a bad one, or merely an average rainstorm?

She had mentioned sensing weather patterns. He reached out with his perception and tried to feel the approaching winds and rain, without success. In this area, he had no more talent than any experienced sailor. So despite the Scottish witch's disclaimer, she did have some weather power.

He gave orders to prepare for a storm, then headed down to his cabin. By morning, he would know how accurate her weather sensing was.

THE TEMPEST STRUCK with a force that heeled the ship over and almost threw Jean from her bunk. The violence of the movement shocked her awake. She'd experienced two storms on the voyage to Marseilles, but they were nothing compared to this one.

Using her improved weather sensitivity, she reached out to study the internal forces of the storm. It was as strong as any she'd ever felt, but she might be feeling that power only because she'd become better at reading weather.

The ship rose, then dropped so abruptly that for an instant she was left floating above the bunk. Dear God, she wished Duncan was here! He could disperse these winds, but she couldn't.

She grabbed the bed rail as she and the mattress connected again. Something in the cabin crashed and broke.

Though she was a good sailor, her stomach roiled with distress. Fresh air would help steady her, but with water crashing against the hull, opening the porthole would surely flood the cabin. For her stomach's sake, she sat up in the bunk and wedged herself into a corner, clinging to what handholds she could find. The ship's violent pitching made her wonder how the *Justice* stayed afloat.

Maybe this storm wasn't as bad as she thought. She was a landlubber. Surely she misjudged the power of this tempest. Pray God she was wrong.

She created a globe of mage light and placed it on the wall beside her. Light made everything seem more normal. The water pitcher on the washstand had broken when it was thrown from the well that held it. The washbasin was lower and still safely in its well. At least she hoped it was safe—she wasn't about to cross the cabin to move it.

As the wind and waves battered the ship, she prayed with the greatest sincerity since the Rising. Then she had asked for divine aid in getting herself and her men home safely. Tonight she prayed that Gregorio was as good a seaman as she thought, and that he and his crew could keep them afloat through this storm.

KA-BOOM! The whole ship shuddered and lurched to

port. One of the masts had given way, she guessed. So much for hoping that her fears were unjustified.

With cold fear, she heard rushing water within the ship. A few moments later, pumps began banging away ominously. The falling mast must have damaged the hull, for the ship still listed to port, shaking under the hammer of wind and waves.

She struggled from the bunk and across the tilted floor to unlock the cabin door. The idea of drowning in a locked cabin terrified her even though she knew that running up to the deck wouldn't save her life if the ship was sinking. She'd probably be blown overboard before she took three steps. But that seemed a better death than drowning like a rat in a rain barrel.

She found her slippers, which had been tossed across the cabin, and put them on to protect her feet from the broken pitcher. Then she returned to her bunk corner and held on for dear life.

She must put her faith in God or Gregorio. Either one would do.

The door crashed open, and Gregorio burst into the cabin. He was saturated and hatless, water streaming from his cloak. He roared, "Damn you, woman, you were right! This is as bad a storm as I've ever sailed in. You're a Macrae, so end it!"

"I can't!" she gasped. "I'm no weather mage!"

"You're the closest we have to one." He grabbed her arm and yanked her from the bunk. "If you don't act, we'll all die, so by God, you will act!"

She drew a deep breath, wondering what the devil she

could do. Though she knew the theory, that didn't mean she had the power to control the tempest. "I'll try. But I'll need your help, and I'll need to see the storm."

"As you wish." He towed her toward the door. "And dowse that lantern! What kind of madwoman has fire in her cabin in the middle of a storm?"

"It's mage light, not a lantern," she snapped.

For an instant he focused on the light with sharp interest. "You can teach me how to do that later, if we survive the night."

She acquired more bruises as he hauled her along a tilted corridor too narrow for them both. He climbed the ladder first, grabbing her when she stepped onto the deck and the howling wind nearly knocked her over. She was soaked to the skin in an instant.

The world was a chaos of wind and water, the elements slamming the ship and the sailors who struggled to save it. An officer shouted orders that could barely be heard, while high above men scrambled to reef the sails. Several had already split, but most had been taken in.

As she watched, one of the sailors aloft lost his grip and fell. He managed to catch a line. For an instant his body waved in the wind like a banner. Then two other sailors grabbed him and pulled him to safety. One of the rescuers was nearly naked. A freed galley slave, she guessed, working alongside the *Justice's* regular crew.

As she'd thought, the ship had lost a mast. The mainmast had crushed a small section of the port hull, and its wreckage dragging in the sea was responsible for the ship's dangerous tilt. Men were chopping at the lines that held the mast to the ship, the sails acting as a giant anchor. As she watched, they severed the last of the lines and the ship returned to a more upright position, though it still bucked and rolled with the waves.

Gregorio wrapped an arm around her and pulled to the wheelhouse, which offered a modicum of shelter. Inside, two men fought with the wheel as they struggled to hold the ship steady into the wind. "Can you work here?"

She nodded and turned to face the open side of the wheelhouse. "I'm not strong enough to do this alone. I'll need to use some of your power."

"Take whatever you need." His dark eyes were haunted. Not fear for himself, she realized, but for his men and his cause.

He saw her shiver with cold, so he pulled off his cloak and wrapped it around her. The wet, heavy fabric dragged on the deck, but it protected her some from the wind.

She braced her left hand on the frame of the wheelhouse and clamped her right hand onto his wrist. Energy always crackled between them when they touched, and this time she followed that into his spirit to explore his power.

He was deep and convoluted, like a labyrinth at the center of the earth. She couldn't begin to guess how much power he had—the roots ran all the way to Africa. Though he might not be able to use that power, it was still there, dark and pulsing. "This won't be comfortable," she warned, "but don't fight me. It's the only way."

Ruthlessly she stabbed into his magic. He gasped as the connection was made but managed to control his instinctive defenses. Forcing herself not to waste time exploring his fascinating depths further, she turned her attention to the storm. Huge and wild, she felt that it had been born in the far north. "The storm stretches in all directions. It must be destroyed, for we cannot outlast it."

His teeth were a dangerous white flash in the dark. "Then destroy it!"

Though she hadn't the weather mage gift, she'd learned in the nursery the technique of controlling weather. First she tuned in to the whirling energy that carried the wind and rain. If it could be unbalanced, perhaps that spiraling power would unravel or twist away on a new course.

As she grasped the full pattern, she realized that she might be able to make a difference. The process was profoundly dangerous—but less so than wringing her hands and hoping the ship survived.

After three deep, slow breaths, she closed her eyes and arrowed her awareness from her body out into the storm. The power of the whirling energy nearly tore her to shreds. She grabbed frantically for Gregorio's power, hanging on to him as a lifeline while she stabilized herself.

Thank God he had the strength to hold her together, though she felt him shudder as she drew on his resources.

Feeling stronger, she tumbled with the storm, seeking a weakness. She found an area where the air had different pressure. She dived into it with the combined strength of her and Gregorio.

Dear Lord, but this was exhilarating! She felt like a soaring eagle. No wonder Duncan had never had words to describe weather working. There *were* no words to describe this wild oneness with nature in its rawest form.

She reached outside the storm for warm, dry air over the Sahara. When she found it, she pulled the strong stillness into the chink she'd created in the whirling tempest. When she had the Saharan air in place, she began to expand it.

The work was bitterly hard, and she felt the strain in every fiber of her body. But she was succeeding, *she was succeeding.* The storm had been feeding on itself, and now it lost its fuel. Like a child's top, it wavered as the center ceased to hold.

Jean also wavered, too weakened to maintain the flow of desert air. Immediately, the whirling storm energy began to coalesce again. Grimly she dug deeper into herself. Her ancestor Adam Macrae had almost died when he tried to conjure a hurricane to stop the Spanish Armada, and he was infinitely more powerful than she. If she died, so be it, but by God, she would take this damned storm with her.

She pulled more power from Gregorio, but it wasn't enough. In a last desperate attempt, she reached a thousand miles to the north, hoping she could connect with her brother. It should have been impossible, yet miraculously, she realized that she had established a tenuous connection. His power flowed into her. Not much, the distance was impossible—but it was Macrae power, and it sang the song of the winds.

Knowing she had only one last chance, she pooled all the available power and stabbed it through the heart of the tempest, driving toward all the quarters of the compass to shatter its structure.

The storm lost its coherence and fell apart. Clouds scattered in all directions, bringing welcome rain to the shores of the Middle Sea. As the winds died to normal breezes, the *Justice* ceased its wild rolling. The damaged section of the hull stopped taking in water. Though the waves were still high, the ship could now handle them.

The storm was broken, and so was she. As her knees folded under her, she said in a raw whisper, "You said I would have my freedom if I saved the whole crew. Remember that, my demon captain."

She was unconscious before she hit the deck.

FAR TO THE NORTH, Duncan Macrae shot up in his bed, his temples blazing with pain. "Dear God in heaven!" he gasped.

His wife woke instantly and took his hand. "What's wrong?"

"Wait." He concentrated on the energy that was being pulled from him. The drain lasted only a few minutes, then faded away. "Jean tapped into me," he said as the pain disappeared. "I think she's discovered that she has some of the Macrae weather ability, because she needed help rather badly."

"Did a storm hit Marseilles? Or was she trying to end a drought?"

"It was a storm, a very bad one, but not in Marseilles." He leaned back into the pillows and put his arm around his wife. "I think she was at sea. Perhaps she decided to come home early."

"Then we will see her all the sooner," Gwynne said comfortably.

Duncan didn't reply. He was no seer who could read the future, but he had a strong sense that his little sister was not having a normal journey home.

CHAPTER FOURTEEN

A PART-TIME HUSBAND was better than none, but Adia missed Daniel desperately during their months of separation. It was harder to have a family, too. Miss Sophie, who lived with her husband, managed to produce three children in the years that it took Adia to have only one. One blessed daughter, Mary Monifa —one name Christian, one name African—and called Molly.

With the aid of an old, infirm Watson slave, Adia was able to keep her baby with her in Charleston. Miss Sophie was tolerant of the times this made Adia a little late, as long as it didn't happen often. But the situation gave Adia another wish. She wanted not only freedom, but to be able to live free with her family.

Someday, Grandmother whispered. Someday.

In the meantime, she and Daniel shared what precious hours they had.

A REVOLT IS BLOOD, *fear, and violence. It is also* opportunity. *When the colonies rebelled against the British masters in 1776, they were much stronger than the slaves who had revolted in Jamaica. Adia read newspapers avidly when she could, trying to make sense of the matter. It appeared that the colonists wanted liberty, though only for themselves, of course. John Watson, head of the Watson family, despised the rebellion because it would be bad for business.*

That is, he hated it until the British offered to free any slave who fought for the British. That pushed Watson to join the rebels. How could he run his plantation with the British threatening his labor? He chose to support the rebels so colonial life could return to normal.

News of the British offer to free slaves who joined them spread through the black community like wildfire. Familiar faces vanished from Charleston. The Watsons lost their coachman and two of the young footmen. One of the footmen was recaptured, whipped, and sent to the plantation to become a field hand.

With a battle being fought over Charleston, the Watson women and children and house slaves were sent to the safety of Magnolia Manor. Sophie's husband, Joseph, stayed in the country to protect the family while his father returned to the city to look out for the Watson business interests.

When they reached the plantation, Adia had to spend the rest of the day unpacking and settling Miss *Sophie and her children. It was near midnight when she was finally free to find Daniel. Half mad with yearning, she rushed outside toward the slave quarters.*

He was waiting for her outside the big house. She gasped

when his great dark figure loomed out of the shadows, then fell into his arms. "Sweet wife," he breathed. "Beloved."

They kissed frantically, trying to melt their bodies into each other. As *he laid her down in the privacy of the bushes, she thought dizzily that this was the only good part of their long separations: when they came together again, the pleasure was shattering.*

After, they lay in each other's arms, silvered by moonlight. "I had to wait until I saw you again," he said huskily.

She stiffened, knowing what this meant. "You're going to run to the British!"

He nodded. "It's our chance, honey child. The British will win, and we'll be free."

"Or dead." She started to sit up. "I'll get Molly. We should leave immediately."

"No." He sat up also, drawing her into his embrace. "I must go alone. I will send for you when I can." He laughed softly. "I wondered why you said I must learn to read and write, but now I can send you a letter."

"And if you go and I never hear from you?" she said, tears running down her face.

"That will mean I am dead, honey child." He traced the lines of her face, as if trying to memorize them. "When I have a safe place for my family, I will send for you. And if I die, my spirit will watch over you and Molly."

She caught his hand, weeping, but she would not ask him to stay because he was right: this was a chance for them to be free, and he could travel more swiftly if he was alone. Grandmother, will I see my husband again? Yes, child. Have faith.

"Be careful." She thought. "Stay another day. I will make you a protection charm and a pathfinder stone, and you will have a chance to see Molly. One day will not matter."

He hesitated, then nodded. "Your magic will help, and I want to see our baby girl again. If... the worst happens, maybe she is old enough now to remember me."

"I will tell her what a strong, brave man her father was, and how much he loved her." She leaned into a kiss, and then they were making love again. Delay meant not only giving him magic and Molly, but one last chance to share flesh and spirit. She had yearned for his touch and scent for months, and now he would be gone in another day.

The protection charm she made herself. The small, painted pathfinder stone came from a wise woman who lived on the neighboring plantation, and the paint used to mark symbols on the pale surface was colored with Daniel's blood. When Daniel was ready for Adia and Molly to join him, he could send her the stone, and it would guide her to him.

As *she instructed him on how to use the stone, she refused to believe they would never be together again.*

After three days of freedom, Daniel was captured and brought back to Magnolia Manor. The overseer tied him between two trees and flayed the skin from his back.

But perhaps Adia's protection charm worked, because he didn't die. With salves and prayers to Grandmother, plus the skilled nursing of the plantation wisewoman, he recovered with surprising speed, though his back was ridged with scars. Adia didn't realize how much she'd loved the feel of his smooth, taut skin beneath her palms until it was gone. But the rough scars were potent in other ways, reminding her always of her husband's courage.

As soon as Daniel had recovered enough, he ran again. This time, he was not recaptured. Adia worked quietly and looked obedient. When questioned about Daniel by the overseer, she said bitterly that she'd begged her man not to run away, damn him. It was so easy to lie to the masters.

A month later, she received a message written on a small, tattered scrap of paper. "I safe, luv you and baby. D." She gave thanks that she'd taught Daniel to write, and that the secret network of slaves passed such messages on.

There were occasional messages, but two years passed before she received the small, painted pathfinder stone. It was wrapped in a ragged piece of cloth on which Daniel had written, "Follow north. Luv. Daniel Adams."

The pathfinder stone had been quiet when she gave it to Daniel, but he had been carrying it for two years, and before sending the stone he had activated it with his prayers for her presence. Now it glowed with power. She held it in her palm and tried walking in different directions. The stone warmed when she headed north. If she headed that way, she would find Daniel. She liked the idea of having a family name. She'd ask Daniel why he chose Adams when they were together again.

She consulted the wisewoman and an old sugar mill man who knew some magic, and with their help she created pouches to be hung around the necks of herself and her daughter. The charms would make people less likely to notice them on their journey. Adia had used a similar magic to keep herself from being bothered by unwelcome male attention, but this was stronger because the wise woman had greater power than Adia.

She made a couple of extra charms, just in case they might prove useful. The pathfinder stone went into her pouch, which was made of thin cotton so she could feel the warmth against her breast.

She had few other preparations. A small bag that could be slung over her back contained a few garments and food. She concealed a small, sharp knife in her waistband. Everything else she left with the wise woman, to be given out after she was gone, assuming she was not recaptured. Adia owned some fine clothing, given to her by Miss Sophie. It would be appreciated by others. She also had a little money that she'd received from guests when she'd performed special services. Using it to run away pleased her.

She chose a moonless night to leave. Mr. Watson was in Charleston for a few days, which meant slow pursuit. Before she left her small, hot attic room, she spent a few minutes communing with her grandmother. Protect us, Grandmother. Let me live to hold my husband again. *There were no words in reply, but she felt encouraging warmth.*

She headed down the stairs, thinking it was strange that if she was lucky, she would never see this place or these people again. With a twist of her heart, she accepted that she would never see Miss Sophie's children. When she reached the second floor, she impulsively turned right to go to the nursery rather than continuing down the servant stairs..

A lantern turned low burned in the nursery since young Amy was afraid of the dark. She and her big brother would soon be given separate rooms for propriety's sake, but for now, they enjoyed being together. The middle child, Henry, had died of a fever. Adia had held Miss Sophie in her arms as her mistress wept for the loss. There had been no white or black then, only two women mourning.

Amy was curled around her battered rag doll, the fabric worn from being taken everywhere. Adia was tempted to touch the soft childish curve of cheek, but dared not risk waking the girl. Young Joseph was sprawled across his bed, looking ready to run at any minute. Lord, she would miss them—they were almost as much her children as Molly was. She hoped they would grow up in a better world, one where there was no more slavery, but that was unlikely.

After saying her silent good-bye, she left the nursery. Defiantly, she headed to the great sweeping staircase that was used only by the family, never the slaves, who had to use the hidden servant steps. She rested one hand on the mahogany railing, lifted her skirt with the other hand, and prepared to descend grandly to the first floor.

She was just starting when a hand touched her arm. "Addie?"

Adia swung around, instinctively pulling her knife as she damned herself for stopping by the nursery. She would have been out of the house by now if she hadn't. But she would not be stopped now, not by anyone.

In the moonlight, she saw Miss Sophie, aghast as she stared at the knife. "Addie?" she said again, her voice quavering. Her gaze darted to the bag slung over Adia's shoulder. "You are running away!"

"I am." Adia held the knife ready while she wondered frantically what to do. She might kill a stranger or anyone threatening Daniel or Molly, but could she kill Miss Sophie?

Her mistress stared at the knife. "Would you murder me, Addie?

Adia lowered the knife a little, thinking how Miss Sophie had taught her to read, about the moments of honesty that they had shared despite being mistress and slave. "I could not do that. But I can and will bind and gag you if I must." If that happened, her chances of successful escape were slim. But she could not change her mind about running, not now. She yearned to breathe the air as a free woman almost as much as she yearned for Daniel's arms.

"Why?" Miss Sophie breathed, less tense as she stopped fearing for her life. "Have I not treated you well? I thought we were friends, Addie."

"You have been a good mistress, Miss Sophie. I am grateful for that." Adia lowered the knife, but did not return it to its sheath. "But slave and master can never be friends. You cannot understand, not truly. How would you feel if forced to work and threatened with whipping or death if you refuse? What if you knew that any white man might rape you at any time? What if you had only a few precious hours a week with your children? Have you thought about such things, Miss Sophie?"

"No, I haven't." The other woman became very still. "You are going to Daniel?"

"Yes. We will be a family again, or I shall die in the attempt." Urged by a feeling from Grandmother, Adia said, "If you promise not to tell anyone that I have left until well into tomorrow, I will not bind you. Will you give me your word?"

Miss Sophie hesitated, then gave a nod. Perhaps she realized that after tonight, things could never be the same between them.

"I promise not to raise the alarm. May God protect you and your family, Addie."

"Thank you." She sheathed her knife. "And my name is Adia." She turned and silently descended the steps.

On the way to the slave quarters, Adia suddenly wondered how much she would have earned if she had been paid for her labor all these years. It would be a fair amount of money. Certainly enough to buy a mule. She took a detour to catch and saddle the placid mule, Daisy, that she sometimes rode. Once more her desire to learn was proving useful.

She hung a don't-notice charm around the mule's neck. Then she collected her sleepy daughter, hugged the wisewoman, and started her long journey to freedom.

MISS SOPHIE MUST HAVE KEPT *her word, for there was no swift pursuit. Though the trip to Daniel was long and tiring, no one paid dangerous attention to the runaways. Adia's charms seemed to be getting more effective. Now that she was free, perhaps she could find a teacher of magical ways.*

Every day the pathfinder stone grew warmer. They traveled the back roads as they made their slow journey north. They asked only black folk for directions. From the Carolinas to Virginia, across Maryland, into New Jersey. She had never dreamed that Daniel had gone so far.

After weeks of traveling, they reached the Hudson River and were able to look across the water to the great city of New York. They hid in the reeds all day, and crossed the river that night in a moored rowboat that

Adia found and cut loose. The faithful mule swam behind them while Adia clumsily learned how to row, fighting the current. Stay with us, Grandmother!

They reached the island of Manhattan as the sun was rising. A Black Pioneer who was cutting firewood for the British Army pointed them toward the military encampment. The pathfinder stone seemed likely to burn Adia's skin as she guided the mule into the sprawling camp. Molly rode on the soaked saddle, tired but excited. A whole section was occupied by black soldiers. Adia baited her mule, weary to the bone and wondering what to do next.

Then a bass whoop sounded over the encampment and she saw a familiar, powerful figure running toward her. Her Daniel was a sergeant, she saw. And his face blazed with the same happiness that threatened to burst from her. As she slid into his arms and he hugged her and Molly, she said with a shaking voice, "Never again will we be separated."

"Never again," he said, weeping, his arms threatening to crack her ribs. "Never again. "-

CHAPTER FIFTEEN

THE SCOTTISH WITCH fell to the deck. Though Nikolai's wrist bore bleeding wounds from her nails, she looked fragile as a child.

Yet she had succeeded. The wind had dropped to almost nothing, and his battered ship rode the waves in peace.

He reached down, and almost fell over. He was weak to the bone, barely able to stand upright. Bracing himself on the door frame, he managed to kneel. When he fumbled for a pulse in her throat, he couldn't find one.

"Captain, what happened?"

He looked up to see Tano, drenched and battered but intact. Tano acted as ship's surgeon when necessary, and he had an uncanny knack for appearing when needed. He also understood about magic since he had some himself. "This female is a weather mage," Nikolai said gruffly. "She saved the ship, but she may have killed herself in the process. Can you do anything?"

Tano frowned as he knelt beside the unconscious girl. After checking her pulse, his frown deepened. He pulled out his knife and held the blade in front of her mouth. A small film of condensation formed. "She's alive, but barely. A great work of magic drains body and soul. She has consumed herself like a candle." Tano glanced up. "You don't look well, either, Captain. Were you helping her?"

Nikolai nodded. Even that effort seemed too much.

"She said she didn't have much power and would need some of mine. While fighting the storm, she entered my mind and... drew out my soul."

"To break a storm so huge took immense magic. She needs much rest and nourishment."

Hoping she could be saved, Nikolai bent over to pick her up, and again almost fell flat on his face. Tano muttered a curse in his native language before saying, "Don't be a fool—you need rest as much as she. I will tend her. After she has taken some broth, I will come to your cabin." His eyes narrowed. "You will be lying on your bunk, yes?"

It was a mark of his exhaustion that Nikolai didn't even argue. At the moment, the ship's cat could knock him over. Gripping the frame of the wheelhouse, he managed to get to his feet.

Tano carefully lifted the little witch and carried her to the hatch, expertly supporting her on the tricky climb belowdecks. She was in good hands, though Nikolai felt Jean Macrae was his responsibility and he should be the one to care for her.

As he followed Tano, he thought that he hadn't been so tired since he'd escaped slavery. Yet he was also exhilarated. He'd worked with magic to the best of his ability since Macrae opened his eyes to what was possible. But never had he been part of such a great manifestation of power. He had been dabbling along the shore, and Jean Macrae had showed him the ocean's depths. Now that he had tasted true power, he wanted more.

AFTER AN ETERNITY OF STRANGE, drowning dreams, Jean awoke feeling that she had been on a very long journey. She was no longer on the schooner. Instead, she lay on a comfortable bed in a room with starkly whitewashed walls. Golden sunshine poured in a window with half opened shutters, and flowers were visible outside. One door beckoned out into that sunshine while another led into the house.

Cautiously she sat up, her head swimming. She wore a shift that was too large. Was she on Santola? The table, chairs, and chest were plain wood, but there was an elegant simplicity that reminded her of a Highland croft. An earthenware vase contained bright blossoms, and the bed was covered with a quilt of soft, colorful fabric squares. The effect was modest but cheerful.

In contrast, the richly patterned Oriental carpet on the tile floor was sumptuous. A pirate's spoils, perhaps.

She climbed from the bed and found a very simple blue gingham gown draped over a chair. It didn't have much more structure than a shift, but she felt more dressed when she put it on. Lying underneath were her knife and scrying glass, still secure in its pouch. She pulled the glass out and held it in her palm for a moment. Apparently no stranger had touched it, for which she was grateful. She considered using it to learn more of her situation, but she felt too drained of power for the attempt.

After donning both scrying glass and knife, she investigated the pitcher and bowl on the table. They weren't washing materials but nourishment—the pitcher held fresh milk, and a half loaf of bread was covered by a cloth. She poured milk into the bowl and dipped in the bread. Her parched mouth welcomed the moisture, and her ravenous appetite made it clear that she hadn't eaten much lately.

Hearing the faint creak of a door, she looked up to see the African who had been with Gregorio in Marseilles. It was hard to judge his age. His face was unlined, but his eyes were not young. "You are awake," he said. "I'm glad. For a while, I was not sure you would wake again."

"How long have I been asleep?"

"Three and a half days. Since you've had only water and broth you must be hungry, but it would be best if you do not eat too quickly."

Three and a half days! No wonder she felt as if she'd been on a long journey. Since her stomach was already feeling full, she pushed the bowl away. "I am Jean Macrae, but you know that already, I think."

He nodded. "I am Tano. On shipboard I act as surgeon when necessary, but here on the island, we have better physicians if you need care."

"I'm tired but otherwise well enough." She studied his calm face. "You speak English beautifully."

"I learned the language in Jamaica. Because I spoke well, I was taken from the sugar mill and trained to be the overseer's secretary."

She stared at him, remembering Gregorio's horror stories about life on the West Indies plantations. "I'm glad you are there no longer."

"So am I." His dark eyes were deeply ironic.

Not sure what she could say to a man who had survived seasons in hell, she asked, "The ship and crew came through the storm safely?" She thought of how much power she'd had to take from Gregorio. "And the captain?"

"All are well. The mainmast broke, and the captain was almost as tired as you, but he recovered well enough to pilot the *Justice* home. Have you seen Santola yet?" When Jean shook her head, Tano crossed the room and opened the outside door, revealing a terrace bright with cascading flowers in pots. "Behold our sanctuary." Feeling stronger for having eaten, Jean walked outside, and stopped dead, enchanted by the circle of light before her. As she looked more closely, she saw that the circle was a huge bowl of turquoise water surrounded by a jagged tiara of dark islands.

The sight was so striking that it took a moment for her to understand what she was seeing. "Santola is the crater of an ancient volcano, isn't it? I've seen drawings of Santorini in the Greek Isles and it looks like this. A volcano erupted and left a circle of islands around the edge. It's called... a caldera, I think?"

"Very good, miss." Tano nodded approvingly. "The volcano that created Santola made the soil rich and created shoals that protect us from unwanted visitors." Shoals combined with magic, Jean guessed, for she sensed the distant buzz of a protective field. The terrace reminded her of courtyards in the Fontaine household, with pots of brilliant flowers and a roofed area that provided shade from the baking sun.

She moved across the terrace to the wall and looked down on a large village that was beautiful in the manner of the Mediterranean. Whitewashed stucco houses climbed the steep hill, accented by vivid splashes of color from painted woodwork and flowers.

This particular dwelling was at the top of the village, high enough to look down on dozens of other buildings. She saw people working in courtyards and walking the narrow cobblestone streaks. Hardy donkeys wearing straw hats patiently carried loads up the hill while children chased one another in a game near the docks. Their complexions were every shade from Nordic pale to rich ebony.

The steepness of the caldera hills meant that the fields visible beyond the village were terraced. The slopes above were grazed by goats and sheep. Santola appeared to be not only self-sufficient, but prosperous. "I've landed in paradise."

"We think so." Tano quietly left.

Glad to be alone, Jean settled on a bench under the awning. In high summer this island would bake, but on a late winter day, there was a pleasant amount of warmth. Far below, she could see the *Justice* undergoing repairs at a dock. The jagged stub of the mainmast had been removed, and men swarmed over the ship making repairs. She shaded her eyes, wondering if Gregorio was there.

He'd show up soon enough. She gazed out at the caldera, idly tracking the path of a small sailboat. She felt empty and not quite attached to the world, a result of the tremendous expenditure of magic the night of the storm. It would take time to refill the well of power, though the process had begun.

When she fought the tempest, she'd used power beyond what she believed she possessed. Various teachers and mages had said over the years that she had a great deal of power—she just didn't know how to wield it. That had been frustratingly true.

Yet though she had sensed power growing within her, she'd had little success using it. Even simple magical tasks were like wrestling a greased pig—her power might squirt off in any direction. More often, she couldn't even get it moving. Eventually, she had stopped torturing herself with her magical failures and concentrated on managing the family estate.

After her brother married, she had done some studying with his wife, Gwynne, who came late to her power. Jean had become a little better at some of the basic skills, like scrying, but Gwynne had quickly surpassed her in all areas.

Except when Jean had led the surviving Macrae rebels back from Culloden. Their flight had been harrowing because companies of Hanoverian troops pursued any Jacobites who had escaped the battlefield. The Macraes would never have made it back to Dunrath if she hadn't somehow managed to use misdirection and illusion spells to protect her men. Desperation had driven her, for she could never have created such powerful spells under normal circumstances.

After Culloden, she had quietly experimented with her abilities, and had been disappointed to find herself as clumsy as ever. So she'd traveled to London to please her relatives and put magic aside, except for the smallest and most daily of spells. That was how matters stood until the night of the tempest. Once again, desperation had given her the ability to tap into deeper power. Though maybe working with Gregorio was part of it—they seemed to spark each other in powerful and rather alarming ways.

Scree! A huge dark shape swooped over her head, its cry shattering. She ducked instinctively, wondering if the island had monstrous bats. She blinked in astonishment to see a gigantic blue parrot. As she watched, it spread its wings and landed lightly on the railing that topped the wall. The creature was dazzling, but was any parrot so large and so blue? The feathers were almost cobalt, and the wingspan over a yard.

"*Bonjour!*" the bird caroled cheerfully.

"Bonjour," Jean said with bemusement. "Pleased to meet you."

"Bonjour!"

As the bird repeated the greeting, Gregorio said behind her, "Meet Queen Isabelle. She's a macaw. They come from the jungles of the New World."

Jean tried to suppress her instinctive flinch at the sound of his voice. "You've been there?"

He shook his head as he sat on the far end of her bench. On a terrace full of sunshine, he was a dark, intense presence. "Isabelle belonged to the captain of a slave ship. With his dying breath, he asked me to care for the creature. So I have." The macaw hopped from the railing onto his shoulder, where it rubbed its beak against his cheek. Seeing the bird perched on a human emphasized how enormous it was.

"I've seen parrots in London, but they were usually green and much smaller. I suppose Isabelle is a parrot cousin." She studied the macaw more closely. Despite yellow facial markings that gave the bird a rather clownish expression, the beak looked as if it could bite off a person's finger with no effort. "The pet parrots I saw had clipped wings. What prevents this one from flying away?"

"A spell surrounds the house." He pulled some nuts from his pocket and offered them on his palm. The bird took the treats with amazing gentleness. "When Isabelle reaches the edge, like this wall, she decides it's time to turn back."

"So even your pet is enslaved," she said drily.

His eyes narrowed, but he refused to take the bait. "You will be freed and returned to Marseilles. By saving my ship and men, you have earned that."

"You never thought that would happen, of course," she said, amused. "But I appreciate that you are a man of your word. When can I leave?"

"It will be a fortnight or so." He gestured down to the docks. "The *Justice* needs repairs, and she is the only large ship in port at the moment."

So he had other ships. "How do you support this community? There must be hundreds of people, and all look well fed."

"Most of our income is from shipping. We have half a dozen ships now, several of them captured from slave traders and refitted as merchant vessels. They are more heavily armed than most merchant vessels, and they are always on the lookout for slave ships to liberate. I have a gift for finding such ships."

"So it was no accident that we were attacked by that corsair?"

"I sensed it from far away, and knew that the master was an old enemy." His expression darkened. "I hope the galley survived the storm. A number of my crewmen were aboard, as well as those slavers who survived their trials. The plan was to drop off the captured crew near Algiers, then return here for refitting."

Without conscious thought, she said; "The ship survived."

"You know that?" he asked quickly. "You are a seer?"

"Not really, but I have a strong feeling that the ship is all right."

"Can you tell me more? Have they reached Algiers yet?"

Thinking she might as well test her power, she pulled out her scrying glass and looked more closely. In the smoky obsidian, she imagined the captive corsair galley. As she held that image in her mind, more information came. "The edge of the storm brushed the ship, but with much less force since it was well south of us." She frowned. "They haven't reached Algiers. Tomorrow, perhaps. They were delayed when some of the captives tried to retake the ship in the confusion of the storm, but they failed."

His dark brows drew together. "Were any of my men killed in the rebellion?"

She tried to see more, but the image of the ship faded away. "I'm sorry, I can't see that much detail. But I don't think there were serious casualties."

"That glass disk. It's magic?" He stared at it avidly.

"Not exactly. A scrying glass is more of a focusing device." She opened her hand to show him, but didn't offer to hand it over. "The more it's used, the more it becomes attuned to the user's power. But it's possible to scry in a glass of wine or a basin of water or any other reflective surface."

The macaw bobbed forward, opening its beak to grasp the scrying glass. Jean hastily yanked the glass away and returned it to its pouch while Gregorio grinned and offered the bird more nuts. "Take care, Jean Macrae. Isabelle likes shiny objects."

"I shall do my best to keep my distance from her." A thought struck her. "Surely the galley slaves are all men. Where do the women of Santola come from?"

A husky woman's voice said from behind her, "We are all whores, of course."

Jean turned to a tall, striking woman of mixed race with dark skin, glossy black hair, and almond-shaped eyes. Her expression was curious and not very friendly as she crossed the terrace to the arbor.

"Louise exaggerates," Gregorio said. "The women of Santola have many backgrounds."

"But many of us were whores." Louise held out her arm and the macaw flew to her with another ear-piercing cry. It seemed even happier with her than the captain. "Whoring is often enslavement by a pimp, though I suppose a lady like you wouldn't know." She managed to make "lady" sound like an insult.

Clearly the beautiful Louise was trying to shock the visitor. Perhaps she was Gregorio's mistress and jealous of his showing interest in another female.

No. With a flash of knowledge, Jean realized that Louise wasn't the captain's woman, though they had probably been intimate in the past. Interesting.

Having traveled with the Jacobite army, where many of the other camp followers were prostitutes, Jean was not easily shocked. "Since men won't be happy without women, rescuing prostitutes is a way to serve two goals."

Not missing the byplay between the women,

Gregorio said, "It has worked well. No one here talks about the past unless they wish to."

Louise's expression softened. "Santola is the island of second chances. I shall see you at dinner, Nikolai." She sauntered across the terrace, her full hips swinging and the towering macaw grooming her glossy dark hair.

The captain stood. "Since Louise has taken charge of Queen Isabelle, would you like to see more of the village, Jean Macrae?"

"I would that." Jean stood. "Why do you always call me Jean Macrae?"

He considered. "Miss Macrae is too polite, and Jean is too intimate."

"I've been in your mind. How much more intimate can two people get?"

She realized what a foolish comment that was when he gave her a look that scorched to the marrow. "Even a prim Scottish maiden should know that answer."

"Call me Jean," she said softly, "for I am not so prim as all that."

He looked away, his face set, and she realized that he was as uncertain about the energy between them as she was.

As they entered the house, she asked herself if she wanted him for a lover. The passionate, physical side of her nature burned to join with him, to take that fierce energy inside herself, but she could see no good end to such an affair. He'd shape her soul in ways that would make it impossible to return home as the Jean Macrae she'd always been. What she'd experienced so far was an adventure, exciting, sometimes too much so, but not yet life changing.

Nikolai Gregorio's bed—that would be life changing. She'd rebuilt her broken soul once after the Rising. She didn't want to have to do that again.

She *would not* do it again.

CHAPTER SIXTEEN

Adia, New York City

The British had lost. *Adia still had had trouble believing that, but the news had raced all over New York. Some of the British soldiers were glad to know that soon they'd go home, others were embittered at the surrender to a ragtag collection of colonial rebels. If they had been given enough soldiers and weapons, they grumbled, Britain could have won.*

But none of the British were as worried as the thousands of former slaves who had taken refuge in New York. Everyone was anxious about how they would be affected by the surrender. How long until the British-held city was turned over to the Americans ? Would the triumphant rebels be in a vengeful mood?

"What will happen to us now?" Adia asked Daniel, her voice soft to keep from waking Molly. He had been patrolling outside the city for several weeks. Now that he had returned, she had a compulsive need to discuss their future again.

"We will not return to slavery," he said firmly. "Major

Blaine says that Carleton, the British commander in chief, believes that the Americans' demand that all their property be returned does not include freed slaves since we are no longer property." Daniel grinned. "I think that Carleton truly believes it would be dishonorable for Britain to go back on its word to us—but he also enjoys irritating the Americans. Even General Washington wants his escaped slaves returned. Carleton can refuse nobly in the name of honor."

Adia smiled. "I don't care about Carleton's reasons as long as he doesn't abandon us." She poured their tea in the early-morning light. Many blacks lived in canvas-topped huts in the sections of Manhattan that had been burned by angry patriots when they lost the city, so she and Daniel were lucky to have this tiny, snug cottage. "Already slave catchers are coming to New York to hunt down escaped slaves." She shivered. "John Watson is just the sort of man to do that. Do you think he will send men after us? I like this city, but how can we live here if we must constantly worry about being captured and taken back to South Carolina?"

"Mr. Watson can't know that we are in New York." Daniel hesitated. "Do not speak of it yet to anyone, but the major told me there is talk of evacuating Loyalists and freed slaves to Nova Scotia. We would be given land to farm."

"Nova Scotia?" She thought about it. "From what I know it's a cold, hard land, but a long way from Charleston."

"We will be safe there, honey child." He gave her a warm, intimate smile, reminding her how they had celebrated his return the night before. "After we are settled, it will be time to have another baby."

Though she yearned for another child, she had taken measures to prevent that during her years in New York. The war made life too uncertain to risk a second baby. But soon the time would come. "We will have a boy," she said, feeling prophecy stir within her. "He will be strong and handsome like you, and I will tell him tales of his father's bravery against the Americans since you will be too modest to sing your own praises."

Daniel laughed and gave her a good-bye kiss, patting her backside as she left to walk to work. Almost as soon as she arrived in New York, Daniel's commander, Major Blaine, had hired Adia to be his housekeeper. The major was a tall, austere man whose rare smiles were surprisingly warm. He treated Adia with grave respect, sometimes talking to her about his wife and children in a way he couldn't with any of the men around him. He was particularly fond of Molly, who often accompanied her mother to the major's quarters. He had a daughter of similar age.

Was Major Blaine fond enough of Adia and her family to protect them against being enslaved again? Perhaps, but even if his intentions were good, he might not be in a position to help. It was time to start planning a way to escape to Canada.

Though Daniel had fought with a company of black former slaves, they were not members of the regular British Army, and his group would soon be disbanded. They could leave the city as soon as that happened, but perhaps they should wait to see if the British would keep their promises to the slaves who had fought for them. If they were evacuated on British ships, their journey would be much safer than if they fled on their own.

Bitterly Adia wondered how often she would have to leave home and friends and start all over again. She and Daniel had created a life here in New York. Not long after her arrival, they were formally married by a blind Methodist preacher who had escaped from slavery and brought much of his congregation with him. Though Adia had always felt that she and Daniel were husband and wife, she was proud that the world and the law now recognized their union.

Daniel had also explained why he had chosen the family name Adams. "One of the rebel leaders is named John Adams, and they say he will not own slaves." He kissed the end of her nose. "And it sounded good with Adia. Adia Adams."

She had laughed and agreed. Having a last name of their own choosing was a mark of freedom. Now they had a home and a bit of garden. Molly was a student at a small dame school and already reading well. If it was safe for them to stay in New York, Daniel could use his carpentry skills to find work and surely Adia would be able to find a place as a servant in some other household when Major Blaine left.

Instead, they would have to escape again to a cold, inhospitable land. Luckily, she had saved most of her wages, so they had a little money. As long as she and Daniel and Molly were together and free, they would be all right.

She was on a quiet street halfway to the major's house when a tall white man stepped out in front of her. "You are Addie Watson?"

She halted, fear crimping her veins. "I know no one of that name."

"They said you are handsome and well spoken," he said as a man grabbed her from behind. "All of you runaways lie about your names. But I have been following you, Addie Watson. I know who you really are. Now you will be returned to your master, along with your pickanniny and your carpenter." He smiled chillingly. "And a fine bounty I'll get for the lot of you."

She struggled frantically against the man who held her. He was tall, lean, black, and familiar. There was also something familiar about the white man's cold blue eyes. She gasped, recognizing the captain of the slave ship that had taken her to the Indies. He must have been very young then, for he was no more than in his forties now. His evil companion, Kondo, had not aged at all. "Captain Trent'. You swine'."

He looked interested. "Did I bring you to the New

World? You should thank me for removing you from the savagery of Africa." He gestured to Kondo. Judging by his rich dress, the slave trade had been very good to the captain. "Chain her and take her to the cell. Then we can go for the brat. With luck, the carpenter will be there, too." The thought of these brutes touching Molly drove Adia wild. Help me, Grandmother! *Calling on the magic she had never properly mastered, she tore herself away from Kondo before he could chain her.* As *she whipped away, violet fire blazed around her.*

Run, child! *As shouts rose behind her, Adia bolted to the end of the block and turned into a much busier street. Many of the people here were black, and there was a good chance that they would help her escape if Trent came after her again. She risked a glance back, and saw Trent and Kondo staggering blindly where she'd left them. They didn't look burned. She sensed that the violet fire had confused rather than caused physical injury.*

Thanking Grandmother, she ran the rest of the way to Major Blaine's lodging. She burst in as he emerged from his bedroom, ready for his breakfast. "Adia!" he exclaimed. "Did someone try to rob you?"

She looked down at her disheveled clothes. "Worse—a slave catcher tried to capture me so he could take me south, and he said he would also go for Molly and Daniel. Does the law allow a slave catcher to steal me and my family away?"

The major frowned. "With the city changing hands, the law is uncertain. Force will rule."

That was what she feared. "Daniel said that the British Army was arranging to evacuate former slaves and Loyalists to Nova Scotia. Can you help us get on such a ship?"

"You and Daniel qualify, but the first ships won't leave for Nova Scotia for weeks. We are still negotiating with the Americans about procedures. They want the right to challenge every black man, woman, and child in the city. There will be registrations and lists and certificates."

"Sir, we need help now!" She caught the major's gaze. "Can you do anything for us?"

His gaze narrowed as he thought. "Though the Nova Scotia transports aren't ready, there's a British naval vessel sailing for England on the afternoon tide. I know the captain, and I believe I can obtain passage for you and your family. Can you leave so quickly?"

"London?" Thinking of the cool evil in Trent's eyes, Adia said flatly, "Yes."

"Then, go home for Molly and your husband. You will be able to take only what you can carry easily. I'll send two soldiers to guard you. When you're ready, come here. I'll arrange for you to be taken to the ship." His voice dropped. "And may God watch over you."

MAJOR BLAINE WAS as good as his word. His men escorted her home by a route different from her usual walk. Daniel was horrified to learn of the attempt to capture Adia. Mouth tight, he began packing the small amount of luggage they could take. The two of them had become very good at leaving. Adia told a neighbor that they were going, and why, but not where. Then they left their snug home forever.

Eight hours later, they were sailing from New York harbor on the tide. Adia and Daniel stood on the rear of the ship, Daniel holding Molly as they watched the city diminish behind them. The child said wistfully, "I didn't have time to say good-bye to my friends."

"I'm sorry, sweeting," Daniel said. "But there will be new friends in England."

"Look!" Molly's sadness vanished, and she pointed toward the bow. "Big fish jumping!"

"We'll go look at them." Daniel set her down on the deck and took her hand.

"I'll join you soon," Adia promised.

Her husband nodded, knowing she wanted to say her private good-bye to the city she loved, which had sheltered them so well. When Adia was alone, she leaned on the railing, blinking back tears. She couldn't say that she was sorry they wouldn't have to cultivate raw wilderness in Nova Scotia. She liked cities, and the idea of London drew her. She and Daniel were hard workers, and Major Blaine had given them twenty pounds to help them get started in England. The Adams family would survive, and Molly would have a better life.

Adia was about to go to join her family in fish watching when a young black sailor passed nearby. On impulse, she asked, "You are a free man, sir?"

He paused, his warm gaze moving over her. "Aye, mistress. You're bound for London?"

"I am." She gestured toward the bow. "With my husband and daughter."

Looking disappointed that she was unavailable, he replied, "You will like London. Many Africans live there."

She noticed that he wore a strand of beads around his neck, and guessed that it supported a medicine pouch. Lowering her voice, she said, "Are there any African priests?"

He instinctively touched the pouch hidden beneath his shirt. "Aye, mistress." He studied her with narrowed eyes. "You are a witch?"

"No. But I have some power, and would like to learn to use it."

"You will find priests and priestesses to guide you in London. Good luck to you and your family, mistress." He inclined his head, then returned to his work.

She turned back to the sea. The American coast was only a thin dark line. Deep, powerful feelings were stirring inside her, and for the first time, she felt that she was not fleeing from something, but running toward something better. Will I find what I seek in London, Grandmother?

Aye, child. Freedom, teachers, destiny. You will find them all there.

Above all, destiny.

CHAPTER SEVENTEEN

NIKOLAI WONDERED what Jean Macrae thought of his house, with its cool tile, white walls, and colorful fabrics. He found the simplicity soothing, but the style was that of peasants, not aristocrats.

Telling himself it didn't matter what she thought, he ushered her outside onto the cobbled street. She studied everything with interested eyes as they strolled down the hill.

The villagers studied her in return. Though Santola had a wide range of nationalities, red hair was rare so everyone recognized her as the stranger who had not been a slave. As they neared the docks, Nikolai made a mental note to get her a hat so her face wouldn't burn. Then he remembered that she would be gone in a matter of days.

She would leave, taking with her that fierce independence, winsome figure—and her knowledge of magic.

As they halted on the terrace above the ship repair

dock, he said harshly, "Don't go, Jean. Not yet. I want to learn more about magic. My education has been erratic. I must learn how to fully use my power. It will make me more effective in my work."

"Surely you also want to learn for your own sake." She glanced up at him thoughtfully. "Talent usually brings a powerful need to use it. You need training, but I doubt I am the best teacher. There is too much between us."

"You are the best because you're the only one available," he said bluntly. A string of pack donkeys was passing, so he pulled the straw hat off one and dropped it on her head. "If you aren't careful, your fine white skin will be bright red."

She laughed and adjusted the hat back so it didn't fall over her eyes. "I will smell of donkey. But I suppose that's better than burning."

"I want you healthy to answer my questions, not perishing of sunstroke."

"Speaking of which, I'm tired. I'd like to return now." Reminded that she had been unconscious for several days, he turned to guide her back up the hill. "When you struggled with the tempest—what was happening then?"

She looked thoughtful. "I'm not entirely sure, but the storm proved that I inherited a good share of the Macrae sensitivity to weather patterns. I've become more aware of weather since sailing from London. Perhaps my talent works best now that I'm farther south.

"But while I can feel the patterns, I haven't the raw power needed to control great storm systems. That's why I needed to draw on you." Her brows furrowed. "I'm sorry there wasn't more time to prepare you. I'm told that having one's power seized so abruptly is disturbing and often painful. Usually power sharing is done only after careful discussion and gradual preparation. And only between friends."

Though it had been painful, he brushed her words away. "Your actions were needful. But at the end, I felt another energy as well, as if another person was present. Did I imagine that?"

"You're perceptive," she said with a nod of approval. "I was about to lose control of the storm's center, and I knew I didn't have the strength to master it again. So in sheer desperation, I reached out to see if I could get help from my brother, who is the most powerful weather mage in Britain."

"Your brother was joined to us?" he said, revolted by the thought. He had to some extent made peace with Jean Macrae, but her brother was another matter.

"Without him, the ship would have sunk and all of us drowned," she pointed out. "I would not have been able to reach him over such a great distance if not for the bond between us. So he, too, was essential in saving us from the storm. Surely that means you should give up your desire to revenge yourself against him."

"Damnation, Jean Macrae, is no one in your family to pay for your father's crime?" he exploded, furious at her brazen request.

"If my father were alive, I would put the two of you in a room to talk about what happened that day you were captured. You might find the truth different from your memories. But even if my father betrayed you..." Her eyes narrowed. "Duncan and I have done nothing to harm you. *Nothing.* In the storm, we saved your ship, your crew, and all your future battles against slavery, not to mention your precious neck. That cancels any blood debt you feel you are owed."

Rage blazed through him. He wanted to slam his fists into the stucco walls of the nearest house or kill a slaver with his bare hands. Anything to release the violence of his long-held fury.

He had lived for revenge, clinging to it as a lifeline when he lay bleeding from the lash on a galley, or perishing of thirst in the desert. He wanted to kill Macrae, who had promised him a home and safety, then casually broken that promise. At least as much, he wanted to destroy Duncan Macrae, the favored child, the true son, who had effortlessly possessed what Nikolai had wanted with such frantic need.

But he could not deny the truth of the witch's words. She and her brother had not harmed him directly, and together, they had saved the *Justice* and her crew. All three of them had been needed—he and Jean Macrae together had not been enough.

He forced himself to remember the touch of her brother's mind at the end of the struggle with the storm. What kind of man was Duncan Macrae? Bleakly he admitted to himself that there had been nothing in the man's energy to hate. Under other circumstances, they might have met and become friends.

Though Nikolai burned for justice, he also valued

honor. Bitterly he accepted that Macrae, the true betrayer, was beyond reach. Any justice the Scottish lord received would have to be at God's hands, if there was such a creature and He believed in justice.

Hating every word, he said, "Very well. I will not pursue my vendetta against your brother or his family. But I will neither forgive nor forget."

"As you wish. Hate us if you must, as long as you don't hurt my family." She halted, swaying, and reached out to a wall to support herself. "I... I need to rest." The damned woman looked on the verge of collapse. Why had he suggested she walk through the village when she had just woken from a three-day collapse? He scooped her up, thinking that she must have burned off weight when using her magic, for she weighed almost nothing. She struggled feebly. "Let go of me!"

She was right, he shouldn't have touched her—the contact between them was profoundly disquieting. He shouldn't be feeling raw lust for a woman who was so feeble. A woman for whom his feelings were so complicated. But the longer they were together, the harder it was to regard her with detachment.

If he set her down, she'd probably crumple up on the street. An unloaded donkey was heading down the hill, so he signaled the driver. The fellow obligingly brought the donkey over so Nikolai could set the witch on the beast's back.

Her fingers locked onto the donkey's scraggly mane. "Thank you." She smiled warmly at the driver, ignoring Nikolai. The driver, a usually cantankerous Berber from

North Africa, stared at her with dazed pleasure. The woman was definitely a witch.

By the time the small group reached Nikolai's house, she was able to slip off the donkey and thank its owner with another smile. When they entered the building, she looked at the steps to her room with some dismay.

"Can you climb the steps? Or should I carry you?" She scowled and began to climb, relying heavily on the railing. He stayed a quiet two steps behind her until she made it to the top. Once sure she was safe, he said, "You need more to eat. And perhaps a cup of tea. That is a very British remedy, I think?"

She turned and smiled crookedly over her shoulder. "I'd like that."

As he headed down to the kitchen, he thought that the sooner she sailed from his island, the better.

He could not bear the thought of her leaving.

Scalding hot tea sweetened with honey and served with bread and cheese went a long way to restoring Jean. By the third cup, she was able to regard Gregorio with equanimity. He had agreed to drop his vendetta against Duncan, so she and her family were safe. Soon she would be back in Marseilles, able to tell her friends about her adventure before sailing for home. For now, she sat on one of the chairs in her room rather than the bed, since that would be far too suggestive.

Of course, there was the matter of the captain

wanting to be tutored in magic. "I could find you a Guardian who will teach you how to use your power. There are surely men in Marseilles who would be willing to do so."

"It would be easier to work with a man than a woman." He frowned over his tea. "But you are here now."

Jean toyed with her dagger. Interestingly, while she had shown some Macrae weather talent, she didn't seem to have sensitivity to iron that male Macrae weather mages did. Magic was so complex no one could ever truly understand it.

But—one could try. "Would you like me to attempt to evaluate your abilities?" she asked. "I need your permission to enter your mind, though it wouldn't be painful. Not like the night of the storm."

His frown deepened as he weighed her offer. "Will you be able to read my thoughts or see the events of my past?"

"Rarely can thoughts be read, though I will certainly be aware of your emotions." She finished her tea. "Details of events are also unlikely, especially since I won't look for them. My only goal would be to map the dimensions of your power. If I'm successful, we will have a better idea of your potential."

"I want to be able to use the power I suppressed to survive." His dark brows drew together. He hated admitting that he needed anyone. "And I can't do it alone."

"I'm not sure I can be the teacher you need, but I can

at least evaluate your power." She extended her hands to him. "Are you willing?"

He hesitated. "It is not easy to trust you."

But he wanted whatever information she could give him. "Do you think it's any easier for me to trust you?" she retorted. "You kidnapped me, threatened me with assault and slavery, threatened the lives of my family. I am willing to help because your mission is a noble one, but if you don't trust me, leave now and let me be."

"Witch," he said, mouth tight, but he clasped her hands.

Once more energy blazed between them. Instead of resisting it, this time she dove into that stream of power, letting it sweep her into the labyrinth of his mind. Despite his complexities, his inner blaze of passion

and anger and idealism were easy to read, to a point. "You're a natural finder. The ability to locate things such as corsair ships can be strengthened. There are great reserves of power in your nature, including your ability to knock others unconscious by pure mental energy, but much of this potential is... I suppose walled off is the best way to describe it."

She probed further, without success. "This goes beyond the way you suppressed your power to protect yourself as you grew. There is another factor at work, one I'm unfamiliar with. I can sense power on the other side of the barrier. I even tapped into that energy during the storm, when I was desperate. But I can't evaluate it now."

"How does one break down the wall?"

"I don't know. I've never seen anything like this." She

let her mind flow around the mysterious well of energy. "I believe the barrier is related to your African heritage. The nature of African magic is somewhat different from the Guardian magic I know. You would be best served by finding an African mage."

"How the devil does one do that?" he muttered.

"One of my friends in Marseilles is African. His family also runs a shipping business, so he set the captains to finding an African priest. The priest visited Marseilles and stayed long enough to teach Moses what he needed to know. Perhaps Sekou would be willing to visit you here. Moses probably knows how to find him."

"Assuming your friend Moses would help a man who had kidnapped you." Nikolai released her hands, frowning. "Tales of slavery made you violently ill. Do you hate the idea enough to help me fight it?"

Her brows arched. "You might not be able to end slavery by yourself, but you've proven that you can make a difference to some people. I can't even do that. While you have my sympathies for your cause, I'm of no practical use."

"Your teaching can make a difference. I will seek an African mage, but that could take years. Anything I learn now will make me more effective while I wait for the right training."

He blazed with passion for his cause, and she envied that. She had never been happier than when she was part of the fight for Scotland's freedom. A burning need for freedom was part of every Scot's soul, and that passion made Gregorio's quest echo within her. Yet there were limits to what she could do. "I'm not African, and I wish to go home. But for what time I have before leaving, I'll teach what I can."

His eyes burned. "Will you swear a blood oath to do that?"

"Is that necessary? If my plain word is not good enough, swearing in blood will not change anything." A vague memory surfaced. "Unless there is a magic in blood that I am not aware of?"

"There is magic in ritual, though you northern Protestants don't seem to recognize that." He drew his dagger and cut across his left palm, then offered the weapon to her hilt first. "And yes, I feel this is necessary, though I cannot explain why."

Jean knew better than to argue with the intuition of a mage, even an underdeveloped one. "I should use my own blade." She turned away from him and bent to lift her hem, then turned back with her knife.

Schooling herself not to flinch, she made a small, neat cut on her left palm. She extended her left hand. The left side, closer to the heart. She wondered if Gregorio was conscious of why he'd chosen the left hand.

As she began to speak, energy rushed through her, pure and transcendent. "I swear that I will always oppose slavery in any way I can, even if the cost would be my life." She wasn't sure where those words came from, but the source was higher than her conscious mind. She caught Gregorio's gaze. "I also pledge to share with you any knowledge I possess that can aid you in your just crusade."

They clasped left hands, blood to blood—and the world turned inside out. Power blasted through the room like a thunderstorm, blinding all the senses in chaos. Jean fell from the chair to her knees. She was in a tunnel of energy that roared from unknown past to unknowable future. Screams of souls and events beyond imagining resonated through her, tearing at mind and body. Her hand locked with Gregorio's, and she was dizzily uncertain who was saving whom.

A thump reverberated and the energy faded away. When her vision cleared, she found herself kneeling on the floor, her fingers still interlaced with Gregorio's. He was crunched into a ball beside her, his face haggard.

And beside them, appearing from nowhere, lay an African woman. Though she wore a neat European-style gown and a white headscarf, loops of beads around her throat and wrists gave her an exotic appearance. In her forties, with smooth black skin and a strong, shapely body, she lay sprawled on her back as limp as death. An embroidered pouch of animal skin was slung over her shoulder.

Wondering where the devil the woman had come from, Jean crawled the few feet between them and tried to find a pulse with shaking hands.

The woman choked, then inhaled, opening dark, stunned eyes. Her gaze went from Jean to Gregorio and lingered. Relief in her eyes, she asked, "When am I?"

"You're on the island of Santola," Jean answered.

"Not *where,*" the woman said forcefully. "*When?*"

CHAPTER EIGHTEEN

When? While Nikolai stared, Jean replied, "It's the year of our Lord 1753."

The woman breathed, "The magic worked." Her eyes closed and she lay still, her chest rising and falling gently.

Jean glanced at him, baffled. "Do you know who she is?"

"I've never seen her before." Nikolai managed to get to his feet without falling, though it was a near thing. Every spark of energy had been sucked from his body, like when he'd helped the Scottish witch fight the storm. "Which is interesting, for I know everyone on Santola. She is a stranger on an island where there are no strangers." He extended his hand to Jean Macrae.

She accepted his help in getting to her feet. Even though she seemed as exhausted as he, a spark hummed between them when they touched.

"She looks like someone who has just performed a great magical work and barely survived it," Jean said as she studied the motionless woman. "The fact that we feel the same way suggests that she had to use some energy from the two of us to arrive here."

Since the woman didn't belong to the island, there was only one other possibility, though it seemed incredible. "Could she have traveled here from another place by magic?" Nikolai asked.

"I've heard that a few powerful mages can travel from one place to another, though I've never met anyone who could. It's one of those magical abilities that may be legend rather than fact. But I don't know a better explanation for her." Jean frowned. "We should try to lift her onto the bed."

"I'm not sure we can manage that in our current state. The carpet will do for now." He pulled a blanket from the bed and spread it over the woman.

Jean tucked a pillow under the stranger's head. "I don't think she is merely from another place. Look at the cut of her gown. I've never seen one quite like it. She may have come from another time. From the future." Nikolai whistled softly. "That would explain her asking when she was. Is such a journey even possible?"

"I've never heard of traveling through time, but that doesn't mean much. I'm no scholar of the lore." Jean knelt by the woman again, her gaze on the bracelet on the woman's left wrist. Large black beads of a curious design were threaded between smaller beads of transparent black stone. "There is magic in that bracelet. If one looks with mage vision, it burns with power. Can you see that? Relax your eyes and look for the energy patterns rather than at the surface."

He stared at the bracelet and tried to relax his eyes. Seeing his scowl, she said, "Try looking through rather than at it."

Using her advice, he let his gaze slip out of focus—and abruptly he recognized that the bracelet really did burn with power. He saw it as brilliant white light with the large beads flaring brightest of all.

There was also a faint, streaky glow around the unconscious woman. A stronger golden glow around Jean Macrae. He stared at his own hand and saw a pulse of transparent color around his body, but the shade was deeper, more red. "Good Lord," he breathed. "Yes, I see. Mage vision? That's a powerful first lesson."

He bent and reached toward the bracelet. Jean caught his wrist hard. "Don't touch it! Not without knowing more. The bracelet is bespelled." She pointed toward a gap on the bracelet. The cord holding the beads looked slightly charred. "This looks as if one of the large beads burned away. That might have been part of the magic that brought her here. Don't touch her pouch, either." Her brows furrowed as she studied the sleeping woman. "What is your story, madam?"

"I presume she'll tell us when she wakes up. For now, she needs rest and nourishment." He had enough strength to pour what was left of the cold tea into a cup. He raised the woman's head and held it to her lips. She drank the half cup of liquid without opening her eyes. He made a mental note to ask his cook to make more broth.

As he stood, Jean smiled wryly. "Are you sure that you want to know more magic? The great mages do not walk an easy path."

"Oh, yes," he said softly. "I want to know more." He studied the mystery woman, who was resting peacefully. "And perhaps the ancestors have sent me a teacher."

ADIA'S HEAD pounded like drums when she woke, but she was glad to see that she really had gone to another place and time. Her ghastly passage through other worlds had not been for nothing. She cautiously pushed herself up on one elbow. She was nicely tucked up with a pillow and blanket on a lush Oriental carpet, her arm curled protectively around her medicine bag.

A soft voice said, "Good morning. I am Jean Macrae. Would you like a drink?"

Jean Macrae was the pretty redheaded girl Adia had seen when she arrived in this place. She looked very young, but she had an air of competence.

"Please." Adia's throat was so dry she could barely speak.

The girl brought her a cool tumbler of fruit juice. After the first long, welcome swallow, Adia pulled off her headscarf and shook out the dozens of narrow braids that confined her long hair. Her coiffure seemed to have made the journey with less struggle than the rest of her. After finishing the fruit juice, Adia said, "I am Adia Adams."

"You have come from the future?"

As Adia studied the girl's face, she realized that Jean Macrae was not as young as she looked at first glance. "You are clever, but of course you are a powerful sorceress."

The girl laughed. "Not so very powerful. But I have lived among great mages."

Feeling stronger, Adia got to her feet. "I have much to explain. Will you summon your husband so I can tell you my story at once?"

"Captain Gregorio is not my husband," the girl said emphatically.

"No?" Adia said, surprised. "When I looked at the two of you, there was a visible bond."

"Perhaps, but it's not the bond of lovers or mates. Opponents, perhaps. Sometimes uneasy comrades." The girl headed to the door. "I'll have food sent up while I look for him." She shook her head as she left. "My *husband*?"

Amused by the girl's unwillingness to accept what was clearly evident, Adia explored the room. She gasped when she stepped onto the terrace and saw the sea and the broken ring of islands. Where was this place? The two people she'd met were white and spoke English, but many of the people she saw in the village below were Africans.

This island reminded her a little of the Indies, but the light was different. Perhaps the Mediterranean? Certainly it was a place she had never seen before. A wave of dizziness swept over her, and she sat on a bench before she collapsed. This was *1753*. Though she had chosen this path, the knowledge that she would probably never see her home and family again made her ache in every fiber of her being. She folded over, wrapping her arms around her body as she shook with shock and grief.

Slowly the dizziness passed. Her reasons for risking such dangerous magic were as powerful as ever, and at the least, she seemed to have come to a kind place. She would survive as she always did.

She hoped the food would arrive soon. She was famished.

NIKOLAI LOOKED up when the door to his study opened. Though he'd been trying to work on accounts with Louise, he was having trouble concentrating, and his companion was irritated with him.

Jean entered the study. After inclining her head politely to Louise, she said, "Our visitor, Adia Adams, has awakened and wants to speak to you and me, Captain."

He almost leaped from his chair. The twenty-four hours since the mysterious woman appeared had crept with painful slowness. "Good. Louise, your accounts appear to be in fine shape, so you don't need me anymore."

"It amazes me that a man who will fight slavers with his bare hands will seize any excuse to run from a ledger," Louise said acerbically.

"Perhaps if the ledger fought back, it would be more interesting," he said as he crossed the room.

Isabelle flew from her perch to land on his shoulder.

He scratched the macaw's neck. "Stay and keep Louise company, *ma belle.*" He returned the bird to her perch, where she rocked restlessly from foot to foot.

"Isabelle will be better company than you have been," Louise said as she bent over her ledger again. "Mam'zelle Macrae, I have a lotion that protects pale skin from the sun. I shall send you some."

"Thank you. That would be welcome," Jean said, a little surprised by the offer.

Nikolai ushered Jean ahead of him and up the stairs. As she climbed, she asked over her shoulder, "Is Louise your housekeeper?"

"Among other things. She has a gift for figures, so her main work is managing the accounts for the shipping business that supports most of the island. She lives two houses down, so she is here often. She cares for Isabelle when I am away. That useless bird likes Louise better than me, I think."

When he entered Jean's room, he didn't see the visitor, so he crossed to the terrace. Adia stood by the wall, looking out at the island and caldera.

When Jean and Nikolai stepped onto the terrace, she turned to greet them. She was a tall woman and a commanding presence. "This is a very beautiful place," she said, her English touched by only the faintest hint of an accent. "I think you called it Santola, Captain Gregorio?"

He nodded. "The island is a sanctuary for those who have been freed from slavery. We are located in the western Mediterranean."

"A sanctuary for freed slaves? No wonder I was brought here."

Guided by intuition, he said, "I was a slave. You also?"

She nodded. "Since this is the Mediterranean and you are white, you might have been enslaved by Barbary pirates?"

"Yes. But I am not wholly white. My grandmother was as African as you."

Adia's eyes widened at what she heard. "I wonder if that is why the magic brought me here?"

"Where and when do you come from, Madame Adia?" Jean asked. "I'm perishing with curiosity."

"Sit, please, this will be a long discussion." Adia moved under the covered area and settled onto a chair opposite the bench. Nikolai and Jean took seats on the bench as far from each other as possible. "I have come from London in the year 1787."

Her words fell into total silence. Though he and Jean had deduced that Adia must have come through time, to hear her say as much was shocking. So many questions were raised that his mind boggled. First and foremost... "Why have you come?"

Her gaze was piercing. "My mission is to find warriors who will join the fight against slavery."

Her words blazed through him like lightning. "Dear God, is slavery being fought in your time?"

"I think we may be witnessing the beginning of the end, though it will be a long struggle." Her expression became abstracted. "I best start at the beginning, I think. I was born in West Africa, not far from the Slave Coast.

When still a child, I was captured by slavers and taken to America. First the Indies, then the Carolinas." She halted. "We are in 1753, you say? I have just been enslaved!"

"I am having trouble grasping the idea of time travel," Jean said. "You can be in two places at once?"

"I must be," Adia said ruefully. "But I do not truly understand it, either."

Impatient to hear more of her story, Nikolai said, "You were a slave in America, but you came here from London? How did you escape?"

Adia toyed with her bead bracelets, her long fingers restless. "That is a complicated tale. Thirteen of the American colonies revolted against Britain in 1776. They wanted their freedom. Many noble speeches were made, but of course they wanted freedom for white men, not African slaves." Her voice was bitter. "So the British offered liberty to any slaves who came to their side and fought the rebels."

Nikolai whistled softly. "Did many take the British up on their offer?"

"Many, many. Some were caught and punished, a few hanged, but nothing would stop men from trying. Even slaves of the great American general, Washington, said to be a good man in most ways, ran away to freedom." Adia rose from her chair and began pacing the terrace, her steps tense. "My husband and I belonged to the same master, but I was kept in the city and Daniel was on the plantation, so we saw each other seldom. He ran to the British and sent for me when he could give our daughter and me a home. Seven long years the rebellion lasted."

Nikolai's own experiences provided too-vivid images to go with her flat narrative. She and her husband were very brave, and very strong. "So you won your freedom when the British defeated the colonists?"

"No." Adia's expression was wry. "The rebels won, and the British left."

"Britain *lost?*" Jean gasped. "How did the colonials defeat them?"

"They cared more. They fought for their homes and property, and the battles were right on their doorsteps." Adia leaned back against the railing, her gaze distant. "Of course the masters considered slaves part of that property. They wanted us back so much that part of the peace treaty demanded the right to retrieve their slaves. As soon as the British surrendered, American slave owners began sending catchers to New York City to seize us and take us back in chains."

"How did you escape from America?" Jean asked in a hushed voice.

Adia's expression lightened. "Many British officers thought it wrong to break their word to us even though we were only Africans, so they arranged to evacuate former slaves as well as Loyalists. Most were sent to Nova

Scotia, but a few of us, including Daniel and me, were put on ships for England."

"You have lived in London ever since?" Jean asked. Adia nodded. "We almost starved the first year for there was no work, but at least we were free and together. Daniel is a skilled carpenter, and eventually he found a steady job. I work in a bakery. We have a home and another child, a son." Her voice hardened. "But we have not forgotten slavery."

"So you and your husband founded an antislavery movement?" Nikolai asked.

"Not us. This is not an issue Africans can win alone, for we have no power. Many think us no more than animals." She chose her words carefully. "White people must be involved for change to come. Indeed, they must lead the change because whites listen best to other whites. In the spring of 1787, a dozen Englishmen, most of them Quakers, founded an antislavery movement, but it is very fragile. Our best seer says that the death of a single man could end the movement for another generation or more."

"So you have come seeking allies in the battle against slavery," he said slowly. "But why have you traveled back to us? Surely there must be people in your own time who are as willing to give their lives as I am."

"The willingness to die is not enough. More is required."

"So you sought mages to help you?" Jean asked, brow furrowed.

"Magic is one thing we do possess," Adia replied. "There are several thousand Africans living in London. We come of many tribes. My tribe, the Iske, is small, tucked between the Yoruba and the Ife, but we are famous for our great magic. Though I come of a priestly lineage, I was stolen from my home so young that I wasn't trained to use my power. I could do small works—magic helped my daughter and me escape to join my husband—but I was no true priestess."

With an interested expression, Jean said, "I've found that my magic works best in a crisis. Was that the case with you?"

"Indeed it was. Desperation is very effective," Adia said with a hint of a smile. "But I have learned much since then, for our London black community is blessed with several true priests and priestesses. They initiated me into my full power, and I became a member of the circle of elders. Given the vulnerability of the antislavery movement, the elders decided to appeal to the ancestors to locate those who can protect and nourish the movement. That is where you come in."

"Whatever I can do, I will," he said intensely. "But why me?"

"You are of my blood, Nikolai Gregorio." She closed her eyes as if listening to an inner voice. "We are both Iske. I believe that my grandmother was the niece of your grandmother, so we are cousins."

"How do you know that?" he asked, startled.

"My grandmother just told me," she said simply. "When the elders did our great invocation in London, we did not know if we would succeed, nor were we sure what success would look like. I think I was drawn here because you and I are blood kin and the ancestors needed that tie to make the magic work."

Jean asked, "Will you be able to return to your family in your own time?"

Adia's expression turned bleak. "I hope so, but I do not know." To Nikolai, she said, "I think the ancestors chose you because you are Iske, yet you also have enough European blood to move among white men. You can walk the streets of London in neighborhoods where a black man would be kidnapped or beaten."

"He will suit your purpose admirably," Jean observed, "but I doubt I would be any use to you. I am no great mage, and certainly no warrior."

Adia turned the full force of her dark eyes on Jean. "You are essential, Jean Macrae."

"How?" Jean asked, puzzled. "I agree that slavery is evil, but I've never had the personal experience of slavery that drives you two. Since I'm not a powerful mage, what can I contribute?"

"African magic is a balance of male and female energies," Adia explained. "For small magic, a man or a woman may work alone, but for great magical works, such as the guardianship of this movement, the protectors must be two—a man and a woman. Both must have powerful magic. Both must hate slavery and be willing to risk their lives to end it." Her mesmerizing gaze held them both. "And to aid in this great cause, they must be mates."

CHAPTER NINETEEN

"MATES?" Jean said incredulously. Her gaze shot to Gregorio, who seemed as stunned as she. They both looked away instantly. "Why would that be necessary?"

"The union of male and female energy creates a power greater than either has alone." Adia studied them thoughtfully. "You also come of very different magical traditions. Those powers will be enhanced if they can be blended harmoniously, but for that to happen, the bonds must be very strong." She smiled. "For a man and woman, the strongest possible bond is the most intimate. If you are willing to risk your lives to end slavery—well, surely it is easier to celebrate life than to end it."

"Simpler perhaps," Gregorio said, his expression grim. "But not easier."

Jean looked down at her fists, face flaming. Though she'd had wild thoughts of what it would be like to take the captain as a lover, that was lust and fantasy. Being told they must become mates for the sake of a greater cause was quite a different matter. She felt shocked. Terrified.

Excited.

Suppressing the thought, she said, "Adia, you told us you needed people of strong magical power, and I think part of the energy that brought you here was drawn from Gregorio and me. But neither of us is a strong mage. I come of the Guardians, European families with a tradition of power and service. Yet though I was raised a Guardian, I am one of the weakest of my kind."

She gestured at Gregorio. "He has a potential for great power, but his abilities are blocked so that he can't use them. How can either of us be the type of warrior you need? Even if we became mates, I doubt we'd have anything like the power needed to end an institution as huge and evil as slavery. Much of the world is in bondage, though it is called different names. What can *we* do?"

"You will not yourselves end slavery," Adia said, her gaze turned inward. "That will come only when a great mass of people rise up and cry, 'Enough!' Your task is to protect and aid the yeast of the abolition movement so it can make that mass rise."

"You say this movement was new in your time. Would we have to travel in time to protect it?" The idea did not appeal to Jean.

"I believe so." Adia smiled ruefully. "I do not have all the answers, you know. I was brought here by the ancestors, and they have given me a sense of what must be accomplished. But their methods are... not so clear as one might like. Even my grandmother, whose presence has comforted me since I was taken by slavers, usually only gives me feelings, not clear directions."

"Magic is often like that," Jean said. "It provides a sketch. We must then figure out how to fill in the missing pieces. And there are far too many pieces missing in what you describe. What would we do in another time? Would we ever be able to come back? How much danger is involved?"

"All I know is that the magic succeeded in bringing me back to this year without killing me. Apart from that, I have no answers for you. I'm sorry."

Jean frowned, recognizing the truth in Adia's voice. If she and Nikolai chose to walk this path, they would do it nearly blind. Yet how much did one ever know of the future? Even seers weren't always right. A great goal was worthy of great risk.

"Tell me more of your Guardians," Adia said. "How is your magic worked? Do you go into a trance and join the ancestors? Do you use roots and herbs and rituals?" She touched the pouch slung over her shoulder. "Do you carry a medicine bag?"

Jean shook her head, wondering how many ways there were to approach magic. "For us, magic usually comes through the mind. One visualizes the desired result and uses power to make it happen. There are mental exercises that help one channel that power. Some Guardians work with potions and ritual magic, but most draw directly on the forces of nature."

"Your people walk a different path from ours. But surely you must go through initiation to achieve full mastery?"

Jean's brow furrowed. "I'm not sure what you mean by initiation."

"One is initiated when one grows from child to adult," Adia explained. "The rites vary from tribe to tribe, but the purpose is to teach the younglings about what lies beyond the world we see."

Jean's mind flashed back. "Though we don't use the term 'initiation,' when a young Guardian reaches maturity, there is a ritual that involves fasting, testing, and deep meditations. Often the young person discovers the full dimensions of his or her talents during this process. At the end, there is a ceremony where one-swears the Guardian oath to use power to serve the greater good." Her own passage had been undramatic. Though she had sworn her oath with great belief and intensity, her meditations had produced no special insights. And, alas, no sudden influx of power.

"So you do have an initiation." Adia turned to Gregorio, and her expression became troubled. "But I see that you have not been initiated. That lack is what stands between you and full use of your magic."

"I do know how to use power," he said sharply. "I can knock a man unconscious with a touch." He glanced at Jean. "Or a woman. I can find a slave ship across many leagues of sea. Surely I can do what is needed for your mission."

She shook her head. "What you can do is only the

barest taste of what you would be capable of if you'd been properly trained and initiated. It isn't just that you might need specific magical skills, but that you would need to live with a magical way of seeing the world. You can't do that."

"Are you saying it is too late for me to be initiated?" he asked harshly.

Adia's frown deepened. "In theory, no, but it would be far more dangerous at your age. Even with lads of thirteen, there is danger. It is not unknown for young people to die during initiation. Over the years you have left parts of your soul in many places. Those pieces must be retrieved for you to survive the rituals."

"Was your soul fragmented by your scattered life?" he asked.

"Indeed it was. The elders were concerned about my survival, and justly so. My initiation was the most difficult passage of my life, far more perilous than the escape from slavery." She hesitated to find words. "Initiation involves... going to different worlds. Seeing different kinds of reality. I know no better way to describe it. The process is painful, confusing, frightening—and dangerous."

"This is what has been missing from my life." He leaned forward on the bench, vibrating with tension. "I will do whatever is necessary to achieve mastery. Teach me what I need to know."

Adia's hand curved protectively over the bag that hung from her shoulder. "I can teach, but the danger is in how you experience your initiation. You are a strong man, set in your ways. I fear that you are too much a leader, a man who gives orders and chooses his own path, to flow with the ancestors. Your death would be a tragedy." Her face twisted. "Your loss in one of the other worlds would be... worse."

"I have risked death many times. I am willing to risk it again." He glanced over at Jean, and his eyes narrowed. "Are you going to forbid me to attempt this?" She gave a startled laugh. "As if I could forbid you anything! Don't worry, if you can persuade Adia to allow you to try, I will not interfere." Her humor faded as she remembered Adia's warning. "Though I am oddly reluctant to see you kill yourself."

"Generous of you." His gaze returned to Adia. "How do I prepare for initiation?"

"First, meditate on the question of whether you should. Ask your deepest self if you are fit for such a challenge." She smiled wryly. "Do you know how to be still enough to meditate, Captain? I do not ask in jest. One must empty one's mind to hear the voices of nature and the ancestors."

"I can learn," he said stubbornly.

"Then practice that, Captain, while I meditate on whether I should send you into such danger. I will not attempt initiation unless I believe there is a chance you will succeed." She stroked the medicine bag again. "I must also seek others of African blood since I will need help to lead an initiation. There are Africans on this island, I think?"

"Yes, plus some of mixed blood. I shall send Tano to

you. He will know." The captain stood, his mouth twisting. "Now I shall go and see if I can find stillness."

Adia frowned after the captain. "He is a brave man, but he does not realize what he is undertaking."

"Most of life is undertaken with insufficient knowledge," Jean said wryly. "If he does not successfully undergo initiation, will he have the power needed to aid the abolition movement?"

"Likely not." Adia wished she knew more. "I do not know which is worse—to permit him to attempt an initiation ceremony for which he is dangerously unsuited, or to send him on a mission that may kill him because he lacks the power to do what is needed. Perhaps it would be best if I do neither."

"Now that you have shown him a vision of the end of slavery, it would destroy him if you took that hope away," her companion said pragmatically. "Best to teach him what he needs to know to survive. He has a fierce will. Perhaps fierce enough that he can learn even stillness and acceptance."

"As soon ask fire to become water," Adia said pessimistically. "That can be done by a powerful priest, but I doubt your captain can master himself to that extent. Submission and release are the opposite of his nature." Jean cocked her red head to one side. "Would the ancestors have sent you here if we were incapable of carrying out this mission?"

"You may be the only two who might have any chance at all. That doesn't mean you'll be successful." Adia spread her hands in frustration. "The invocation of the London elders was powerful and desperate. We asked the ancestors for a chance, any chance at all, no matter how remote. I hoped the ancestors would choose Daniel and me. One of the other elders would have taken in our children if we died, and both of us would do anything that might end slavery, even if the chances are ten thousand to one."

"You're obviously a very powerful priestess, and you have the commitment required. Do you have any idea why the mission didn't come to you and your husband?"

"Now that I have been brought here, the answer is obvious," Adia said slowly. "Daniel has very little magic. Certainly he is no priest. Also, he is Ashanti, and there are no Ashanti among the elders in London. If there had been a blood tie, perhaps we would have been chosen. Instead, I am here and he is there, a lifetime away." She had considered that they might both go, or both stay, but hadn't realized that only one of them would be drawn through time. At least Daniel was still with the children.

"So the ancestors might have settled on Gregorio and me as the best of a bad lot," Jean observed. "Would my power increase if I also undergo initiation? Like Captain Gregorio, I have been told that I have abilities I haven't learned to use."

"You have already been initiated in your tradition. It would be wrong to walk such a different path," Adia said, shocked. "But it is true that you are not fully realized as a priestess. If you like, I will see what I can discern."

"Please." Jean extended her hands.

Adia clasped the other woman's small, fine-boned hands and felt an immediate rush of power. Slowly she sank into Jean's consciousness, down to the levels where magic dwelled. "This is curious. There is a... a tangle in your mind that makes it difficult for your power to connect with your will. Such things are not unknown. There are those who cannot speak clearly, and the family that enslaved me had a son who could not learn to read, though he did not lack for intelligence. You have a mental tangle when it comes to using magic."

Jean frowned. "That sounds right. I've often felt that I have a fair amount of power, but I simply can't summon it effectively. How do I unknot these tangles? Is it even possible?"

Adia clicked her tongue. "I have no idea. There is so much I don't know. But at least you have been initiated.

You have a better chance to resolve your problem than the captain does." She cocked her head thoughtfully. "Are there any kinds of magic that come easily to you? Times when power manages to pass through the tangled ways?"

"In times of great danger, I have been able to perform strong magic. Particularly when my clansmen and I were trying to escape after the Battle of Culloden. Government troops were everywhere as they sought rebels to slaughter, but I was able to shield my men well enough to get us home."

Adia was beginning to understand why the magic had

brought her to Jean. “So you are a woman warrior?” Jean looked bemused. “Perhaps. I’m too small to be much good with a sword, though I’m not bad with firearms. My most useful talent during the Rising was my magic, which worked fairly well because I was desperate. There was another occasion only a few days ago. A great tempest struck Gregorio’s ship, and she almost foundered. I found that I possessed some of the family weather ability. By borrowing power from the captain and my brother, I was able to dispel the storm.”

“So you can manage in disaster, and you have worked successfully with Gregorio. Both of those are good,” Adia said, nodding. “Do any other magics come easily to you?”

Jean shrugged. “I can scry a little, but mostly I only manage small domestic matters such as keeping my clothing and appearance neat. Very trivial magic that I really don’t think about.”

“You can do that? I’d like to know the trick of it. With danger, necessity slices through the tangle to allow you to access your magic. With clothing and appearance”—Adia studied Jean’s neat, stylish appearance with frank admiration—“you have the most wonderful hair, and you say you do this without thought. Surely that is significant.”

“You think that my problems come when I try to access magic consciously, but there is not enough danger to make me desperate?” Jean considered. “That fits. I wonder how I can use this knowledge to stop me from tangling up in myself?”

"You say Guardians work through mental visualizations. Can you visualize clear, free-flowing channels between the depths of your power and your conscious mind?"

Jean's eyes narrowed thoughtfully. "It's worth trying. Thank you, Adia."

"If you are successful, the result may send you to your death," Adia said softly.

"It's possible," Jean said, and she did not look at all young and fragile. "But death comes to us all. Gregorio and I might have died at sea last week along with dozens of others, some of them newly released slaves who had barely had time to draw breath as free men. Death by drowning would have no meaning. Fighting slavery, that has meaning." She hesitated. "When I was leading my men away from Culloden, with thousands of English troops hunting rebels, I prayed to God to get us home safely. I even bargained with God, offering my life in return for the lives of my men. I promised I would make any sacrifice He demanded of me."

The flat words outlined the desperation the girl must have felt. "I, too, have tried to make bargains with God. It never seems to work."

Jean smiled faintly. "Perhaps it did this time. My men and I did make it home safely. For years, it appeared that nothing more would be asked of me. So I spent half my time in London drifting aimlessly from one ball to another. Those years taught me that I must have meaning in my life. I think that through you, God is taking me up on my offer to risk everything for a higher cause."

So the Scottish girl's decision was made, and not done lightly. Quietly Adia said, "You're a brave woman, Jean Macrae."

"Braver than you? I think not." She hesitated. "Before I go in search of Gregorio, would you be able to help me use mind touch to reach my brother and my friends in Marseilles? I want to let them know that I am well, but I don't have enough power to reach them since I'm not in dire straits."

Adia thought wistfully how she would have liked to reassure her family in Africa that she was well. "Of course. What must I do?"

"Let me hold your hands and borrow some of your power."

Adia clasped Jean's hands and deliberately relaxed. She felt the light, swift touch of Jean's mind as the girl established an energy connection between them. There was a long silence during which she could feel a pull on her power. Then Jean gave a sigh of relief and released her hands. "Thank you. I was able to reach them clearly enough to give reassurance and tell them not to worry."

"They will still worry, Miss Macrae."

Jean smiled. "Yes, but not as much." She stood and bowed her head respectfully. "Call me Jean. I'm tired of hearing my full name all the time. Now to find Captain Gregorio. He and I must talk."

After Jean left, Adia closed her eyes. *Thank you,*

Grandmother, for bringing me to two such strong people. Will they be enough to achieve our goals?

Over the years, as Adia's life had become smoother, Grandmother spoke less and less frequently, though Adia still sensed her presence. Today, Grandmother's reply was clear, but uncertain. *I do not know, child. But I know that there are none better.*

CHAPTER TWENTY

NIKOLAI'S THOUGHTS churned as he left his house. By rights, he should go to the docks and see how the repair work was proceeding on the *Justice.* Instead, he turned away and headed into the hills. His favorite walk was a goat path that led through a dip in the rim of the caldera, then down the steep opposite slope to the sea.

A priestess had come through time to recruit him to fight against slavery on a scale far beyond anything he could ever do with his ships. And he must do it as Jean Macrae's mate. The idea gave him chills and fever both. The fever was easily understood, for sexual tension had burned between them from the start. If it were a matter of bodies only, he'd bed her in an instant.

But even the most lustful people brought their minds to a bed, and matters between him and the Scottish witch could never be simple. Did he fear her? In some ways, yes. Not physical fear—he was twice her size, and his magic was equal to hers, though different. But she had an emotional power over him that kept him away for fear of... what? Adia had said that he'd left pieces of his soul in many places. Joining with Jean Macrae would take a very large piece of his soul, and he might never get it back.

He picked his way down the slope to a sheltered cove, wondering how to become still enough to meditate. His mind jangled with thoughts of Adia, the antislavery movement, and Jean Macrae. There were too many questions, too many possibilities. What did an initiation involve? How could he prepare? Could he help end slavery?

The cove was a favorite place of his, almost invisible from the sea but with a peaceful black sand beach. He settled on a rough stone wall that bounded the narrow strip of sand and watched the waves roll in while he tried to meditate.

He was able to force his body to relax, muscle by muscle, but he had less success with his mind, and as the hours passed his concentration worsened. No sooner did he banish one thought than another dashed in. He tried to focus on the question of whether he should attempt initiation. His heart said yes, but was that his deepest self?

The sun had passed the meridian when he heard, "Making any progress?"

He flinched, angry with himself for not being aware that the Scottish witch was approaching. She moved as quietly as a cat.

He glanced up as she perched on the wall several feet

to his right. The wind blew around her, pressing the light fabric of her gown against her slim, elegantly female form. His painful physical awareness destroyed any shred of stillness he'd achieved.

Wrenching his mind away from thoughts of bedding her, he said, "I am a long way from being adept at meditation, but I did complete Adia's assignment. I feel that I am meant to undertake her initiation despite the risk." From Jean's ironic glance, she was unsurprised by his conclusion. He gestured at the bag she carried. "Have you taken to carrying a medicine pouch like Adia?"

"Adia informs me that I should stay with Guardian traditions," Jean said peaceably. "So being a practical Scot, I brought food, not magical implements."

She pulled out a stone jug of wine and set it on the wall between them, then produced a lump of cheese wrapped in light cloth, and a small loaf of bread. She divided the bread and handed him the larger piece, then did the same with the cheese. "Fasting may be good for achieving spirituality, but most of the time, I prefer to be fed."

He grinned and took a bite of the cheese. "You have your uses, Jean Macrae."

"If the ancestors want us to be mates, you should call me Jean." She tilted the jug for a drink of wine, the muscles in her pale throat working as she swallowed. He was acutely conscious of every breath she drew, every muscle she moved. Of her scent, which was erotic and individual and made him think of Scottish heather, though he'd never seen or smelled real heather in his life.

She handed him the jug. "While I was in Marseilles, I developed a fondness for these light French table wines. Better than ale. Do you get yours from France?"

"Yes, but one of the island farmers is planting vines. In time, we'll make our own wine." Why was he talking about wine? Because it was easier than discussing anything important.

She studied the wall between them more carefully. "Surely your people didn't build this here merely to make a nice place to sit."

"No, the island was inhabited in the past. Many of the houses in the village are built on old foundations. Santola is scattered with ruins."

"There is great age in these stones." She brushed her hand along the roughly dressed wall. "Do you know who those early people were?"

"Greeks, perhaps. Or maybe Phoenicians. Or both. Quite possibly pirates of many races." He scooped up a handful of the black volcanic sand and let the grains sift through his fingers. "The many and varied people of the Mediterranean. Ancestors of mine, I suspect. Malta is the crossroads of the Middle Sea, and the blood of a hundred nations runs through Maltese veins."

"Adia said that your grandmother was her kin. Did you know her?"

"Oh, yes. My grandmother, Folami, had the largest share in raising me." He scooped up another handful of sand, gazing at the black glitter of the volcanic grains. "I can see a resemblance between her and Adia, in their faces and in their natures. Both are strong African women, loyal and a little mysterious."

"How did your grandmother come to Malta?"

"She never spoke much of her past, but I believe she was a slave in North Africa when my grandfather found her. He was Maltese, a sailor." Nikolai smiled a little. "Probably a bit of a smuggler as well. But not a slaver. He stole her away and married her in Malta. I never knew him; he died at sea when my mother was a child."

"So your grandmother raised your mother, then you. A strong woman indeed."

"She was. My mother was... less strong." She had been beautiful, though, and had enjoyed her life as a barmaid in a waterfront tavern. Sailors had complimented her, given her gifts. One gave her a son. Another had given her the fever that took her life.

He closed his eyes, thinking that if African spirituality included a connection with the ancestors, he would like to feel that Folami was with him. But he felt no sense of her presence. He opened his eyes and took another swallow of wine, wiping the mouth of the jug before handing it back. "You are the Guardian. Do you believe Adia's story?"

Jean smiled as tendrils of bright hair danced around her face from the breeze. "Her story is impossible, but yes, I do believe it because there is no other explanation that is less impossible. We were there when she appeared from nowhere, on an island where there are no strangers. I think it was the mingling of my blood with yours as I swore my vow that brought her here. Blood has great power. You and I created a beacon of antislavery energy that drew her through time. Impossible, yet here she is." He realized that he'd needed Jean to confirm what had happened. Now that she had, it was easier to allow himself to believe. "As much as I wanted to end slavery, I have always known that my efforts are trivial in the great pattern of life. I am chopping off one evil tentacle at a time, helping a few people, but no more.

"Yet as soon as Adia said that slavery would end when the mass of people cried 'Enough,' I understood. You are typical of a decent person who never thought much about slavery since it took place at a distance. Yet now you are revolted by it."

She nodded. "The little black boys kept as pages by London ladies never seemed like slaves. More like pampered pets. Seeing men chained to their oars, their backs a mass of scars, made slavery vividly real. I think most Britons would agree with me that slavery should be abolished if they understood its wickedness."

"If Britain stands up against slavery, it will make a huge difference. The largest number of ships carrying slaves from Africa to the New World are British."

She stared at him. "I didn't know that."

He looked toward the horizon, wondering how many slave ships and corsair galleys were cruising the high seas. He sensed one just at the edge of his range of perception. Too far to go after, even if the *Justice* was repaired. "Much of the wealth of Liverpool and Bristol and even London is drawn from human flesh. If British ships stopped carrying slaves, it would be a start to ending slavery."

He halted to allow the exhilaration of that prospect to rush through him. "It's possible to end slavery, Jean! It's possible, and I can help that happen."

"Ending slavery would be right, but incredibly disruptive," she said, her face troubled. "The sugar trade is a huge economic force. If it collapses, the economy of Britain and the Indies will be badly damaged. Countless lives will be turned upside down, and many of the people affected will be average men and women who own no slaves. Nations might fall into civil war. Do we have the right to undertake something whose consequences might be even more evil than what we hope to end?"

He wanted to explode with anger, but he reminded himself that her knowledge of slavery was mostly of the mind, not the flesh. She had never known the lash, the confinement, the breaking of the will.

"I don't care if ending slavery produces catastrophic consequences! Slavery is wrong, and no amount of intellectual qualms will alter that. Yes, ending it will be disruptive, but the world has survived other disruptions. If people want sugar, plantation owners can pay wages and fire the overseers who carry whips. If decent wages are paid, there will be workers. Sugar will cost more, but it's a luxury, not a necessity of life.

"If sailors lose work on slave ships, let them find other ships with more honest cargo. If European workers are injured by the change—they are still in better condition than most slaves. There is no excuse for allowing evil to thrive simply because we don't know what will happen if it ends."

"It must be comforting to be so sure of what's right," Jean said drily.

"There are few things I am sure of, but the evil of slavery is one of them," he said, voice edged. "If I could end it today, I would, and be damned to the consequences. I hope you can overcome your doubts, since if Adia is right, we must work together to be effective."

"We're better at quarreling than working together." She finished her bread and cheese, not looking at him.

Mates. Male and female energy joined together. Deciding honesty was called for, he said, "We have had much to disagree about, but from the beginning, I have desired you. I think the reverse is true. So why are we so wary of each other?"

She laughed a little as she gave him a slanting glance. "Have you forgotten that at first you despised me as your enemy? You wanted me to suffer terribly for the sins of my father. Such an attitude is hardly romantic." When had she stopped being his enemy? Step by step, she had dismantled his anger, using courage and logic as her tools. "Somehow we have become friends."

She turned to him, her hazel eyes burning. "Oh, no, Captain. We are not friends."

She was right—friendship was of a different nature. But they could be—should be—lovers. So he leaned over and kissed her.

She gasped. *Annihilation.* Perhaps she could have pulled away, but his dark gaze held her captive like a rabbit enthralled by a serpent. All his strength, his fierce will, were concentrated on her, and she wanted to absorb those qualities into herself. Yet she sensed that lying with this man would destroy the essence of what she was.

But the stakes were high, involving far more than their two lives. As the familiar energy flared between them, she forced herself to accept it rather than retreat. Kissing Gregorio was like diving into a bonfire, becoming flame without being consumed. Without conscious thought, she raised her arms and locked them around his neck. He made a rough sound and embraced her, his muscled body both prison and protection.

With Robbie, there had been the sweetness of first love. They'd known each other their whole lives, running the hills, getting into mischief together, always laughing. When he died, a part of her died with him.

Gregorio filled her with scalding life that was both terrifying and exhilarating. His hand moved to her breast. She wanted to press into his palm, but doing so would be stepping into the abyss. She pulled away. "There is no doubt about the lust," she said shakily. "But I am not yet ready to act on that, Captain Gregorio. I don't know if I ever will be ready."

He started to reach for her, then dropped his hands, the fingers clenching into fists. "I want you, yet I fear you would drive me mad, Jean. Though I'm not sure that would be entirely a bad thing."

She smiled wryly. "That fear is mutual, Captain."

"My name is Nikolai. If you wish me to call you Jean, you must use my name in turn." He looked away to the sea, his dark expression unreadable. "Few people have done so since I was a child."

"Very well, Nikolai." She touched the back of his hand lightly. "Time to return to the village now?"

As a vigorous wave splashed a yard from their feet, he turned and asked, "Will you marry me, Jean Macrae? That will force us to come to terms with each other." She jerked away from him. Surely he was joking! No, his dark eyes were utterly serious. "Good God, no! Adia said we needed to be mates, not married. I don't know you well enough to marry you."

"Yet you contemplate lying with me?" His smile was edged. "Of course, well-bred ladies might bed mixed-blood bastards, but they won't wed them."

She would have thought him impervious to insult, but she saw that her instant rejection of his proposal had hurt. She studied the strong-boned face, wondering if it was possible ever to know a man composed of so many layers.

"I don't want to marry you, but not for those reasons." She concentrated on packing the empty jug and cheesecloth back into her shoulder bag. "We come from different worlds, Captain. Nikolai. I hope we will be successful in aiding the abolition movement. Succeed or fail, I think it likely we will die in the attempt. But if by some faint chance we both survive, I would like to be able to go home again. That will be difficult if I have a husband whose life lies elsewhere."

"I wouldn't have thought you would be too weak to abandon a husband when you tired of him," he said, his voice cool. "You could go back to Scotland and claim to be a widow if you wish to settle down into your staid, well-bred life again."

"I won't marry a man with the thought that I'll leave if I tire of him," she snapped. "And I certainly won't commit bigamy. It's not you, Nikolai. I haven't had the desire to marry since Robbie died. Even then, I was in no rush to reach the altar."

His gaze raked over her, so intense that she felt naked. "So marriage itself makes you wary. You surely didn't lack for opportunities to wed."

Trying not to react to the heat of his gaze, she said, "Lord above, I believe that's a compliment!"

He almost smiled. "An accident on my part."

More seriously, she said, "Marriage can be a form of slavery, too. Perhaps that's why I have no taste for it."

"But you were willing to consider wedding your young Robbie."

"I was younger." She grinned. "And he knew better than to tell me what to do."

Nikolai laughed. "Then he was a wise man, indeed. But I think I am equally wise. I recognize that you can be persuaded, but not coerced. If I were fool enough to try to force you into anything, you would put a stop to that instantly. So why not marry me? You've proved that your shields are equal to my assaults."

He looked so irresistibly handsome in his laughter that she almost jettisoned judgment and said yes to his proposal. But she was no green girl who thought of nothing beyond desire. She drew a slow breath. "I no longer fear physical harm at your hands, but I fear what you will do to my spirit. Not that you would choose to harm me, but that your forcefulness will destroy everything I am."

"Perhaps you will do the same to me, Jean Macrae," he said intensely. "Perhaps that's what the ancestors want."

"That's possible, but opening my body and soul to you on the chance that it's the right thing to do is like leaping from a cliff to learn if God wants me to grow wings. If I'm wrong, it will be too late to save myself."

"What a very melodramatic view you take." He took her bag and slung it over his shoulder, then offered a hand. "Come. It's a hard walk back to the village."

She let him help her to her feet, glad that he was willing to let the subject of marriage drop.

She should have known better. His dark eyes sparked with determination, and he used his grip on her hand to pull her into another hot, demanding kiss. Their bodies molded together full length, her breasts flattening against his chest as her knees weakened. This time he deliberately used the full force of his will in an attempt to reduce her to mindless desire.

He came very near to succeeding. She felt as if her body was melting, and she offered no protest as he laid her on the black sand. His hard, vibrant body trapped her against the yielding sand as their hips ground together, seeking union despite the clothing that separated them. More than anything on earth, she wanted to dissolve in his fire and let his passion remake her.

"Gods above, witch!" His eyes were glazed with

desire. "We must wait no longer!" He braced his weight with one hand and slid his other hand under her skirt. Cool air touched heated flesh, and the skim of his fingers on her thigh almost persuaded her to surrender to the liquid fire that blazed through her.

Yet the small, stubborn core of her spirit refused. She threw her defensive magic at him, at the same time rolling violently away. Her roll ended with her crouched on the sand, panting, "Do not try to overpower my will with passion, Nikolai, for we will both regret it!" Nikolai had been blasted onto his side by the force of her magic. He stared at her, face fierce and eyes wild. For an instant she feared that his determination to possess would overcome his distaste for rape. Were her defenses strong enough to protect her?

The tension broke when he buried his face in his hands, his breathing harsh and shoulders shaking. She quietly stood and was edging away when he raised his head and got to his feet. The wildness was gone, but he glittered with menace. "You're right—marriage would be a mistake, for the two of us would explode if joined in holy matrimony. But the mating—If we travel together, it will surely happen in time. There is too much fire between us to be quenched."

"Perhaps. But now is not the right time." That she knew beyond doubt. "Bank your fires, Captain Gregorio. We cannot work together like this."

"Then bank your own fire, you damned witch!" He glared at her as if she was a scorpion. "You can't expect a man not to react when you stand there looking like every man's fever dream!"

Absurdly, she was pleased that she had such an effect on him, but that could not be allowed to continue. "That's only fair." She closed her eyes and consciously tamped down her energy, starting with the lust that still hammered through her veins. When passion was under control, she concentrated on her emotions until she was fully in balance.

When she opened her eyes again, she saw that he was watching her intently and his energy had also calmed. The fierce desire that had seethed between them was gone, dissolved into sea air and sunshine. For a treacherous moment she regretted the loss. But only for a moment. Much better that they had returned to their previous relationship, where they had achieved a degree of friendly relaxation.

He picked up her bag, which had ended up crumpled over the stone wall, then made a courtly gesture toward the narrow trail. "What now, mistress witch?"

As she started up the steep hill, she said, "We must both become better mages. Adia has suggested a technique I might use to become more effective at wielding my magic, so I shall practice that."

She skidded on a patch of loose gravel. Quick as a snake, he caught her arm and kept her from falling. She flinched, but his touch was impersonal, with nothing beyond the spark that occurred whenever they touched. Though he might not be a trained mage, he had learned well how to control his energy.

"Take my arm," he said brusquely. "I know this path

better than you."

Conceding the point, she took his arm, trying to convince herself that she was holding a walking stick rather than a strongly muscled male body. Talking to distract herself, she said, "If we don't improve our skills, Adia might refuse to enlist us in her cause. In the abstract, she was willing to pay any price, but having met you and me as individuals, she is reluctant to send us to possible disaster if there is no hope of success."

"If she doesn't use us, she is wasting the magic created by the London elders. She will have come all this way, accomplished nothing, and probably be unable to go home again." He glanced up momentarily from the treacherous footing. "The decision to risk everything for a cause is easy for me, but what of you, Jean Macrae?

Do you have doubts about undertaking such a mission to solve a problem that is not your own?"

"None." She scrambled along without talking for a dozen steps, wondering how much to say. "I once made a bargain with God, and now it is time to pay the bill. There will be no chance of ending slavery unless many people who are not directly affected are willing to fight for the freedom of men and women they have never met. They must roar with such outrage that kings and ministers will be unable to ignore them. Am I not a good example of the work that must be done?"

"Since you put it that way, yes." His brows drew together. "If we travel through time and space to Britain, I shall need you for a guide. As a foreigner, I would waste much time and perhaps call too much attention to myself on my own in London. Even decades in the future, you will understand Britain better than I."

"We will make a good team, then," she said, trying not to pant too obviously. She thought of herself as fit, but the volcanic slope was a stiff climb. "I will be in charge of dealing with society, and you will be in charge of mayhem."

"A team indeed." He scowled. "But before we go anywhere, I must be initiated, and I can scarcely bear waiting. I want to make a difference *now.*"

"The movement will not begin for many years, so we have time to perfect our skills," she pointed out. "There might even be enough years available for you to outgrow your impatience." She smiled a little. "But I doubt it."

CHAPTER TWENTY-ONE

THEY REACHED the crest of the path that ran over the rim of the caldera and paused. Jean was pleased to see that even Nikolai was breathing hard. The path ran between two spiky peaks made of black volcanic rock. Behind them the barren wind scoured the outer island. Below was the cupped sea, an amazing shade of blue, and the fertile fields and trees of the community. Whole terraces were devoted to almond and olive trees.

In the center of the caldera was a small island—the cone of the volcano, she guessed. "I didn't really appreciate this when I walked in the other direction," she said, shading her eyes against the sun's glare. "What a magnificent view. Your island is a place of great beauty, Captain."

"I never tire of it," he said quietly. "For someone who has lived in chains, beauty is almost as healing as freedom."

She realized that she still held his arm, so she released her clasp. He smiled with a touch of malice. "I wonder which of us will surrender to passion first? Probably me, since nature gives women good reasons to be wary."

"True, but Guardian women tend to be better protected than most."

"I noticed. My ears are still ringing from the energy blow you struck me with." Returning to the prospect before them, he pointed into the distance. "From here, you can see the outlines of different ruins more clearly than from lower down. See those square shapes halfway down the hill? There was a cluster of buildings there once —a farm and stables, perhaps."

"I see!" she said, delighted. "There are faint outlines of buildings in several places. What is that hollow over there to the east? It seems too regular to be an accident, but perhaps it's a volcanic formation?"

"That's the remains of a small amphitheater. It seems to be a natural space that was reshaped for gatherings and entertainments." His finger moved to the left. "On this side of the caldera are orchards. For some reason, there is more rain there. We have olive trees, almonds, oranges, and lemons. I'm told the trees are very, very old. They ran wild when the island was empty, but now that they're cared for, they produce for us."

They started down the hill, which was easier than the climb, though still strenuous. As they neared Nikolai's house, he asked, "How did you find me?"

"I used my scrying stone." She chuckled. "Plus, when Louise gave me a lotion to prevent sunburn, she said that there was a walk behind the village that you're fond of."

"Would the scrying glass have been enough?"

"I'm not sure. I can often see friends and family if I look for them, but I don't necessarily know where they are unless I recognize the background. I saw you watching the waves, but didn't know where the beach was." He frowned. "You can watch me?"

"Yes, but I don't scry very often. It's very tiring."

He didn't look mollified, but they were coming to wooden latticed gates that led into his courtyard house. He said, "I want to find Adia and ask some questions." They found her drowsing in the courtyard, which had potted plants and chairs and areas of sun and shade, much like the terrace but without the view of the sea. She woke and sat up when they joined her. "I have been enjoying the warmth," she said. "It was wet and wintry when I left London, and the journey through time was long and cold."

"That sounds like London all right." Jean took a chair in the shade. Louise's herbal lotion might help keep her skin from burning, but surely it had limits. "What is it like to travel through time?"

Adia couldn't suppress a shudder. "Like being chopped into a thousand pieces, dragged through a tunnel full of shrieking demons, then reassembled. It seemed to take a long time, but how can one know? It might have been seconds or days. I felt I was being pulled through the tunnel. Perhaps it was your energy, as you suggested."

"This doesn't sound as if it will be amusing," Nikolai said drily. He sat on Adia's other side. "Will you tell us how the magic will work? Or will you wait until we have improved our abilities?"

Adia slid the bracelet with the large, unusual beads from her wrist and held it on her open palm. "The large beads were made by an elder gifted with clairvoyance. He asked the ancestors to help him create a number of beads equal to the number of critical points where the fledgling abolition movement would need aid. It was a great and powerful magic, and I think creating the beads took a dozen years from his life."

Jean bent closer to look. "The large beads are all different shapes."

"Each is tuned to a particular crisis. They must be used in sequence, starting here"—she pointed—"and working around in order. There were seven originally. The first bead was destroyed in my passage here, leaving six. I think each bead will vanish as it is used, but I'm not sure."

"Will the final bead take you home to your own time and place?" Jean asked.

"I'd like to think so, but truly, I have no idea."

"How did you end up with the bracelet if all of you worked on the ritual together?" Jean asked. "Did it appear on your wrist as you came through time?"

Adia shook her head. "Each of the seven elders had a bracelet like this one, and we invoked the power together. I believe I was the only one to be taken through time because of the blood bond between me and the captain." She rolled one of the large beads between her fingers thoughtfully. "I wonder if the matching beads vanished on the other bracelets when I was taken." She sighed. "I may never find out."

"How will we know what to do when we have used the bead to travel to a critical place?" Nikolai asked. "To be dropped into a strange location, not knowing where or when we are, will be confusing. What if we fail from ignorance of what we should do?"

Adia's mouth twisted wryly. "We must hope that the ancestors know what they are doing."

Jean exchanged a doubtful glance with Nikolai. "There is an old Christian saying that God helps those who help themselves. I should think the same would be true for ancestors. Is there anything we can do to improve our chances of success?"

"We also wished to improve the odds," Adia replied. "While preparing for the invocation, we gathered all the knowledge we had about the abolition movement—the events, people, issues. We have also included information about the London African community." She pulled a plump folder of papers from her ever-present medicine bag. "Here is a summary of all we could learn. Much was written by me. I wish you to copy it over, Jean, so that you will know it well. I will also talk with you about what I know of the time between now and when I left London—fashion, news, politics. You must be the source of worldly knowledge during your mission." Nikolai arched his formidable brows. "You think me unworthy of knowing?"

"Your time and energy will be taken up with the initiation." Adia slid the bracelet back on her wrist and handed the papers to Jean, "You may leave now. I must talk to the captain. You have your own tasks."

Jean accepted her dismissal with some relief. She was tired from her hike, and a nap sounded good. She also needed time to think—both about clearing her mental tangles, and about Nikolai.

NIKOLAI WATCHED Jean depart with relief. He was still shaken by what had happened between them by the shore. Even his passion for revenge had not matched the intensity of his desire for her. He had come painfully close to losing all control and behaving unforgivably. On some deep level, was his desire for revenge twisted up in his attraction to Jean? No, this raw need for her existed separately from his long-time hatred of her father. Something in her spirit called to something in his. He hoped it Wasn't long until the time was right for them to come together.

Adia called him back to the present by saying, "We must discuss initiation."

"What must I do?" He tried to read her energy field, hoping that might increase his understanding. The colors around her were deep and pure—blue, gold, indigo. He sensed that they represented truth and power.

"I have spoken with Tano and other Africans here," she replied. "There are three other priests, one woman and two men. Though we come of different tribes, we have enough in common to work together. We will place you on the initiate's path."

"There are priests on the island?" he asked, surprised. "Were they trained in Africa, before they were taken as slaves?"

"One was. The other two learned their magic in slavery. Here they have blended their individual pathways to create a Santolan tradition of magic."

"But virtually all of the islanders are Muslims or Christians," he said, puzzled. "We have a mosque and two churches here."

"Africans do not forget their knowledge of what is true," she said patiently. "For safety's sake, a woman may build an altar to Oshun and decorate it with a statue of the Virgin Mary. When she prays to the Mother, she is invoking more than the Christian mother goddess. Under the mantle of Christianity and Islam, African traditions remain. We are very adaptable." She smiled a little. "My Jamaican mistress thought she was doing the Christian god's work by forcing all the family's slaves to convert, but underneath the Christian rituals, our spirits were free even if our bodies weren't."

"So you only pretended to convert?"

"Not at all. Jesus is a very fine spirit for worship, and I'm told that Muhammad is, too. An African can pay reverence to many gods." Mischief showed in her eyes. "To honor only one god seems paltry."

He laughed. His religious training had been mixed but monotheistic. He'd been baptized Catholic in Malta, and performed a lip-service conversion in Islam to save his life. Now he found that he liked the idea of multiple gods. Or perhaps multiple faces of one god. "What will the priests have me do? What preparations should I make?"

Her expression sobered. "I have decided you should start as soon as possible. The longer you have to ponder initiation, the more you will think. Better that you experience, not speculate and analyze. Tonight you will attend a ritual at the African gathering place. Then we priests will take you to Diabolo to begin your initiation."

Diabolo was part of the caldera, an uninhabited arc of island opposite the main village. Only goats grazed on its steep slopes. "What will I do there?"

"We will set you to different tasks so that you will experience nature in new ways. The goal is for you to learn awareness of other ways of seeing."

That didn't sound too bad. "How long will the initiation take?"

"At least a fortnight, probably longer."

He hesitated. "I have duties here. I must oversee the repairs to my ship, and I have leadership responsibilities in the village."

"Does the village collapse when you are at sea?" Her brows arched. "What is most important, Captain? Choose."

His concerns vanished. "You're right. The village runs perfectly well without me when I'm gone, and the mission you have offered is the most important undertaking of my life. Do you have any instructions?"

"A few. This will not be easy, Captain. For years you

have lived in the world of action and will. You must release that if you wish to survive initiation." She sighed. "I say again that this is dangerous, Captain, especially for a full-grown man who has not lived among Africans. Even in Africa, there are always some boys who die or become lost between worlds, a fate far worse than simple death. You do not have to do this."

"Will you send me through time if I am uninitiated?" Her troubled expression was answer enough. "Then I shall make the attempt, and do my best not to think."

"Not thinking is one of the hardest things one can attempt."

"I discovered that this afternoon," he said drily. "Where is the African gathering place I must visit for tonight's ceremony?"

"Tano will meet you here at dusk and guide you there." Adia leaned back in her chair. "And I shall nap. The night will be tiring."

He stood. If there was a chance he might die of his initiation, he must speak to Jean first. Though he wasn't quite sure what he'd say to her.

JEAN WAS FROWNING over a letter when a knock came on her door. "Come in," she called.

Nikolai entered, looking tall, dark, and sober. "Adia has decided to launch me into the unknown this evening," he said without preamble. "I thought I would bid my farewells in case her direst predictions come true." Nerves clenching, she set the quill aside. His dark face was calm, but it was easy to see the tension thrumming through him. He was not precisely afraid, she guessed, but even the boldest man was wary of the unknown. "This seems very sudden. I thought she would spend more time teaching you how to think like an African."

"She says I think too much already, so the less thinking, the better." Instead of sitting, he wandered to a window and looked over the caldera, where the water shimmered like bronze in the late-afternoon light. "Is she right about the dangers?"

So he was here for reassurance. "I know nothing about African initiations, but I was taught that dark energies exist side by side with the world we know. Spirits, demons, creatures—call them what you will, but they can cause damage."

She tried to think what else should be said. "Our spirit and body are connected but separate. If the spirit goes traveling, there is a risk it might not be able to find its way back. Or it might be attacked by one of the creatures of the spirit realm. Either of those things can cause the body to die."

"And damn one's spirit to suffer everlasting torments?" he asked drily.

"I wouldn't know about that. Few Guardians travel on the inner planes regularly, and I know of none who have died that way. But... death is possible."

"Spirits and demons would be easier to accept if I

were a religious believer." He stared sightlessly out the window, his profile like granite.

She doubted he'd welcome the idea that initiation might make him a believer—he must work that out for himself. What useful advice could she offer?

She thought of the ceremonies she had undergone when she came of age. "If your spirit travels so far there is danger of not returning, try to think of what is most deeply *you.* The captain, the protector, the outsider—recognize what is the essence of Nikolai Gregorio. That might help bring body and soul together again if they become separated."

He turned from the window. "I hear the words, but on some level they seem meaningless, like a child's rhyme."

"I think the words will come alive during the initiation."

He shrugged, accepting but not believing. "What are you working on?"

"Letters to my friends in France and my family." She indicated the number of sheets already covered with fine, neat handwriting. "With Adia's help, I managed mind touch with my friends and my brother, so they know not to be frantically worried, but there is concern, of course. Hence, letters to assure them I am well. Louise said that within the next week or so, it should be possible to send messages to France."

He nodded. "Even if the *Justice* isn't repaired, another ship should be in soon."

"No rush. I need time to work on the letters." She

smiled wryly. "It's awkward to explain that one has been kidnapped by a revenge-seeking pirate, but really, all is well. One's family tends to disapprove of kidnapping."

"You fear that your brother will come chasing after you and get himself killed?"

"That, or that he might kill you," she said tartly.

"You're a dangerous man, Nikolai, but so is Duncan. Better you not meet like two rams banging heads."

He smiled at the image. "I have promised not to seek vengeance against him.".

"He has made no such promise about you." She toyed with the quill. "There are two sets of letters. One set addresses the current situation. The other is a farewell if you and I go flying off through time. I assume that if that happens, we will probably not come back to this year even if we're successful. I want my family to know that I go willingly, and am glad for a chance to serve." Her smile was a little brittle. "That I went to my death as a proper Guardian."

His gaze returned to the view outside the window. "It's hard to believe in death in a place of such peace and beauty."

"Death can come in a heartbeat even in a drawing room."

"Or on an uninhabited island. Adia and the other priests are taking me to Diabolo, across the caldera. It should be... interesting." He crossed the room to her desk. "If we don't meet again in this lifetime, I hope you know peace in your future, Jean Macrae." He bent and kissed her, not with the passion they had shared earlier, but with wistful tenderness. His mouth was warm and inviting.

"I don't want peace," she whispered, blinking back tears. "I want life. Challenge. Meaning." All of those qualities that were so visible in Nikolai.

She stood to return his kiss, her arms sliding around his broad chest. Her lips were slow and tender as she tried to express what she could not fit into words. She felt the same yearning and concern in him. They had traveled far from the passionate embrace on the black sand beach, and she felt closer to him now than when their bodies had been intertwined.

For a mad instant she considered lying with him so she would at least have that memory if he failed to return, but her inner guidance still said that intimacy would be profoundly wrong now. Refusing to accept that they might never meet again, she said briskly, "You will be back, Nikolai. Battered and tempered and shaped in ways we can't predict. But you will be back." She managed a teasing smile. "Because we have unfinished business, you and I."

CHAPTER TWENTY-TWO

NIKOLAI SPENT the rest of the day taking care of as much business as possible. The pile of work prevented him from thinking too much. He managed to submerge himself deeply enough in his accounts that he was surprised when Tano arrived at the house at dusk. His friend appeared in the door of the study wearing only a loincloth and beads, his dark skin shining as if oiled.

Nikolai blinked. "Am I overdressed?"

Tano smiled a little. "Most will be dressed as I, but the choice is yours."

Nikolai didn't like the idea of exposing his bare skin to a group, though he supposed that was the kind of vanity he should release. As a compromise, he said, "For future ceremonies, I shall devise a loincloth. For now, I'll remove my coat and waistcoat." He stripped off his outer garments so that he wore only shirt and breeches and boots. Then he followed Tano into the falling night. "Where are we going?"

"Our ceremonies take place in the cellar of one of the ruins on the west side of the island," Tano explained. "That is the largest of the old villages."

"Ceremonies have taken place regularly?" Nikolai asked, surprised.

"Of course. Surely you have heard the drums."

He had, but hadn't thought much of it beyond assuming that some of the African-born liked drumming. Despite his own African blood, he had never been invited to join any ceremonies. Was he not African enough? Too intimidating because he was the leader? Or too well known as a man who concentrated on the visible world?

All of those things, perhaps. Even if he had been invited, he probably wouldn't have accepted.

Now that he was listening, he became aware of the drums. Though drumming wasn't uncommon on Santola, he'd never truly listened to the sound. The closer he came to the source, the more the pounding rhythms saturated his body, echoing the beat of his blood through his veins.

They reached the ruins of the largest of the old villages as full dark fell. Tano led them on an erratic route through the weeds and tumbled stones.

Then he vanished. It took a moment for Nikolai to realize that his friend had ducked into a twisting tunnel that led downward. Nikolai followed, using caution after he banged his head on the irregular ceiling.

At the end of the short tunnel was light, and the full power of the throbbing drums. The ceremonial space appeared to be the cellar of a sizable building. Open to the sky, it was lit by a blazing fire in the center. Perhaps two dozen people, both men and women, sat in a large circle around the fire. Only the men drummed. Tano said quietly, "Because we are few and of many tribes, both men and women attend. We need to share our heritages to keep us strong."

Nikolai knew them all, of course—there were no strangers on Santola—but those present looked different tonight, and he couldn't immediately identify everyone. The men wore loincloths, the women little more. Some also wore ropes of beadwork, headdresses, and other more exotic body decorations that included feathers and animal skin and painted markings slashed across dark skin.

Not all the skin was so dark—as his eyes adjusted to the erratic light of the fire, he saw that some of the mixed-blood Santolans were present. One was Louise. He always thought of her as French, but tonight she was African.

Silently Tano found a place in the circle and sat down. Nikolai sat next to him, wanting a friend close in this strange place. He looked around for Adia, but didn't see her. The only sound was the drums.

He closed his eyes and let the drumming penetrate his body. The thundering waves numbed his mind, eased the separation between his body and the world around him. There was magic in these instruments. They were a choir of harmonious rhythms, he realized. Sometimes a solo drummer would explode to the foreground with virtuoso work, then later fade back into the chorus and another player would take the lead.

The rhythm changed and a cry pierced the night. He opened his eyes to see Adia dance into the circle. He recognized her more from her energy than her appearance, for she was almost unrecognizable. Nude except for beads, she was slashed with white paint in a skeletonlike pattern. She whirled around the circle several times before halting and gesturing at the fire with both hands. The flames turned violet and flared high into the sky, taller than the average house.

The violet light dazzled, making it difficult to see anything else. Even closing his eyes didn't eliminate the light. He opened them again, his senses filled with the light and the bone-stirring hammer of the drums. Gradually he began to see hints of movement from the corners of his eyes, movement that vanished when he looked directly at it.

He forced himself to be still and wait. Abruptly he realized that he was seeing small people, men and women perhaps two feet tall. They were unmistakably Africans, dark of skin and dressed in the simple wrapped garments of the Dark Continent. Were these the ancestors?

Perhaps. Or maybe they were another kind of being that possessed spirits but not bodies. One, an old man, walked toward him. *Through* him, causing a clammy shiver.

Adia began speaking in a language he couldn't identify. The sounds were ancient, primal, as if this was the first tongue spoken by mankind. Her voice rose and fell.

Sometimes it was so soft it was obliterated by the drums, other times so powerful it echoed from the lava stones of Santola. The small beings drew around her, watching and dancing to the sound of her voice and the drums, weaving in hypnotic patterns.

He realized that sweat was pouring off him. Some of the heat was from the fire, whose towering flames still burned as high as a building, far brighter than the fuel could support. But heat also blazed from Adia, a human heat more potent than the flames.

She raised her hand, and he saw that she carried a long polished stick crowned with beads and feathers. Had she always held it, or had it appeared from nowhere?

She gave a call of summoning, and three of the people sitting in the circle rose to join her. There were two men and a woman, and they were painted with the same white skeleton marks. One of the men was of mixed blood, his skin noticeably lighter than the others. Nikolai was glad to see that a mixed-blood could achieve priestly power.

She pointed her staff at Nikolai. Without words, he knew that meant he should come. He rose and joined her. The four priests surrounded him, and they walked from the gathering place, surrounded by the thunder of the drums.

He could think a little more clearly when they were out in the open air, farther from the drumming. The rest of the island was silent, and he saw only a bare scattering of lights from the main village. He had discovered

Santola with his mage's intuition and thought he knew every square yard of the main island, yet he felt as if he'd been transported to an alien land. Was this one of the different worlds Adia spoke of?

No, Santola had not changed, he was the one who had moved from his normal awareness. He felt like an observer, set apart from his body, as the group reached the shore. A narrow, crudely made log canoe was pulled up on the coarse sand. He hadn't known there was such a craft on the island. It was becoming very clear that he knew less of Santola than he'd thought.

The two priests launched the boat. Nikolai started to help, but a sharp gesture from Adia stopped him. He was motioned into the center of the boat with a man and woman in front of him and the other two behind.

Moonlight silvered the water as they glided across the caldera to Diabolo. Nikolai tried to remember the island, which he'd visited once or twice in his early years on Santola. It was a narrow, jagged crescent that jutted up from the sea, smaller and more vertical than the main island.

They reached the shore, and the priests pulled the boat onto a sliver of beach, the hull scraping harshly. The shore was fairly flat for fifty feet or so before rising into a steep hillside. Adia stepped from the canoe and scooped up a stack of blankets, then walked to the middle of the flat area. The other priestess brought several sacks of supplies.

"Where...?" Nikolai's question was stilled when Adia touched her finger to her lips in the gesture for silence. The white slashes of paint made her look inhuman in the moonlight. She was no longer the civilized Londoner who had learned the language and manners of a well-bred Briton, but a dangerous priestess of dark mysteries.

Still without speaking, each priest picked up a blanket and settled down to sleep for what remained of the night. Nikolai was glad to see that there was a blanket for him, for the night was chilly without a fire.

He rolled into his blanket and prepared to sleep, knowing the morning would begin the real initiation. He should get what rest he could.

But sleep wouldn't come. Stars splashed lavishly across the sky, and he found he couldn't close his eyes to them. As a sailor he knew stars and constellations well, but tonight the stars seemed alive. They pulsed and shimmered with meaning, brighter and more compelling than he'd ever seen them before.

They seemed to be singing, too. Not in words. More like a chorus of notes, individually discordant yet somehow in harmony when taken together. He listened in case there was a message for him, but heard nothing except haunting, distant chords.

He fell asleep to the music of the spheres, and woke when a soft voice said, "Captain."

He tensed even as he remembered that he was on Diabolo, the barren, hell-born island opposite Santola. Adia stood beside him. The body paint was gone, and she wore a simple wrapped gown and turban. No longer African priestess, but an African woman who reminded him of his grandmother, who had always worn a similar turban.

He sat up and she handed him a cup of steaming tea

and a bread roll. The tea was sweet and flavored with cardamom, the roll a little stale. The other priests were consuming a similar breakfast. Though it was past sunrise, the interior of the caldera was still shadowed.

When everyone had finished the meager meal, Adia rose and gestured for them to follow. Medicine bag slung over her shoulder, she picked her way along the edge of the water for some distance before turning up a twisty ravine. The group was about halfway to the top of the hill when she turned left into a cave, which was interesting since Nikolai had never heard that Diabolo contained any caves.

Yet this was certainly a cave. The narrow entrance opened into a sizable area. Most caves had scents of animal occupants, but not this one. It smelled—ancient.

As she entered, Adia raised her hand, and violet fire appeared on her palm. The light illuminated a large space, roughly circular in shape and with a roof perhaps ten feet high. At the back, a cleft led deeper into the hill.

Adia placed the violet fire on one wall. It clung to the stone like a torch, burning steadily without fuel. She threw a handful of powder into the flame and acrid smoke began to fill the cave. Nikolai coughed, blinked his eyes, and realized that the subtle glow of magic was also beginning to fill the space.

Turning away from the fire, Adia drew her companions into a circle. "You must find the missing pieces of yourself, Captain. We will do what we can to set you on the right path, but ultimately the journey is one you must make alone. I do believe it is possible that you can do this successfully, or I would not allow it."

Not exactly an enthusiastic belief in his chances for success. "I know the risk." He glanced at each of the priests in turn. "If I do not survive, I do not want you to feel guilt for what I choose of my own free will."

The tense atmosphere eased a little. At a gesture from Adia, the younger priest began ringing a crudely made metal bell with a deep, hollow tone. The other priestess started to shake a rattle made of a dried gourd while the older priest chanted low in a foreign tongue. Nikolai had identified him as Omar, who had been freed from a corsair galley. The man had been deeply grateful to regain his freedom and a new home. He had settled down into farming, but he'd never mentioned that he was a priest.

The crude music was strangely compelling, and Nikolai found himself swaying to the beat, his mind drifting and unfocused as he breathed the acrid smoke. Adia also began chanting, her voice deep and powerful. Out of the corner of his eyes, he sensed movements and realized that the small beings had again been drawn by the music. The night before, he'd found them disconcerting. Today they seemed... natural.

As the rhythms echoed from the stone walls of the cave, Adia opened her medicine bag and poured a collection of objects on the ground. There were stones, pebbles, feathers, and stranger things Nikolai couldn't identify. He narrowed his eyes and realized that all of them glowed with magic, some brighter than others.

The last object Adia produced was a polished, Y-shaped stick about fifteen inches long. It burned with violet fire.

Still chanting, she clasped the stick and held it upright. Omar grasped the wood above her grip, and the stick immediately soared upward, as if propelled by unseen hands. It twisted about before diving toward the ground. The descent slowed, and the stick touched a pebble in the middle of the collection of medicine objects.

Adia nodded and set the pebble aside, then said a phrase that sent the stick soaring up again. After another whirl, the stick came down and tapped a small knuckle bone. It joined the pebble. The ritual repeated half a dozen more times. Nikolai noted that the objects chosen were those that shone the most brightly with magic.

The acrid smoke made him dizzy, and he had no sense of how much time was passing. Minutes? Hours? Eventually the stick no longer moved when Adia spoke to it. Omar let go, and Adia bowed respectfully to the stick before stashing it back in her bag. The bell and rattle slowed, then stopped, and the cave was once more silent.

She scooped up the objects selected and placed them in a small leather pouch with painted symbols on the side. After producing a needle and thread from her bag, she carefully sewed the pouch shut and attached it to a leather thong. Then she approached Nikolai and placed the thong around his neck. "For protection."

She stepped back. "The time has come for your first test. It will be a journey of pain, but it is not too late to withdraw. Think carefully, Captain. You have accomplished much on the seas and here in Santola. To attempt initiation is to risk losing all."

Her voice triggered eerie images of doom and disaster. He had a brief, horrifying vision of himself trapped and helpless in the midst of screaming demons. For the first time, he felt the visceral recognition that he really might die if he continued. He did have a good life, valuable work. Why throw it away?

Because he would never forgive himself if he had a chance to work toward slavery's end and was too much a coward to try. He had risked danger many times. The danger of the unknown was more fearsome than any blade or cannon, but the stakes were so high it was worth the risk. "I wish to go forward."

She inclined her head, expression troubled. "Very well." Omar stepped forward, a dagger in his hand. "Be still." He rolled Nikolai's left sleeve up to his elbow, then made a quick slash in his forearm.

Nikolai flinched but said nothing even when Omar rubbed a harsh, stinging liquid into the cut. The older man stepped away. "For protection against fire."

Fire? The four priests moved into a formation around Nikolai. Even underground, he sensed that they were taking the four compass points. Then Omar said in a deep, booming voice, "Learn the fire!" He swept his hands up and blue flames exploded from the earth, surrounding Nikolai.

He gasped in panic as his clothes, his hair, his flesh, were consumed by the flames. Unable to bear the pain, he stumbled from the blazing circle—and found himself in a strange, sun-blistered land.

Jean was finishing a letter to her brother and his wife when her hand jerked, spattering ink across the page. *Nikolai was in danger.* Though she had known initiation was dangerous, she hadn't expected him to be threatened so quickly. Nor did she expect the danger to be so hard to define.

She laid down her quill, careful not to spatter more ink, and closed her eyes.

She had been connected to him since they met, but now that connection was gone. He had vanished from her internal awareness. Heart pounding, she searched for him with increasing desperation.

Nothing.

She forced herself to calm down before she fell into shrieking pieces. He was undergoing a magical initiation, surrounded by African priests, and it was certainly possible that the ritual might cut him off from her questing magic.

Adia had believed that Nikolai had a good chance of surviving. And if she was wrong and Nikolai was dead—well, the priests would bring the news to Santola soon enough.

Since there was no longer a connection between Jean and Nikolai, it wasn't even possible to send him any of her energy. There was nothing she could do but try the oldest magic of all.

Locking her hands and closing her eyes, she prayed that somewhere, the damned man was alive and well.

CHAPTER TWENTY-THREE

STUNNED, Nikolai scanned the sun-drenched plain that extended in all directions. The cave and the priests had vanished. A burning sun scorched a land that was flat and covered with bleached golden grasses. The few scattered trees were oddly shaped, the limbs stretching out rather like umbrellas.

Except for the pouch around his neck, he was naked. He saw the last blue flames flicker out on his forearm. He had *felt* himself burning, yet there was no damage to his skin or hair. Was he really in a different place, or was this some kind of dream? He felt real enough. The cut Omar had made on his arm still stung.

The wind sighed across the plains, a breath of coolness on his bare body to mitigate the fierce sun. What the devil was he doing here? What task was he supposed to accomplish?

He felt painfully exposed and wished he had a

weapon and clothing, in that order. And a place to take cover, but the harsh landscape offered no shelter.

What should he do?

In a strange land, look for water. He had learned that while working as a slave on the North African salt caravans, which traveled through the most desolate lands on earth. He was already thirsty in the heat, so he consulted his intuition about water. His ability to find water had saved him and his companions on his last trip to the salt mines.

There, to his left. Some distance away, but reachable before thirst and the sun would bring him down.

Before he left, he should mark this spot in case it was the only gateway that could take him back to his own time and place. Assuming he would be able to return at all. When Adia had spoken of other worlds, he had thought of them as dreams or metaphors, but this scorching land was acutely real. Now it was his home—Santola, the *Justice,* Jean—that seemed to be a dream.

He tore up the grass around his feet, then piled what stones he could find on the bare patch. While seeking stones, he found the bleached bones of an antelope that had been picked clean by predators. He thrust several longer bones into the piled rocks, then mentally marked the location. His sense of direction was another ability that had served him well on the trackless seas. He hoped it would hold true even in this strange world.

Having done what he could to mark his place of arrival, he started to walk to the west. As a child and a slave he'd usually gone barefoot, and his feet had been tough as elephant hide. Years of wearing boots had softened them.

No matter. He'd learned early to ignore discomfort, and that skill he had retained. As he walked, he studied the plain, thinking it looked like what he'd heard of East Africa. Though he'd never been there, a fellow caravan slave named Rafiki had described his native land, and these plains and trees fit the description. Omar was also from East Africa, if he recalled correctly. Might the elders have sent him to a different place in the world Nikolai knew, or was this some other reality?

He fretted about the questions for a while, then dismissed them since he didn't know enough to find answers. *Think less.* Tonight when he saw the stars he should know if this was his world or another.

A huge antelope with curled horns thundered up from behind him. As it bolted past, he thought, *"Kudu."* How did he know that name? He glanced back and saw a dozen tall, lean black men running toward him—and they all carried spears.

After an instinctive rush of fear at his helplessness, Nikolai realized that the newcomers were hunters pursuing the kudu. Rafiki had described this ancient way of hunting. A group would run down a beast during the hottest part of the day and kill when the prey could run no more.

The hunters didn't appear surprised or hostile at seeing him. They simply continued to draw nearer and nearer. Most were naked or clothed only in loincloths, though they carried spears in their hands and hide bags slung over their backs. Their black skin glistened with sweat, yet they ran easily, without strain.

The group of runners swept past him. The nearest, a youth of perhaps twenty, called a greeting, his teeth flashing white against his dark face. He threw one of the two spears he carried in a sideways toss as if they were playing ball. Nikolai pulled the spear from the air. The weapon was balanced and natural in his hand. Guessing that this was part of his mission, he turned and began to run with the group.

Soon the long, loping stride of the hunters felt as natural as the weight of the spear in his hand. Though his feet were sore and his breathing labored, he was able to keep up. He welcomed the burn of his muscles as he stretched them to the limit. A sea captain didn't have much opportunity to run.

They were heading in the direction of the water he'd sensed. His awareness of it grew stronger. They passed over a slight rise and looked down on a watering hole edged with shrubs, a scattering of umbrella trees, and several birds and small beasts drinking. In the center of the water was the dark snout of a submerged hippopotamus.

At the approach of the humans, the birds took flight with loud cries, great wings beating while the small beasts darted into the undergrowth. The kudu ran past the watering hole, its gait faltering. Too tired to run farther, it folded to its knees and collapsed in the rutted ground beside the water.

The hunters closed in, and the leaders killed the kudu

with brisk efficiency. Three of the group pulled stone knives from their leather pouches and began to skin the carcass. The other hunters gathered fuel, either wood or dried dung. When it was stacked into a pile for burning, several of them glanced at Nikolai.

Without words, he realized that it was his job to light the fire. But how? He had no tinderbox, no flint. Perhaps he was the priest of this group and should be able to summon fire? Omar had said he must learn fire.

He knelt by the stacked fuel and held both hands above it. Jean's Guardians would visualize flames, thinking the fire into existence. Since he knew no other technique, he tried that. His palms heated up, but no flame appeared.

What if he added the heat of the blazing African sun? He did that, imagining the fierce sun joining with the essence of fire, concentrating till sweat dripped from his face.

Flames flared between his hands, setting the fuel alight. His companions made noises of approval and slung a haunch of the kudu over the fire. As the meat browned and fat dripped into the fire, Nikolai found he could barely wait to eat. How long had it been since he'd had a decent meal? The bread and tea that morning hardly counted.

While the haunch cooked, the young hunter who had given Nikolai a spear walked around the watering hole, scanning the ground. Halfway around he stopped and dug into the earth. Then he returned with tubers that he buried in the coals. He made a laughing remark that

Nikolai almost understood. He also realized that the boy's name was Sefu, though he didn't know how he knew.

The rest of the meat was dressed and packaged. Again, without knowing how, he realized that in the morning two of the hunters would carry it back to their village, along with the hide and horns and whatever else was useful from the kill.

The sun was setting by the time the meal was ready. Never had meat tasted better. Nikolai and the hunters ate their fill amid much laughing and talking. Though he didn't know the language, he found that he had a general sense of the conversation. He was accepted as part of the group, though set a little apart because he could do magic.

When it was full dark, several of the hunters produced small, flat drums from their bags, and they began drumming. The others rose to dance around the fire. It was a hunter's dance, mimicking the movements of the antelope—a way of honoring the beast that had been sacrificed. The rhythms pounded through Nikolai, the drumming and dancing inextricably linked. He wanted to participate, but he didn't know how.

One of the drummers rose and tossed his small drum to Nikolai, then joined the dance. Startled, Nikolai caught the instrument. The tautly stretched head was warm where the drummer's hands had pounded, and it called to him.

He tentatively began to slap his open hands on the drum, trying to match the rhythms of the others. His companions laughed and called encouragement. He kept the beat very simple, and soon his drumming was in harmony with the rest of the ensemble. They were joined as one, twined together with the dancers as one rejoicing entity.

The dancers suddenly broke from their movement and bent before the drummers to pound the earth, honoring them. After a last flourish, the drummers stopped and handed over their instruments and the two groups changed places.

Nikolai felt awkward as he joined the dancers. He'd done little dancing in his life, and his body didn't understand the movements of the kudu dance. He was clumsy, sticklike, a European surrounded by Africans.

Sefu touched Nikolai's arm, saying without words that clumsiness didn't matter. A warm relaxation spread through him, and he stopped worrying how he looked to others. He let the drumming thrum through blood and bone, opening himself to the movement of the dance, and he became one with the group.

Despite his lighter skin, his ignorance of the language or even of where he was, he felt that he was part of this life. The dance ended and the hunters lay down to sleep, except for one who sat up with his spear to watch over the camp.

Nikolai held a palm to the fire. *Burn low but steady through the night.* Then he lay back on a thin pile of grasses, tired to the bone and ready for rest.

He had just enough energy left to study the stars. Maddeningly, they were similar to the sky he knew, yet not identical, and not because he might be farther south than he'd ever sailed. The stars were not quite the same. Perhaps this was another world, one that lay close to his own, but was slightly removed.

Don't think. He closed his eyes and slept.

As the days and nights passed, Nikolai fell into the rhythm of life with the hunting band. They called themselves the Dahana, The People. For the first time in his life, he felt that he truly belonged somewhere. He was not a mixed-blood Maltese, not black or Arab or European. He was one of The People, not only accepted but honored for his magical abilities. They called him Nikai.

After two handfuls of days, they returned to their village. There was a feast to welcome the hunters home. Nikolai's drumming was improving, and he enjoyed learning new dances. These were the African roots he had never known, and he gloried in the ancient traditions of life lived in harmony with nature. Vital force was in all creation, connecting all that lived.

He had found a missing part of himself.

His hunting group traveled in search of game about half the time. The rest of the time they relaxed in the village with friends and families. As memories of his old life drifted away, Nikolai practiced his mastery of fire. He found he could call it in carefully measured amounts, lighting a cook fire or raising a great bonfire for the tribe's dancing.

He also learned how to store fire in a stick so that saying a brief magical word would cause it to burn for some minutes. Such a fire stick could be used by anyone, which made it a valuable gift. He was much praised for the invention, for now other hunting groups could easily carry fire with them.

He vaguely remembered someone he'd known in the past who could call fire—a woman. Ah, that was Adia, a priestess who could call violet fire. But her name quickly slipped away again. As did the name of the woman who had hair like fire...

He practiced drumming and spear throwing, and humbly asked an elder for lessons in playing the flute made from a twisting kudu horn. He'd always enjoyed music, but never learned how to make it. The lessons were a delight, both for the music and the elder's shy, pretty daughter, who watched him with special warmth. Soon he was smiling back and thinking it was past time to take a wife. But there was no rush.

The days drifted by, placid and satisfying. For the first time in his life, he was content, though he could no longer remember why he'd been discontented.

After many handfuls of days had passed, his group of a dozen hunters left the village to make a trading journey to a town that lay at the fork of two rivers. Sefu explained that many peoples visited Timtu and that great wonders could be seen there.

Nikai and the hunters ran for three days, moving

from the grassy savanna to a harsher, drier landscape. Over time, the sun had darkened his skin so that he looked more like his hunting brothers, for which he was glad. He did not want to be a man apart.

The hunters took turns carrying their trade goods until they reached Timtu in late morning of the fourth day. The square mud buildings teased a distant memory. He had visited a town like this long ago, in his dream life. Why had he done so, and where was it? He couldn't remember.

The market bustled with traders displaying fruits and bright cloth, worked metal and carved wood, and a dizzying area of other goods that had traveled the rivers and trade routes. He admired a small drum, tapping the head to hear the rich sound. What might he trade for such a fine object? Perhaps he could offer a pair of his enchanted fire sticks? A husband and wife were selling the drums, and their pretty little daughter shyly offered him a different one, tapping the head to demonstrate the tone.

He was about to try the little girl's drum when shouts sounded in the distance, accompanied by thundering hooves. The market square dissolved into screams and panicky flight. Sefu shouted, "Run, Nikai! Raiders from the north are attacking! If we run, they will not pursue because we are armed, but we must go quickly!"

Nikai spun about and followed his friend and the other hunters as they fled the attackers. He was leaving the square when horsemen thundered in from the opposite side. Veiled and dressed in voluminous robes, they bellowed and waved curving swords, using blades and horses to herd the townspeople into the center of the square.

Nikai spotted the drum sellers. The father caught up his little girl and ran with his wife toward a narrow alley, but he was too late. A raider swooped down and pulled the little girl from his arms, kicking the father in the gut to make him release the child. The raider tossed the little girl in front of his saddle, then used the flat of his sword to force the parents toward the group of captives.

Nikai halted, shocked by the scene. "What are they doing?"

Sefu paused and turned back to answer. "They are slavers. They'll take young, healthy captives to the coast to be sold and shipped to distant lands. Come now, while they are busy!"

"If we fought together, we could drive them away." Some traders were fighting back, but they were too few to make a difference. Nikai started forward with his spear.

"These merchants are not The People! Their fate is nothing to us." Sefu grabbed his arm. "Come!"

For an instant, Nikai accepted his friend's words. What did it matter if foreigners were enslaved if all of The People were safe?

The instant passed, and he shattered into rage and memory. He was Nikolai Gregorio, sworn to fight slavery everywhere. He had been sent to this world to learn fire, and thought it meant only the burning flames. But fire was also passion. Outrage. A demand for justice. The fire in his soul had come near to flickering out, until today.

He had a sudden, vivid memory of a small redheaded female with blazing eyes. She had told him that if he was in danger of losing his way home, remember what he most truly was. The essence of Nikolai Gregorio was the fire of justice. "They are all my brothers," he said grimly. "Flee if you will. I fight."

He ran forward into the square and raised his hands to summon fire from the skies. A great ball of flames materialized, and he hurled it at the raiders. Their flowing cloaks ignited, and the attackers began screaming and wrenching off their garments. Horses threw their riders and bolted while the armed traders began cutting down those raiders who didn't run away.

In the shambles of the market, he saw the horseman who had taken the drum sellers' child. He was cornered against a building, looking for a way out, still clutching his prisoner. Grimly Nikolai stalked toward him. When he was several yards away, he hurled a spear of fire.

While the raider screamed and covered his eyes, Nikolai swept the little girl from the horse. She was crying but unhurt. As soon as he set her down, she ran for her parents. Her mother caught the child up in the safety of her arms while the father used a broken post from his stall to stab up at the man who had tried to steal his daughter. The jagged end plunged deep into the raider's belly.

The rider folded over in his saddle, blood splashing his pale robe. But before he died, he had enough strength left to raise his sword and drive it into Nikolai's chest, damning with guttural fury the man who had ruined this raid.

Recognizing imminent death, Nikolai pulled his energy inward and tried to dodge, but the sword slashed into his chest, crushing bone and slicing flesh. As strength fled and he collapsed, he was mildly surprised to realize there was no pain.

He didn't fall to the ground, but *through* the ground, into dark chaos. He was trying to puzzle out what was happening when he slammed into a hard surface on his back. Blinking, he looked up—and found that he was in the cave on Diabolo and the four priests who had sent him to that distant land were watching him.

He had survived the first test.

CHAPTER TWENTY-FOUR

NIKOLAI BLINKED up at the priests. "You're still here?"

"We had to hold the gateway open so you could return," Omar explained. "*If* you returned."

The priests certainly were a pessimistic lot. Nikolai sat up and noted that he was wearing the same shirt and breeches and boots as when he'd entered the cave. "I was gone for many weeks. Months. You've waited here the whole time?"

"The time might have been months in that other world, but here it has been only hours." Adia offered him a hand up.

He lurched when he rose, disoriented. "What happened to me—was it real?"

"As real as this cave and this island. Look at the color of your skin." He did as she said, and saw that he had tanned many shades darker from the fierce savanna sun. "Everything that happened there is now part of your spirit."

"I think I died there," he said slowly. "I had just been stabbed in the chest when I was brought back. Did my death bring me home?"

Omar's brow furrowed. "Perhaps, if your death was caused by what you learned on your journey."

"It was." He had discovered the fire inside, the passion that had faded when be became too comfortable. That fire was essential to his mission.'

But he had discovered a missing African piece of himself among the Dahana. He thought of the peace and joy he had known running with his fellows, and of his discovery of dance and music. He had been one of The People—and he felt a piercing sadness because that life was closed to him. Once more he was in a place he didn't fully belong.

"Drink." The other priestess, Nayo, gave him a cup of hot, sweet tea. He swallowed thirstily. He would miss the Dahana, but at least he had tea again.

SIMPLER TESTS FOLLOWED, taking him to places where he'd lived such as Malta, Algiers, his ships, Santola. In each place, he drifted ghostlike through familiar scenes, becoming more complete as he saw himself with the detachment brought by distance.

He lost track of time, but after some days, Adia decided that his soul was whole enough and informed him that the next test would be of a different nature. She led the group to the top of Diabolo's highest hill, where the younger priest, a former galley slave called Enam, performed a ritual as the sun rose. At the end, Enam sketched a circle in the air the size of a man. "Enter now and learn the spirits of air."

Nikolai stepped through, and found himself falling endlessly through dark space.

If the first test of his initiation was a dangerously appealing heaven, this one was hell. The fall itself was terrifying. Even worse was the noise: a mind-numbing scream of fear and intimidation that was high and low at the same time and that pounded his very marrow. He tried to block his ears with his hands, but the cacophony was in his head, impossible to escape. He panicked, desperate to escape, but the hideous noise was getting worse, worse. He hadn't realized that sound could produce such pain.

He was on the point of madness before he realized that the greater his fear, the more painful the sound. The only way to survive was to overcome his fear.

What did he fear most? Not death—that would almost be a relief. As he recognized that, the hideous noise diminished a little.

What else did he fear?

Failure. He had a responsibility to his men, to those he'd rescued and to the sanctuary he had created on this island. If he failed his people, he feared he would take them with him into hell.

But that wouldn't happen, he recognized. Santola had many strong, capable men and women. If he died, the community would survive. His fear was ungrounded.

Once more, the painful noise diminished, and he was no longer falling so fast.

Loss. As a boy, he'd lost everyone he'd ever loved. He thought he'd dealt with that fear by refusing to care, but somewhere deep inside, the fear lingered on—as did the desire to care and be cared for. Recognizing that fear diminished the hammering noise so that his body no longer vibrated with it.

Betrayal. As a boy, he'd given his trust too freely, and the pain of betrayal had nearly cut his heart out. Fear and loss had created a consuming fury that had turned him to bitter revenge. That vengeful rage had made him more than a little mad.

Injustice. He'd kidnapped Jean, would have cheerfully killed her brother, and that would have been a great injustice. He lived for justice, yet in his fear and anger, he had very nearly become what he hated most.

The noise was now bearable, and he was no longer falling. He hung suspended in the air, floating like a soap bubble. Each fear had been a lost piece of his soul, he realized. As the fears were vanquished, his soul became stronger.

The punishing noise faded to nothing. As he hung in the void, he wondered if it was possible to fly here. He'd had dreams where he swooped through the sky, arms and legs extended while he concentrated fiercely on staying aloft. He tried that now, and found to his delight that he could indeed fly once he relinquished the fear of colliding with the earth or a mountain.

The experience of flight was magical. He laughed

aloud as he swooped through darkness, improvising loops and dives like a playful seabird. He decided to see how high he could fly. Using all his will, he soared up and up and up—and burst through the portal that led back to Diabolo.

He fell clumsily to the ground and rolled, his skin abrading on the rough stones. His priestly mentors stood around him. This time, Enam helped him up.

"That was... interesting." Nikolai glanced at the sky to judge the position of the sun. "How long was I gone? A day?"

"Only a few minutes." A wicked glint showed in Omar's eyes. "There is time enough to do another test today."

Nikolai concealed his groan. Initiation was difficult in ever-changing new ways—but the sooner he was done, the better.

"JEAN, ARE YOU HERE?" Adia's voice called from the entrance to Jean's room.

"On the terrace!" Jean leaped to her feet, her heart in her throat as she greeted her visitor. "Has... has something happened to Nikolai?"

"Much has happened, and more will come, but he is doing well so far," Adia said quickly. "I'm sorry if my appearance alarmed you. I wasn't needed on Diabolo for the afternoon, so I decided to come to the village for supplies. I also thought it was time to see how you were doing with the abolitionist notes. Is there anything that is unclear?"

Relieved beyond measure that her captain was doing well, Jean gestured to the piled notes on the table where she worked. When her eyes tired, it was a pleasure to gaze out at the caldera. At Diabolo. "I'm about halfway through my copying. There are several places where I don't fully understand your notes. Also, I've been working to create a time line of abolition-related events. Could you look at it to see if I'm correct?" She handed over the paper where she had drawn a long line with different events flagged on different years.

"This is very fine as far as it goes," Adia said after she studied the diagram. "But there is more." She sat down and recounted several important incidents. "I did not experience these things myself, but the elders spoke of them."

"This is wonderful!" Jean scribbled notes hastily. "One can say so much more in words than in writing."

"We had time only to record what was most important. I did much of the writing since not all the elders have the skill. Now, let us go over your questions."

Jean relaxed as she opened the notes to her first question. Surely Adia would not be taking time to work with her on this unless there was a very good chance that they would be going forward in time. And that meant that Nikolai would survive.

THE DAYS MERGED into a blur of tests, some frightening, others merely strange. Learning earth was terrifying because Nikolai thought he had been buried alive and would suffocate. When he didn't die, he gradually realized that he was a budding seed, learning earth in the most literal of ways. All was texture, weight, temperature, and slow time as he mindlessly struggled up toward the sunshine.

Being touched by a passing earthworm was strange indeed. After an eternity of fighting his way toward the sun, he emerged into a world of wonders and new dangers. He stretched his leaves—and found himself curled into a ball in the cave on Diabolo.

He visited places that were as familiar as his own hands, and worlds so strange he didn't have words to describe them. Sometimes he knew fear, other times excitement, occasionally boredom. He never found another place where he fit as he had with The People. Bleakly he accepted that it was not his path in life to feel that he belonged completely to a group.

The experiences left him feeling spiritually battered, but also more aware of the world around him. Would that be enough for him to become fully initiated? He spent little time worrying about that, because he was indeed learning to think less.

He lost himself so thoroughly in changing experiences that it was a surprise when Adia said one morning, "Come. It is time for your final test."

He swallowed the last of his tea, then followed her as she set out briskly on a goat path that angled back and forth as it ascended the steep hill. The other priests did not accompany them.

They reached the summit, then headed down. The sun was well above the horizon by the time they had descended to a rocky edge several feet above the crashing waves. The waves were larger here than inside the caldera, and the wind harsher. Adia stopped at the water's edge and gave him a pouch that contained a water bottle and half a loaf of bread. "Sit here and watch the sea."

"What shall I look for?"

"I cannot say. But cultivate patience, Captain. Wisdom does not come quickly." She smiled. "You are better suited to this now than when you first came to Diabolo."

"How will I know when I have learned this particular wisdom?"

"You will know." She turned away and began climbing again.

He found himself gazing after her because she was human in an inhuman landscape, so he forced himself to turn back to the sea. He had tried meditating before starting his initiation, and been a flat failure.

Today, meditation seemed a little more possible. All day he sat as still as he could manage, watching the waves splash in and the light change on the rocks. The sun was hot and the rock under his backside was damned uncomfortable, but he did his best to clear his mind.

Seagulls glided over with haunting cries, occasionally diving into the sea for fish. A lizard came from the rocks and passed so closely that Nikolai could have caught it. Three goats wandered by, cropping at the scattered greenery. But of wisdom, he found none. Though the challenges he had experienced had slowed his thinking some, his mind was still a jumble of thoughts and questions and digressions.

As the sun set, he realized that Adia would not return for him today. That was why she'd left bread and water. He ate and drank a little, not sure how long his supplies must last. When it became too dark to watch the waves, he found a protected niche among the rocks. The goats ignored dried grasses, so he collected as many as he could find to make a thin pallet. He settled for the night, thinking he'd never spent a more boring day in his life. Maybe accepting boredom was the lesson he must learn?

As he fell to sleep, the stars sang to him.

BY THE NEXT MORNING, hunger, cold, and lack of stimulation were beginning to weigh heavily on him. Reminding himself that he'd survived much worse, he finished the bread and took a swallow of water, then returned to doggedly watching the sea. In midmorning, he saw a far-distant sail. It was the high point of his day.

By late afternoon, he was light-headed. He drank the last of the water, thinking that if he was unable to see anything by the morning, he'd have to hike back to the camp. He wasn't sure which was worse—the hunger and thirst, or the overpowering desire to do something, *anything.* Even solitary confinement in a prison cell would be better than this—he knew because he'd experienced imprisonment.

Dusk was falling when he saw a waterspout in the distance. He thought it must be the result of some distant storm. Then another spout formed, and another and another until the horizon was full of whirling towers of energy. All had their own nature. Some were dark and frightening, causing his mind to flinch away. Others were distant, seemingly not of this earth. A few were warm and beckoning.

With a shock, he realized that they were spirits. African religion included spirits of nature, some good, others evil in human terms. What they all shared was great and dangerous power. Where the ancestors were intimately connected to mankind, these spirits were mighty entities that could do great damage without having anything humans recognized as conscious awareness.

It was another shock to realize that his mission would involve such great, inhuman powers. The knowledge was terrifying.

As he stared at the spirit beings, they began to whirl together until they had combined into a single vortex of energy that towered to the heavens and beyond. It glided across the sea toward him in eerie silence. Within that twisting form were flashes of dark and light, colors with no names, the essence of creation and destruction.

He began to shiver in the cool wind from the sea. As it came close, the spirit formed into a shape that was almost human, but indistinct so that he couldn't tell if it was male or female or—something else.

Yet he didn't feel fear. Whatever the entity was, he felt no malice. Rather, there was a sense of cool, clear wisdom and benevolence.

The spirit paused before him and began to shimmer through many shapes. He saw his mother, his grandmother, a dark Malti man who was surely his grandfather, a fair northerner who might have been his father. The images extended back in space, a line of ancestors that branched from Africa, Europe, and Asia.

The spirit reached the shore and cupped great hands around Nikolai's trembling body. As warmth flooded through him, he heard in his mind *"Be still and know that I am God."* The words blazed into the dark core of his being, which had never known stillness.

Be still and know that I am God.

Though the words were Christian, he knew they reflected the essence of all faiths. Christianity, Hinduism, the nature spirits of Africa—all of them flowed from one great source of truth and mystery. Stillness would always be a challenge for him. But if ever he needed to find peace, he now knew the path.

As the realization filled him, he felt the spirit being embrace him. The energy was distinctly female now, and in those arms he felt his grandmother, his mother, Ulindi, Adia—and most of all, Jean Macrae. Over the years he had lost the feminine aspect of his nature, and now it had been restored to him again.

He bowed his head, and wept.

By the time Nikolai had collected himself, the sea spirit had vanished and it was full dark. Creakily he rose to his feet, wondering if he could make his way over the steep hill without breaking his neck in the dark. He looked up and saw a glow of light above. Adia was coming for him.

She smiled when she reached him, her violet fire shining around her. "You have done well, Captain. You are now initiated into the mysteries of the ancestors. Come back with me now, for you are surely cold and hungry as well as wiser."

"Do the great spirits come to everyone?"

"Each person has a different experience. Not everyone is set to watch the sea, but you are of that element, so this was the place for you to start." She handed him a water bottle and a piece of cheese before turning to lead the way back to the camp.

He took a grateful swallow of water, then a bite of the cheese. Her provisions kept him going until he reached the camp. It was a relief to rejoin the others and warm himself with hot soup.

With the initiation successfully ended, the priests were more relaxed than he'd seen them before. He learned supplies had been ferried across from Santola. The supplies had included small drums, and he discovered that his fingers had retained some of the skill he'd acquired with the Dahana.

At the end of the evening, in a small ritual, Adia presented him with a smaller version of the leather medicine bag he'd worn during the initiation. The original bag had been to protect him against the wrenching challenges of that ordeal. This one was to wear forever, a tangible sign of his African blood.

When he rolled into his blanket, exhausted but content, he tried for stillness. For just a moment, he felt the warmth he had experienced when the sea being had touched him. *Be still and know that I am God.*

SINCE THERE WAS no news from Diabolo, Jean clamped down on her anxiety and continued her work. Occasionally she had a faint sense of his energy, but it was so elusive that she couldn't be sure she wasn't imagining it. Whenever she felt traces of him, she stopped what she was doing and sent power, just in case he needed it.

She had no idea if her efforts were of any use, but ironically, her concern was improving her ability to access and channel her magic. If she had to worry about him all the time, she'd end up a first-class mage.

A fortnight had passed when her door flew open and Nikolai swooped into her room, where she was sipping her morning tea. She jumped to her feet, barely remembering to put the cup aside. "You're back!"

"Are you disappointed?" Laughing, he scooped her up and deposited her on the bed in a flurry of skirts, covering her body with his while he gave her a thorough, exuberant kiss.

Jean responded with delirious joy, intoxicated by his

scent and warmth and strength. This kiss was a celebration, not driven by mindless lust or aching farewell. "I shouldn't be doing this," she breathed before kissing him again.

"Probably not." He pulled out her hairpins and freed the thick red tresses. As he buried his face in them, he murmured, "Your hair smells of lavender. Irresistible." It would be easy, so easy, to flow with this joyous energy, but her inner voice was quite clear that this was not yet the time. She buried her fingers in the thick waves of his hair and studied his face. Dark and dangerous he would always be, but he was now centered in a way she hadn't seen before. Apparently he had found the lost pieces of his soul. "The initiation was successful," she said, and it wasn't a question.

"Indeed. A most interesting experience, but not one I should care to repeat." He bent to lick her throat.

She shivered and allowed herself a few more heartbeats to enjoy his embrace before saying, "Now we both get up and sit in chairs that are not within touching distance. Today we need talk, not passion."

She thought he would disagree, but he didn't. He pushed himself to a sitting position. "Regrettably, you're right." His eyes narrowed thoughtfully as he studied her. "I have a sense that we must keep our distance while our personal powers develop. Does that make sense?"

"Actually, yes." She sat up and swung from the bed, her newly freed hair tumbling around her shoulders. "If we were lovers, we would influence each other's energies.

Sometimes that's a good thing, but not for us. At least,..not yet."

She crossed to the table to pour tea, then froze. Even though he was right behind her, she couldn't sense his energy. She felt as if she was alone in the room. Spinning around, she asked, "Are you suppressing your energy in some way?"

He looked surprised. "I'm not sure. Let me see..." His expression became abstracted. A moment later, subtle colors swirled around him and she once more felt the thrum of connection. "Did that make a difference?"

"It certainly did." She sank into a chair, mind racing. "It's rare for a person with power to be able to shut his energy down so completely that a nearby mage can't tell that he's alive. As soon as I turned from you, it was as if you didn't exist. Did you do that consciously?"

He frowned. "There was an incident early in my initiation where I was attacked by a sword-wielding horseman. I believe that I instinctively pulled in my energy, like a shell, as I tried to dodge. For a moment I thought I would surely die, though I didn't. But my energy must have stayed drawn in until now because I didn't think to open it up until you mentioned the subject. I must learn to be more aware of what I'm doing."

She didn't know whether to laugh or cry. "Now I know why my father seemed to betray you. In his later years, he developed cataracts, a clouding of the eyes. His magical senses worked well so it usually didn't matter that his vision was weak. But if you drew into yourself when captured by the corsairs, he wouldn't have been able to locate you on an adjoining ship even if he was looking right at you. He must have thought you were dead since he couldn't find your live energy."

Nikolai looked as if he'd been kicked in the stomach. "And in the middle of a pitched battle with a close friend lying bleeding at his feet, he could not spend much time looking for a boy he believed dead." He closed his eyes and swore in low, heartfelt tones. Then he was silent for a long time before he opened bleak eyes. "All my life I have taken pride in my ability to conceal myself when in dangerous circumstances. It was my own bloody damn fault I was enslaved."

"There is no fault involved when a frantic child is trying to protect himself." Jean tried to imagine what he must be feeling. "If my father had known you were alive, he might have died trying to save you. Or he might not have been able to do anything, and would have lived with the guilt of that till he died. We just don't know, Nikolai."

She moved to sit by him on the bed and took his hand. "And if you hadn't become a slave yourself, you would not have developed the fury and the compassion that have led to freeing so many other slaves."

His hand locked around hers. "You're saying my capture was for the best?"

"Perhaps. We cannot know divine will." Her smile was wry. "I'm trying to imagine what it would have been like if you'd reached Dunrath and been raised as my brother. I do not think of you as a brother."

He laughed as his hand squeezed hers. "And I certainly do not regard you as a sister." He bent and gave her a light kiss, then crossed to the table where the teapot sat. He topped off her cup and handed it to her, then poured tea in the second cup. "Were you expecting company?"

"I've kept a spare cup since you left, just in case." Before he could reply, there was a shriek of avian bliss and Isabelle rode into the room, her claws clenched around the outside doorknob. Apparently the door had not latched shut behind Nikolai, and she used the beat of her powerful wings to swing it open. Once inside, she flew to her master, who quickly raised an arm for her to land on. The macaw rubbed his cheek excitedly with her beak, making cooing noises.

As he greeted the bird with equal enthusiasm, Jean asked, "What was your initiation like? What strange places have you visited?"

"It is not the sort of thing one talks about." He scratched the macaw's throat, his expression thoughtful. "Adia was right to warn me of the dangers. Your advice to seek my true self if I became lost saved me from sinking into another world. Thank you, Jean Macrae."

"I'm glad my words helped. Now we can finally undertake our mission. I've been going mad with boredom," she said fervently.

"You and I are much alike in preferring action. It was the stillness that I found most difficult in my education." Isabelle hopped to his shoulder, so he reclaimed what was left of his tea. "How have you been occupying yourself?"

"Mostly I've been copying the notes Adia and her

London friends assembled about the future and the abolitionists. I've tried several times to scry about what we might need to do, but I saw nothing clear enough to be useful."

"Have you devised exercises to improve your ability to use your magic?"

From the glint in his eyes, she guessed that he'd decided that the faster she learned, the sooner he could bed her. "Mostly I visualize clear, straight pathways with white light flowing easily from the center of my spirit to my will." She hesitated. "Also, since I couldn't sense that you were alive, I worried about you. Several times I thought that perhaps I felt a trace of your energy. When that happened, I tried to send some of my own energy to help, and I think my concern helped straighten the channels a bit."

"Then, we must hope you are desperate again soon." He looked pleased by her admission that she'd been concerned for him. "The waiting is over, my Scottish witch. Now we're ready to fly into the future."

"Despite Adia's presence, it's still difficult to believe that travel through time is possible." Jean stopped, startled by a memory. "So much has happened that I forgot a conversation I had with Moses in Marseilles. He said he'd undergone an initiation where he walked on other worlds. He also told me that some African shamans have special abilities to work with time and place." She smiled ruefully. "It seemed so improbable that I made a note that we must talk further, and then forgot about it."

"So you now have confirmation about traveling

through time from another source. We have Adia, your friend Moses"—he extended his hand—"and soon enough, we'll know for ourselves!"

She clasped it, grateful for the warmth and acceptance between them. They were not lovers, and perhaps they never would be. But today she felt sure that they were friends and comrades. "May our actions be equal to our ideals!"

BOOK THREE

FANNING THE FLAMES

1753 – Onward

CHAPTER TWENTY-FIVE

TONIGHT WAS THE NIGHT. The new moon meant bright stars and powerful energies afoot. The time had come to risk themselves to Adia's magic. Jean touched the bag slung over her shoulder with nervous fingers, hoping the carefully chosen contents would provide for them in whatever emergencies they might encounter.

She and Nikolai also wore money belts stuffed with coins and notes that would be accepted from their time to Adia's, and probably well beyond. If, God forbid, they were separated, they must be able to manage independently. The chance of separation was one more thing to worry about.

Though Jean almost vibrated with anticipation, she was also profoundly aware that she was leaving everything and everyone she'd ever known, probably forever. The knowledge was gut-wrenching. Nikolai's life had taken so many unexpected turns that he was skilled at adaptation, but she had lived among family and friends, secure in the heart of the Guardian community, for most of her life. She could hardly bear knowing that she might never see family and friends again.

Before she broke down entirely, she reminded herself that the Guardian community would surely exist in the future and would include Macraes. She would adapt as necessary, and if she died—it would save the effort of adaptation.

She tugged her cloak around her. Again at Adia's direction, the Santolan tailors had created garments that were neutral enough not to draw attention over the next several decades. The travelers should look unfashionable but not in a way anyone would particularly notice. Jean didn't mind, but looking dowdy pained Nikolai.

She remarked, "I didn't expect it to take more than a fortnight for us to make the preparations to go, but at least we've been busy, not bored."

"My suntan had time to fade to normal." Nikolai donned his own cloak. "The more unremarkable I look, the better."

" 'Tis impossible for a braw lad like you to look unremarkable." Though Jean's usual speech was that of an educated English lady, she now spoke with a broader accent that identified her immediately as Scottish. Unless England changed greatly over the following decades, being Scottish would explain any oddness on her part.

Perhaps sensing they were about to depart, Isabelle flew anxiously to Nikolai's shoulder and dug in with her claws. He lifted her down and set her back on her perch with a last caress. "Be happy with Louise and her family, *ma petite.* They will worship you as you deserve."

He offered Jean his arm, and they headed out the door of his house. She was very conscious of the gold band on the third finger of her left hand. The wedding ring was part of their masquerade. The fraudulence of the ring bothered her more than the sinful fact of her traveling with Nikolai even though they were unwed.

They walked to the African gathering place in the abandoned village and found Adia and the other priests waiting. When they were all ready, Adia said in a deep voice, "I call North." She conjured a violet fire on the north side of the space. "South." More fire. "East. West." As she called each point, one of the priests went to stand in front of the fire she created. Adia herself took South.

When she finished, the six of them stood bracketed by fire. As the flames blazed upward, Adia said soberly, "I have done all I can to prepare you. I hope and pray that it is enough. Do you have any last questions?"

"Not unless you can tell if the bead spells will take us beyond the time you know," Nikolai replied.

"Or whether disaster will ensue if we meet anyone from this past," Jean added. "And if the magic can bring us home again."

"You will learn all that before I do," the priestess said wryly. "Much of your journey is a mystery. All we can do is trust that the magic of the ancestors is true, because we are asking for miracles."

"Your arrival here was a miracle." As the critical

moment neared, Jean found she was vibrating with excitement. "Why shouldn't we find more?"

Nikolai clasped Jean's hands. The bespelled bracelet was wrapped around her right palm with the first bead pressed between them. "I could not ask for a better partner in adventure," he said softly. "Shall we be off?"

For an instant she was tempted to flee, to break the circle and return to the world she knew. But her certainty that she was destined to follow this path steadied her nerves. She glanced around the circle of priests. "I hope to see you all again, but if not, thank you, Adia, and all of Santola. You have helped me find meaning in my life."

She raised her gaze to meet Nikolai's. "Now!"

They both poured their power into the charmed bead. Their energy was joined by that of Adia, Omar, Nayo, and Enam. Each priest added his individual note to the rainbow of swirling power. Three men, three women, male and female balanced, the energy filling mind and body.

The enchanted bead that would take them to the first critical event dissolved in a flash of heat that scorched Jean's palm. The world turned violet, the same shade as the fire that blazed before them. Pure energy engulfed them in a vortex of magic and destiny that drew them down and down.

With all her passion and determination, Jean hurled herself into the vortex—and she took Nikolai with her.

As Jean and Gregorio vanished, Adia fell to her knees, near fainting. She had burned so much of her power that she could barely manage to close the magical circle the priests had created. When she had done that, Nayo walked to her side and laid hands on Adia's shoulders, sending energy. "You have done all you can," the other woman said softly. "Now it is up to them, the ancestors, and the gods."

With Omar's help, Adia managed to get to her feet. "Slavery has been with us since mankind first emerged from the sea. Is it even possible to end it?"

"It is possible," Nayo said. "But for now—let us eat and restore our energy."

Adia smiled as the four of them left the gathering place. Great issues mattered, but so did dinner.

Jean felt as if she was being torn apart, fiber by fiber. The only reality was Nikolai's hands, his fingers locked around hers.

For a horrible moment she thought they would be wrenched apart and lose each other in the vortex. Then her body solidified and she became whole, though she fell gasping to her knees in the process.

Nikolai managed to keep his feet and his grip. "Gods!" he swore. "I much prefer travel by ship, even through a tempest!"

"Or on a runaway horse." With his help, she got shakily to her feet. It was night, and they were in a city.

She smelled the stench of too many people living too close together, sensed walls confining the narrow, empty street even before her eyes adjusted to the darkness. The sky was cloudy and the air dankly cold. She shivered and pulled her cloak tight. With no lights anywhere, the darkness was deep and intimidating.

He wrapped an arm around her shoulders. "Do you know where we are?"

"It could be London," she said uncertainly. "But I haven't been in enough great cities to tell one from another."

"If this is London, it's certainly dark."

"I've heard that London is the most ill-lit city in Europe. The law says there should be lamps on main streets, but this feels like an alley." Her eyes were adjusting to the dark. "It looks lighter down there, so perhaps there is a larger street."

They started walking in that direction. She asked, "Was your journey here like what you experienced during your initiation?"

"Somewhat similar, though this was worse." He paused thoughtfully. "I wonder if traveling through time is a matter of being drawn into one of Adia's other worlds and reemerging here at the correct time?"

Jean considered. "It's a good theory. I like having a way of imagining what we're doing. Step into a world that lies alongside the one we know, move to a different place, then step out in our world in a new time."

"Let's hope that the travel becomes easier with practice, and that we have enough power to make the next trips on our own," he said pragmatically.

"If not, Adia told me about the African community in the East End. In particular there is a priest, very old in her time, but he had lived in London for many years. She said we could go to him for help. He was a member of the circle that sent her to us."

"It's good to know there is help nearby, but I hope we don't need it." His brow furrowed as they reached the end of the street. "The map in my head says we are where London should be. The bigger question is *when* are we?"

Jean nodded wordlessly. This larger street had lanterns hanging outside a few of the houses, which helped a little. It didn't look any different from the London she knew. She frowned at the corners of the buildings that framed the alley. "There's always talk of requiring street name tablets on corners, but it doesn't seem to have happened yet."

She drew closer to Nikolai. She hadn't realized how disorienting it would be not to know her location or even the date. Thank heaven there were two of them.

Glancing to her left, she saw a ragged man staggering toward them. "Help me," he gasped before he collapsed on the filthy ground.

Groaning, he tried to struggle to his feet, but collapsed again. Nikolai raced to the man's side, Jean a step behind. While Nikolai knelt next to the man, Jean created a small mage light on her palm, directing it downward to illuminate the dark-skinned face. "He's just a lad!" she exclaimed, thinking he couldn't be older than sixteen or seventeen.

"An African boy, and he's been badly beaten," Nikolai said grimly. He pulled out a handkerchief and began to blot blood from the young man's eyes. When he was done, the boy's lids opened and he looked up with a dazed expression.

"We'll help you," she said, sending warmth and reassurance. "Were you attacked by footpads?"

The boy blinked blearily at her. "Master Lisle did this," he said through swollen lips. "Master beat Jonathan with a pistol till barrel and stock broke."

"Why?" she asked, horrified.

"He be drunk," the boy mumbled. "Always hits me when he drunk. Said I was worthless and he shouldn't have spent the money to bring me here from Barbados.

Not worth feeding me, he said. Kicked me and said I should go away. S-so I did."

Nikolai swore. "Then you're not a runaway," he said, his voice more controlled than his expression. "Your name is Jonathan, you say?"

"Jonathan Strong," the boy said, his voice despairing. "But Master kill me, sir. I be dead soon."

"You will not!" Jean said, her mouth tight. She held his head between her hands and sent healing energy into him. Even more vital, she sent hope and a desire to live. As always, her magic was strongest when the need was greatest. She combined her desire to help with her practice at channeling power, and felt that her healing was improved. Pray God her ability was strong enough to help this poor lad.

With a sigh, he closed his eyes and went limp in Nikolai's grasp. "I'm not a powerful healer like my mother, but I think I've stopped the worst of the bleeding." She sat back on her heels. "Adia told me about this young man. After his master, a lawyer named David Lisle, half killed him, Jonathan Strong managed to reach the clinic of a surgeon named William Sharp. Sharp is surgeon to the king, and he and his family are all musicians who travel around the country on a barge making music." Nikolai stared at her. "You are making this up."

"No, really," Jean said. "As he waited by the clinic, he was noticed by the surgeon's brother, Granville Sharp. The brothers took him to St. Bart's hospital to heal."

"Our job is to find this man Lisle and kill him?" Nikolai asked with a dangerous flash of teeth. "I would enjoy that."

She shook her head. "I think our task is to deliver him to the Sharp brothers because later that will lead to important legal progress. I'll explain more later, but now we need to get Mr. Strong to shelter before this cold damp gives him a lung fever on top of his other injuries."

"Maybe I can kill Lisle later." Nikolai carefully lifted the young man's limp body. "Where do we find William Sharp's free surgery?"

"I'm not sure—it's somewhere in the East End, I think."

"Where are we?"

"I'll see if I can recognize any landmarks." She moved

into the intersection and scanned the skyline. "I think we're close to the Tower of London, which means we're also close to the river."

She tried to remember what Adia's document had said about this incident, then gave up and pulled out her copy of the papers. Using just enough mage light to read, she said, "William Sharp's clinic is near here, on Mincing Lane. We need to make sure Jonathan survives the night, then help him to the clinic in the morning. According to this, the assault happened in 1765."

"Only a dozen years in the future. I find that oddly comforting." Several church tower clocks began chiming in ragged disharmony. "Two o'clock. Might there be a coaching inn nearby that would stay open all night?"

"There are several major roads near, so we should be able to find an inn or perhaps a livery stable." Jean rose and brushed off her skirt. After tucking her documents back in her bag, she slung it over her shoulder. "Which way, Captain?"

He thought a moment. "To the right." They set out down the street. Jonathan Strong was so thin that his weight didn't seem to slow Nikolai down at all.

Two blocks west, they found a small coaching inn. They walked under the arch into the courtyard. The stables were to the left, with a bored man half asleep in front, keeping watch over the courtyard and inn from a wooden armchair. A lantern hanging above the stable door revealed that he had a tall flagon in one hand and a clay pipe in the other. "Here, I think," Jean said softly. "I'll do the talking."

She approached the watchman, who immediately set down his flagon and rose to his feet, expression equal parts wary and curious. Jean looked up at him earnestly. "Sir, would there be a room we can hire for the rest of the night? My husband and I were looking for lodging when we found this poor boy beaten in the street. We couldn't just leave him, so I thought I could bind his wounds and in the morning we'll take him to a hospital." She let a coin show in her hand. "Unless you know a physician nearby who might see him tonight?"

The watchman glanced at Jonathan Strong. "Poor sod looks half dead. An escaped slave, maybe. Don't know any surgeons round 'ere who'd be willing to look at him at this hour. The inn is full up, too." He took the shilling piece Jean offered. "The streets aren't safe at this hour. You can spend the rest of the night back in the hay room. It's warm and dry."

"Thank you." She gave him a shining smile. The watchman blinked, then lit a second lantern and led the way into the stables between a double row of dozing horses. The hay room was at the back. There were deep piles of hay, plus a stack of roughly woven horse blankets. "If you don't get blood on 'em, you can use some of the horse blankets to make up beds in the hay."

"Would it be possible for you to leave the lantern?" Jean gave him another shilling, then spread a blanket on the hay.

He took the money and hung the lantern on a wall hook. "Sleep well, mistress." Then he hesitated, studying Jonathan's battered body as Nikolai laid him on the improvised bed. "Want me to bring a bucket of water to clean the lad up?"

"I'd be very grateful," Jean replied.

The watchman headed off for the water. Nikolai said, "What kind of magic did you use to make the fellow so cooperative?"

"A very old kind of magic." She grinned. "The kind Eve was blamed for in Eden."

He smiled a little. "Is there anything I can do?"

"Try to send Jonathan emotional warmth—the feeling that he is cared for."

Silently Nikolai took one of the boy's hands while Jean examined his injuries more carefully. Even using her new magical techniques, she couldn't fix Jonathan's broken bones, nor the terrible damage to his eyes. He would be fortunate if he didn't lose his sight. But she was able to stabilize his flickering life. When the watchman brought a bucket of water and clean rags, she washed blood and dirt from his worst wounds and applied some crude bandages.

She finished by enveloping Jonathan in a cocoon of physical warmth to protect him from the chill of shock. The boy had come perilously close to dying of his misery. What kind of life had he had, being beaten regularly by a drunken brute? But there was hope for him. She sensed that if he survived this crisis, a happier, freer life lay ahead.

When she'd done all she could, she covered him with another blanket and settled back in the straw. "He'll survive, I think, though his recovery will be long." She dragged her wrist over her tired eyes. "How can one person be so cruel to another?"

"Men are not so very far removed from the beasts." Nikolai shifted so that he was lying next to her in the straw. After pulling a blanket over them, he tucked her against his side. "Can you tell me more about our mission?"

"Better not to speak in front of Jonathan Strong. My mother said that people who seem unconscious can be affected by what is said in their presence," she said drowsily.

"So I must wait. No doubt the discipline of that will be good for me." Nikolai's arm tightened around her. "Rest now, Jean. You've had a demanding day."

She relaxed against him, burying her face against his shoulder. He exhaled softly against her temple as he also relaxed into the embrace. She loved his scent, which made her think of desert winds and sunshine.

His warmth and strength brought her perilously close to weeping with gratitude. She and Nikolai had shared passion and conflict, but this was the first time she'd felt such kindness and simple caring. It was as if they had moved beyond lust to the trust and affection of a long-wed couple.

Not that passion was gone—she felt it simmering deep inside him, and she was alarmingly aware of how easily her own desire could be unleashed. All she need do was raise her face and kiss him, and their carefully constructed barriers would shatter.

But mages became very skilled at controlling their

personal energy, and that included passion. With desire firmly locked away, she and Nikolai were free to comfort each other in an uncomplicated way.

The scent of hay reminded her of the barns of Dunrath. There had been nights when she and Robbie had rested in similar barns while following the damnable Stuart prince to war. It was hard to imagine two men more different than Robbie and Nikolai. Yet both fought for freedom.

And both made her feel safe.

CHAPTER TWENTY-SIX

NIKOLAI HAD LEARNED to take catnaps during his years at sea, so he dozed through the rest of the night. His well-honed reflexes brought him awake whenever there was an unusual sound. He gave up sleeping when the livery stable began stirring with early-morning business. He was glad to see that Jonathan Strong was still breathing steadily. When they'd first found the lad, Nikolai had feared he wouldn't make it through the night. He wouldn't have survived if Jean didn't have some healing ability.

He glanced down at her as she slumbered against him. Tendrils of red hair had escaped their bindings and lay against her smooth, pale skin. She looked lovely and a little fragile. She must have used a great deal of power in her efforts to save Jonathan. As her father had said long ago, magic always had a price. At the least, fatigue.

He leaned forward to give her a butterfly kiss, too light to disturb the delicate balance of passion between them. Then he stood and brushed stalks of hay from his garments, thinking how satisfying it would be to find David Lisle, late of Barbados. He would dearly love to inflict on the lawyer the same kind of brutality that the man had visited on a youth who couldn't fight back.

But such vengeance would do nothing to fight the larger cause of slavery. Changing opinions and laws were required if there was to be real change. For now, he would go exploring and see if he could find Mincing Lane.

The streets that had been so empty now bustled with people heading to their work. Nikolai's unremarkable appearance did its job—no one looked twice at him. Well, a few women did, but they weren't criticizing his clothing. Even his dark coloring didn't attract attention—this part of the city seemed to be home to a diverse population. Now to find the good surgeon Sharp.

JEAN WOKE when Nikolai entered the hay room. "I've found Mincing Lane and Sharp's surgery," he announced. "They're quite close. Everyone knows Sharp because of his free clinic. How is Jonathan Strong doing?" Suppressing a yawn, she leaned forward and checked the young man's pulse and breathing. "He's a little stronger this morning, though his injuries are still grave. He should be well enough to survive the trip to the surgeon's office."

As she rose and stretched, the night watchman

entered the hay room with a tray. "I thought the lad might need something soft to eat, if 'e's still alive," he said gruffly.

"He lives. You're very kind." Jean took the tray, which held a bowl of porridge as well as a pot of tea and a chunk of bread. "Nikolai, do you have a coin?"

Nikolai was reaching for his purse when the watchman made a dismissive gesture. "No need. The poor young devil needs a little kindness. 'Twas good of you to help him." Embarrassed at revealing softness, he pivoted and left.

"He's seeing Jonathan as a real person, not an object," Jean said softly. "Minds are changed one at a time." Jonathan groaned and opened his eyes. Jean knelt beside him. "Mr. Strong, we'll take you to a surgery soon, but first, here's something to eat."

The boy's bloodied gaze moved hopefully toward the bowl she held. After Nikolai helped him sit up, she patiently fed small spoonfuls of the porridge into the boy's bruised mouth. He ate like a man who hadn't had a good meal in far too long. Halfway through the bowl, he said, "I can manage now, ma'am."

Jean gave him the bowl, then poured tea for the three of them. It was a mint mixture, pleasant and refreshing. She also divided the bread into three and they all ate. Jonathan was well enough to eat his share of the bread, though he winced when he bit into it. When they were all finished, Nikolai returned the tray, cups, and spoon to the kitchen of the inn.

He returned to the hay room and helped Jonathan

stand. The boy cried out with agony even though Nikolai supported most of his weight. "I'm sorry, Mr. Strong," he said. "The surgery is a bit of a walk. Would you rather I carried you?"

"No," Jonathan panted, biting back his pain. "I walk on me own feet."

And so he did, though with considerable help. Nikolai supported the youth with an arm around the waist while Jean walked on his other side, in case extra help was needed. The walk that had taken five minutes the night before now took closer to half an hour, but Jonathan staggered along with a determination that boded well for his survival.

When they reached Mincing Lane, they saw a short line of shabby people standing beside William Sharp's surgery. Nikolai halted. "There is the surgery, Mr. Strong," he said. "Join the people waiting there and you will be helped."

The youth blinked to clear his vision. "No one never called me Mr. Strong before."

"They will now," Jean said fiercely. She took his bruised hand between hers and caught his gaze. "You will heal, Mr. Strong, and find work here in London as a free man. But remember the two Mr. Sharps. If ever you are in trouble in the future, let them know. They will help you."

"I'll remember, ma'am." He straightened, moving away from Nikolai's supporting arm. "Thank you for helping a black boy, sir, ma'am. Never would have thought it might happen."

"You deserve the aid and respect we all owe each other," Jean said softly. "Go with God, Mr. Strong."

He bobbed his head at the two of them, then turned and made his uncertain way down the street to join the line of people waiting at the surgery. Though everyone in the group must have been ill, none had been brutalized like Jonathan. Jean bit her lip as she watched his painful movements. "Let's find a quiet place where we can watch. I know what Adia said, but I want to see for myself that he's taken care of."

"So do I. Let's buy some muffins from that peddler." The morning bread hadn't been much to start the day, so this would serve two purposes. Nikolai guided Jean to the peddler and bought them warm muffins scented with cinnamon. They lingered as they ate, concealed by the muffin man's stream of customers.

Nikolai was swallowing the last bite of his muffin when two gentlemen emerged from the surgery. There was a clear resemblance between them, though the younger man had fiercer, sharper features. They were talking casually, but they stiffened when they saw Jonathan Strong, clearly shocked by his condition.

They asked the youth questions. Though Nikolai and Jean were too far away to hear what was said, the two gentlemen seemed even more shocked by Jonathan's answers. The hawk-faced man took Strong's arm and helped him into the house while the other made an explanation to the other patients about needing to take care of this emergency first. No one who had seen Jonathan's condition argued the point.

Jean gave a sigh of relief. "So far, it's exactly as Adia said, which gives me faith that other events will unfold as she said. The Sharps will bandage Jonathan up, then take him to Bart's hospital. He'll be there for months, but when he recovers, the Sharps will find him a job as a servant and he'll work there as a free man."

Nikolai frowned. "I'm glad for Jonathan, but how will that affect the future of slavery?"

"In two years or so, David Lisle will see Jonathan working," she said tersely. "Since he'll be healthy then, Lisle will realize that his former slave represents money, and he'll secretly sell him to another West Indies planter."

Nikolai swore. "Are you sure I can't kill Lisle now?"

"Alas, no. Lisle will send two slave catchers to capture his 'property.' While Mr. Strong is in jail waiting to be shipped to his purchaser, he'll get a message to Granville Sharp. Mr. Sharp will be so outraged that he will take the matter to the lord mayor of London. Lisle can't afford to go to court, and Mr. Strong will be freed. When Mr. Sharp's eyes are opened to the evils of slavery, he will fight it for the rest of his life. Currently, the status of slaves in England is unclear, but Sharp will step in to defend other men in situations similar to that of Jonathan Strong. Eventually, because of Sharp's work, a court will produce a ruling that essentially says that any slave is free in England."

Nikolai exhaled roughly. "That will indeed be a major step forward. I suppose it's worth letting Lisle live."

"I shall hope that he receives justice in the next life if

not in this one." Her brows knit together in puzzlement. "I wonder how Jonathan Strong would have found his way to the surgery without our help?"

Nikolai shook his head, as uncertain as she was. "Perhaps someone else would have helped him. Or maybe he managed on his own. Or perhaps we *had* to be here to help. The last seems most likely, since he might have died without your healing."

"Part of me wants to understand how this time-travel business works. And part of me is afraid to know more." She swallowed her last bit of muffin. "Now that Mr. Strong is in good hands, what shall we do? Are we ready to attempt the next bespelled bead?"

He considered. "Despite my usual impatience, I'd like to spend a little time here. I've never been in England before, so I need to develop a better sense of the country. Also, learning about this time period should make it easier for us to adjust when we move farther into the future."

"That's a good idea. We can find a nice respectable inn, perhaps in the city or Westminster." She sighed. "I wonder if any of my family is in London. Heavens, Duncan's children must be almost grown by now!"

He gave her a sharp glance. "It wouldn't be wise to visit them."

"I know." She pivoted, taking Nikolai with her. "But it's hard not to think about them. Let's walk along the river a bit. The shipping is the reason the city was built here, and as a sailor you should find it interesting."

She was right, he would. Maybe studying the port

would take his mind off David Lisle. He allowed himself to relax as they strolled down to the waterfront, then along the river. They had traveled safely through time, and successfully accomplished their first task. Not only had they saved Jonathan Strong's life and liberty, but they had helped to form a link in the chain of freedom. Not a bad day's work at all.

Nikolai had seen his share of ports. London was both the same and different. Despite being on a river well inland, it was one of the busiest ports he'd ever seen. Great ocean ships loaded and unloaded alongside compact coastal vessels. Small boats darted up and down the Thames, carrying passengers and merchandise.

He enjoyed the familiar sights and sounds. He was also intrigued by the light, which was cooler and more blue than the blaze of the Mediterranean.

They were heading west and had passed London Bridge when a young naval officer approached them. "You have the look of a sailor," the officer said in a suspiciously hearty voice. "Are you one?"

Bemused, Nikolai said, "Why do you ask?"

Jean's grip on his arm tightened warningly. "He's a foreigner, Lieutenant," she said to the officer. "Maltese." The lieutenant glanced at her wedding ring. "But you are British, madam, I hear Scotland in your voice. A foreigner married to a Briton is eligible for the press." He turned to Nikolai. "Do you have a Protection?"

He frowned. "What the devil is a Protection?"

That was the wrong question. "Since you have no Protection, sir, I am impressing you into the king's navy."

The officer gestured and two heavyset men behind him moved forward. They looked like dockyard scum, and they wore dark blue bands on their right arms.

"What are you talking about?" Nikolai snapped.

Jean interposed herself between him and the officer. "You're making a mistake, sir. This man is not my husband, so the British Navy has no right to impress him."

"All the wives say that," the lieutenant sneered. "He's mine to take, and it's up to him to prove otherwise. If he objects, he can appeal to the Maltese consul for help. Now come along." The officer's men closed in around Nikolai.

He wasn't afraid of the men, but it might be bad form to knock them unconscious with magic. He was wondering what to do when Jean quietly offered a handful of gold to the officer. "You are supposed to take only experienced sailors. Mr. Gregory is neither a common nor an able seaman, nor is he British. Seek elsewhere."

The lieutenant glanced down and evaluated the amount of the bribe. "If he isn't a sailor, you're right, ma'am, he is not eligible for impressment. Sorry to have disturbed you." He pocketed the money, then collected his men and moved away.

Nikolai asked incredulously, "They were going to take me by force and make me work as a sailor? I thought there was no slavery in England!"

"Except for sailors who are needed by the Royal Navy," she said drily. "The press-gangs are only supposed to take qualified seamen, but they are not always careful. A Protection is a document that says you can't be pressed. Generally men with money have them, but heaven help them if a press-gang sweeps them up when they don't have that Protection on them."

"So you bribed him for my freedom?"

"It seemed the simplest solution," she said candidly. He swore in several different languages, including Malti, which he saved for special anger. Before he ran out of phrases, a ruckus erupted halfway down the block. A woman began beating a man over the head with a mop. "You'll not take my man, you devils!" she shrieked " 'E's the support of me and my children and his old mum!"

Her victim, one of the lieutenant's bullies, raised his arm to block her blows but kept a firm grip on his struggling captive. "The king needs 'im more. You can starve for all 'is majesty cares."

As the lieutenant tried to intervene, a dozen more people joined the fight. Half were women wielding brooms and frying pans, while the others were workingmen. The mop woman's husband had been rescued from his captors when a dozen more men with blue armbands arrived. The newcomers had three prisoners in their midst and several weeping women behind them.

A full-scale riot exploded, civilians against the press-gang. Men, women, and children poured out of buildings and shops and began fighting the gangers. Jean took a firm grip on Nikolai's arm. "Time for us to leave."

He ignored her tug. "This is like corsairs taking slaves for the galleys."

"Not quite as bad. Pressed men can get a bounty if they declare themselves as volunteers, and they get paid for their service. If they stay in the navy long enough, they'll even get a pension. But it's still being taken by force." She frowned. "I've heard that sometimes a man will set the press-gang on another man he dislikes. Or a father who doesn't approve of his daughter's sweetheart will bribe the press to take the lad away."

"None of *these* men will be taken away," Nikolai said grimly. He waded into the mob, heading straight to the nearest member of the press-gang. He threw a solid punch at the man, with a dash of the magic he'd used to knock Jean unconscious when they met.

He laid the ganger flat on the ground. Though less satisfying than beating David Lisle to a bloody pulp, Nikolai still enjoyed bruising his fists and punishing men who were little better than slavers.

He knocked down only three of the press-gang since the other civilians had taken care of the rest, but that was enough to relieve his simmering anger. As he stood panting over his last victim, a young man with a bruised cheek said, "Well done, sir!" He offered his hand. "The bluidy bastards had taken me from my wedding!"

As Nikolai shook the proffered hand, a pretty young woman with flowers in her hair came to the young man's side. "My thanks to you and the others," she said softly. "Losing my darling to the press would have been a poor start to our marriage."

Nikolai bowed to her. "I am new to London, and I

find myself most impressed with her liberty-loving citizens. My best wishes to you on your marriage."

As the young couple left, Jean arrived, picking her way daintily among the fallen. "I trust you feel better now, my dear?" Her eyes were mischievous.

"Indeed, I do." He took her arm and continued along the street, still heading west. "Is it common for locals to fight with the press-gangs?"

"I believe so. We didn't see this in rural Scotland, but citizens in port cities must always be alert to the possibility of being pressed. When the navy is particularly hungry for men, the gangs will even go into the countryside." She shivered. "Until today, I hadn't thought about how truly wicked impressment is. You're right. It's slavery."

He stopped dead in the street as an insight struck. "This may be why opinions in Britain can be swayed to abolition! People here live with the fear of being taken by violence and forced into slave labor. Surely that will make them more sympathetic to the plight of slaves everywhere?"

Jean caught her breath. "You may be right. Britain's power comes from her navy, and that means many seamen must serve, willing or not." She smiled up at him. "Perhaps we have found another piece of the puzzle." His eyes narrowed as he tried to define what he sensed. "There are strange energies in this area. Some dark, some light. I feel that a battle has been fought that is beyond the men and women who struggled here today. It's like a pressure in my mind. A riot. Can you feel that?"

"Cities are notoriously intense," Jean said. "Guardians usually feel tired the first few days after arriving in a city, and London is the most tiring one of all. Since you are newly initiated, perhaps you're more aware of mass energies than in the past."

"Perhaps." He mentally explored the clashing energies again. "But my intuition says that what I feel is something more specific to our mission."

"In that case, we both need to pay attention." She smiled. "But for today, let us just be visitors enjoying one of Europe's great cities."

CHAPTER TWENTY-SEVEN

TO JEAN'S RELIEF, they were able to find a pair of adjoining rooms in a respectable inn. She wasn't ready to share a room with her partner and his rather overpowering masculinity. He seemed equally relieved to have some distance between them.

Still tired from the power she'd expended on Jonathan Strong, she lay down for a nap in midafternoon and woke up the next morning. It was embarrassing to have slept more than the clock around, but she felt strong and refreshed.

After washing up and dressing, she tapped on the connecting door to Nikolai's room. There was no answer. Wondering if he was sleeping or perhaps had already risen and gone out, she quietly opened the door—and found him sitting on the bed clad only in boots and breeches. He was staring intently at his hands as he poured light back and forth from one palm to the other.

Shirtless, he was... quite magnificent. His shoulders

were broad and a hard life had produced hard muscles. She was so entranced by his half-naked body that it took her a moment to notice the small leather pouch he wore around his neck.

As she entered, he looked up, startled. The light between his hands winked out as sensual tension flared like sparks in tinder. They stared at each other, on the brink of forgetting the compelling reasons for staying apart.

Jean took a step toward him, yearning to run her hands over his beautiful chest. At her movement, Nikolai chopped off his energy with unnerving abruptness, then grabbed the shirt that lay beside him on the bed. "I thought it was customary to knock," he said drily as he yanked the garment over his head.

Jean drew an unsteady breath and forced desire back into the box where she'd locked it away. "I did knock. You didn't hear."

When his face merged from the white linen, he said, "I was concentrating too hard to hear you. Light and fire are fascinating."

"And you're getting very good with them." She strolled over to the window, giving him privacy to finish dressing while removing temptation from her sight. Realizing that her hands were clenched into fists, she forced herself to relax. They were adults. They could control desire. Then she realized that his image was reflected in the window glass. She shut her eyes against the sight. Control had its limits. "Is that a medicine pouch around your neck?"

"Adia made it," he said in an unforthcoming voice.

"African magic is a great deal more fun than the Guardian sort," she said wistfully. "We're so mental. You get drums and feathers and other interesting objects."

That startled a laugh from him. "I hadn't thought of that, but you're right."

Feeling the energy between them return to normal, she turned to see that he'd finished dressing. After debating whether to refer to what had happened or stay silent, she said, "Perhaps next time we should not get adjoining rooms."

"That might be easier." His mouth quirked into a smile. "But easier isn't always better. I think I like being driven mad by you now and then."

She thought of the delicious shock of finding him half dressed. "I take your point, but I don't know if my self-control is up to such challenges."

"Mine barely was this time," he admitted. "After we break our fast, do you have a particular goal for the day?"

"I want to visit a bookshop. We need to find some newspapers so we can learn what is happening in the world." She shook her head. "I still have trouble believing that American colonists have defeated the British Empire. I wonder if there is any hint of that in current newspapers?"

"That war is still years in the future, but the causes must be building now." He reached for his tricorn hat. "After we inform ourselves, what then? I want to walk and explore the city, but that will happen no matter where we go."

"I'd like to try to find Kofi, the African priest Adia told me about."

His brows arched. "I thought the plan was to be as quiet as possible."

"In general, yes, but I think we should find Kofi. We might need his help to trigger the next spell bead."

"Given how much power it took to come here, you're probably right," Nikolai agreed. "The two of us might not be strong enough to do it without aid."

"Besides needing magical assistance, we are likely to be in London more than once since it's the political heart of Britain. We might need allies and a base of operations, and who better than the African community?"

"And they can tell us more about what's going on now. Do you have detailed directions for finding Kofi?"

"Fairly so, though Adia isn't sure of his exact location at this early date." Jean smiled ruefully. "Adia said that there's nothing like collecting information to make one realize one's own ignorance. She and her friends did their best to write down anything about the abolition movement that might be useful, but there is much I don't know."

"I'd like to read her notes and historical summaries," he said as he ushered her toward the door.

"Adia said I shouldn't allow anyone to read the notes, even you. Knowledge of the future might be dangerous. The fewer people who know, the better." Jean shivered. "I feel as if we're playing with fire, and can't even see the flames. The more we limit our effect on this time, the better."

"I take your point, but what if something happens to you?"

"You can read the notes then," she said cheerfully. "But they'll give you a headache as you think about the time travel. Are we changing what will happen? Or already part of the flow of events? Has it always been foreordained that we attempt this mission and help the abolition movement? Or is it ordained that we will fail?"

"No wonder your head aches." He took hold of the doorknob. "Nonetheless, I should like to see what she says about abolition."

"Alas, you'll have to wait." Not that she blamed him for wanting to know. Even secondhand knowledge was better than none.

IT TOOK two days of searching, plus Nikolai's skill as a finder, to locate Kofi. The African community was suspicious of white people, and Nikolai didn't look African enough to allay fears.

But eventually they found Kofi, who owned a small cooper's shop. They had been referred here by another African after reassurances that they meant Kofi no harm. "That's him," Jean said quietly. "Look at the magic around him."

Nikolai invoked mage vision, which was getting easier. As Jean said, the tall, broad-shouldered man radiated power. He was assembling staves within a metal jig, his hands moving with startling speed. He stopped work and straightened as they approached, his expression wary. Parallel scars slashed across his cheeks.

"You are Kofi?" Nikolai asked.

The cooper's eyes glanced toward an axe that leaned against the wall next to him. "Who wants to know?" he growled in a deep, rumbling voice.

"I am Jean Macrae, and this is Nicholas Gregory," Jean said peaceably. "A friend said you can help us."

"Why would I?"

"She said to tell you that we are here because of Mattie."

Kofi sucked in his breath as if he'd been struck physically. "In the back garden."

He led the way through the shop and into a long, narrow garden stacked with weathering wood. The piles were so high that the space between was like a small, private room. Kofi crossed his arms over his chest and waited for an explanation.

Jean exchanged a glance with Nikolai, silently suggesting that he tell their story. He nodded and began, "We have come to you because we are working toward the abolition of slavery, and we were told you might be able to help." He took a deep breath. "And we have come through time to do this."

Instead of scoffing, Kofi examined them both with sudden intensity. His gaze caught on Jean's beaded bracelet. "You are witches using African time magic." His gaze moved to Nikolai. "You have African blood and African magic. Tell me more."

They sat on piles of timber, surrounded by the scent

of fresh-cut oak, and told the tale of Adia and their mission.

Kofi listened with the alertness of a wildcat. When they were done, he said, "What do you wish of me?"

"We need allies. Magical help and information," Nikolai said bluntly.

Jean added, "Adia told me that you will be living in London for many years, so you will be a good ally, if you're willing." She caught Kofi's gaze. "Adia also said that you were the most powerful African priest in London."

Kofi dropped his gaze and stared at the ground. "Tell me about Mattie."

"She was your wife," Jean said softly. "She died at a white man's hands in the Virginia colony."

Kofi swallowed hard. "I strangled him with my bare hands, then fled to Upper Canada. From there, I worked my way to England on a ship. I have another wife now, and children. Few know of Mattie."

"That is why she was chosen as the key to your confidence," Jean said. "You yourself suggested to Adia that Mattie be used to establish us with you."

Eyes narrowed, Kofi reached out and grasped Nikolai's hand. Energy blazed between them. Nikolai realized dizzily that he was being scoured, tested, judged. After the first shock, he found that he could see into Kofi as well as vice versa. The man had led a turbulent life. He had survived by always being ready to fight, and by having a gift of magic that he only gradually came to understand.

After working his way to England, he found work at this small cooperage. When the owner died, Kofi had married the man's daughter and they ran the business together. There had been a few who objected to a black man marrying an Englishwoman, but most of the people in this neighborhood accepted it with a shrug. As his life became stable, Kofi had studied magic with the London elders. Powerful and determined, he would make a formidable ally.

"You will help us, then," Nikolai said, and it was not a question.

Kofi nodded before turning his gimlet gaze to Jean. "You will need white allies also. You are English. Do you have friends you can call on?"

"I am Scottish, and yes, I do have friends and family in London. I shall have to think who I might ask." Her mouth quirked. "Adia had the advantage of starting from the future, so she knew what had happened and that you would be here now. Coming from the past, I look to the future in ignorance."

"Use your instincts, girl. They will carry you."

"Is time magic something only Africans can do?" Nikolai asked.

"I don't know," Kofi said. "I have little experience of European magic. Even among Africans, time magic is very rare. One of the elders who initiated me said that Africa is the mother of mankind, with roots that go back to the beginning of time, and this is why only Africans can do time magic." Kofi shrugged. "He may have been right. I do not have the gift for it myself, but some of the other elders have known priests who could move through time." He rose. "Come. You must meet my wife if you are to use us for a touchstone through the coming years."

Jane Andrews was a calm woman who had seen enough of her husband's magic, and hosted enough gatherings of the London elders, that she didn't even blink at the idea of travel through time. She merely said, "If you need us, we're 'ere. When the young 'uns are old enough to be told, they'll 'elp, too."

"We may need help soon to activate the next spell." Jean took Nikolai's arm. "Thank you both. It's good to know we're not alone."

After they left the cooper's shop, Jean removed her hand from his arm. He firmly replaced it. He enjoyed the quiet magical buzz between them when they touched. He asked, "Are you thinking of telling your brother of your presence and our mission?"

She shook her head. "He's not the right person, and not only because he spends much of the year in Scotland. It would be too complicated to involve him in our mission. We are too close. He might become too protective."

"Do you have another candidate in mind?"

"I'd love to talk to Lady Bethany Fox, but she might not even be alive now—she was old when I left England." Jean frowned. "I'm thinking of Lord and Lady Falconer. Simon is almost like a brother to me. A rather alarming brother because of his power, but I would trust him with anything, including not talking to Duncan. He is an earl and has a good political understanding. Simon and Meg are often in London, which could be useful. Meg is also very powerful, and because she spent years enslaved, I'm sure she and Simon would support our work."

"This countess was enslaved?" he asked, surprised. "Not by corsairs or plantations owners, but a rogue mage," Jean explained. "He kept her enthralled so he could use her power. Joined to his own magic, that made him very dangerous. She wasn't a countess then, of course. Just a girl of unusual potential. He enthralled several others for the same reason."

"Slavery is even more widespread than I realized." What Jean described was mind rape combined with slavery. The countess must be a very strong woman to have survived that. "I look forward to meeting the Falconers." Seeing Jean's frown, he asked, "Is there a reason you don't wish to?"

"I'm afraid of what I might find out, Nikolai. What if Simon or Meg has died? What if others I care about are gone? What if I'm told of my own death? I don't want to know!" Her fingers tightened on his arm like a vise. "I hadn't realized how necessary ignorance is to carrying on with one's life. I'm glad I'm not a seer. Seeing too much would make me mad, I think."

"Then we shall visit your earl and the first thing you shall say is that you don't want any knowledge of the fates of your intimates," he said. "If he and his wife listen well, I presume they will honor that."

"They both listen very well." More relaxed, Jean glanced up at him. "Now to find a bookstore and a coffee shop, for there we will learn the temper of the times."

For several days after the ritual that sent Gregorio and Jean Macrae into the future, Adia did little but sleep, eat, then sleep more. She felt so drained that she wasn't sure if she'd ever do magic again. Even her dreams were empty.

But eventually, she awoke feeling energetic and ready to face life again. The question was, What should she do? She was staying in a guest room of Gregorio's house, sharing the same balcony that Jean's room opened on. A maid had delivered a breakfast tray with bread and fruit and tea. Adia had never lived in such luxury—in the future, she had always been the one who delivered the food, not the one who received it. She found that she didn't like being waited on. She preferred managing for herself.

After eating, she headed down to the office where Louise worked mornings. The Frenchwoman glanced up from her ledgers. "Welcome back to the land of the living."

"Is it that obvious?" Adia paused by Isabelle's perch to offer the macaw nuts.

"The last several times I've seen you, you looked like a ghost—gray and wan." Louise pushed her chair back.

"If you want company, you are always welcome to join my family and me for dinner. My husband's ship has returned, and he'll be here for several weeks, and of course you already know the children."

"That's kind. I will join you this evening." Adia began

pacing the office. "But what am I to do with myself? I've worked my whole life, I don't know how to be a woman of leisure." She stopped by the bookcase that covered half of one wall. "What a wonderful library Captain Gregorio has. I've never seen so many books in one place. Will he mind if I read some?"

"He will not mind." Louise's expression became bleak. "Particularly if he never returns to Santola. Do you think that he and the Scottish witch will return?"

"I don't know. Probably not," Adia said honestly. "You and he are close?"

"He brought me out of whoredom and taught me that I had value. We were lovers for a time, but that was never the most important part." Louise used her penknife to carefully sharpen a quill. "Will you stay on the island? One of our ships can take you to France or Spain or Italy. From there, you can return to England."

"There is nothing for me in England now. My husband is a boy in Africa today. My children have not yet been born." She fought the despair that lanced through at that knowledge. She had known what she was losing when she called the magic. Though she hadn't realized quite how much it would hurt. "Besides, I feel that I must stay here as... as an anchor for them if they are to have a chance to return. So I must stay, and find occupation so that I will not go mad."

"You will find no more accepting place than Santola, and there is plenty of work. Would you like to help me? There is much figuring and correspondence, and I could use an assistant who can read and write a fair hand."

"I would like that." Adia pulled a volume from the bookshelf. *Tom Jones: The History of a Foundling.* She had heard of this story, but never had a chance to read it. She and Daniel didn't have money to spare for books.

"Why don't you write your own story?" Louise suggested. "You could get it published in London. The moving tale of an innocent African girl stolen from her home and sold into slavery could help educate people about slavery. There is much ignorance, and people are more touched by tales of individuals than mere numbers."

The suggestion resonated within Adia. "Perhaps you're right, but I don't know if I can write well enough. Even if I can, how could I get such a story published? How can I write about events that are in the future from our time?"

Louise frowned. "There are always printers looking for exciting tales to publish. I know of no journal that tells a story like yours, so I think it would attract interest. Your other question is more difficult. I think you would have to write the tale without events that could be dated easily. Write as 'An Anonymous African Princess.' "

"I was no princess," Adia protested.

"You are now," Louise said, clearly enjoying herself. "Describe the exotic places where you have lived, especially Africa—people love a travel tale. Tell of the great love between you and your husband and how cruelly you were torn apart, how you risked all to be together—women in particular love a romance. And speak of the great blessings of becoming Christian. All will approve of that."

"I am not so very good a Christian," Adia said drily.

"You are now!" Louise smiled wickedly. "Think of this as a way to reach people's hearts. Emphasizing certain aspects of the truth will help in that task. You know something of Christianity, don't you?"

"I have been baptized," Adia admitted, "but we also used Christian symbols to worship African gods."

"No white man needs to know that. The story of how you were stolen away as a child, of how you fell in love and married—those are real, are they not?"

"They are indeed," Adia said softly.

"Then shape them into a tale that will have truth at the core, but is also designed to make men and women weep at the horror that is slavery." Louise leaned back in her chair and grinned. "But save your mornings to work for me."

"May I have pens and paper?"

Louise gestured toward a cabinet. "Gregorio's lap desk is in there. You might as well use it." Her expression had turned serious. "I have a touch of seer in me, Adia, and I feel that a journal such as yours could be important."

"I think you're right." Adia opened the cabinet and removed the lap desk. As she surveyed the contents, she added, "At the least, it will keep me from fretting."

As she headed up the stairs, she wondered how long they would wait for the return of Jean and Nikolai before giving up. Would she eventually become so lonely that she would take an island man as a lover? Would Daniel find another woman to warm his bed? She didn't want to think of it. For herself, it would be a long time before the need for warmth would overcome the vows she had exchanged with her husband.

She set up the lap desk on the table in her room, then paused to think about where she wanted to start. Paper was expensive and should not be wasted.

Despite Louise's suggestion that she remove events like the American Revolution, she decided it would be easier to write her life as she had lived it. When she was done, she could go through and make a fair copy, removing details that might give her away. She must change names also.

After her thoughts were ordered, she dipped her pen in the inkwell and wrote, *"I have changed the names and details of those I met during my enslavement. Some are good people who were part of an evil system; I do not wish to shame them.*

"The evil I leave to God's justice."

CHAPTER TWENTY-EIGHT

"WHY DO you wish to find a coffeehouse?" Nikolai asked.

"I don't know about other cities, but in London, they are the places where men gather to talk and discuss the news of the day," Jean explained. "There are usually copies of newspapers for customers to read. You can learn what engages men's minds now. If you think it appropriate, you could mention slavery and see how others react. Adia was right when she said the slave trade will not end until the mass of people protest it. Britain's press is very free. The newspapers and debating societies will discuss anything. It will aid our cause if they start talking about slavery."

He nodded thoughtfully, understanding her point. "Are women not allowed?"

"No, which is why I will find a bookstore." She smiled. "Besides learning what has been published in recent years, I'd like to have a book to read in the evenings."

He studied her winsome face and the tendrils of red hair escaping her bonnet and could think of other ways of spending evenings. Though his mind believed that they must develop as individual mages before they became lovers, other parts of his anatomy were harder to convince.

Patience.

THE COFFEEHOUSE WAS low-ceilinged and smoky, the long tables scattered with newspapers and writing materials. In early afternoon, the place was about half full. Nikolai was surprised at the range of men present. While a number were dressed as clerks or merchants, others were clearly laborers. A few men sat alone with newspapers and mugs of coffee, but most gathered in friendly groups. Half a dozen were debating a subject vehemently while others conversed with moderation. Several men looked up when Nikolai entered, but there was nothing hostile in the curiosity.

He spent a few moments getting his bearings. After hanging his hat on a peg with the other hats, he approached the only woman, who presided over a counter by the fireplace. Coffeepots stayed warm by the roaring fire. The woman poured a tall, steaming mug for Nikolai at his request.

On the counter were a pitcher of milk and bowls of cracked sugar. He gazed at the sugar a moment, thinking that it had been harvested with blood and sweat by slaves in the Indies. But he didn't intend to start a revolution today. He merely wanted to learn. He added milk and sugar to his mug, then took a seat at an empty table where a rumpled newspaper waited.

The contents of the newspaper were a shock. The tone was positively treasonous. They could print such things without being jailed? After scanning the first newspaper, he picked another one from a different table. It was even more seditious than the first.

He looked for more newspapers. A man in one of the groups noticed his gaze and offered a gazette lying in front of him. "Would you like this, mate?"

"Thank you." Nikolai accepted the gazette. "I am newly arrived in Britain, and I find the freedom of expression rather startling."

"Aye, we're the freest people in the world," the man said complacently. From his dress, he might have been a stevedore. "Englishmen have our rights, even the least of us."

"Some 'ave more rights than others," another man said. "Why shouldn't all decent workingmen be able to vote? Why only property owners?"

The others in the group laughed. "You 'ave strange ideas, Tom," one said. "Only folks who really count are those with money."

"If enough of us say it's wrong, things'll change," Tom said stubbornly.

"Next thing, Tom will be sayin' women should vote, too." The comment set off a roar of laughter, followed by a lively political discussion. Nikolai said little, but he was impressed by the knowledgeable speech of even the most roughly dressed.

His expression was thoughtful when he left and met Jean at the bookstore on the next street. "I see why you sent me to the coffeehouse. Are all Englishmen so independent and well informed?"

"Not necessarily." She took his arm and they headed back toward their inn. "Coffeehouses tend to attract those who are interested in discussion. Different coffeehouses have various kinds of customers—there is one called Lloyds where men meet to underwrite shipping insurance. Ship captains usually go to a different coffeehouse. For those who want only to drink, there are plenty of taverns and gin shops."

"I was amazed at the inflammatory writing in the newspapers. In Paris, the editors would all be in jail." Jean's brows arched. "I didn't realize that the French controlled the press so tightly. Complaining about the government is normal here."

"Are Scots as concerned with their rights as Englishmen?"

"Scots are equally independent, but there are differences." She grinned. "The English complain about the government while Scots complain about the English."

"This independent spirit might be why abolition will take root here," he said thoughtfully. "Just as fear of being violently impressed into the navy might make the common man more sympathetic to slaves. If we keep going forward in time, it will be interesting to see how British notions evolve."

" 'Interesting' is one of those all-purpose words," she observed. "Ever since I met you, my life has become 'interesting.' I'm not sure how much more I can bear."

He smiled teasingly. "Would you really rather be part of London society, powdering your hair and attending too many entertainments?"

"Some days, yes." Her smile lit her eyes. "But not today."

ENTRANCE TO FALCONER HOUSE was not easy for a stranger who could say little about his business. Nikolai was dressed in his sober best while Jean had gone to a used-clothing shop and bought a black mourning gown and bonnet with a veil so heavy that even Nikolai could barely recognize her.

By prearrangement, Nikolai did the talking to get them into the earl's Mayfair home. Jean kept silent, but he felt her use her magic to "lean" on the butler and persuade the man that Lord Falconer would want to see these strangers.

Falconer knew it, too. When Nikolai and Jean were ushered into a handsome study, the earl looked up with a dangerous glint in his eye. "You used magic to persuade my butler to bring you up, Mr. Gregory, which is interesting. I trust you will make this worth my time." Jean had warned him that the earl was one of the sharpest men in England. It was hard to guess Falconer's age, though he must have been near fifty. He had fine lines around his eyes and mouth, but he was lean and fit. Nikolai thought the man was wearing a wig, then realized it was his natural blond hair accented with silver.

He was every inch an aristocrat. "You will not regret this, Lord Falconer. Please allow me a moment to explain our unusual circumstances."

"Proceed."

"Jean Macrae and I have come through time to support the abolition movement," Nikolai said bluntly. "Jean doesn't want to know anything about her personal life, or about the deaths of family and friends. She said you would respect her wishes in this."

"Jean?" Falconer's gaze moved to the black-clad figure holding Nikolai's arm. He was utterly still.

"Indeed it's me, Simon." She pulled back the black veil to reveal her face. She looked pale and tense at this meeting. "As Nikolai said, I don't want to know of personal tragedies—I would rather think that all my family and friends are alive and well even if I can't reveal myself to them. And I don't want to hear that I'm dead, either!"

"Most are indeed well, but I shall say no more. You have come through time, you say?" He studied her thoughtfully. If he was shocked, he concealed it well. "It must be true since you look barely out of the schoolroom. Tell me everything, starting with the identity of your companion." His eyes narrowed as he studied Nikolai. "He is no Guardian, but he is certainly a mage."

"So I have discovered." Jean removed her bonnet and the trailing veil. "His true name is Nikolai Gregorio, and he has a most interesting background."

"Then, we shall need refreshments to carry us through your story." The earl gave instructions to a servant, and they took seats around the fire. Jean told most of the story. Nikolai thought that there was an appealing symmetry in the fact that they were seeking the aid of a black African workingman and a pale English aristocrat. Falconer was everything that Jean had said—focused, intelligent, and radiating power.

Jean ended by saying, "Are we chasing rainbows, Simon? Adia, our African priestess, says that a serious abolition movement will be founded in about twenty years. Has it any chance of success?"

A line formed between Falconer's brows. "Slavery has been with us since the first tribal warrior defeated another and forced him to work. But society is changing. There are already people who think slavery is wrong, and more will come to agree. It's quite possible that the groundwork for a broad movement is being laid now." He frowned. "Though I do not approve of slavery, I must admit I haven't examined my investments with an eye as to whether any of them support the slave trade. I must do so."

Jean had said that Falconer was one of the most progressive members of the House of Lords, so the fact that he hadn't thought much about slavery was significant. Would that all men were so willing to consider the subject when it was brought to their attention. "Society has many troubles that need addressing," Nikolai said. "Can abolition compete with issues that are closer to hand?"

"Eventually. Inventions are being developed that will reduce the need for slave labor. Will it happen in our lifetimes?" Falconer shook his head. "That I cannot say."

"There are really two issues," Jean said. "First we must stop the slave trade so people are no longer captured and shipped across the sea. Then those already in slavery must be freed."

The earl nodded. "Ending the trade is a good beginning and it's more achievable than emancipation, but powerful forces will oppose you. The West Indies lobby is vastly wealthy, with connections to every corner of the ruling class. One of the largest plantations in Jamaica is owned by the Church of England."

Nikolai's lips tightened. "Not very Christian behavior."

"The good bishops would be shocked at such an accusation," the earl said cynically. "They do not see the blood and pain and misery of the slaves who produce their wealth. It's easy to ignore what you've never seen. They nod complacently and tell one another that the poor Africans are fortunate to enjoy the benefits of Christian living."

Nikolai swore under his breath. Falconer's brows arched. "Such language in front of a lady."

Jean gave an unladylike snort. "Surely you know me better, Simon."

His gaze softened. "Indeed. You've chosen a noble crusade, Jean. You and your... husband?" His glance touched Jean's wedding ring.

"The ring is part of our masquerade," Nikolai said. "To make it easier for us to work together."

The earl's lifted brow was eloquent. He didn't need to say a word to convey that the lady had her defenders, and anyone who injured Jean Macrae would be in serious trouble. It was just as well Jean hadn't mentioned that she had been kidnapped.

Jean leaned forward, her expression intense. "Simon, you are close to the Guardian Council. Will they assist us in ending slavery?"

Falconer shook his head. "You know that our policy is to interfere with the mundane world as little as possible. If the council gave your efforts official support, it would create great dissension."

"How could anyone with Guardian sensitivity favor slavery?" she retorted.

"You'd be surprised," he said drily. "Like the good bishops who run Jamaican plantations at long distance, most Guardians have not seen slavery close up. Many will think it is not our business to interfere. Had you thought much about slavery before you left for the Mediterranean?"

"No," she admitted. "But we can educate people about how evil it is."

"For every sad tale of slavery you produce, there will

be ten West Indian planters saying how happy their slaves are. Some will start calling slaves 'assistant planters' because it sounds better. They will talk about how their 'assistant planters' receive food and clothing and shelter and medical care, making them more fortunate than the poor of our own cities. They will claim their slaves give thanks for having been removed from the heathen lands of Africa. And they will say that blacks are born to be slaves—it is their place in the natural order of things."

"That's all rubbish!" Jean exclaimed.

"Of course it is," Nikolai said. "But Falconer is right—such lies will be spoken in all seriousness. Countering the lies will require the efforts of many people. That is why a large-scale movement is needed. If you and I were the greatest mages in the world, we couldn't do enough to make a real difference." He glanced at the earl. "I am not very familiar with Guardian powers. Is it even possible to change the minds of large numbers of people through magic?"

Falconer shook his head. "Not in any lasting way. Minds must be changed slowly, though logic is often led by the emotions. Make people gasp in horror at slavery and they are well on their way to opposing it. There was a dreadful case several years ago when the incompetent captain of a slave vessel called the *Zong* tossed more than a hundred sickly slaves overboard. Then the captain claimed them as an insurance loss, saying he'd had to drown almost half his cargo because he was short of water. That certainly created abolitionist feeling in many of the people who heard of the case.

"In contrast, even the most powerful mage could do no more than create a temporary revulsion if he cast a spell over a group. Magic would barely touch the surface of people's minds, and the effect would not last long."

"So the trick is to bring the genuine horrors to people's attention," Nikolai observed.

"I thought there was a form of magic created by groups?" Jean asked.

"Yes, but that is different. The energy is generated by the people themselves," Falconer explained. "Everyone has at least a touch of magic in his soul, and when beliefs are strongly held, the group creates a kind of spirit that reflects the essence of their beliefs. It is not a conscious energy, but it has power and its nature tends to attack those that oppose it. The pro-slavery forces have created such a spirit. To counter that, many people must believe intensely that slavery is wrong and should be ended."

Nikolai frowned. "I don't understand."

"I'm not sure anyone does," Falconer said. "I was taught this many years ago, and since then I have seen such energy in action when large groups feel strongly about an issue. Sometimes that spirit is positive, as in a church group. Other times it is negative and destructive. The struggle between pro- and antislavery groups will take place on many levels. The most visible is the political, for only a parliamentary law can stop the slave trade. But the political will be echoed and energized by the opposing spirits. It is your job to win hearts, minds, and souls to your cause."

Nikolai glanced at Jean. "Do you understand what he's talking about?"

"Not really." She shrugged. "Perhaps the concept will make more sense later."

Falconer looked amused. "If you come to understand the principles of group energy, pray explain them to me. I have only the vaguest grasp of such things."

Fuzzy as the idea was, Nikolai's intuition said it would be important in the future. "Adia said that slavery would end when the mass of people reared up and cried 'Enough!' Perhaps that's what she meant."

The earl nodded thoughtfully. "Her explanation is better than mine."

"You said that the Guardian Council won't help us. Will you help, Simon?"

"Of course. There will be other Guardians who will wish to aid your cause, starting with Meg." He rose from his chair. "I believe she is home. I will explain the situation and bring her to you."

After the earl left, Nikolai said, "We have acquired a formidable ally.".

"I knew Simon would be on our side, but I'm disappointed that he thinks the council will not help." Jean rose and began circling the room restlessly. "I didn't really think they would, but I hoped I was wrong."

"Falconer is in a position to influence others. Perhaps engaging his interest is part of our task. As he said, the groundwork must be laid today for change in the future."

Jean looked thoughtful. "That's true—the notes that

Adia wrote up concern mostly public events, but behind-the-scenes encounters like this matter, too."

The Countess of Falconer was another surprise. Nikolai expected a woman as intimidatingly aristocratic as the earl. Instead, Lady Falconer was dark-haired and petite, with an otherworldly quality that was balanced by the warmth of her gaze. She and Jean fell into each other's arms. "Jean, you look so young! Simon says you've been having such adventures."

Jean laughed as they ended their hug. "You sound envious, Meg."

"Only a little." The countess turned to Nikolai. "You will take care of Jean?"

He bowed. "If she will allow me to, ma'am."

"Jean is not the most biddable of allies." Lady Falconer subsided on a sofa by the fireplace, gesturing for the others to be seated. "I have always believed slavery was wrong but never thought anything could be done about it. What do you want from us?"

Her husband sat next to her, and Nikolai was startled to see the way the energy flared between them. The bond was palpable. So this was what a true marriage of mages looked like. The energy between him and Jean was strong, but nothing like this.

Answering the countess, Jean said, "Two things. First, to speak against slavery when the subject arises. Say it is wrong and cruel and un-Christian. If you speak up for abolition, others will develop the courage to do the same. Second, we may need to use your household for aid and sanctuary as we travel through time." Her mouth twisted.

"Though we haven't the vaguest notion of how far the magic will take us."

"Simon and I shall be here for a good few years to come." Lady Falconer sounded quite certain of that, and since she was a mage, she might actually know.

The earl said, "We shall need some kind of password that you can offer to the household staff if Meg and I are not here. We shall also speak of this to our children so they will know to offer aid if you appear. Do you need money for your expenses?"

"Not now, but we may in the future," Jean said.

"You have only to ask when you need it," he said gravely.

"I'm so glad you're on our side!" She smiled at Simon, grateful that he was as generous and honorable now as when they'd been children together. "For a password, shall we use 'liberty'?"

They agreed on that, then Nikolai and Jean prepared to leave. Falconer said, "It is probably best not to come here again unless necessary. You might run into someone you shouldn't meet, Jean."

She nodded. After hugging both Falconers, she took Nikolai's arm and they left. As they stepped into the street, Nikolai tried to analyze the meeting to find hints of whether he and Jean—or Jean, at least—would survive and return to 1753. Falconer hadn't seemed very surprised to see Jean, which could mean that she had returned to her starting place and told him about the time travel. But he wasn't the kind of man who showed surprise easily, so there was no evidence there. Even if he was genuinely surprised to see her, it might have been because Jean decided not to tell Falconer about her journey through time, even if she did manage to return to her own time.

The countess had seemed overjoyed to see Jean, which could indicate that she thought her friend had died after disappearing from Marseilles. But clearly the women were close friends. Maybe Lady Falconer had seen Jean in normal time the week before, and was merely happy to see her again.

A man could go mad trying to deduce what would happen. Time travel was definitely a source of headaches. He wanted to think that Jean would survive and return home because that mattered more to her than to him—yet he couldn't just ask Falconer, because he agreed with Adia that the less said about this mission, the better. It was simpler to stay with things they knew. "You're happy to have seen friends, I think."

She nodded. "It was a shock to see them aged a dozen years, for it brought the reality of time travel home as nothing else has. Yet I'd been afraid I would never see anyone I loved again. Now I can imagine that my brother and his wife will be joining Simon and Meg for dinner and I just missed them." Her smile was shining. "I feel less alone."

She had never complained or shown her fears when he'd kidnapped her. He felt a wave of guilt for what he had put her through. Like him, like Adia, like countless thousands of Africans, she had been taken from the world she knew by violence. But if he had not done so, he would not have her for a friend and ally now. "I am only now fully realizing that I gave you the experience that makes it possible for you to sympathize so deeply with slaves. But it was a harsh gift."

"Very." She gave him a wicked glance. "I forgive you the kidnapping. But I will not let you forget it."

JEAN DROPPED Nikolai's hands with frustration. "We will have to ask Kofi for help in activating the next bead spell. We can't do it with just the two of us."

"We came close." Nikolai's face showed the same strain she felt. "I sensed the whirlwind trying to form, but there wasn't quite enough energy to bring the magic alive."

Jean had felt the same. She studied the bead, which had become warm but was stubbornly intact. "We must learn how to work this magic without help. We can't be sure that we'll always land in London, or even England." They had been in London for a month, long enough for Nikolai to get a sense of the city and its people. Now they were both impatient to move on. She reminded herself that another day in this time period would not matter to their mission. But they did need to learn how to manage their own time magic. It would be hard to find other African priests outside of London, and there was a good chance that Guardian magic wouldn't be as effective.

"I don't know what we would do without the information Adia collected for us," Nikolai observed. "It will be interesting if and when we move beyond her period into terra incognita."

" 'Interesting.' There's that alarming word again." Jean looked around the room, double-checking that nothing had been left behind. "Onward to Kofi and our next adventure!"

CHAPTER TWENTY-NINE

ONCE MORE THE vortex dragged them through time, flaying and dissecting body and soul before painful reassembly. Jean blacked out, hands still locked with Nikolai's to keep them together in the time tunnel.

Her head cleared with a fresh breeze. She opened her eyes and found herself beside a road that ran between country fields. The day was pleasant, probably late spring or early summer. She was leaning against Nikolai, who looked as dazed as she. A pony cart stood beside them, the pony placidly nibbling at the lush grass growing on the verge.

Nikolai wrapped an arm around her shoulders, though she wasn't sure who was supporting whom. "Jean, have your wits returned?"

She exhaled roughly. "That wasn't quite as bad as the first time."

"Practice improves."

She looked at the bracelet and saw that the second bead had been consumed. "Do you know where we are?"

He closed his eyes as he tried to locate them on his mental map. "I believe we're in England somewhere northeast of London."

She studied their surroundings. "I think I traveled along this road once some years ago. It runs between London and Cambridge." She turned to the pony cart. WELSH'S LIVERY, HIGH STREET, WARE was painted on the side in faded letters. "One wouldn't rent a small cart like this for a trip of any length, so we must be in Hertfordshire. But what the devil are we doing here with a cart? Would the ancestors be able to provide us with transportation?"

"If they can move us through time, a hired cart can't present much challenge." He grinned. "I would have been more impressed with a coach and four."

"This is easier to handle. I suppose that since a cart is waiting, we should drive somewhere." A thought struck her. "Can you drive or ride?"

He shrugged. "Not particularly well. I spent time on the salt caravans, so I'm rather good with camels, but there are few horses at sea."

"I'm afraid your camel skills will be of little use here." She gathered her skirts with one hand and climbed into the cart. A covered basket was set behind the seat. She looked inside with interest. "The ancestors are even feeding us. Can you tell which way we should go?"

He closed his eyes a moment. "To the right." Opening

his eyes, he swung into the cart beside her. "Luckily, the odds are even no matter what I say."

She smiled as she stowed her bag under the seat, then signaled the pony to start moving. It stopped grazing with reluctance and began ambling along the road in the direction she ordered. "Let us hope that our mission reveals itself."

They drove along the road peaceably, seeing a few grazing cows but no humans. After about ten minutes, they crested a long hill and started down the other side. Halfway down, they saw a man sitting on the left under a tree, his horse's reins in his fist as he frowned into the distance.

"Do you think he might be our mission?" Nikolai asked quietly. "Jonathan Strong was the first person we saw after our last jump."

Jean caught her breath as she saw the young man's red hair and lanky height. Remembering Adia's notes, she said, "I think this might be Thomas Clarkson! Adia said that he is perhaps the single most important abolitionist. He won a contest at Cambridge for a Latin essay on the subject of the morality of slavery. It's a huge honor—for the rest of his life, people will say that he won the Cambridge Latin essay contest.

"But after winning the prize, he couldn't stop thinking about the subject. It is said that on his ride from Cambridge to London, he committed himself to working for the abolition of slavery. Perhaps he is pondering what to do now. If so, we're in"—she thought for a moment—"1785,I think."

"Twenty years farther into the future? We're getting close to the time where the movement will start to grow," Nikolai said thoughtfully. "Perhaps the magic brought us here because he needs some persuasion. Stop the cart beside him."

As Jean pulled the cart to a halt, Nikolai called to the young man, "Sir, has your horse lamed? If you need assistance..."

The young man looked up, startled. "No, though I thank you for your kindness, sir. My horse is well. 'Tis I who am troubled."

Nikolai swung from the cart. "Would the ears of strangers help? I've found that sometimes discussing a problem can help me find the solution."

Jean added, "Food can help, also. We were looking for a place to rest the pony while we dine. There is plenty to share, if you don't mind our joining you."

The fellow scrambled to his feet and bowed to Jean, a smile brightening his long face. Jean had learned early that all young males were hungry all the time, so food would be welcome.

"Why, thank you, ma'am, you're very kind." Clarkson sketched a bow. He was impressively tall, and he wore the black garments of a cleric. "My name is Thomas Clarkson. Late of Cambridge University and now on my way to London."

"I am Nicholas Gregory and this is my wife, Jean." Nikolai pulled the heavy basket from the cart and set it under the tree. He whistled softly when he lifted the lid.

"My dear, you have outdone yourself. We and Mr. Clarkson shall dine well." He pulled out a lap robe and spread it on the ground to protect them from grass stains.

Jean opened her eyes wide as she swung down from the cart. "Are you the young Deacon Clarkson who won the Latin essay prize at Cambridge?"

"Indeed, I am," the young man said, blushing with embarrassed pride. "I have been most honored."

" 'Tis honor earned, sir," she said firmly. "Will you tell us of your most recent essay? I heard that it was about whether slavery was lawful and moral."

Clarkson lost some of his animation. "That is the source of my disquiet. I did much study on the subject of slavery. Though I began merely hoping to win literary honor, my studies filled me with horror. The more I learned, the less I could sleep."

"Did you speak to those who have seen slavery first-hand?" Nikolai asked.

Clarkson nodded, expression deeply troubled. "My own brother is a naval officer who has served in the Indies, and he sent me letters describing unspeakable acts. Now my essay has been acclaimed and I am on my way to London to seek a post in the church. Yet... yet what I have learned troubles my sleep. I feel that someone should do something about these horrors, but who?"

"Why not you, Mr. Clarkson?" Jean asked, her expression earnest and admiring.

"I should not know where to begin," he said frankly.

"What can one plain ordinary man do alone in the face of such vast evil?"

"You are not alone," Nikolai said. "There are others who share your concerns, and if you look, surely you will find them."

Jean nodded agreement and called on more of Adia's notes. "The Quakers have been doing their best to make the evils of slavery known for some years, but they are considered eccentric and not listened to. They could use a man like you, who has youth and intelligence and passion—and is ordained in the Church of England."

"Men will listen to you, where they might dismiss a Quaker," Nikolai observed.

"That is true," Clarkson said slowly. "Being a man of the cloth would grant me a hearing in some circles."

"You should translate your essay into English and get it published," Jean said. "There are many people who would like to read it but haven't the Latin."

"That's a splendid idea! I could also add material from my studies to show the current state of slavery." He hesitated, in need of reassurance. "Do you really think anyone would want to publish it?"

"There is a Quaker printer and publisher in London who has produced other works that speak against slavery," Jean said. "I believe his name is James Phillips. I should think he would be very interested in your essay." Clarkson fell silent as he attacked another sandwich of ham and cheese, but the energy around him flared yellow, the sign of intense mental activity. After swallowing the last of his sandwich, he said, "You are both well informed about slavery. Have you lived in the Indies and seen it firsthand?"

Nikolai's mouth twisted. "I have indeed seen slavery, but not in the Indies. I was captured by corsair pirates as a boy and I spent years as a slave. I was beaten in the galleys, whipped on caravans crossing deadly deserts, and gained my freedom by leading a slave revolt on a galley."

Clarkson stared at him. "You have experienced this great evil yourself?"

"Do you doubt me?" Smoldering with emotion, Nikolai rose and peeled off his coat and waistcoat, then turned and yanked his shirt free of his breeches to reveal an ugly, crisscrossed mass of gnarled scars on his back. "The proof is written on my body."

Jean and Clarkson gasped. Wanting to weep, she leaned forward and traced the deepest of the scars. Nothing Nikolai had said about his slavery was as wrenching as the sight of these scars. Now she better understood why he had been so determined to revenge himself on the Macraes.

He jerked away from her touch, and she guessed that the scars spoke to him of humiliation and helplessness. He restored his garments and sat down, controlled again. "If you work against this great evil, Mr. Clarkson, I guarantee that there are many like me who will join you. I am foreign-born and could never lead such a crusade, but I believe that you might become such a leader."

"Do you truly think so?" Clarkson asked quietly.

"I know so." Jean caught his gaze, mustering all her sincerity. He must be persuaded by truth, not by magic.

"I'm a Scot, and I have a touch of the Sight. I believe that you can truly make a difference in fighting the slave trade. Perhaps it is divine will that led my husband and me along this road today." Divine will, or the ancestors. She wasn't sure there was a difference.

"Perhaps... perhaps I shall do as you suggest." Clarkson's energy flared again, this time with resolve. "I shall pray on it."

As Jean remembered what Adia had written about Clarkson, she knew that today they had done another good day's work.

After their picnic had ended and Jean had sent Clarkson off to London with another sandwich wrapped in cheesecloth so that he wouldn't starve along the way, Nikolai packed the basket into the pony cart. "I suppose we should return the cart to the livery in Ware. Then London, I think?"

Jean nodded. "Twenty years have passed since our last visit. We need to see what people are thinking, not to mention get newer clothing."

"I'd like to drive the cart. I need the practice."

"Feel free," Jean said as she swung up on the passenger side. "This placid old pony is a good choice for a sailor." He was glad to drive, and not only because he had so little experience. Learning to use the reins properly was a convenient distraction. For years he had concealed his scarred body, hating the idea that anyone would see how he'd been used. Now that Clarkson was gone, he expected Jean to say something about the scars, but mercifully, she said nothing. A man could fall in love with a woman who knew when to stay silent.

Fall in love? Where had that thought come from? Yet when he studied Jean's delicate profile from the corner of his eye, he admitted to himself that he was at least half in love with her. Their partnership and mutual dedication to this mission was bringing them closer together than many wedded couples.

He was tempted to pull the cart over, pull the lap robe from the basket, and take her to some private place where they could become closer yet. Just thinking about that made his pulse quicken. But his damnable intuition insisted that it was not yet the right time. They were both still developing as mages, and he suspected that they would need their full abilities before their quest was completed.

He must hope that he didn't expire of frustration first.

LONDON WAS TWENTY YEARS BUSIER, noisier, and smellier. Perhaps it was a coincidence of the route, but Jean saw more blacks than on any past visit. Many were obviously poor, looking to gain a few coins by holding horses or sweeping the streets clean for more prosperous citizens. She wondered if she was seeing refugees from American slavery who had fled after the war, like Adia and her family. Adia had said that London had thousands of black residents in her time.

She and Nikolai found a clean, modest inn not far from where they had stayed before. They deliberately chose a different inn this time since it was not impossible that they might be recognized even twenty years later. But they chose to go to the same coffeehouse and bookseller as before, since the establishments were convenient and the likelihood of being recognized almost nonexistent.

Smythe's, the bookshop, was quiet when Jean entered. She looked around with pleasure, enjoying the scents of paper and fresh ink and the brimming bookshelves. On tables at the front, new titles were stacked enticingly.

A middle-aged man approached her. She vaguely remembered him as a Smythe, the son of the old proprietor. Probably he now ran the business. "Good day, madam," he said. "Are you looking for a particular title, or do you prefer to browse?"

Jean asked the same question she'd asked twenty years before. "Do you have books about slavery and abolition? Perhaps accounts by former slaves?"

Smythe beamed. "We have as fine a selection of such titles as any bookseller in London. In fact, I've set up a display." He led her to one of the front tables, where several dozen books were stacked. "Ignatius Sancho's *Letters* are extremely popular. The author was born on a slave ship in the mid-Atlantic as his parents were being transported to the Americas. Later he came to England. His story is most compelling."

He placed a copy in Jean's hands. "If you haven't a

copy already, you might also enjoy Phillis Wheatley's *Poems on Various Subjects, Religious and Moral.* The book has been out for a dozen years, but it remains very popular. She is an American slave who showed such quickness that her mistress had her educated. She has even visited London and was much acclaimed for her intelligence and sensibility."

Jean looked at the poems, then added the book to Sancho's *Letters.* "I was looking for exactly such books. What else do you have?"

"I have tracts by the American Anthony Benezet as well as the work of our own Granville Sharp and the reverends John Wesley and James Ramsay." He spoke like a man who had read the books in question, and agreed with the contents.

Jean looked at each book Smythe produced, then added it to her pile, trying to conceal her excitement. Twenty years earlier, there had been almost no publications about slavery or abolition. There had been an explosion of interest in the subject since then.

As Jean was paying for her purchases, Mr. Smythe said, "Do check back with us soon, madam. Any day now, we will be receiving a new book written by a female former slave. The printer said that it's very powerful. He has received more advance subscriptions for the title than for anything else he has ever published."

A half-grown girl emerged from the back carrying a basket of books. "Papa, you said to bring these up as soon as they arrived."

"Just in time!" Smythe exclaimed. "Here is the volume

I was speaking of, madam. *My journey to Faith and Freedom* by An African Princess." He opened one of the copies and began reading it himself.

Jean opened the book and saw that it had been published by James Phillips, the Quaker printer whom she'd learned about from Adia's notes. She flipped to the first page and stiffened with shock. "I'll take this one, too."

Because of the number of books she'd bought, Mr. Smythe himself carried her purchases in a basket to her inn. She thanked him, then raced upstairs. She couldn't wait to tell Nikolai what she'd discovered.

NIKOLAI FOUND the coffeehouse talk exceptionally interesting, so it was late afternoon when he returned to the inn. He went straight to Jean's adjoining room. When he entered, he found her reading by the window.

As she glanced up, he said exuberantly, "Jean, the world has changed greatly in twenty years. Men were discussing the slave trade when I came in, and almost everyone present was against it. There was a slave ship officer who tried to say that the trade was kindly and essential, and whenever he spoke, he was heckled down. The subject is now one that average men feel passionately about."

"I found the same thing at the bookseller's." Jean gestured to the stacked volumes on the table beside her. "There were a number of books and pamphlets written against the slave trade, and several accounts written by former slaves. Including this one written by An African Princess." She handed him the volume she was reading. "Look."

He glanced at the engraving of a handsome African woman in the front. "Good God, it's Adia! Why didn't she mention that she'd written a book?" A thought struck him. "Could she have lied and told us another woman's story? She might have read this book and used the information to deceive us. But why?"

"I think Adia did write this, but not in her early years in London before she left her own time and came to us," Jean said slowly. "She must have written the book on Santola after we left. But if so, why was it only published now?"

"Perhaps it took her thirty years to write. Or it took that long to find a publisher." Nikolai frowned. "Or perhaps she held it back so it could be published now, when public support for abolition is growing."

"So she is living in London right now but probably she doesn't know about her book because in her personal time, she hasn't written it yet. I'm sure she would have told us if she had written it before she came back in time." Jean made a face. "Whenever I think about traveling through time, I feel a headache coming on."

"Better not to think of it," he advised as he paged through the book.

"From what the bookseller said, her story will sell very well. I'm sure her family will welcome the money." Jean sighed. "No doubt Adia made arrangements for them to benefit even if she herself can never return to them."

Nikolai gave her a quick glance, hearing her own wistful hopes. "Perhaps the ancestors will help her to return, for she is serving them well." He glanced down at the book. "I see that she has changed some of the names, but the events are very detailed and convincing."

"And some are horrific," Jean said softly.

He reached the description of Adia's rape when she was little more than a child. There were few details, but emotion raged under the words. "Someday slavery will end." He closed the book, his expression grim. "And you and I and Adia will have done our share in ending it."

CHAPTER THIRTY

KOFI HAD SCARCELY CHANGED at all in twenty years, apart from a few white hairs mixed with the black. He accepted the appearance of Nikolai and Jean calmly. "I had wondered if I would see you again. I see the time magic still works."

"Yes, and we still need help," Nikolai said ruefully. "We have accomplished our mission, and it's time to unleash the next spell. Can you aid us again?"

The older man nodded. "My daughter has grown into a powerful priestess. Together, we should be enough when joined with your power. Are you ready now?" They had brought their small packs of possessions and wore their nondescript traveling clothes just in case. It took only a few minutes to arrange for the ritual. Kofi's daughter Mary was a slim girl with skin the color of caramel. Like her father, she glowed with power. She already knew their mission, so explanations were unneeded.

The circle was sealed, Nikolai and Jean held the bead between their palms, the energy was called—and once more they were pulled through time.

Perhaps the process was a little easier. But not much.

THEY LANDED IN A GRAY-SKIED GALE. Nikolai gasped as a blast of wind tore at his hat. He captured it with one hand while maintaining his grip on Jean with the other.

"Now, this is jolly," she said breathlessly. "Do you have any idea where we are?"

He glanced up at wet warehouses. "I smell the sea, so this can't be London." He stretched out his perception to learn more about the location. "There is a poisonous feel to this place—as if the devil and his demons are holding a party. Do you feel it?"

Jean's expression went blank as she turned to inner sight. "This place was built on blood and suffering."

"It was." He took her arm and they began to walk toward the water. "My guess is that we're in one of the west-coast slave ports—Bristol or Liverpool. Probably Liverpool, since it seems more northerly."

Their street ended at the waterfront. A fresh blast of wind might have knocked Jean over if Nikolai hadn't been holding her. She clutched at her cloak with her free arm. "More than any other city, Liverpool's wealth is built on the slave trade."

"I wonder what our mission is. It sounds as if there is

much to be done here." He turned right and they began walking along the waterfront, Jean tucked under his arm. The few others out in the storm were scudding quickly along the streets, heading for warmth and shelter. None of them looked liked they needed the help of time travelers.

"Good Lord. Could that be Thomas Clarkson?" Jean pointed to a tall, lanky figure who was heading out onto a pier. He must have wanted to watch the storm, since there was no work being done. "He might recognize us, so I suppose we shouldn't approach him. Unless he's in danger of being blown off the pier."

"Do either of us have any magic that could help in such a case? It would be difficult to fish him out of such rough water," Nikolai observed. He tried to sound unconcerned, but the pervasive dark energy was too intense to ignore. "To me, this city feels like it contains the evil spirits of Africa come to steal men's souls."

"Given Liverpool's history with the slave trade, perhaps their souls have already been taken."

He nodded, feeling so suffocated by the negative energy that he didn't want to talk. As they studied the scene, a group of eight or nine men emerged from a shabby tavern, fighting the wind as they stepped onto the waterfront. One of the group pointed out the lone man on the pier and spoke to his companions. It was impossible to hear the words over the wind, but the group turned purposefully onto the pier. They were halfway out when the man at the end turned and saw them approaching.

"It's Clarkson, all right," Jean said tensely. "And I think he's going to need help."

Nikolai quickened his step as one of the group began yelling at Clarkson. Though the gale winds made it impossible to hear the words, clearly Clarkson was being threatened. In his black clerical clothes, he looked like a scarecrow being attacked by a mob. Two of the men grabbed Clarkson and began dragging him toward the edge of the pier despite his struggles.

"Dear God!" Jean gasped. "He probably can't swim, and even if he does, these waves might be impossible!" Nikolai broke into a run. All around him he could feel the spirit of evil pulsing with rage and hunger for destruction, and the pressure attacked his breathing. Grimly he kept running. Clarkson managed to fight free and almost broke through the sailors, but he was dragged down again. His attackers began kicking as they shouted insults. "Meddlin' bastard! Teach 'im to mind 'is own business!"

Protecting his head, Clarkson managed to roll away from the kicks and stagger to his feet, but he was too badly outnumbered to have a chance. He was being dragged toward the water again when Nikolai exploded into the group.

This time he felt no restraint in his attack, using fists and feet and magic to knock out Clarkson's attackers. From the corner of his eye, he saw Jean arrive. Her image was blurred by some kind of magical shield, and he could feel his gaze sliding away. If not for his own magic, he would never have seen her latch onto Clarkson and haul him to his feet, then guide him away, taking half his weight on her own slim shoulders.

The sailors were fighting back, but their alcohol-fueled rage was no match for Nikolai. He had knocked the last down and was ready to drag the leader to the edge of the pier when a voice in his head cried, "No!" He hesitated as cool clarity rushed through him, countering his hot rage. He had been caught up in the spirit of destruction, he realized. His goals might be different from those of the bullies who had attacked Clarkson, but the rage for destruction had been the same.

He clenched his fists and turned away, shaking. The voice of his ancestors, which sounded just like his grandmother, had pulled him back from the brink. He invoked light to push the dark spirit away as he caught up with Jean and Clarkson. He wrapped an arm around the deacon, taking most of the young man's weight as they left the pier.

"There's a tavern on that side street," Jean said. "He needs time to recover."

Nikolai nodded and headed in that direction. Clarkson was walking better now, though his pace was still uneven. "I must thank you, sir," he said a little unsteadily. He blinked owlishly at Nikolai, then turned to Jean. "Why, it's Mr. and Mrs. Gregory, I believe! Are you my guardian angels?"

Jean laughed. "No, only abolitionists who happened to show up at the right time." They had reached the tavern, and she opened the door for the two men. The place was shabby but clean, and the few other patrons were quiet and orderly.

After they hung their dripping cloaks on pegs, Nikolai guided Clarkson to a booth while Jean ordered steaming tankards of punch made from hot water, lemon, sugar, and whiskey. As soon as the drinks were delivered, Nikolai took a deep swallow, grateful for the warmth. Next to him, Jean said, "We've been mostly away from England since we met you, Mr. Clarkson. What have you done to inspire such fury?"

Clarkson sipped his tankard more slowly, his long fingers clasped around the heated pewter. "I knew I had angered many people here in Liverpool, but I didn't expect anyone to try to murder me," he said unsteadily.

"I think their assault was the impulse of drunkenness," Jean said. "Though the results would have been no less fatal."

"One of the men who attacked me is a slave ship officer. I tried to have him charged with murder because he killed a sailor on his ship." Clarkson's mouth curved up without humor. "Drunk or sober, he'd gladly dance on my grave. This is a city that has grown fat on the misery of slaves."

"I heard that the two men who owned the slave ship *Zong,* where the captain massacred so many slaves, were both former mayors of Liverpool," Jean said.

"You heard true." Clarkson's intense blue eyes were grim. "And it is not only slaves who suffer. I have been studying the ship's manifests at the Custom House, and the results are shocking. On slave voyages, as many

British sailors die as slaves. The officers don't care—dead sailors need no wages. Yet it is hard to persuade sailors to bear witness against the captains because they fear for their jobs. The trade is very nearly as destructive to them as to their unhappy victims."

"You should not be venturing out in the streets without protection," Nikolai said. "A pistol, a guard, or both."

"Often my friend Falconbridge accompanies me, and he's a stout fellow, but today he was otherwise engaged. He's writing a book on his experiences as physician on several slave voyages." Clarkson sighed, looking more like a man in his thirties than his twenties. "I do not wish to live like a frightened rabbit, constantly in fear."

"No one does," Jean said softly. "But your life is precious, Mr. Clarkson. If you die at the hands of ignorant men, it will set the cause back by years. Perhaps decades."

"I shall bear that in mind." He smiled a little. "The abolition committee wishes me to return to London. Perhaps, on the way, I shall visit Manchester. I have heard that new ideas are welcome there."

"Have you considered starting a petition in support of abolition?" Jean suggested. "If Parliament sees the signatures of thousands of abolitionists, they will realize that we are a force to be reckoned with."

"The abolition committee has discussed the possibility of petitions. Perhaps Manchester would be the place to begin." His eyes brightened. "In the two years since I first met you, so much has happened! I translated my essay, and James Phillips published it. I thank you for sending me to him—his suggestions were as helpful as his printing press. The book has done very well. A slow discontent with slavery had been building for years, and suddenly abolition leaped into flames. My essay helped strike the sparks."

"You mentioned an abolition committee," Nikolai said. "Is that new?"

Clarkson nodded. "Earlier this year, a dozen of us met at Phillips's print shop and formed an abolition committee. Nine were Quakers, three of us Anglicans." He smiled affectionately. "One cannot ask for better allies than Quakers. They live and work for their beliefs."

"How do you hope to achieve your goals?" Jean asked.

"Through the law, of course. We must persuade Parliament to declare the slave trade illegal." He leaned forward, his enthusiasm radiating from him. "I met a most remarkable man, William Wilberforce. He's only a year older than I, and already a Member of Parliament. He is a devout Evangelical who believes abolition is a moral crusade. There is much work to be done, but with men like Wilberforce in Parliament, surely one day we will succeed."

He accepted a refill of his punch, then began to speak of what he had learned in his research and interviews with those in the slave trade. Nikolai could understand why the ancestors' magic had brought them to Clarkson twice. The man was a powerful and passionate advocate for his cause.

When the storm abated, Nikolai and Jean escorted

Clarkson back to his lodgings. Then they went in search of a respectable inn for themselves. "I'm ready for a nap," Jean said as she covered a yawn. "Traveling through time and saving lives is tiring."

So was feeling the relentless dark energy that had engulfed Nikolai since their arrival in Liverpool. A nap might help. But he doubted it.

"THIS IS INTERESTING." Jean looked up from the local newspaper she'd bought when they booked rooms at a nearby inn. They had dined well in the private parlor, and now she and Nikolai were reading before retiring for bed. They'd come forward a bit more than two years—no need for new garments this time.

"This whole strange land of yours is interesting." Nikolai glanced up from Adia's book, the only one they'd brought with them. "What has caught your attention?"

"A by-election was just held to replace a Member of Parliament who died. The custom in this area is to provide ale to the voters to engage their loyalty. This time someone decided to save money because he thought the results of the election were a foregone conclusion. So a different fellow opened up a few hogsheads of ale and won."

Nikolai grimaced. "This great English democracy is fueled by ale and bribery?"

"Sadly, yes." She glanced back at the newspaper. "But what caught my attention is that the newly elected MP is called Captain James Trent. That's the name of the master of the slave ship that carried Adia to the Indies. He was also the slave catcher who almost captured her in New York when the American war ended."

"I wonder if it's the same James Trent? The name doesn't sound uncommon."

"This Trent is from a prominent family that owns one of the largest shipping lines in Liverpool, and they specialize in slave trading. If he's the same man, that would explain why he captained a slave ship at such a young age." She closed the paper and handed it to Nikolai. "Tomorrow Trent is sponsoring an ale fest for his supporters to celebrate his victory."

"Perhaps we should attend," he said thoughtfully. "The event might not be on the schedule of the ancestors, but it could be educational."

She nodded, wondering if the men who voted for Trent supported slavery, or if they were just grateful for the ale. She wasn't sure which answer she liked less.

By the time Nikolai and Jean reached the market square that was the site of Captain Trent's victory celebration, the crowd was mellow with drink. Nikolai kept Jean well back from the speaking platform that had been erected. He didn't expect the crowd to turn ugly, but drunks were unpredictable. If necessary, the two of them could make a rapid escape down an alley.

A brass band that made up in noise what it lacked in

tunefulness played a fanfare while a well-dressed gentleman climbed onto the platform to introduce the new MP. The lengthy discourse on the captain's experiences in the slave trade and the Americas certainly fit Adia's James Trent.

The crowd applauded as the new MP moved forward to speak. Trent was a sleek, heavyset man, expensively dressed and reeking with self-satisfaction. Evil in its most respectable form.

Nikolai's attention sharpened when he saw a lean African a few steps behind Trent. He had ebony skin, military bearing, and a sharp gaze that roamed over the market square. Beside him, Jean gasped, "The African is a mage! Look at his energy field."

Nikolai adjusted his vision, and suddenly the African flared with dark pulses that mirrored the city's dark light. Did the mage create that energy, or feed from it?

"Adia mentioned that Trent always had a dangerous-looking African with him, a man named Kondo. He beat other slaves and helped in the slave catching. This could well be Kondo. Since he's a mage, I wonder if he helped in Trent's victory?"

"Very likely. After all, he was willing to brutalize his own people in return for special privileges." Nikolai had known such men. They were particularly hated by the slaves they terrorized. He probed at the African, wanting to learn more. Kondo was from East Africa, it appeared, and Trent had taken him into his crew even before the slave ship had reached the Indies. Trent had recognized a kindred evil spirit, perhaps.

He probed deeper, trying to get a sense of the man's nature—then staggered back under a shattering blast of power. He would have fallen if Jean hadn't grabbed his arm.

"What's wrong?" she gasped.

"Not... sure." It was difficult to form words. He felt that he was suffocating in foul-smelling black tar.

She pulled him into the alley and pressed him against a brick wall. Just around the corner, hoarse voices were shouting approval of the new Member of Parliament, but in the alley there was privacy and calm. The dark energy began to leech away, leaving him weak and shaken. "Are you doing something?" he managed to say.

"Shielding you. Protection and shielding are what I do best. It saved us after Culloden." She spread her right hand across the center of his chest with firm pressure. The darkness retreated farther.

He managed to say, "You have become more adept at using your magic."

She smiled wryly. "I've always been good in times of disaster, and you, Master Gregorio, are currently a disaster. Are you strong enough to walk?"

He collected himself and tried to step away from the supportive wall. His heart hammered like drums, and he almost fell again. Jean pushed him back against the bricks. He drew a long, ragged breath. "Apparently not."

"Whatever struck you drained away most of your energy, and it will take time for that to return. I wonder..." Her arms went around his chest and she tilted her face up into a searing kiss. It had been—thirty years?

—since they had kissed like this, and he tumbled headlong into the passion they had so carefully banked. Her slim body was pressed full length into his, and he was profoundly aware of rich femaleness hidden beneath corsets and petticoats.

"Jean..." He breathed, his hands running down her back to cup her beautifully rounded backside. "Why have we been waiting?"

Flushed and laughing, she pulled from his embrace. "We can discuss this later. If you're recovered, let us return to our inn."

Most of his strength had returned, he realized. He felt as if he'd just arisen from a fever bed—tired but whole again. "I want to look at Trent and Kondo before we leave."

"That would *not* be wise," she said firmly.

He allowed her to take his arm and steer them away from the market square. "What happened in the square? I've never felt anything like that, even during initiation."

"I have a theory. That we can also discuss later." She tucked her arm in his, sending quiet strength as she did. "Liverpool is turning out to be most interesting."

CHAPTER THIRTY-ONE

LUCKILY IT WAS LESS than a mile to their inn. Jean made a swift transaction with their landlord for a bottle of brandy on their way up to their rooms. When they were safely behind locked doors, she gave Nikolai a straight shot of the brandy and mixed a watered drink for herself.

The jolt of the brandy burned away the last of his scrambled wits. "Your theory about what happened?" She curled up in a chair opposite his, turning her glass restlessly between her palms. "Remember Lord Falconer saying that passionately held beliefs can create a kind of spirit that is an expression of people's emotions?" When he nodded, she continued, "That pro-slavery energy hovers over Liverpool like a poisoned cloud. You are particularly aware of it, perhaps because of your experiences with slavery. I feel it also, but not so intensely as you." He cautiously sampled the energy that saturated even this quiet room. "That explains the pervasive negativity, but what about Trent's rally?"

"Kondo is a dark mage, and I think he magnifies the city's darkness. He used it as a weapon against you, though I don't know if he realized he was doing that. He might have just instinctively shoved against your intrusion. Since you both have African magic and that is rare in these parts, you may be vulnerable to each other."

"A charming thought." He frowned. "Adia and her friends created the bead spells to find people to protect the abolition movement. She said that at the beginning the movement was so fragile that the death of a single man could cause failure. Having met Thomas Clarkson, I can see how vital he is to the cause, and no doubt there will be others who are equally vital. But as I feel the voracious evil energy of this city, I wonder if part of our job is to defend against the pro-slavery spirit. Is that possible?"

"Your guess is as good as mine." She sipped her brandy absently. "I wonder if the evil spirit of slavery is what possessed the sailors to attack Mr. Clarkson. They could have easily passed on by. In the middle of a gale, ignoring him makes more sense than trying to murder him. But the circumstances were right to do murder. Perhaps the slave demon was drawn to their anger and resentment, and it triggered the attack."

"Lord Falconer said that such spirits tend to attack those who oppose what the spirit stands for. He also said that the struggle against slavery will take place on many levels." Nikolai reached for the brandy bottle and poured more, feeling the need for fortification. "We can't help with the politics, nor in raising public awareness of slavery, so perhaps our chief task is fighting the pro-slavery spirit." He closed his eyes, feeling the corrosive energy gnawing at his soul. "I don't know if I am strong enough."

Jean leaned forward and covered his hand with hers. "We were sent together because we have complementary abilities. You are sensitive to African magic, including this wicked spirit, but that also means you are specially gifted in fighting them."

He opened his eyes, wondering how he had ever thought her fragile. "What is your part of our task?"

"I'm the expert on Britain and how it operates," she said promptly. "Plus, it's my job to keep you in working condition since you are more central to this task than I."

"Is that why you kissed me? Part of your maintenance program?"

"Of course," she said primly. "Why else would I want to?"

He laughed, his dark mood lifting a little. "After we've seen a bit more of Liverpool, I'd like to visit Manchester and see if the energy really is different there."

"That's a good idea. The more we know, the better." And the more they knew, the more difficult their task seemed. Fighting drunken sailors was straightforward. But how did one fight demons of greed and violence? "We need a name for this force that supports slavery," he mused.

"Can't we just call it the Slave Demon?"

He thought a moment, then shrugged. "Very well, the Slave Demon he is. The Demon for short."

"From now on, we will fight for the safety of key abolitionists, and against the evil of the Demon." Jean sighed. "It's easier to fight drunken sailors than wicked spirits." He caught her hand and kissed it. "And perhaps someday there will be time for just us. Thank you for saving me today, Jean."

She blushed and her hand curled into his. "Any time, my captain. Any time."

MANCHESTER WAS INDEED VERY different from Liverpool. It was a city of hope and new ideas and hard-working people who expected to do well by the labor of their hands. Though there was no strong pro-abolitionist sentiment visible, Nikolai and Jean agreed that Manchester would be fertile ground for the abolitionists.

After several days exploring the city, Jean suggested, "It's time to activate the next spell. Shall we see if we can do it on our own? The energy in Manchester is strong and positive, and it might help us move forward without having to go to London to find Kofi and his daughter."

He nodded. "Let us gather our possessions and find a quiet place to try."

They found their quiet spot outside the city, in a copse off a small road. "Why here?" Nikolai asked.

"There is a ley line—an energy line in the earth," she said when they reached the quiet clearing. "Can you feel it?"

He concentrated. "Yes, but not well. I wonder if Guardians are more in tune with the energy?"

She skimmed her palm a yard above the earth, feeling

a strong buzz from the ley line. "Perhaps. We really need to write about the differences we're finding between Guardian and African abilities. My sister-in-law, Gwynne, is a scholar of Guardian lore, and she would love to know." She stopped short, overwhelmed by feelings of loss. "That is, she would be interested if Gwynne still lives and there was a way to get the information to her."

"Let us write up our experiences anyhow." He settled his travel bag over his shoulder. "We can't know about your sister-in-law, but we can leave the information at Falconer House and know it will reach the right hands." His words steadied her. No one lived forever, but the Guardians had existed for time beyond measure. Even if their information didn't reach Gwynne, every generation produced keepers of the lore. Knowledge endured, not like frail humans. "Are you ready?" She positioned the next spell bead in the middle of her palm and clasped Nikolai's hand.

They took turns speaking the ritual, and she could feel the energy rising around them. Personal power, nature energy, the positive energy of the nearby city. The vortex formed and swirled around, but it was not strong enough. "We're so close!" Jean exclaimed. "Just a little more energy and we would be able to trigger the spell!" Nikolai's dark face was tight with strain. Then he suddenly laughed. Still holding her hands, he said, "We have another method of raising energy."

He bent to kiss her, and sexual energy exploded between them. She gasped, dizzy, exhilarated, spinning through time and space...

THEY LANDED IN A CHURCHYARD, so closely wrapped that she was barely aware that they had moved through time until Nikolai pulled away from her, slowly. His mouth quirked. "We have found the secret of raising our energy enough to travel through time by our own efforts." Every part of her body was pulsing with the most personal and primitive of energies. "It was smoother and less unpleasant than the other times, at least for me," she said, trying to sound calm rather than burning with lust.

"It was better for me, too," he murmured, his eyes dark with promise. "I think the right time for us to come together is near."

He turned his attention to the churchyard. Ragged tufts of grass grew around tombstones and a chestnut tree shaded one corner. The church was on a hill, and from their vantage point they could see streets and buildings spreading into the distance. "Where are we now? London, I think?"

She scanned the horizon. "I believe so. I wonder when."

Nikolai closed his eyes. "Not too much further into the future, I think, though I'm not sure why. I might be developing an ability to judge time similar to my ability to judge location." He offered his arm. "We have become experts in arriving in new eras. Let us find an inn." She took his arm and they left the churchyard through the lych-gate, finding themselves on a busy street. It wasn't long until they came on a respectable inn. The few people they saw on the streets wore clothing that seemed identical to what they had seen in their last time.

There was only one room available, not a pair of adjoining chambers. Jean eyed Nikolai warily, but nodded acceptance. Whatever might happen between them would happen even if they had separate rooms.

The innkeeper had a newspaper that had been left in the taproom, so she took it with them. As soon as they were in private, she glanced at the front page. "It's April 1788, so we came forward only about six months. And we've moved past Adia's knowledge."

She plopped into a chair and swiftly skimmed the pages, with occasional glances up to admire Nikolai as he prowled around, settling into the room. He moved like a graceful wild creature, and she never tired of watching him.

He caught her looking at him, so she said, "There are several articles relating to slavery and abolition. This piece says that a lady spoke to a debating society on the immorality of slavery, and was most effective in her words. Naturally, no name is given, but the article says it may be the first time a woman has ever addressed a debating society. Are you familiar with the societies?"

He slung his bag over one of the bed's foot posts, then hung his hat on the top knob. "Not really, though you've mentioned them a time or two."

"They are public lectures and discussions on topics that are likely to interest enough people to make a profit for the organizers. Entrance costs only sixpence or so, and people from all levels of society attend," she explained. "Twenty years ago, I saw no debates advertised about slavery. Now half the debates listed are about slavery and abolition. The one where the lady spoke voted on the subject at the end and carried almost unanimously against slavery. Public opinion has come alive and is on our side."

"Interesting, indeed," he agreed. "In our time, few people thought about abolition because they assumed it was impossible. They are no longer assuming that." Before he could continue, he was interrupted by a knock on the door. He opened it to find one of the inn's maids. "This note just arrived for you and your wife, sir." She handed over the message, bobbed a curtsy, and left.

Nikolai broke the seal and read, his eyebrows arching. "We have been invited to a reception at the home of William Wilberforce, MP. The purpose is to honor those who support abolition."

Jean's jaw dropped. "How do the ancestors do that? How did they manage an invitation and know where to send it? We didn't know we'd be here until half an hour ago! How did they get us an invitation?"

"Better not to think of it and get another headache," he advised. "That's what I've decided. But if I had to guess, I'd say the ancestors are weaving a great tapestry whose subject is abolition. The threads are interwoven, so events connect. Wilberforce is obviously a force for abolition, and so are we. As soon as we arrived here, we became part of the pattern, and that connected us to the abolition movement."

"I'm not sure that makes sense, but it sounds good." She flipped the newspaper to another page. "When is the reception?"

He glanced at the invitation again. "Tonight."

"Good God!" She shot out of the chair, horrified. "We need to find suitable clothing!"

Nikolai frowned. "Is that possible? There is no time for proper tailoring."

"In London, all things are possible. I'm sure the innkeeper here can refer me to a shop that deals in quality used clothing and can do tailoring in a few hours." And so it proved. The rest of the morning was spent finding the shops recommended by the innkeeper, choosing garments that were proper for the occasion and a reasonable fit, then waiting while quick alterations were made. Jean found that clothing silhouettes were narrower for both men and women than in her own time. Assuming that the 1750s could still be considered her time.

Jean found an attractive gown whose fine cotton fabric had narrow stripes of white and two shades of green. The costume suited her without being dramatic enough to call attention. She also bought powder for her hair. Though she disliked powdering, covering up her red locks removed her most identifiable characteristic.

Nikolai was impossible to disguise. Women would notice him immediately in his handsome dark blue frock coat, and men would react to his aura of masculine power. "You look splendid," she said. "I hope no one challenges you to a duel."

He looked startled. "Why would anyone do that?"

"Husbands will resent their wives hovering around you," she explained.

He laughed. "I doubt that. But I do wonder why the ancestors want us to attend this event. Maybe Clarkson will be there and in trouble."

She fluttered the Chinese silk fan she'd bought to go with the gown, glad she hadn't lost the knack. "More likely he'll be off in the provinces stirring up abolitionist trouble, and more power to him."

Nikolai offered his arm and they headed down to the light carriage they'd hired. The reception was being held in Wilberforce's home in Clapham, a village three miles south of London, so it seemed best to arrange their own transportation.

They arrived to find a jam of carriages and a crowd of energetic people. As they walked from their carriage to the spacious house, Nikolai said under his breath, "This area radiates light and positive energy."

"The newspaper mentioned that a number of Evangelicals live here, all of them working to improve society." Jean thought back to Adia's notes, which had two pages of information on Wilberforce. "Mr. Wilberforce shares his home with a cousin, Henry Thornton, who is also an active Evangelical reformer. So many good people in the area must drive off the Demon's darkness." Nikolai's expression grew vague as he studied the energies around them. "I can feel the darkness just outside this beacon of light. It's like a wolf prowling around a fire, hoping that some weak or foolish person will wander close enough to become prey."

"A charming thought." She clutched his arm more tightly as they climbed the entry steps. "Let us hope the wolves keep their distance tonight."

"You may wish for that," he said, a wicked gleam in his eyes. "I prefer to hope for excitement and progress."

CHAPTER THIRTY-TWO

JEAN AND NIKOLAI entered the house and found themselves in a short receiving line. At the head was a small, pale young man not much taller than Jean. Even his side-whiskers couldn't make him look worldly.

To her surprise, the young man smiled and said, "I'm William Wilberforce. It's a pleasure to welcome our movement's strongest supporters to my home."

Nikolai introduced Jean and himself, and they chatted a moment with their host. Wilberforce might look unimpressive, but he had a remarkable voice and a warm charm that made him seem six inches taller.

As Nikolai continued talking to their host, Jean moved on, exchanging greetings with Henry Thornton, cohost and cousin to Wilberforce. She met several more abolitionists before a familiar voice said, "Mrs. Gregory, I believe?"

Jean looked up into Lord Falconer's amused eyes. He must have been past seventy, she guessed, thinner and with his hair all silver, though he still looked capable of besting a man half his age. It was strange to see him and realize that the man who had been like an older brother now looked more like her grandfather. But he was still her friend, and blessedly alive and well.

She caught his hand in hers. "Lord Falconer, I didn't expect to see you here." Though her words were neutral, she couldn't hide the pleasure in her voice.

"I am now considered the leading voice of abolition in the House of Lords," Simon explained. "Some days it seems like I'm the only voice. My lordly colleagues do not believe that all men are their equals and therefore should be free, but they sometimes respond to a plea for pity." She wanted to ask about Meg, but didn't dare. What if she had died? Perhaps seeing that in her expression, Simon said, "Lady Falconer is somewhere in the crush. I'm sure she'll be delighted to see you."

Jean smiled gratefully and moved on as Simon and Nikolai shook hands. Most of the crowd was gathered in the grand, high-ceilinged library, sipping wine and talking enthusiastically. Though she didn't see Thomas Clarkson —even in such a crowd his great height would have stood out—it wasn't long before Meg found her.

Like her husband, Lady Falconer showed her age in her snowy white hair and a hint of fragility, but her hug was vigorous. "Jean!" She stepped back and surveyed her friend before saying under her breath, "Did I ever look so young?"

"Younger. You seemed about fifteen when I first met you." Jean surveyed her old friend, who was elegantly dressed and radiated dignity. Though she showed her years, she was no less lovely than when she was a girl. She reminded Jean of Lady Bethany Fox, who had been old and wise and wonderful when Jean was newly arrived in London. "You seem to have come to terms with being a countess."

"I've learned to be quite a good countess in public. Anything is possible with the right man." Her gaze drifted to her husband, who was still greeting guests. "Speaking of which, what about that gentleman of yours?"

"I'm not sure he's the right man and he's probably not a gentleman, but my life has certainly become more interesting since we met!" Jean glanced across the room to where Nikolai was talking with a well-dressed African. "Do you know who Nikolai is speaking with?"

"That's Gustavus Vasa, a former American slave who earned enough to buy his freedom and lives in England now. He's well-known for his writing and speaking on abolition." Meg's smile turned cynical. "Even the most fervent abolitionist usually supports blacks from a distance. Only a man as eloquent and charming as Vasa will be found in a drawing room."

"Distant charity is better than none at all," Jean observed. "But Gustavus Vasa? Wasn't he a Swedish king?"

"Mr. Vasa's first owner thought it amusing to call a slave boy by a grand royal name," Meg explained. "Now Mr. Vasa is writing a book of his experiences, and Simon is encouraging him to publish it under his African name."

"He sounds most interesting." Hoping she would have a chance to speak with him, Jean surveyed the crowded room. "I thought I saw another African when I came in."

"That would probably be Quobna Cuguano, another African writer and lecturer who is accepted in respectable drawing rooms." Meg sighed. "Perhaps someday one might attend a reception of whites and blacks and Red Indians and Chinese and no one will notice complexion, but we are a long way from that."

Thinking of Santola, Jean said, "I know a place where people of all colors live in harmony, so it's possible. But it will not happen in Britain any time soon."

"I will settle for an end of the slave trade. Freedom first. Equality will come eventually." Meg's gaze moved past Jean. "There is someone I must see. You and I will speak again before the reception ends."

The countess moved away, leaving Jean to quietly study the crowd, using mage vision as well as her eyes. Some guests were very fashionable like the Falconers, and others were soberly dressed Evangelicals, but their mutual desire to end the slave trade was genuine. Many had dedicated great amounts of time and money to the cause.

Yet the Demon was not far away. As Nikolai said, it was possible to feel that negative energy outside this beacon of goodwill. Slave supporters might act from selfish motives, but they were as passionate as the abolitionists. Even here, in William Wilberforce's drawing room, the spirit of slavery was near.

Uncannily near. She glanced around uneasily,

wondering if the West Indian lobby had sent a spy and she was sensing that energy.

Her speculations ended when Wilberforce climbed onto a portable podium that had been set up only a few steps from where she stood. Even with the extra height he was barely above crowd level, but when he began to speak, he commanded the attention of everyone in the spacious chamber. "My friends, it is good to welcome you here today as we celebrate the great gains we have made toward ending the slave trade."

The room erupted in applause. Wilberforce waited patiently, a slight smile on his face. Jean saw Nikolai quietly working his way through the crowd toward her. He reached her side as Wilberforce began speaking again.

"I thought you would be interested in our strategy for the parliamentary session that is about to begin," Wilberforce said. "Hearings are being held that provide massive, irrefutable evidence of the wickedness of the trade. I intend to present this evidence to the full house. My colleagues may choose to look the other way, but they will never again be able to say that they do not know!"

There was another burst of applause. Wilberforce continued, "Legislation has been drafted for a law that will render the trade illegal. Great rolls of petitions supporting abolition are being delivered to Parliament from every corner of Britain—more petitions than have ever been received on any other topic. Support increases every day!" More applause. Wilberforce knew how to raise a crowd's enthusiasm. Under cover of the noise,

Nikolai murmured to Jean, "Falconer says that even if the law passes the House of Commons, it will never pass the House of Lords. Too many of the lords derive wealth from slavery, and few have real sympathy or understanding for the less fortunate."

Jean nodded ruefully, knowing that was all true. "At least Wilberforce will be introducing abolitionist legislation into Parliament. That is huge progress. It will probably have to be introduced again and again before there is a chance of success."

Wilberforce resumed speaking, this time detailing specific plans and support. His voice was as mesmerizing as ever, but Jean saw that he was sweating and he was holding tightly to the edges of the podium. "I think he is ill," she whispered.

"Dark energy is swirling around him," Nikolai replied softly. "Can you see it?"

She refined her vision, and was startled at the blackness crowding around the MP. As she probed, she realized it had the flavor of the Slave Demon spirit. "How can it penetrate all this positive, supportive energy?" Nikolai's eyes narrowed. "It seems to be coming from the far side of the room—see that dark, wispy trail?" Jean followed the direction of his gaze. It took a moment for her to find the smoky trace of power that ran from Wilberforce to an unknown location on the other side of the crowd. "I see it."

"I'm going to find the source," Nikolai said grimly. He glided away. Jean turned her attention back to the speaker. Rather than attacking his opponents, Wilberforce used his captivating voice to describe goals and dreams. He inspired people to live up to their highest ideals rather than stirring up anger and hatred.

But the mellifluous voice was faltering. In the middle of his next sentence, Wilberforce said unsteadily, "I... I'm sorry, my friends. I am feeling... unwell."

He moved to step down from the podium. Hands reached up to help him, but before Wilberforce could take one, he gave a choked cry and crumpled to the floor. His frail body was so engulfed in dark energy that Jean could barely see the outlines.

Instinctively she darted toward him, wriggling between taller people. She saw that Simon was doing the same, but he was coming from the entrance to the library and he was too large to move through the crowd easily.

Jean used a jab of power to force her way into the inner circle around the fallen MP. He looked on the verge of death. His friends were frightened and concerned, and none knew what to do. Projecting an aura of competence, she dropped to her knees beside Wilberforce.

Undoing his cravat, she placed her hand on his neck. There was no pulse. His heart had stopped. All her senses were extended, and she realized that his spirit was beginning to detach from his body.

Though she was not the healer her mother had been, the work she'd done to strengthen her power came to her aid. She reached for the light that saturated the house and channeled it into Wilberforce's still form, surrounding his heart with life and vitality. *Please God...*

Time seemed to hold still. She was a conduit for a

higher power, and the stricken man under her hands was critical to the greatest cause in human history.

She felt a pulse beat, then another. He was not yet beyond saving. *Please stay,* she begged silently as she continued to send healing energy. *You are needed.*

His heart was beating weakly when Simon knelt on Wilberforce's other side. Simon was a gifted healer, as strong as Jean's mother had been. As soon as he laid a hand on the fallen man's chest, Jean felt the rush of his power.

After long moments, she sensed a shift of energy and knew that Wilberforce's soul had settled back into his body. The MP opened dazed eyes. "So sorry to cause such trouble..." he murmured.

His cousin Henry Thornton pushed through the group, his face pale. "Is he...?"

"I'm well enough." Wilberforce tried to sit up, then fell back onto the carpet, shaking. "I... I think I need to rest."

Several of the Evangelicals moved forward, and Wilberforce was tenderly lifted while Thornton climbed onto the podium. "Mr. Wilberforce is not feeling well, but he is not seriously ill. I shall briefly cover the rest of the material he wished to share with you."

With the relieved crowd's attention on Thornton, Jean rose and said softly, "Thank the Lord you were here, Simon."

"My knees are not fond of such treatment," he said as he got to his feet, grimacing. "If you hadn't been close enough to pull Wilberforce back from the brink, I would not have been in time. He is still very ill—every organ in his body has been weakened. He is not likely to introduce his bill into Parliament this session."

Jean sighed. "I feared that. Do you think this is coincidence? He was engulfed by very negative energy as he collapsed."

Nikolai appeared, his face dark with suppressed anger. "It was no coincidence. Come. I must speak to you both."

Simon nodded, waiting a few moments before he followed Jean and Nikolai. They exited the library and found a small empty room off the corridor. When they were inside and the door safely closed, Nikolai said, "Captain James Trent's African mage Kondo was here, and he was the one who almost killed Wilberforce by using the Demon energy. I tried to capture him, but he managed to escape."

"The Demon?" Simon asked.

"That is what we call the spirit generated by the proslavery forces," Jean explained. "The energy is very powerful and destructive. We think that in Liverpool, it was the trigger that caused slavers to attempt the murder of Thomas Clarkson."

"Good God, Clarkson was almost killed? That would be a disaster equal to the death of Wilberforce." Simon looked troubled. "I know of Trent, of course. He is one of the best-known slavery supporters in Britain, and now that he is in Parliament, he has a powerful platform. You say he has an African mage working for him?"

Nikolai nodded. "I don't know if Kondo is slave or

servant. I'd guess servant, since a mage would not allow himself to stay enslaved. He has been Trent's tool for more than thirty years, according to Adia Adams."

"And he can apparently channel and control the Demon spirit," the earl said. "You're right—antislavery advocates will need more protection. Not just physical guards, but mages who can keep the destructive spirits at bay."

"Perhaps the African priests can help with that," Nikolai suggested. "From what I've learned, African magic has a special connection with such spirits."

"Maybe a protective shield could be created by the African priests, and Guardians could help maintain it. I have an idea how this can be done," Jean said slowly. "But it will be a commitment of years."

"Protection is essential if there is to be any chance of success," Nikolai said. "And I think it is our job to provide this protective shield. The Demon energy is intense because it comes from humankind's basest, most selfish impulses. Greed, anger, and hatred have more raw power than kindness, compassion, and reason. For better qualities to bloom, we must counter the Demon energies."

Simon nodded. "Schedule a meeting between African priests and Guardians willing to support such a shield. Jean is exceptionally gifted at protection, but determining how such a shield will be created and maintained will require all of us. I would like to bring my son and daughter, and Meg will want to participate."

"We will speak to the priests and find a time and

place that will suit." Nikolai glanced at Jean. "You look exhausted. It is time to leave, I think."

His words made her aware of how drained she was. "I've never done such an intense healing before. I'm glad I had enough power to help."

Simon regarded her thoughtfully. "You have much more ability than I realized."

"Adia told me that I have power, but the channels for using it are twisted. I have been doing visualizations to try to straighten them out." Jean smiled wryly. "Also, I do best in emergencies, and there have been plenty of those lately."

His gaze became intense. "You have cured yourself, I think."

She thought of her years of magical frustration, and contrasted them to the way her skill had increased since starting on this journey. She hadn't realized how far she had come. "It would be nice to think the emergencies have some positive use!"

Nikolai put a welcome arm around Jean. "We'll leave now, before the reception ends and all the carriages are summoned at once. Until later, Lord Falconer."

She was so tired that she barely noticed as Nikolai escorted her outside and got her into their carriage. Dusk was approaching as they started back into the city. He scooped Jean up onto his lap, cradling her close. "You did well, little witch."

"Wilberforce lives, but the movement has been delayed."

"What matters most is that he survives." Nikolai

rubbed Jean's back gently. "We knew that changing the world would not be quick or easy."

He was right, of course, but she had never yet met a redhead to whom patience came easily. With a sigh, she burrowed against Nikolai's warm body, feeling safe. Safe, and unbelievably tired..

CHAPTER THIRTY-THREE

JEAN SLEPT in Nikolai's arms for the whole ride back to London. Even when they reached the inn and he carried her up the stairs, she didn't wake. He told himself that Falconer wouldn't have let her leave if she had drained her life force to a dangerous level, but the longer and more heavily she slept, the more concerned he became.

He laid her on the bed, then removed her gown, stays, and petticoats. Even being undressed didn't wake her. It was an effort not to caress her alluring body, but he managed to keep desire under control. When they became lovers, he wanted her to be awake.

With her powdered hair, she looked ghostly pale. He wet a towel and patted her face. No response beyond her slow, shallow breathing. He gave her shoulder a little shake. "Jean, are you all right?"

When she didn't respond, he gently probed her with his mind. She was like a banked fire. Though coals of life glowed, she was deeply unconscious. He frowned.

"Before I call Falconer for help, I'll try to return some energy to you. You started today by giving me yours, so I suppose it's no surprise you're depleted now."

He stretched out beside her on the bed and leaned into a kiss, visualizing a stream of clear, bright energy channeling from some high place. As the light poured through him and into her, her lips moved slightly. He stroked her hair, wondering what fool had come up with the idea of covering beautiful hair with ugly, messy powder.

When she inhaled deeply, he took the opportunity to kiss her throat. Her pale skin put rose petals to shame. She gave a small hum of pleasure.

Encouraged, he asked, "Jean, are you awake?"

Eyes closed, she whispered, "What a nice way to wake up."

"You were so deeply asleep that I was worried," he said, relieved. "I decided to see if I could transfer energy to you."

"I've never been so exhausted in my life, but you did a good job of restoring me." She raised a hand and slid her fingers into his hair, pulling his head down for another kiss. He was happy to oblige.

Desire danced between them, rich and enticing. When he paused for breath, he said warningly, "You realize where this will end if we don't stop now."

"I know." Her eyes opened, the hazel depths blazing lucent gold with deep, ancient wisdom. "The time has come to put away our fears and truly become mates."

"Is it our fears that have kept us apart?" He caught

her hands, wanting to believe that it was time to join as one, but still uncertain. "I thought we were waiting until we'd both developed our powers."

"So we were," she agreed. "But now you have been initiated and have learned to recognize and oppose the Demon spirit of slavery. For me, I have practiced faithfully since Adia identified my problem. Keeping Wilberforce alive brought together all I had learned, and finally I feel that I'm in full control of my magic. The power I channeled to save Wilberforce burned through me, clearing the twisted pathways for good, I think."

He frowned, remembering. "I saw the flare of that from across the room. The power was extraordinary."

"We both needed to fulfill our potentials, but the fear was real, too." She raised her hands to him, mischief in her face. "We each fear having our soul consumed by the other. My fears are perfectly justified, of course, but yours are quite foolish."

He laughed, knowing that she was well if her sense of humor was intact. "You underestimate your power, witchling. Any sensible man would find you alarming." She blinked demurely. "My kin considered me harmless and useful."

"They weren't paying proper attention." He hadn't fully appreciated how long her auburn lashes were. Her hazel-gold eyes were an invitation to riot even without looking at the rest of her. "It pains me to admit it, but you're probably right about the fears. You're a terrifying woman, Jean Macrae. And I wouldn't have it any other way."

Hungrily he reclaimed her mouth, this time kissing with passion, not healing. Lightning seared between them. Her arms wrapped around his waist, and she pulled him down on top of her. Having their bodies pressed together full length was fire to tinder. He untied the ribbon at the neckline of her shift so he could kiss her breast, round and perfect in proportion to her slender frame.

She gasped and arched her back, her fingers clawing at his garments. He was wearing far too much. Panting, he rolled onto his side and yanked at the buttons of his waistcoat. Her fumbling fingers slowed the process, especially when she reached for the buttons of his breeches. He stiffened, paralyzed, before having the sense to swing from the bed and remove all his garments in one frantic rush. Through habit, he faced her as he disrobed, hiding the scars that crisscrossed his back.

Jean was an irresistible antidote to habit. She slid from the bed and moved behind him, her palms caressing the ridges and furrows of his back. He stood rigid, distantly aware of laughter in the taproom below, a wagon clattering by in the street. Remembering why he always avoided exposing his bare body to others.

Her warm lips pressed against his back, her tongue soothing an old scar. "Badges of courage," she said softly. "What would you be if my father had not changed the course of your life for both better and worse?"

He'd never thought to ask himself that. After a few moments of hard thought, he said, "Probably I'd be a Maltese sailor. Not a deckhand. A bo'sun, maybe." He took a deep breath. "And perhaps I would still have ended up a galley slave. It's not an uncommon fate for those who sail the Middle Sea."

Her arms circled his waist and she pressed against him, only the thin chemise separating them. "A peaceful life may be easy, but it's hardship that builds character. Without your difficult past, you would not be the champion of freedom that you have become. You redeemed the lives of many with your courage. Your efforts now may help countless thousands of other slaves. This would not have happened with an easy life."

All true. Nor would he be able to hold this amazing woman in his arms. He turned and embraced her. "So I should thank your father for shattering my life?"

"That would be too much to ask, I think. But you might look on him as part of the tapestry of your fate. If you hadn't met, you would not be the man you are."

"I will start by thanking him for you, my Scottish witch." The night was cold, so he pulled the covers down before scooping her up and laying her on the cool linen sheets. He had done an admirable job of controlling his passions since they had begun this crusade, but no longer. He wanted her, needed her, with every fiber of his being.

And she felt the same. As he covered her with his body, her hips rocked against him, pressing them together with intoxicating intimacy. "Consume my soul if you wish," he breathed as his hands cupped her breasts, his thumbs stroking the nipples to hardness. "I no longer mind."

"Your soul would be too rich a brew for me." She

raised her head and nipped his ear. Heat blazed through him. "But your body—that is a different matter entirely." He pulled her shift upward and slid his hand between her thighs to find moist, heated flesh. She gasped when he touched her, her muscles rippling. For a frantic moment he wondered if he would last long enough to enter her.

Her urgent hand guided him into her taut, welcoming body. As he sheathed himself, she cried out and bucked frantically. He climaxed immediately with an intensity that echoed the time vortex, whirling and splintering his awareness, only this time pain was transmuted to pleasure. Their energies flowed together, melting and being reforged. In the very marrow of his bones, he knew that they had changed each other forever. It was what he had feared since they met—and yet now that change was perfect, inevitable, and *right.*

He almost blacked out, returning gradually to the awareness that she was panting in his arms, her body still clasping his. "That was... quite extraordinary," he managed.

"We have been denying the attraction since we met, so desire has built up like the pressure in the steam engines Simon builds." She laughed a little. "Engines are very dangerous when they explode. And so is passion."

They would not have been able to join so easily if she had been a virgin, so her Scottish sweetheart had been her lover in all ways. Nikolai was not surprised—where Jean loved, she would give herself completely. As he rolled to one side and pulled her close, he said, "I did not think to control myself to avoid the risk of a child." She covered a yawn. "I have some ability to control quickening. A Guardian woman with healing ability seldom has babies when she doesn't want them."

He blinked. "How amazingly useful."

"It certainly was during the Rising, when we were caught up in long marches and ambushes and ragged retreats." There was a long silence. "Later I wished that I had borne Robbie's child. As we followed the prince into England, I was too young to truly believe that Robbie could die. I assumed there would be time for a family-"

He kissed her forehead since he had no words that could assuage such a loss. "You said before that it was time to come together. Now that we have, I feel that we have been transformed in ways I can't describe."

"I feel that, too," she said quietly. "I believe we have been tempered into a stronger weapon for our cause." He tested the concept, and found that he agreed. "We really did need to reach a certain place in our magical growth before we could be bonded in this way, so I suppose the frustration was necessary."

She grinned. "It's rather like cooking. Soak the dried apples before making the pie. If the ingredients aren't ready, the result won't be good."

For some reason, thinking of them as an apple pie struck him as uproariously funny. She joined in, and they laughed together until they were both gasping for breath. As they relaxed, intertwined, Jean said, "Adia told me about the magical power of blending male and female energies. Remember, that's why her elders sought a couple to undertake this mission. I didn't really understand until tonight. Look!"

She gestured with her hand, and a ribbon that had fallen from her hair floated from the floor and draped itself over her palm. "Proof that the twisted pathways in my mind are now working properly. I've never been able to move solid objects. Casual magic has always been difficult." She twined the ribbon between her fingers. "Between trying to save Wilberforce and lying with you, my mental knots are gone."

He touched the ribbon, amazed. "It makes sense that the ancestors are forging us into the tools needed for our task. But it's unnerving to think that they might have been looking over our shoulders here."

"I doubt that we shocked them, the old rascals." She turned so that her back curved against his chest. She fit beautifully. "And if we did—I hope we shock them again and again!"

"I HAVE FINISHED LISTING expenses in the ledger." Adia pushed back her hair with ink-stained fingers. "Do you have other tasks for me?"

Louise shook her head. "No, you may go for your walk." She glanced at the floor. "And take that ugly beast with you."

"He comes or goes as he wills." Adia leaned over and scratched the neck of the large, scarred orange tomcat. He must have reached the island by stowing away on one of Santola's sailing ships. The island had its share of cats, useful for catching vermin, but none of the others had the swagger and arrogance of this ginger tom.

Not long after the captain and Jean vanished into time, the cat had attached himself to Adia, following her around during the day and usually sleeping on her bed at night. She called him Bruiser. The cat and Isabelle, the macaw, could spend hours in the same room without ever acknowledging the other's presence by so much as a twitched whisker or feather. "I shall see you at dinner, Louise."

"Fish stew and rice tonight. Very tasty."

"I look forward to it." Adia stood and stretched, thinking what a good friend Louise had become. The Frenchwoman had a sharp tongue but a kind heart, and she welcomed the chance to learn more about Africa. Adia had become a de facto family member, dining nightly with Louise and her children. Though Louise's husband was often at sea, he welcomed Adia like a sister when he was home.

But it was not the same as having her own family. Even her grandmother had largely faded from Adia's awareness, apart from an occasional touch of warmth. Adia supposed that was because she was now safe, free, and had accomplished her part in the great crusade to end slavery. She no longer needed Grandmother's regular encouragement and guidance. But she missed the old woman's tart, loving presence.

As she left Gregorio's house, Adia donned a broad-brimmed straw hat to protect her from the blazing midday sun. She had fallen into a comfortable way of life during her weeks on the islands. She helped Louise with the island's ledgers, worked on her journal, which was proving unexpectedly interesting, and took long walks to burn off her restlessness. She had good food, interesting work, and friends.

Her life would be almost paradise, if not for how much she missed her husband and children. When Adia left London, Molly was being courted by a handsome young Englishman whose father owned a pub. Would they marry? Would her son be accepted as a charity student at the school that would teach far more than Adia could? How was Daniel managing without her? They had thought they would live or die together. They had not considered the possibility of another endless separation.

Bruiser fell into step beside her, looking bored. She guessed that he felt it beneath his feline dignity to be seen following a human as if he was a mere dog. Or perhaps he had been a dog in another life and hadn't yet acquired the habits of catliness. Whatever his reasons, she welcomed his company and missed him when he was off on mysterious private business.

Her walks always began by heading down to the small harbor to see what was going on. She had never lived by the sea, and she enjoyed the waterside activities. Fishing boats sailed out and returned with bountiful fresh fish for the islanders. Sometimes a Santolan trading ship would be in port, loading or unloading or being refitted. Gregorio's *Justice* had been repaired and was at sea again.

Today the harbor was quiet. No trading ship was in port, and it was too early for the fishing boats to return. A captured Barbary corsair was being fitted into a sailing ship on the edge of the harbor, but the workers were at lunch. Behind her, she could hear the occasional shrieks of children at play, the cackles of chickens, the braying of donkeys. The sounds of paradise.

She sat on a weathered bench that overlooked the harbor, absorbing the peace and blazing heat. The summer sun reminded her of the Indies. Bruiser jumped up beside her, shaking the bench when he landed. He turned several times, then settled into a nap, his furry body pressed against her thigh.

Though she did not quite expect him, she was not surprised when Tano appeared and sat down on the side opposite the cat. She and Captain Gregorio's aide found it easy to talk. Both were well-educated and had curious minds.

Both were lonely.

Tano pulled a piece of whalebone from his pocket and began to carve. "What are you working on today?" she asked.

He showed her the nearly finished carving. "Isabelle. I saw her shape in the bone and sought to free her."

"How lovely!" Adia said admiringly. Tano had captured the macaw's large head and playful expression. Every feather seemed to have been delicately etched into place.

He returned to his carving, meticulously deepening the lines around one wing. "My son will be ready for initiation soon. There are several other boys in the village who will also be ready."

"I will speak with the elders and we will choose a time." She and the other priests and priestesses had been teaching the young Africans. Though initiation could never be taken for granted, she didn't expect any of the Santolan youths to be at risk as Gregorio had been.

She had already led an initiation for several girls, and the results had been deeply satisfying. Like the boys, the girls had learned to walk between worlds. They had emerged stronger and more confident. Tano's daughter had been part of the group.

Tano rubbed his thumb over the curving bill. "Do you think our travelers will ever return?"

"I don't know." Adia felt the tightness in her chest that occurred whenever she thought about the couple she had sent off into the unknown. "I think it unlikely."

Tano nodded, sad but unsurprised. "The captain will not regret his choice if he can make a difference. The young witch is cut of similar stone. But what of you, lady? What will you do if they never return?"

"Stay here and make myself useful." She smiled mockingly. "Every village needs maiden aunts."

"You need not be alone forever," he said quietly. "You are a beautiful woman in the fullness of your life. Santola needs such women."

In his voice, she heard the unspoken offer. Tano would welcome her to his home and bed, and he was a wise, kind man. She would be lying if she said she had not noticed his interest, or wondered about what kind of mate he would be. "I have a husband. I would not betray him."

"A husband who is only a child in this year." He blew a particle of bone from the carving. "A husband you are unlikely ever to see again."

She touched the small pouch that hung under her tunic. Inside was the pathfinder stone that had once led her and Molly to Daniel. "But he exists somewhere in time."

"My wife exists somewhere in time also. If I could go back five years, she would be alive." He stared down at the carving. "But now she is gone, and she would not wish me to be alone forever. Would your husband wish that for you?"

She thought of generous, loving Daniel. "He would not. Yet we have not been apart for very long in real days. Not as long as we were separated by the American war. He is still my husband in my heart, and my dearest hope is that we will be reunited."

"How long will you hold to that hope?" He looked up from the carving, his dark eyes more intense than his words.

"I don't know." She and Daniel had been separated for two years in America, but she had known he was alive. This was different. "At least a year. Likely longer. But... the day may come when I can hope no more."

"Tell me when that day arrives."

"I will."

He smiled and gave her the carved macaw. She ran her fingers over the polished bone. A loop was carved in the back so that the ornament could be hung on a cord and worn around the neck. "You do beautiful work."

When she tried to hand the carving back, he gestured no. "It is for you, because you soar unlike any other woman I have ever known."

She held his gaze for a long moment. "I shall cherish this always." She cradled the carving in her hand, the bone still warm from Tano's touch. She would hang it around her neck, outside the tunic, a sign of her connections to Santola.

She no longer felt alone.

CHAPTER THIRTY-FOUR

OVER A DOZEN PEOPLE had gathered in the spacious room above the tailor's shop. Jean was not surprised that the English aristocrats were on one side and the Africans on the other. She and Nikolai were in between.

The Africans, except for Kofi, were clearly nervous in the presence of the Falconers, their children, and several other Guardians. Not that Jean blamed them—they had not fared well at the hands of wealthy, influential Britons. Many of them were part of the circle of elders that had sent Adia into the past.

Despite their wariness, they had power. Between the Africans and the Guardians, the room contained enough energy to set London ablaze.

It had taken over a fortnight to arrange this meeting and decide on a location. The tailor who owned the shop was a Quaker abolitionist, and his business was located in a busy commercial area. With entrances on both ends of the building, no one was likely to notice the unusual nature of the gathering.

Falconer strolled over to Nikolai and Jean. "Wilberforce has gone to Bath to take the waters and improve his health. His recovery will be slow."

Jean nodded, unsurprised. "That's a pity, but the movement is growing. Perhaps by the time he is well again, there will be more support for his legislation."

"We will have had more time to counter the pro-slavery forces." Nikolai scanned the room, counting the number present. "Everyone is here. Time to begin."

Jean said softly, "I hope this works. What we are going to try is without precedent, I think." She wished she could ask her sister-in-law, Gwynne, the Guardian scholar, about what this group was going to attempt. Gwynne would know if such a shield had ever been created before.

Tall and commanding, Nikolai moved behind a table set at one end of the room, facing a number of chairs. Usually the chamber was used for cutting fabric, so there were other tables stacked with rolls of fabric. "Please find seats so that we may begin." Though he didn't speak loudly, years of giving orders on shipboard had produced a voice that carried easily.

When everyone was settled, he continued, "I am Nikolai Gregorio and this is Jean Macrae. We have all come here because of our mutual desire to see the end of slavery. Perhaps we should start with each of us saying who we are and why we are working for abolition. I will begin by saying I was born on Malta of mixed blood. I was raised mostly by my grandmother, a former slave who came of the Iske tribe of West Africa. As a boy, I was captured by Barbary pirates and spent years as a slave. My life since I escaped has been dedicated to combating slavery in any way I can." He nodded to the African side of the room. "Kofi, will you tell us about yourself?"

Kofi rose, whipcord lean and fit despite his years. "First I want to know why these white men are here. You trust them, but I would hear from their own lips why they wish to fight with us when most whites prefer to feed off the blood of slaves."

Simon started to rise, but Meg laid her hand on his arm and stood in his place. "Once I was a girl known as Mad Meggie," she said quietly. "I was enslaved for ten years by an evil mage who stole my will, my identity, my mind, and my power. No one should ever have to endure such servitude. I wept with happiness the day I learned there were people fighting this great evil." She sat down, face calm.

Simon rose next. "Even if my wife had not been used so ill, I believe I would be here today because, quite simply, opposing slavery is the right thing to do. All Guardians are sworn to do their best for our fellow men and women. We are human and don't always know what is right, so in general, it is our practice not to interfere in society. But on this, there can be no argument. Slavery is *wrong,* and we share a moral obligation to end it as soon as possible."

Kofi nodded and briefly described his own background. His tall, striking daughter Mary Andrews spoke next. "I was born free because of my father's courage, but as long as those of my blood risk being enslaved, I pledge myself to this cause."

By the time everyone in the room had spoken, the atmosphere had relaxed. When the last Guardian had introduced herself, Nikolai said, "You have all agreed to become wardens who will help to create and maintain a protective shield against the pro-slavery forces. Jean Macrae is our expert on shielding, so she will explain her proposal."

Jean took a deep breath, then rose and stood next to Nikolai. "For those of you who are unfamiliar with the energy beings created by group emotions and beliefs, they are like great dark clouds, or a flood of mud that flows and engulfs. The energy beings—spirits—are not really conscious like we are, but they have a primitive instinct that draws them to support similar energies, and to try to destroy opposing energies.

"Twice Nikolai and I have witnessed manifestations of what we call the Slave Demon spirit. In each case, a prominent abolitionist was almost killed. There are many people who share our beliefs, but the antislavery energy is less focused. We must learn to concentrate the positive power so that whenever the Demon threatens our movement, the shield will prevent it from causing harm."

"Who were the men nearly killed?" a priestess asked.

"Thomas Clarkson and William Wilberforce," she replied. Gasps filled the room.

"How will the shield work?" The speaker was Lord

Buckland, Falconer's son. In his mid-thirties, he was dark-haired, quietly intelligent, and had an air of latent danger.

"I will create a binding spell that joins the positive and negative energies together. When the Demon energy manifests, the shield will strengthen to balance it."

"Why not try to destroy the pro-slavery spirit?" a young African priest asked.

"It's much easier to shield from bad effects than to eliminate the dark energy altogether," Jean replied. "I don't think the spirit *can* be destroyed when there are so many people supporting slavery. Their emotions are like a lake continually renewed by the rivers that flow into it. Believers will keep the Demon alive until the day comes when everyone agrees that slavery is wrong." Her remark produced wry laughter.

"You wish to protect all of Britain?" Mary Andrews asked. "That is a huge task. Beyond our abilities, I think."

"My plan was to concentrate the shield in London. Parliament is here, and ultimately the members are the men who must be persuaded to change the law," Jean said. "If our shield is effective, it will be easier for MPs to vote their consciences because we will reduce their fear of opposing wealthy West Indian planters."

"The members will also be more inclined to listen to wives and mothers," Mary said thoughtfully. "Many of the most passionate abolitionists are female."

"Perhaps because women know what it is to lack freedom." Jean and Mary shared a glance of understanding.

Jean continued, "If the London shield is effective, later we can think of shielding other cities, or shielding particularly valuable members of the abolitionist movement." She halted, thinking of Wilberforce. "In fact, that's a very good idea. But London first. What we are going to attempt is unprecedented. We should proceed a single step at a time."

"How will the shield be constructed?" The question came from the Falconers' daughter, Lady Bethany March, a young married woman. She had her father's blond hair and her mother's misleadingly otherworldly air.

"The freedom energy will be gathered and concentrated. Then a binding spell will be invoked to link it to the Demon. The shield will be maintained by the wardens who have committed to holding the energy. I think that there must always be at least two people holding the energy so that if something happens, such as one warden being struck by a carriage, the other will be able to maintain the shield."

"It would be wise to also have a backup warden whose energy will be activated if both the frontline wardens fail." Falconer frowned thoughtfully. "It will require some clever spell construction, but I'm sure it can be done." His son nodded agreement.

A young African priest asked, "How do we hold the energy?"

"It's simple, actually," Jean replied. "You imagine a line of power running from you to the shield. Then you allow some of your power to flow into the shield. Most of the time, very little power will be required, and very little attention. Once the connection is established, it will continue to flow while the warden goes about his or her usual duties. If the warden wishes to do other spell work while warding, he will have less power available, but in general, it shouldn't be a demanding task. This is a commitment that will surely last for years, though. It is vital that a schedule be developed so that the shield is never left unattended."

"There will be times when the energy draw is much greater," Nikolai said. "When the pro-slavery forces rally to suppress legislation, for example."

"Usually we should have warning, but it's not impossible that there might be an unexpected draw on everyone who is connected to the shield." Jean turned her palms upward. "I can't predict what will happen. Everyone here is a powerful adept who believes in this cause. I think we will find solutions as needed. But if anyone feels that this task is too much of a burden, feel free to leave now. There is no shame in circumstances that make such a commitment impossible."

She stopped speaking. People glanced at one another, but no one moved. Feeling encouraged, Jean said, "Now it is time to build the shield." She had already designed her binding spell, and it could be invoked with a few words when they were ready. "We need to do this in a circle, holding hands."

She came around the desk and extended her hand to Kofi. He stared at her hand as if it was a snake before warily taking it. "Alternate black and white," she added.

"Our powers are a little different, so we need to weave them together."

"What about those of us who are both?" Mary Andrews asked ironically.

"Use your intuition about whose hands to take," Jean said promptly. "The goal is to balance the energies." Rather awkwardly, they joined hands, the long room making the shape more oval than circular. No matter. "First I will seal the circle." Jean closed her eyes and spoke the words that joined them.

"That's it?" one of the priestesses said incredulously. "No herbs, no ritual?"

Jean laughed. "Guardian magic is mostly very simple. Now each person should send a pulse of energy into the circle so it will flow around and back to you." Immediately she began to feel individual notes, from Kofi's deep, earthy gong to the light, fluting ring of the youngest Guardian girl. Together, they made a matchless chorus. When all the notes were in harmony, she said, "Now we collect and focus the positive abolition energies. Nikolai will guide this."

"It's rather like picking berries," he said conversationally. "Berries of light. Close your eyes, and we shall harvest them."

Jean knew that he had developed this ability as a result of his initiation. When she closed her eyes, she felt him swoop the spirits of her and the others up onto a magical flying carpet that soared above nighttime London. Here and there lights flickered, some sharp and star bright, others like faint embers. As Nikolai touched each bright spark, it was incorporated into a larger fabric, a glittering net of light.

Within the net, Jean could feel individual minds. Some were workingmen, staunch Britons who cherished their own liberty and felt everyone deserved the same. Some were deeply religious people who believed it was a sin to own another human who was made in God's image. And there were the Africans, many of them former slaves, who had struggled to regain their liberty and would fight to retain it.

The newly created net was a gossamer but resilient web that floated both through and above the fabric of the city. When the last spark had been incorporated, Nikolai said, "As others come to believe in abolition, their energies will automatically be incorporated into this shield. Now that it has been constructed, little energy will be required for maintenance unless it is challenged by the Demon. When that happens, those of us who are wardens of the shield will be tapped for more energy."

"What if more power is demanded than we can spare?" someone asked.

"You can control the amount you give, or cut yourself off from the net entirely. But if too many people cut the connection when the net is being challenged, the net will fail, so leaving should not be done lightly."

"How does this shield control the Demon spirit?" a man asked.

"This is the hard part," Nikolai said. "Jean?"

"Earlier I created a spell that will bind our net to the pro-slavery spirit. You will probably feel a jolt when that happens." She hesitated. "I've never done anything quite like this before. Please... be prepared."

She waited until she felt assent, then invoked her spell. As she saturated the net with binding energy, Nikolai brought the Demon into focus. The entity was smaller than their net, and much more dense. Within it, Jean sensed flashes of greed, anger, cruelty, and lust for power, all of them darting about like minnows in a murky sea. These were the primal components of slave owning—a nasty brew that made her want to bathe in scalding water.

She moved her charged net so that it lay parallel to the dark cloud, then supplied the last words that completed the binding spell. Instantly the two energy beings fused together, the net like a pale spiderweb that covered the surface of the dark cloud.

After an instant that resonated with shock, the Demon bucked like a spooked horse trying frantically to rid itself of its rider. Its shock blasted through the circle and she heard a man cry out. "Hold tight!" Jean snapped, terrified that someone would break the circle and they would all be subjected to blasts of wild, destructive energy.

"Hold, hold, hold..." Falconer repeated the words calmly. She felt the deep strength of his power, joined a moment later by Kofi and Meg and other senior priests. Gradually the shock faded. The Demon settled down as a horse becomes accustomed to its saddle. It hadn't the awareness to realize that it had been bridled as well.

Jean exhaled with relief. "We have succeeded. The

Demon represents the opinions of many powerful men, but I think we have countered its ability to damage the abolition movement and its leaders. Does everyone feel their connection to our shield net?"

After murmurs of assent, Jean closed the circle, then stretched her tight muscles. Lord, it was good to be able to call her magic easily in circumstances that weren't desperate! The sky outside was darkening. They had been working here for hours. But they had succeeded. Now she was anxious to return to their inn so she and Nikolai could replenish their strength with passion.

They had finished their work here. Where would the time spell take them next?

ADIA WOKE with her head buzzing. The feeling was strange, as if she was in the middle of a dozen conversations but couldn't make out any of the words. She would have laid in bed longer, but Bruiser yawned and came to stand on her chest.

"Mrrwop?" he inquired.

It wasn't hard to decipher the question. "Yes, it's time for breakfast."

Adia got up from her bed, washed, dressed, and descended to the kitchen. The cat was fed first, always, since Bruiser was not known for his patience.

It had taken Adia time to adjust to the quiet of the captain's villa after the busyness of her London home. Now she enjoyed being able to have a peaceful breakfast of tea and bread and honey. She took her tray up to the terrace so she could watch the caldera as she ate. The morning was a little overcast, but she thought it would clear later.

The buzzing in her head had faded into the background as she had cleaned up and prepared breakfast, but now that her mind was at rest, the buzzing became more obvious. Wondering what was going on, she closed her eyes and meditated on the buzzing. Which wasn't really a sound, more a low level of activity that was—magical?

She mentally captured a chunk of the buzzing to study more closely. To her surprise, the energy that composed it was familiar. It felt like... people she knew, startling as the thought was. She concentrated and picked up traces of the priest Kofi, then several of the other London elders. But they were all more than thirty years in the future, not in her time.

She investigated more, and was shocked to identify the signature energies of the captain and Jean Macrae. Were they connecting the time she was in now and the time she had left? They must be. She dived into the buzzing and realized that it was a mass of conflicting energy, part of it pro-slavery, part of it abolition. The proslavery part was like a bottomless pit, while the abolition energy was a lifeline in the darkness. The two energies seemed bound together.

The buzzing she felt was a binding constructed by her friends and other abolitionists with power, she realized. Was it some kind of spying device so they could learn the plans of the pro-slavery forces? But that seemed unnecessary—the West Indian lobby had plenty of money and even more boldness. There was no need for them to keep secrets, nor for the abolitionists to spy.

Perhaps the abolitionist energy was designed to counterbalance the pro-slavery forces? Jean and the captain must have joined with the council of elders to create a protective Spirit. If she was right, they had successfully traveled into the future and were doing the job they intended. But why was she feeling this buzzing in 1753?

She frowned. No one really knew how time magic worked, but there was a theory that one of the other worlds that lay alongside of this one was a place with no time. To move from one time in her world to another time, one moved through the other world. Since there was no time there, one could enter and exit at any point. The bespelled beads were the gates to the other world.

If so, perhaps the energy buzzing in her head also went through the other world. Because she was connected to Jean and Kofi and the captain, she was also connected to the protective spirit they had created. Perhaps. It was as good a theory as any.

Firmly she told the buzzing to be quiet. It subsided into the depths of her mind, no longer distracting but still there. Perhaps someday she could find a way to use it.

CHAPTER THIRTY-FIVE

NIKOLAI AND JEAN spent another fortnight in London after forming the shield, but no other tasks seemed necessary, so they enjoyed life. They saw the lions in the Tower of London and visited the Ranelagh pleasure gardens and attended plays and exhibitions. Since their money was running low, they had to request funds from Falconer. Though accepting aid made Nikolai a little uncomfortable, he had to admit that Jean's Guardian connections were invaluable.

And they made love. Now that they had come together, it was hard to remember why it had been necessary to stay apart for so long. But the ancestors had known what they were doing. In the course of their travel, Nikolai and Jean had changed on deep levels, and now they were bonded as tightly as the Demon and the shield net.

The bond was not romantic love, or at least, not only

that, even though Jean entranced him. More profoundly, this was the mating that the ancestors had wanted. Their complementary magical abilities had transformed them into a tool against slavery that had more power than either of them could muster alone.

Would the bond dissolve once their task was accomplished? Or would they not survive long enough to find out? He had a suspicion that the bond was so strong that if one of them died, the other would be unable to survive. It was not a thought he wanted to dwell on.

Whatever the future held, Jean was the best companion he'd ever had, and the best mistress.

After their fortnight of relaxing, they packed their belongings and returned to the quiet churchyard where they had arrived in 1788. "I liked 1788," Jean said with a wicked glance. "We learned so much. I wonder where we'll go next."

"It's up to the ancestors. Now that we are beyond Adia's time, we're flying blind. Or rather, even more blind than before." He kissed the end of her elegant little nose, then clasped her hands with the next spell bead between their palms. "I hope we can use the spell without extra help again."

"If not, at least help is near," Jean said pragmatically. Together, they invoked the familiar spell, ending it with a kiss.

He braced himself for the trip through time as they summoned the magic. He felt an odd, rolling sensation rather like a ship wallowing in the trough of a wave. The bead held between their palms dissolved in a flash of heat. It was the first time he'd felt that—always before, the disappearance was overwhelmed by far greater sensations as they were chopped and churned and dragged through time.

Wondering if the magic had failed, he opened his eyes and looked around. An alley again—the ancestors were very fond of them. Jean released his hands. "We appear to have gone somewhere, but the passage was much too easy. I wonder if we didn't move through time at all." She glanced up. "We must have moved somewhat—it's early afternoon now."

"We're still in London, though in a different place." He studied the walls and the ground. "This appears to be a higher class of alley than we're used to. Maybe we just moved across the city?"

Jean walked to the end of the alley and looked out.

"The clothing doesn't seem very different except in some details. It looks as if we're in a fashionable neighborhood. Perhaps Mayfair—this street looks vaguely familiar."

"Shall we go exploring?"

"First I want to check the shield net." Jean's eyes drifted out of focus. "It's alive and well. I recognize the energy of some of the people who were there when we created it, so I don't think we've gone far."

Knowing he should have thought to do that himself, he turned his attention to the protective net, looking at the energy rather than individuals. "The Demon is much stronger than before, but the shield net has the strength to balance."

"Perhaps the public in general is more concerned with slavery, so that would feed both spirits," Jean suggested.

"You're probably right. There is a vast amount of energy involved here. There are also other group energies that are large and strong in the background. I don't recognize them." He studied the bound pro- and anti-slavery energies more deeply. "Our shield energy has actually become relatively stronger, but the pro-slavery energy is still denser and more focused."

"I wonder why we're here," Jean mused.

"Given the efficiency of the ancestors, we'll find out soon enough." He offered Jean his arm. "Time to be off?" She took his arm and they moved into the street. Two blocks walking and Jean said, "Definitely Mayfair. The streets now have nameplates on the corner buildings."

"A nice improvement." Nikolai was about to say more when a carriage pulled to a halt beside them.

The door opened and an elegantly dressed man stepped out. It was Lord Buckland, Falconer's son, looking not much older than when they'd met him in 1788. "Ah, Mr. and Mrs. Gregory," he said casually. "Will you allow me to offer you a ride?"

"It would be our pleasure," Jean said as Nikolai handed her into the carriage and they took the rear-facing seat.

Once they were all inside and the vehicle was moving

again, Buckland's casual expression was replaced by an enthusiastic welcome. "It's good to see you again! I had a vague feeling that I should tell the coachman to take this route, but I didn't know why. Apparently it was to find you."

"Are you a seer, Lord Buckland?" Jean asked.

He shook his head. "I have the family abilities, but that doesn't include seeing the future. I think I must have sensed that you were coming because of our connection through the shield net. Though I wasn't consciously aware, it seems to have been enough to influence my choice of route."

"Speaking of which," Nikolai said, thinking that if he was going to stay in this time, he'd like to know the name of Buckland's tailor, "when are we? And do you know why we've been brought here?"

"1791," Buckland said promptly. "As to why—today the House of Commons will probably vote on Wilberforce's bill to end the slave trade."

"Really?" Excitement blazed through Nikolai. "Is it likely to pass?"

"I'm not sure," Buckland replied slowly. "Much has changed in the last three years. Antislavery sentiment has become a fever among the general public."

"Good!" Jean exclaimed. "If Parliament won't agree, it's time for new MPs."

"MPs can be changed, but not the House of Lords." The other man frowned. "Today's outcome is very uncertain, and the political winds are shifting. If the bill doesn't pass today, it may not have another chance for a very long time."

"Why not?" Nikolai asked, feeling uneasy.

Buckland restlessly fingered the leather portfolio beside him. "There is revolution in France, a popular uprising for freedom similar to the American Revolution. At first progressive Britons were optimistic that the nation would become more fair and democratic, but the French Revolution is turning sour. The best Guardian seers believe that the country will fall into civil war. With France chaotic, the forces of conservatism are on the upswing in Britain. No one wants to see civil society break down here."

"Understandable," Jean agreed. "Chaos benefits only the violent. But such fears can't be good for abolition."

Buckland nodded. "To make matters worse, the slaves have revolted in the West Indian island of Dominica. Proslavery forces in Britain are arguing that ending the trade would be disastrous and create still more turbulence that would endanger every European in the Indies."

Nikolai's brows arched. "Surely that's unnecessarily alarmist."

Buckland's mouth twisted. "When people are afraid, reason doesn't stand a chance. It's remarkable how many people have come to support abolition even though they have no direct experience with slavery. But revolution in France and the fear of it in Britain are very close and alarming. Avoiding major changes begins looking like the safest thing to do."

"Which is why if the abolition vote fails today, it may be years before it is seriously considered again," Jean said flatly.

"Exactly. Even if the bill does pass, it would also have to be approved by the House of Lords and the king, and they may well refuse. But success today in the House of Commons would be a powerful step in the right direction."

Nikolai closed his eyes and spread his attention through the energies generated by the teeming population of London. "I feel the fear and the conservatism you described, and already they are influencing how people look at slavery. But there is a chance of success today, I think, if our shield net can hold the Demon at bay."

Buckland's expression turned thoughtful. "That might explain why you've been brought here. We've maintained the shield net without a problem, and no prominent abolitionists have died. But none of us works with the shield as well as you two, perhaps because you created it. The pro-slavery forces have been adept at delays, continually demanding more evidence, more hearings, saying there wasn't enough information. It's taken three years to finally get to the point of a vote. Maybe you've arrived to tip the balance in our favor by your power over the shield net."

Nikolai exchanged a glance with Jean, and saw that she was as uncertain as he. "We can try, of course. By the way, where are we going?"

"Parliament. I know of a nice, private balcony where you can watch the proceedings without danger of being seen." Buckland sighed. "The odds are not good, but the fact that you are here gives me a little hope."

The carriage rumbled to a halt outside the Palace of

Westminster, home of Parliament. Jean pulled the veil of her bonnet over her face. "Lead on, my lord." .

As they entered the looming building, Buckland said, "This is the second day of debate, and the vote should take place toward the end of the session. You will hear some of the most amazing arguments from the proslavery people. One member claimed abolition would destroy our Canadian fisheries because it's the Indies slaves who are fed the worst fish."

"What?" Nikolai said incredulously.

"Don't expect it to make sense." Buckland led them through the palace and up to the gallery level, stopping outside a section of blank wall. He made a gesture that flared with magic and a door appeared. As he ushered Jean and Nikolai in, he said, "I masked this room yesterday in case it was needed today. Which was an odd thing for me to do, now that I think of it. The shield net must have been prodding me."

"Whenever the ancestors are involved, strange things happen," Nikolai observed.

The room was like a theater box seat next to the large public gallery on one side of the chamber where the House of Commons met. The galleries on both sides were packed, but their little box had half a dozen chairs and a good view down into the chamber. Because of the masking, no one seemed to notice them.

"I must go—I'm an MP myself." Buckland pulled a handful of papers from his document case. "If you become bored, you might want to look at this. It's a summary of the slavery accounts given in nearly two thousand pages of hearing notes. We wanted a document short enough that even the dullest MP could find the time to read it. I shall see you later. Good luck. Perhaps you can turn the tide."

He left just as the session below was called to order. Jean said quietly, "Simon must still be alive or Buckland would be sitting in the House of Lords rather than Commons. I'm glad to know that."

So was Nikolai. Even in his seventies, Falconer had been a formidable mage, and they might need his power before this day was done.

As Buckland had said, the speeches were interesting. Wilberforce spoke, saying in his calm, rich voice that ending the slave trade could only help the West Indies plantations because slaves would be treated more gently and productivity would increase. A flamboyant man in a dragoon's uniform leaped up, waving a hand with only three fingers as he claimed that the Africans themselves had no objections to the slave trade.

When the next speaker rose, Jean clutched Nikolai's arm. "It's Captain Trent, from Liverpool!"

Sure enough, Trent was here, several pounds fatter and several years more unctuous. In a booming voice he declared, "You have all heard of the slave revolt in Dominica, one of the fairest of our Indies sugar islands. That revolt, sirs, is a direct result of the abolition movement! Unpatriotic fools have stirred the passions of the heathen Africans, and now the wealth and health of Britain herself are threatened!"

As Trent ranted, Nikolai felt the pro-slavery energy

intensifying. He also felt a familiar dark energy. "Trent's priest, Kondo, is nearby and active," he said tersely. "I am going to find him."

"Be careful," Jean said. "He's surely working to increase the Demon energy."

So she felt it, too. He touched her shoulder. "I will be all right."

He left their private box and paused outside, turning his locater skills to finding Kondo. He had felt the priest's energy very clearly at Wilberforce's house. Now it was just a matter of identifying his individual energy amidst the signatures of the hundreds of other people in the palace. Kondo was so distinctive that tracing him didn't take long. Especially since his energy was braided into a flood of Demon power.

Nikolai followed the trail up a flight of stairs and down long corridors, finding that the energy strengthened as he moved closer to the source. This area of the building was almost empty since there was a controversial bill being debated.

The energy track led to a latched door. Nikolai used one angry burst of power to open it. He had become quite adept at using his power as a tool, or a weapon.

The door opened to a small, comfortably furnished office. Behind the desk was Kondo, his eyes closed and his clothing that of an English gentleman. Demon energy pulsed around him as sluggish black light, coursing through the building to the House of Commons. There it would strengthen the pro-slavery forces and weaken the abolitionists.

Guessing that Kondo had chosen the office at random because he needed a quiet place to work, Nikolai stepped inside. The African's eyes opened and filled with recognition. "You," he said in a guttural, heavily accented voice. "The English slave. I knew we would meet again. You shall not stop me this time."

"I am not English, and I am not a slave." Nikolai focused his power and slashed at the rope of energy that connected Kondo to the Demon. If he could quickly sever the man from the evil spirit...

It was like hitting steel. His energy bounced back at him with agonizing force. Kondo laughed. "You cannot hurt me. I protect the dark spirit, and it protects me." As Nikolai struggled to collect himself, he asked, "How can you work against your own people? You have the power to achieve wealth and freedom without serving a swine of a white man like Trent."

Kondo looked bored. "African slaves are not my people. Why should I exhaust myself trying to help useless beasts of burden?" His eyes glinted. "I live better than any African king, and I have found that Englishwomen are very curious about African lovers. I have exactly the life I wish."

"So you are still a slave?"

Scarlet energy flared around the African. "I am not! I have my freedom papers. I serve Trent because I choose to, and he pays very, very well."

From Kondo's reaction, he might feel rather less free than he wished. But that was the African's problem. "Very well, you do not wish to exert yourself on behalf of slaves. But why work for the pro-slavery forces? There is no need to do that. As a mage, you could support yourself well by other means."

"Because I have power, and I enjoy using it." Kondo rose to his feet, his posture threatening. Though he must be over fifty, he had the fitness and aura of danger, of a warrior, and the demonic energy swirling around him emphasized the darkness of his soul. "More power than you have, and now I shall prove it!"

He raised his arms and hurled an annihilating blast of Demon energy at Nikolai, who reeled back into the door. He was paralyzed, sliding to the floor—yet as he fell, a net of diamond white brilliance flared around him, pushing back the darkness.

Kondo staggered and had to grab the edge of the desk for support. "Damn you!" he gasped.

As his numbness began to fade, Nikolai realized that the shield net had defended him just as the Demon had protected Kondo. "Stalemate," he managed to gasp. "I cannot kill you, and you cannot kill me."

"Not by magic, perhaps. But there are more primitive methods." Kondo whipped a dagger out from under his elegantly cut coat and stabbed down at Nikolai's heart. Nikolai tried to dodge, but he was still too weak to move quickly.

The blade struck with bruising force and slashed his shirt and waistcoat, but it skittered away without penetrating Nikolai's chest. Kondo swore with vicious fluency. "You and your bitch built your shield well! But I can still rattle your brains."

As the Demon expanded and grew more powerful, Kondo reversed the dagger and slammed the hilt on Nikolai's head. Nikolai fell into darkness—and to his horror, around him spun splintering fragments of the shield net.

CHAPTER THIRTY-SIX

DURING QUIET PARTS of the debate, Jean skimmed the hearing summary notes. The stories were shocking and sometimes stomach turning. She was beginning to wonder what had happened to Nikolai, when the door to her box opened. She glanced up, expecting to see him, but a young woman wearing the sober garb of an Evangelical peered inside. "May I join you? I arrived late, and there are no seats left in the gallery."

"Of course. They are nearing the vote, I believe." Jean guessed that Nikolai hadn't masked the door when he left. She made a mental note to show him the trick of it. He was an interesting mixture of great power and odd gaps in his knowledge. In the meantime, she wouldn't mind having a companion.

"Pray God Mr. Wilberforce's legislation passes!" The newcomer sat down with an empty seat between her and Jean. Though she looked no more than twenty or so, she wore a wedding ring. "My name is Elizabeth Heyrick. I traveled down from Leicester to hear the debates and watch the voting."

"I am Jean Gregory. I've only just arrived back in England, but like you, I am praying that the law passes."

"I have scarcely been able to sleep since I saw the *Brookes* diagram," Elizabeth confided as she set her draw-string bag on the floor and removed her dark shawl. "It is still hard to believe that men can treat other men with such cruelty."

"The *Brookes* diagram? I don't know what that is."

"You haven't seen it?" Elizabeth exclaimed. "But of course, you have been out of the country. Here, let me show you. I always carry my copy to remind myself." She opened her bag and pulled out a stained, folded piece of paper. Handing it to Jean, she said, "It's a diagram of a real slave ship named the *Brookes,* and it shows how the slaves are packed into the space for the Atlantic passage."

Jean unfolded the large sheet and caught her breath. Despite all she'd learned about the trade, the actual image of slaves jammed together like salted herring was horrifying. "This is appalling! No wonder so many die during the passage."

"This diagram shows four hundred eighty-two slaves," Elizabeth said bitterly. "I counted to be sure. On some voyages, the *Brookes* carried half again as many slaves."

"No one who sees this could be unmoved," Jean whispered.

"The slave captains and plantation owners manage that," the other woman said. "When a very mild law was passed saying that slaves must be allowed more space, the slavers claimed that it would cause the deaths of all the whites in Jamaica. And then they failed to provide even that mild improvement."

Jean shook her head as she returned the diagram. She was becoming used to the hysterical political rhetoric of the slavers. "Perhaps that will change after today's vote." As they turned their attention to the chamber below, Jean was swamped by a paralyzing flood of Demon energy that took dark, bloody-minded joy in greed, control, and cruelty. The influx was so intense she could barely breathe. Horrified, she realized that the shield net was starting to rip apart, overwhelmed by the power of the spirit it had been created to control.

Fight back. She threw her awareness and power into the shield, drawing strength from the collected energy of her friends and allies. She could feel shock and disorientation as the net's demand for power overwhelmed the two wardens on duty and began drawing from everyone connected to it. She became one with the net, feeling its rifts as if they were agonizing wounds in her own body.

She shuddered as several panicky wardens cut the connection, but more wardens began pouring their energy into the shield. In the background were more diffuse energies from regular abolitionists. Gradually the jagged tears in the net began to heal.

As the rifts disappeared, Jean's pain faded away. The shield net would survive, but it did not have the strength to prevent the Demon from influencing the present voting.

When the last links of the shield net had been

repaired, Jean drew a deep, dizzy breath and withdrew back into her own body. She felt as if she should bear scars from the energy wounds she'd suffered in the net, but she looked normal enough even though she'd probably collapse if she tried to stand. Luckily Elizabeth Heyrick was so intent on the voting that she hadn't noticed anything wrong with Jean. From the young woman's taut expression, the vote was going against them.

Weary to the bone, Jean watched the final votes being tallied. By the end, two-thirds of the MPs present voted against abolishing the trade. The chamber erupted as the pro-slavery supporters whooped with joy. Abolitionist MPs sat stunned by the magnitude of their defeat. After Buckland's warning about the uncertain outcome, Jean was not really surprised, but she was profoundly disappointed.

Elizabeth began sobbing uncontrollably, her body shaking with despair. "Everyone I know in Leicester opposes slavery," she gasped. "Where are these slave lovers hiding? How can any decent man vote in favor of the trade?"

"Money and power are intertwined like serpents. Slavery is the source of great wealth, and that gives men power. Enough power to buy as many politicians as they need." Jean gestured toward the floor of the house, where men were churning back and forth, slapping one another's backs and congratulating themselves on their victory.

"It is *wrong* that a minority of men can allow wickedness that is despised by the majority." Elizabeth's tears were drying as anger began to replace grief. "Yet what can common people like me do to fight such evil?"

"Hit the slave industry in its pocketbook," Jean said slowly as an idea began to form. Pamphlets she'd bought in 1788 had described the sugar trade in pounds and pence. "Huge amounts of sugar are sold in Britain every year. If enough of us stop buying it, the plantation owners will see their profits fall. If one in ten Britons refuses to buy sugar, the planters will notice. If one in five stops, it will change the industry forever."

Elizabeth caught her breath as she considered Jean's suggestion. "I wonder if such a thing is possible. There are many of us who would agree to stop buying sugar, but there are many more who would not wish to give up their sweetening, not even to save lives. My own mother is a staunch abolitionist, yet she would give blood from her veins before she would drink her tea without sugar."

"I've read that sugar from India is not produced by slaves." Jean smiled wryly. "The conditions of the Indians who produce it might not be much better than those of Caribbean slaves, but at least they are free. Indian sugar costs more, but wouldn't that be a small price to pay for a clear conscience?"

Elizabeth's face lit up. "That would work! We could also refuse to buy from bakers who use slave sugar, or from grocers who carry it. If enough people join the campaign, the merchants will have to use Indian sugar or lose much of their custom."

"Such a campaign would take time," Jean warned. "At first it would not be taken seriously, I suspect."

"But refusing to eat sugar is something that anyone, even a child, can do. There will be many who will join us, that I know. Especially if they can buy Indian sugar." The prospect of action put determination in Elizabeth's eyes. "When I return to Leicestershire, I shall begin with our local antislavery group, and we shall write to other groups across the nation. I vow that a year from now, we will be taken seriously!"

Jean was not a seer, but she had a very powerful sense that this young woman would make a difference in the abolition movement. "I shall watch for reports of people refusing to buy sugar, and I will spread the word myself." Elizabeth stood, already looking beyond this defeat to the next battle. "The forces of commerce may have carried today, but there will be other, better days."

She lifted her shawl and wrapped it around her shoulders. As she did, Jean noticed that the other woman's muslin kerchief was pinned by a brooch that showed a kneeling African in chains. There was lettering engraved around the edge, but Jean couldn't make out the words. "Excuse me, but what does your medallion say?" Elizabeth touched the embossed metal. "It says, 'Am I not a man and a brother?' The design was done by Mr. Wedgwood, the pottery manufacturer, to remind us of the common humanity of African and European."

Like the ship diagram, it was a potent image. "I must get one for myself."

"Here." Elizabeth unfastened the clasp and offered the medallion. "It is yours."

"Oh, no, really," Jean protested, a little startled. "I can buy my own."

"Take it, please." Elizabeth smiled. "A brooch is a small return for hope."

Jean offered her hand, and the other woman took it. Once more, intuition spoke. "You will make a difference, Mrs. Heyrick. Indeed you will. Go with God."

"Thank you, Mrs. Gregory." The younger woman hugged Jean, then left the box, head high.

Now that she was alone, Jean was free to give in to her worry about Nikolai. He had been gone far too long. She settled into a chair and sought him mentally. She had just decided that he was alive but injured, when the door to the box opened and he entered. Jean gasped when she saw his slashed garments. "Good heavens, what happened to you?" She went into his arms, careful not to hug too hard.

"I found Kondo, and he bested me," Nikolai said ruefully. His embrace was not careful at all—he held her with rib-bruising force. "The shield net protected me from his energy blasts and his attempt to stab me to death, but he managed to knock me out of my wits. I thought then that the shield was being overwhelmed, but it feels sound enough now. What did I miss?"

Before she could reply, Lord Buckland entered the box, looking drained. "That was the first time that the shield net demanded such power from us. The shield barely survived. We need to find more qualified wardens."

"We must learn to draw on a broader range of abolitionists. Perhaps we can reach beyond the London area." Jean briefly explained what happened to Nikolai before adding, "I don't think that we arrived here to bring success. I think the ancestors sent us here to prevent total disaster. We came close to losing the shield net—even one less warden might have been the difference between saving it and complete destruction. The consequences might have been dire. Also, a young lady joined me here, and when she recovered from her disappointment, she left determined to persuade every abolitionist in Britain to stop using slave-grown sugar."

Buckland's brows rose. "Hit them in their profits! What a fine idea. I will do my best to spread the word."

"Sympathizers will be glad to have something solid to do," Nikolai predicted.

"The movement is alive. Even if the political tides are against us, we will persevere." Buckland gave a tired smile. "But it would have been altogether more pleasant to have won."

His comment was a masterpiece of gentlemanly understatement. Jean leaned against Nikolai, wanting to sleep the clock around. "Is there a nice inn where you could leave us on your way home?"

Buckland nodded. "Will you be staying here for long?"

Jean glanced up at Nikolai. By this time, they didn't need words to arrive at such decisions. "For a few weeks. We should visit our African friends, then learn how to draw general abolition energy into the shield net."

"I think I know how to do that." Nikolai smiled

tiredly. "There is nothing like being mauled by negative energy to understand it better. Let me think about it for a few days. Then we can have another meeting of wardens."

Looking a little more cheerful, Buckland said, "I'll look forward to it. As for tonight, or rather this morning, I know just the inn. It's very quiet and comfortable." They followed him through the palace to the street and saw that dawn was just beginning to show in the east. Parliament sessions usually began in midafternoon and ran into the night, and debates could last until the sun rose. Jean tucked her hand into the crook of Nikolai's elbow. "A new day dawning. I like the symbolism."

"We knew this would take time." He gave her a half smile. "And we have more time than most."

At first Adia didn't understand the tremendous pull on her mind and power. She staggered to her bed and fell back dizzily. What...?

Gradually she realized that her power was being pulled into the web that she suspected had been constructed by Jean and the captain to battle slaver energies. A great struggle was taking place, and the web was reaching through time to Adia. She felt Jean very vividly, the captain rather less.

Gradually the drain on her energy faded and she knew that the web had survived its test. A pity she would never know what happened.

But at least she was able to help, even buried here in the past.

THE INN WAS all that Buckland promised, and a clerk was willing to check strangers in at dawn. When they reached their room, Nikolai was tempted to fall onto the bed without even undressing, but he'd feel better later if he stripped. With a sigh, Jean did the same. "It's been a long day. Three years long."

"But we survived. For a few moments there, I thought I might not." As Kondo's knife descended, Nikolai had been struck with two thoughts: He didn't want to die before their mission was done. And he didn't want to leave Jean.

As she released her hair and loosely braided it, he found that he was not too tired to admire her. If she hadn't had the strength to hold the shield together when it began to unravel, men like Clarkson and Wilberforce would be vulnerable again. Though antislavery sentiment had grown strong, leaders were still needed, and it would take time for new ones to appear if the present ones were struck down.

He came up behind Jean and put his arms around her waist, bending to kiss the side of her neck. She melted back in his arms, eyes closed. "You can do that again if you like," she murmured.

Encouraged, he kissed her ear as his hands came up to cup her breasts. "You're probably too tired for this," he said, not wanting to be too demanding.

She laughed and turned in his arms so she could slide her arms around his neck. "I work with energy all the time. Why is this the only activity that gives us both more energy than when we started?"

"An interesting question." He lifted her and laid her on the bed. "We can talk about it tomorrow."

Jean was right. Afterward, he had more energy than when he started.

IT TOOK OVER A MONTH, but Jean and Nikolai were able to enhance the shield net by drawing on the energy of abolitionists across a good part of Britain. Though the new people had little power individually, together their support of abolition strengthened the shield net substantially.

Having visited Kofi and his family and the Falconers, it was now time to move on. They paid the bill at the inn and found a half-empty storeroom at the back of the building that would be a convenient departure point.

Jean pulled Adia's bracelet from her wrist and contemplated it. "There is only one spell bead left. I've been hoping that it will take us home again—to 1753 and Santola. Is it possible that the work we've done so far is enough so that we can go home now? Or do you think that another critical point needs our attention?" She sighed. "Or is slavery too huge and intractable for the ancestors' magic to make a difference?"

"I don't know," Nikolai said quietly. "Since our first visit twenty-six years ago, we have seen great change in the hearts and minds of the British people. Just as Adia said, the mass of people are rising up and saying 'Enough!'"

"At the beginning, you and I protected individuals," she said thoughtfully. "Now we are protecting the spirit of the movement itself. Within a few years, the movement and the desire for liberty may be so strong that we are not needed. That would be my hope. That, and having the last bead take us back where we began. But... it might not. It may take us further into the future and leave us there."

"Can you bear it if we must live our lives out in a distant time?"

"I'll have no choice, will I?" She smiled wryly. "I will be sorry not to see family and friends again, but thinking of the separations and privations that Adia has endured puts my situation into perspective. I can learn to prosper in a new time. And I won't be alone—the Guardians never abandon their own."

"You are fortunate to have so many people you cherish." He almost managed to keep envy out of his voice, but not quite.

She looked up at him, thinking how far they had come since they met in the warehouse in Marseilles. "What of you, Captain? When the great goal of your life, ending slavery, is accomplished, what will you do?"

He shrugged. "I am still a sailor, and I can always find work on the sea. I would want to visit Santola to find if the island still flourishes, and if there is a place for me. If I'm even still remembered."

"You will be remembered." She noticed that neither

of them spoke of their relationship. Would they separate and go their individual ways? Or would the bonding that had made them an effective antislavery tool remain when their task was done?

Impossible to say. She got to her feet and positioned the last bead in the center of her palm. When it was gone, the bracelet would be a rather plain collection of small beads strung too loosely for the length of its cord. "Shall we take the final step and see where it leads us?"

"Let us hope for no surprises." He clasped her hand, and together they began to activate the spell. Jean closed her eyes and prayed that she would open them again to find Santola in her own time.

CHAPTER THIRTY-SEVEN

THE PASSAGE through time was very smooth, hardly more distracting than walking through a dark room. They landed with a thump in a house—and it wasn't Nikolai's villa in Santola. Jean swallowed hard, trying not to weep at the knowledge that she would never see her home and family again. Despite her attempts to be philosophical about this possibility, the reality was crushing.

Fighting her disappointment, Jean released Nikolai's hands and studied the room. "This appears to be a bedroom in a London town house, a rather grand one. Can you sense our location?"

"Definitely London." He sighed, as disappointed as she. "I'm sorry, Jean. I would also like to go home, but the loss is greater for you."

"At least we're in England, not High Barbary." She walked to the window and glanced down into the street. It was midafternoon, judging by the light, and sometime in winter. The house was set on one of London's pretty squares designed around a small park. "Mayfair, I think, though I don't believe I've ever been inside this house. Clearly we have more work to do."

She saw several women walking past and sucked in her breath. "We may have traveled a great distance forward. I see women wearing gowns that are scarcely more than shifts!" The high-waisted gowns were flowing and pretty, but wouldn't have been decent in any time period Jean had seen.

"As a man, I approve of the style," Nikolai said when he joined her at the window. "The men's clothing hasn't changed as much, and those women over there are wearing fuller garments. Perhaps a new style is coming in but not yet established."

Jean studied the street scene more carefully. "You're right—I was so startled by the new that I missed the familiar. Perhaps we haven't moved as far as I thought." They heard firm steps approaching and looked at each other warily. They were in a stranger's house with no more reason than if they were burglars. Nikolai took her hand. "The ancestors haven't let us down yet."

The door swung open, and she squeezed his hand hard as a woman entered. It took Jean a moment to recognize Lady Bethany March, Falconer's daughter. She had been part of the shield net from the beginning, and she upheld the family tradition of great power. As controlled as her father, she scarcely blinked at seeing them. "My brother told me how he found you on a street, but thumping into my house definitely trumps that. Welcome, travelers!"

"The ancestors are developing ever better aim, I think," Jean said. "What year is this? Clothing has changed considerably."

"We are in 1807, sixteen years after your previous visit." A mature woman in her fifties, Bethany looked well in one of the slim, graceful new gowns. "Wilberforce has introduced antislave trade bills faithfully over the years. One even passed, only to fail in the House of Lords. But conditions have changed, and this time there's a good chance of passage." She looked hopeful. "Perhaps you are here to tip the balance for victory."

"Lord Buckland thought that in 1791. Instead, we seemed to have arrived there to limit the damage," Nikolai said wryly. "How have conditions changed?"

"Come to my sitting room for tea while I explain."

She ushered them through the length of the house to a handsome set of rooms that looked into the back garden. After ringing for tea, she moved to a side door and opened it to say, "Mary, some old friends have arrived. Will you join us?"

A tall, dark-skinned woman entered. Nikolai exclaimed, "Mary Andrews! How good to see you again." She smiled. "It's Mary Owens now. I'm Lady Beth's secretary."

"And I'll wager you create much mischief between you." Curious, Jean added, "Owens is a Guardian name, though not exclusively, of course."

Mary nodded. "My husband is a Guardian. Our children have some interesting skills among them!"

"Much of Mary's work involves abolition," Bethany

said. "My husband is a government minister, so the house has no shortage of politics. Come, sit down, and Mary and I will educate you on what has happened since your last visit."

After tea and cakes arrived, Bethany and Mary gave a swift summary of how the situation had changed. "When the French Revolution turned into the Reign of Terror in 1793, Britain declared war on France. We've been fighting ever since, except one brief period," Bethany explained. "Because of the war and the general fear of anything that might be considered radical, the government did its best to suppress all groups calling for reform, which hurt the antislavery societies. The movement fell into near paralysis."

"There was also a great revolt by slaves and mulattos in the French colony of St. Domingue." Mary picked up the thread. "Both the French and the British fought to suppress the rebellion, but they failed. The colony has become the free black nation of Haiti." She made no attempt to keep the pride from her voice. "Not only did it prove how well Africans can fight, but since the island is not under French control, British planters in the Indies can no longer say they must keep their slaves in order to compete with the French. Also, British soldiers who fought the black rebels do not want to fight them again to support slavery, which many common soldiers despise."

"A successful slave revolt would make all the planters in the Indies anxious," Nikolai said thoughtfully. "If slaves can be successful on one island, they can be successful on others. So perhaps it is better if they are not slaves."

Bethany refreshed the tea in the cups. "The French have vacillated—so very French! In a burst of idealism, they declared all slaves free. In 1794, I think. But then one of their generals, Napoleon Bonaparte, declared himself to be an emperor and France is no longer so free and idealistic. One of the effects of that is that the French are now trying to restore slavery."

"They've opened a Pandora's box." Jean took two more cakes. Time travel always made her hungry. "Men who have been freed will not willingly accept chains again."

"So the French have found." Bethany smiled mischievously. "A delightful aspect of this is that now Britons can prove themselves more virtuous than the French simply by opposing slavery. It has been a great boon to our cause."

Jean and Nikolai laughed. "Make a man feel superior for agreeing with you and the battle is half won," she said. "So all of these developments are making abolition of the slave trade more likely?"

"All this, plus there was one other master stroke," Mary said.

"One of the staunchest abolitionists is a very clever marine lawyer named James Stephen," Bethany continued. "He lived in the Indies for some years and truly loathes slavery. He wrote a book explaining how even though the British Navy has blockaded France, the French have maintained a most profitable trade by using the ships of neutral nations such as America. If our navy captured such ships, it would impede the French and be very profitable for the naval vessels making such captures. Stephen persuaded Wilberforce to introduce a bill granting permission to capture any neutral ships aiding France. It sounded very patriotic and passed without much notice." Mary offered the plate of cakes around again. Both Jean and Nikolai accepted more. Jean was glad to know she wasn't the only one who was ravenous. "What most people didn't realize," Mary explained, "is that many of those so-called neutral ships are really British. The only thing American is the flag. So Mr. Stephen's law has ended up hindering the *British* slave trade!"

"Is that not delicious?" Bethany said. "Even though abolition groups were suppressed during the nineties, it turned out that people's feelings hadn't changed. The movement has come back and is stronger than ever. In the last parliamentary election, more abolitionist MPs were elected to office. Wilberforce's bill to abolish slavery is being debated even as we speak, and soon there will be a vote."

Nikolai closed his eyes. "The pro- and antislavery spirits are locked in a mortal embrace, aren't they? With so many people passionately caring on both sides, there is a huge amount of energy involved."

"The shield net is stronger now than when you were here before, but it will need all of its strength to keep the Demon at bay during the voting," Mary said seriously. "If left to their own consciences, a majority of MPs would vote for the bill, I think. We must make sure that nothing happens to poison their minds and change their votes."

"Which is where we come in." Jean set down her empty teacup, feeling very calm. "If the bill passes in the Commons, will it have a chance of passing in the House of Lords and being signed by the king?"

"There is reason to believe that the movement has become so strong that they will agree." Bethany bit her lip. "I keep telling myself that because I don't want to believe otherwise. We shall find out soon enough, I think. If you're ready, we can go to Westminster now."

"Could we refresh ourselves first?" Jean asked. "Sorry, I should have thought of that," Bethany said apologetically. "You can use the guest room where you arrived."

"The accuracy of the ancestors is truly amazing." Nikolai stood. "Is the voting likely to take place today? The spirit energies feel very, very intense."

Bethany nodded. "It should be in the next few hours. I thought to take you to the same box where you watched before. Will that do?"

"It will." Jean also rose. "Let us hope we need do nothing more than watch."

NIKOLAI FOUND it a little eerie to return to the site of their last encounter with Parliament. The private box was the same, if a little shabbier. The galleries were just as full, though clothing fashions had changed. Many of the faces were the same, though worn by almost twenty more years of living. Even the background energies were the same, though they were now perilously intense.

After he settled down with Jean, Bethany, and Mary, he tuned in to the dueling entities. The shield net was balancing the Demon, but it was difficult. The proslavery energy was tense and skittish, as if dimly aware that its existence was threatened. He tuned in more and more finely, ignoring the debate below, until he found what he was looking for. He caught his breath.

Acutely aware of him, Jean said, "What did you find?"

"Kondo has traveled into a parallel world and is lashing up the dark energy like a man whipping a team of horses." Even as he monitored Kondo, he felt the Demon grow. "Damnation! He is drawing dark energies from other parts of the world—Africa, Asia, the West Indies. Anywhere there is slave energy and intense misery."

Jean frowned. "Can he use that energy to flood Parliament and poison people's minds against abolition?" Nikolai analyzed what he was sensing. "I think that's what he intends. He may have enough power to physically harm some of the most passionate abolitionists, as he did with Wilberforce."

Jean's face whitened. "The shield net won't be able to hold him off?"

"He is drawing from a much larger population. Even if you could connect with the energy of every abolitionist in Europe, I don't think it would be as strong."

"Maybe not, but I will certainly try," she said grimly. Nikolai thought back to his initiation and the many parallel worlds he had visited. Now he saw that his travels had all been preparation for this. "I think I can reach him on that other world and perhaps stop him there before he can release his destruction."

"That sounds dangerous."

"Very likely. But this is the climax of our mission, Jean." He caught her gaze. "We both pledged our lives if necessary. Up till now, there has been little danger to us. Tonight we face the ultimate challenge."

She nodded, grief in her eyes, but she made no effort to dissuade him. "I shall make the shield as strong as I can. Take whatever protective energy you need. I swear there will be enough." Bethany and Mary, who were listening, nodded grave agreement.

"Then, I shall begin, and pray I reach him in time." Nikolai moved his chair back so he could rest his head against the wall. He relaxed his body while focusing his mind to a narrow blade. Then he followed the track of the dark energy.

He spun through a kaleidoscope of sensations—light and dark, form and chaos, cacophony and bone-chilling silence, searing flames and paralyzing cold. They were different worlds that must be crossed to reach the hell where Kondo's spirit was working.

Nikolai found his enemy in the dark night on an endless red plain. The air was full of groans and cries of agony, as if all the universe's tormented souls resided here. As soon as he halted, his naked body began to fracture into grains of dust. Gasping, he collected himself as tightly as possible, struggling to stay whole.

He realized that Jean had accompanied him as a gossamer, unbreakable thread of light. Through her, he was able to gather the glittering shield net around himself. Its power held mind and body together.

Prepared, he turned slowly, scanning until he saw a dark funnel in the middle distance. It was Kondo in the form of a tornado as he prepared to channel all the dark energies of slavery to that crowded chamber in Westminster.

Nikolai wished himself closer, and in the blink of an eye he was beside Kondo. The African priest spun into his human form and glared at Nikolai with eyes that glowed red. "You should not have followed me, fool, for in this world you are vulnerable."

"As are you." Nikolai envisioned a great silver sword. It formed itself from the diamond-bright shield and fitted itself perfectly to his hand. A river of light poured through him and into the blade.

He slashed at the dark energy, aiming not at Kondo, but at the swirling mass of pain that the priest had collected. His blow divided the mass into two parts. There was a great shriek from Kondo and the howling multitudes, but an instant later the cries of pain diminished.

He was on the right track—dividing the energy reduced its power. He managed one more blow before Kondo retaliated with a mass of black, flaming material like burning tar. The flames spread over Nikolai's body, scorching his skin and etching away at the shield net. He cried out. The pain was indescribable.

Once more Jean poured power into him, a sweet silver stream that neutralized the fire. He felt her and the original wardens of the shield net, and they drew from a vast horde of people who believed that slavery was wrong. Not only English, but Europeans and Americans and others in lands for which he had no name. With amazement, he realized that she was drawing from people in the future, a miracle that must have been possible because he and Kondo were in a place without time.

No longer devastated by pain, he attacked the Demon once more. He wasn't restricted to the surface of the plain—using pure thought, he was able to reach higher and higher into the dark energy. He was unable to eliminate it, but splintering the power reduced its effectiveness. Chunks of dark, pulsating evil collapsed across the plain.

All the while, Kondo clawed and cursed and snarled at him, but the shield was too strong—the priest could do no damage. Though every one of the priest's blows yanked at Jean, straining her to near breaking point, she never faltered. She was channeling half the light of the world into Nikolai's hands and sword.

After a timeless eternity, he neutralized the last molten hell of Demon energy. He turned to face Kondo, at the same time allowing himself to drift to the surface of the plain. The shrieks of agony had diminished to a bare murmur in the background.

Kondo was barely recognizable as human. His form was almost demonic, yet there was something tragic and human about him. Remembering that Kondo had also been enslaved and that captivity had warped the priest's whole life, Nikolai said with compassion, "You have pledged yourself to evil, Kondo. Turn away from that and live your life as a free and honorable man."

"I am free," Kondo hissed. "Trent gave me papers."

Nikolai's mouth twisted. "Do you think they would have protected you against a gang that wanted to sell you back to the Indies as a slave? A free African cannot safely walk the streets without a dozen friends at his back. You are not truly free as long as the law says that men can be held as slaves. The papers Trent gave you are worth nothing."

"You lie!" Kondo's fury increased. "I am free and as good a man as he!"

"As good or as bad," Nikolai agreed. He lowered his sword, feeling pity. "But he could sell you back into slavery or beat you bloody and no one would try to stop him. Except perhaps Granville Sharp, who fought to save black men simply because it was right. Can Trent say the same? Your captain used you as a weapon against his own sailors. He had children murdered because their crying annoyed him. Would he have allowed you freedom if it wasn't to his advantage? You are still a slave despite your precious papers, for you serve your master's wickedness."

"Captain Trent is my friend!" Kondo howled with anguish. But in his face was the stark knowledge that Nikolai spoke the truth: Trent was evil, and he would have betrayed Kondo in an instant if there was benefit to him.

"Evil is a poor friend." Weary beyond measure,

Nikolai allowed the sword to vanish. Then he reached across time and space to touch Jean so he could follow her silver strength home.

The last thing he saw was Kondo's despairing rage as he howled his fury into the black sky. May God have mercy on the man's wounded, twisted soul.

JEAN SHADOWED NIKOLAI, shielding him with one part of her power while searching for more support with the other. Bethany and Mary were solidly with her; as were the other experienced wardens.

To her shock, she found that she was also able to reach beyond previous borders to people in times and places strange to her. Even Adia was there, contributing strength from fifty years in the past. The strain of channeling came near to ripping Jean's mind apart, but she was able to send Nikolai the support he needed as he shattered the power of the Slave Demon.

She'd moved her chair next to Nikolai's, needing to hold his hand as he traveled to unimaginably far places. Beyond her own strain, she was dimly aware of the debate taking place below. The arguments were similar to what she'd heard before, but the balance had shifted. More and more people were coming over as the Demon faded.

Mary snorted. "That hypocrite was pro-slavery for years! Now that he sees which way the tide is running, he is supporting abolition."

"A hypocrite to be sure," Bethany said pragmatically, "but for now, he's *our* hypocrite, and that's what counts."

A new speaker's voice filled the chamber, and this time it was familiar. Jean opened her eyes and looked down to see a raging, red-faced Captain Trent declaiming on how slavery was the foundation of Britain's wealth, and anyone who disagreed was a wicked traitor, by God! His voice was frenzied, as if by sheer fury he could swing votes to his side.

Jean was turning her attention back to Nikolai when sudden shouts filled the chamber. Startled, she looked over the railing to see that Trent had collapsed. Fellow MPs clustered around him. One was Lord Buckland, who checked for a pulse in Trent's chest and throat. He shook his head and stood. In a compassionate voice that filled the chamber, he said, "The honorable member from Liverpool has passed on."

Another clear voice—surely not Wilberforce?—said, "God has struck him dead for his wicked beliefs!"

There was a shaken intake of breath from the chamber. "Oh, well done!" Bethany said softly.

A gruff voice said, "Perhaps we should adjourn this session."

"The time for delay is over," Buckland replied in a steely tone. "We have all spoken our beliefs. Perhaps if there had been fewer delays, the honorable member from Liverpool would yet draw breath. Put the bill to the vote *now,* I say!"

A murmur of agreement followed. There was a brief pause while Trent's body was moved from the chamber.

Jean's attention returned to Nikolai when his hand tightened on hers. She spun in her chair, shocked to see that his dark hair had grayed at the temples. "Nikolai?"

He opened his eyes wearily. "I don't want to return to that world, ever."

"No need. I think you have carried the day. The voting is about to begin." As they moved closer to the railing, she said, "Captain Trent died on the floor a few minutes ago in the middle of a pro-slavery speech."

Nikolai was silent for a long moment. "At the end, I challenged Kondo about Trent, telling him that his former master would willingly sell him back into slavery if he had a good reason. I think I must have touched on a secret fear. Perhaps Kondo lashed out at Trent, and that caused the failure of the man's heart. Certainly the energy he was building could have stopped abolitionist hearts if he had used it as he intended."

Though John Donne had said that each life lost diminished everyone, Jean couldn't work up too much regret for Trent. "What happened to Kondo?"

"I don't know. He was devastated by his defeat and my challenge to his fears. I don't know if he is alive or dead." Nikolai looked abstracted for a few moments. "I just don't know. But he is no longer a danger."

A mighty roar rose in the chamber below. Bethany and Mary rose and hugged each other, weeping. "The bill has passed," Mary said brokenly.

"And by a huge margin as men moved to the winning side," Bethany exclaimed. "The people of Britain spoke, and Parliament has listened!"

Jean's gaze met Nikolai's. Their long journey had ended. He leaned across the space separating them and kissed her. "We did it, little witch," he whispered. "We, and countless others."

She wrapped her arms around him, shaking with reaction. They had won.

Now what?

CHAPTER THIRTY-EIGHT

For the next few weeks, Jean mentally held her breath. She was shocked when the rock-ribbed conservatives of the House of Lords passed the abolition bill. Conservative they still were, but the times and some minds had changed.

Finally, amazingly, King George signed the bill into law. "It is done!" she said jubilantly when Lord Buckland's note reached them in the inn where they were staying. "I feared that the king would never sign. Not when his son Clarence has been one of slavery's most enthusiastic advocates."

Nikolai grinned from his chair on the other side of the fire. He looked most distinguished with silvered temples. "I said we needn't worry. There are men who will go to their graves believing slavery is right and proper, and probably that includes the royal family, but the evil spirit created by their thinking has broken into splinters. No longer can a decent Englishman support slavery with a clear conscience. For all his weaknesses, your King George is a decent man who tries to do the right thing."

"Now that the slave trade will end on the first of May, the next step is emancipation of those still held in bondage."

Nikolai's expression sobered. "That will come. Not as soon as we might hope, but it will come. Like a genie that has been released from its bottle, freedom will not be crushed again. Not only will slaves become free, but poor men and women in this country will demand justice and better treatment for themselves and their children. The world as we know it has irrevocably changed, and for the better."

She thought about his words. The society she had grown up in was far more rigid than this of year 1807. Not so much at her home in Scotland, where a crofter knew himself the equal of his laird, but certainly in England. The classes of society were locked in their places. Since she had occupied a position near the top and life had been comfortable, she hadn't really questioned her society, but that was no longer possible. "You like this brave new world, don't you?"

"I do. Lady Bethany tells me that there is growing support for electoral reform so that more men will have the vote."

Jean's eyes gleamed. "What about women getting the vote?"

He laughed. "You are even more radical than I, my little witch. I think that will also come in time."

"Do you want to stay here?"

He hesitated. "Though I like this year, our original plan was to complete our mission if possible, then return home."

"I don't know if we can," she said bleakly. "I asked Mary Owens if any London elders can do time magic. She said that only one man had the special talent, and he died not long after the bespelled bracelets were made." Jean fingered the small, remaining beads of the bracelet. "No one else in London's African community has the ability, and it doesn't seem to be a talent possessed by Guardians."

Nikolai became very still. "No one?"

"So Mary says." Jean sighed. "This is indeed an interesting time, full of new ideas. But my family and friends are over fifty years in the past. I feel I must at least try to return to them. I will understand if you don't wish to make the attempt."

He leaned forward and clasped her hands. "I wondered if the end of our mission would be the end of our closeness, yet we are now closer than ever. You are my family, Jean, and where you go, I will go."

She caught her breath. "You will?" She had hardly allowed herself to hope he would want to return. "If we try and fail and stay here, I promise that I won't complain. But I must try."

"I've been thinking." She pulled the bracelet from her wrist. "Though all the large beads have been consumed, the small beads absorbed some of the same energy. If we do the ritual and think very hard about where we want to go, perhaps we will return to Santola. But it could be dangerous to try."

He took the bracelet and studied it, frowning. "The time magic is weak, but it might work if I can open a portal to another world where the magic is stronger. As you say, it would be dangerous, but there is some chance of success."

"Then you'll come with me?" she asked, still not quite believing.

"On one condition."

She watched him a little warily. "And that is...?" He lifted her left hand and kissed the gold band on her third finger. "We make this wedding ring real. We are already so closely bound that it almost seems unnecessary. Almost, but not quite." He smiled at her. "Marry me, Jean Macrae, and I will have my revenge on your father, who surely would have wished you to wed a good Guardian."

Laughing, she went into his arms. "I always knew I wouldn't marry a Guardian, but I lacked the imagination to guess that I would marry a pirate."

THEY MARRIED QUIETLY in the ballroom of Falconer House in front of an audience of British Guardians, African priests, and those who were both. Petite and serene, Meg was Jean's matron of honor, and Buckland stood up with Nikolai.

Over the wedding breakfast, Jean said to Simon, "You're going to live forever, aren't you?"

He laughed. "No, but the unicorn magic I acquired all those years ago has kept Meg and me healthy for more years than most people have." His gaze went unerringly to his wife. "When we leave, it will be together, and not so very long in the future. But first we will help you on your way home."

Jean and Nikolai both drank lightly—one didn't walk between worlds with wits scrambled. After a long round of hugs and good-byes, it was time for the ritual.

She slung the travel bag she'd carried for half a century over her left shoulder and clasped her new husband's hands. The mass of small remaining beads were trapped between their palms. "We'll have to have another ceremony in the past, since the date 1807 on our wedding lines will look rather odd."

He laughed, his dark eyes warm. "I'll marry you in any year, Jean Macrae. Now let us venture into the abyss once more."

Everyone present joined the circle. Jean centered herself and closed her eyes, feeling the energies swirling around them. Surely the wardens of the shield net would lend them enough power to send them home. The wardens, and the ancestors.

The ritual began, and the world dissolved around her. The feeling was both like and unlike other time passages. No longer able to see Nikolai, she clung to his hands as the only anchor in a world of mists. The small beads burned away, scorching her palm.

"Steady," he said hoarsely, his hands gripping with numbing force. "I see a path that may take us home." On other trips through time, she had not really been aware of anything but the tumult of the vortex. Now she recognized that they were traveling through a world she didn't know. The journey went on and on, carrying them through strange and painful places. Nikolai's clasp never faltered. After an endless time, light became visible through the mists. Her pulse—did she have a pulse here?—began to quicken. "Is that Santola?"

"I hope so," he said grimly. "This is the only gateway that I've seen, so I think we must take it."

With a last devastating wrench, they were swept through the portal and onto a carpeted floor. The world spun dizzily and Jean almost fell. Something huge and dark like a bat swooped down at her, and she gave a suffocated cry as she ducked away.

But Nikolai was laughing. "Isabelle!" The great blue macaw settled on his shoulder and crowed ecstatically as she rubbed her fierce beak on Nikolai's face.

Jean shook her head to clear it. Isabelle? And this looked like the office in Nikolai's villa. Merciful heaven, they had done it!

"Welcome home, travelers," a woman's rich voice said.

Jean spun around and saw Adia watching them. "Adia!" She threw herself into the other woman's arms, laughing and crying. "Our mission was successful! The slave trade was abolished in 1807, and full emancipation will soon follow."

"What wonderful news!" Radiant with happiness,

Adia settled down in her chair. "Tell me everything." They did, interrupting each other as they talked about the different eras they had seen and how the abolition movement had grown from a wild idea to an irresistible force.

Adia listened intently, one hand stroking the great orange cat that sprawled on her lap. Jean ended by saying, "And a book that you wrote about your life became a bestseller. But it won't be published for another thirty-five years." She grinned. "I didn't realize that you were an African princess."

"I'm not, but Louise said that it would sell better." Adia looked down at the cat. Voice taut, she asked, "Are there any time magic beads left?"

Jean's excitement stilled as she realized what that meant for Adia. Softly she said, "No. I'm sorry. All the large beads had been used on our mission, and we needed all of the small ones to make our way back here."

After a long silence, Adia said, "Santola is a good place. I have made friends here." She looked up, her face a mask of control. "I shall make myself useful."

Her courage was heartbreaking. Nikolai said, "Perhaps we can find an African priest who works time magic in this era."

"I will have died of old age by then," Adia said drily. "The talent is very rare."

"Perhaps my African friend in Marseilles, Moses, will know how to find a priest who can work time magic," Jean suggested. "A shaman came from Africa to France just to teach him. So Moses may be able to find someone."

"You have more optimism than I." Adia shrugged. "If there is one thing I have learned, it's that one must make the best of what life brings."

Adia had learned her wisdom in a hard school. Jean wished there were more grounds for hope. Changing the subject, she asked, "How long were we gone?"

"About eight months. It's 1754 now."

Nikolai's brow furrowed as he calculated. "That's about the length of time we spent traveling."

"So we moved forward as much in time as if we'd stayed here?" Jean asked. "That makes a certain amount of sense."

Adia set the cat on the floor and got to her feet. With a smile that looked genuine, she said, "I must announce that you have returned, so we can celebrate your success!"

EVERYONE ON SANTOLA poured into the village to welcome Nikolai home. Down by the harbor, wood was stacked for a bonfire and the island women began preparing a sumptuous feast. Jean knew she would be welcomed lovingly when she returned to Britain, but that would be restrained compared to this exuberant gathering.

She didn't have a chance to talk to Nikolai privately until the feasting had ended and dancing had begun. The sun was nearing the horizon when she sat next to him on a crude bench and leaned back against the wall. Drumming filled the sky and made her vibrate with happiness. As she watched Adia dance with Tano, she looked up at Nikolai and said dreamily, "This island is amazingly beautiful. A good place to live."

He wrapped an arm around her shoulders and gave her a very private smile. "I hear tell that Scotland is beautiful, too. I thought we might divide our time between here and Britain. And the high seas, of course." She stared at him, not sure she'd heard right. "I was prepared to be like Ruth and go whither thou goest, which would be Santola and the sea. You really won't mind having a home in Britain?"

He pulled her closer, resting his cheek against her hair. "You love your family and friends, and it would be wicked of me to deprive you of them. And them of you." He hesitated. "And if we should have children, they deserve to know their family."

She hugged him, blinking back tears as she thought of how alone Nikolai had been for much of his life. "My family is now yours, my dear pirate. Even you and my brother will like each other once the two of you are done tossing your horns and pawing the turf like bulls."

He laughed. "Is that what you think we'll do?"

"Without question," she said promptly. "But Gwynne and I won't allow you to actually bare steel."

"I believe that I am turning into a domesticated husband," he remarked. "The victory is yours, my love."

"Victory is mutual in a good marriage, and I will

settle for nothing less." She slid her arm around his waist, wondering how long they must wait before they could retire to their quarters. Slanting a glance up at him, she said, "You used the words 'my love'?"

He looked uncharacteristically awkward. "It is easier to be indirect than to come out and say 'I love you.' Such a very large thing to reveal. Yet... true. You are my heart, my dearest witch."

She swallowed hard. "I couldn't have said this before we became lovers because I was so afraid that your strength would overwhelm me, yet now I know that we are both better and stronger together than apart. I love you, Nikolai. I think I have through many lifetimes with you, with more to come."

"Many lifetimes together? What a very wonderful idea." He bent and kissed her.

She responded with every fiber of her being, knowing this moment was their true marriage, more than the ceremony they'd had in 1807, more than the ceremony they would have again soon.

He gave a sudden chuckle. "In all these lives, will we be antagonists before we become lovers?"

"No doubt," she murmured. "I'm trying to remember when I fell in love with you this time."

"When I kidnapped you, of course." His dark eyes danced as he kissed her again. She didn't think she had ever been so happy in her life. Tonight they would make love, and perhaps she would tell her body that it was time for a child...

Reluctantly he ended the kiss, though he kept her

within the circle of his arm. "We have much work to do in this era, so we shall never grow bored. The first foundations of abolition are being laid now, and we can contribute to that. For example, we must arrange for Adia's story to be published at the right time, when antiabolition sentiment is rising."

She nodded. "I should also write a message to our friends in 1807 to let them know that we made it back safely. A firm of solicitors can hold it until then."

He grinned. "You may be alive yourself in 1807. We built such careful partitions between our current selves and the future that it's impossible to say. Perhaps we were both there in London and longing to come to the wedding, but we had to stay away to keep from adding to the confusion about our time-tossed lives."

She groaned. "I will never understand the repercussions of travel through time!"

"There is no need to understand. What matters is that we managed to do what was necessary, and even to return home safely."

"Perhaps it is part of our mission to come back because of work that we will do in normal time," she said mischievously.

It was Nikolai's turn to groan. "You're right, only the ancestors understand time travel." He drew his brows together. "I didn't realize until now, but I felt the ancestors' presence throughout our travels. Especially my grandmother. Now that feeling is gone. The ancestors have left us."

She looked inside herself, and realized that a thread

of wild magic so gossamer she hadn't realized it was there was now gone. "I'll be glad for the privacy. But... I shall also miss them. It was a great privilege to become a thread in their tapestry of fate."

She felt rather than saw Nikolai's nod. Then he spoke, his voice different. "There's a strange ship coming into the harbor." He set her to one side and stood, every line of his body taut. "Not one of ours. That has never happened before."

She scrambled to her feet, as wary as he. "I thought it was impossible for regular ships to find their way here."

"Indeed it is. So who is on that ship?" Nikolai headed down to the harbor with long strides, Jean moving swiftly to keep up.

There was a flurry of activity as mothers took their children home and men armed themselves. The two-masted vessel flew a white flag that suggested peaceful intentions, but one could never be sure. The crowd watched in silence as the ship drifted to a halt by the longest pier.

As mooring ropes were cast over the side, Jean studied the vessel, thinking there was something familiar about the people she saw on deck. Surely... She broke and ran out onto the pier. "Moses! Jemmy! Breeda!"

Moses laughed and leaped down onto the pier, as dapper as when he was in his office in Marseilles. Gripping her shoulders and studying her with mage vision, he said, "You led us a merry dance, my girl. We used every form of magic we could think of to locate you, and I was beginning to think we never would. For the longest time, it was like you had vanished into thin air. Then suddenly, we knew where to find you. What happened? You seem to be flourishing."

"I am, and I did vanish into thin air. But now I'm back and done with adventures. At least for a while." A moment later Jemmy and Breeda were within hugging distance. Incandescent with happiness, Jean asked, "Where is Lily? Is she ill?"

"Not at all," Moses said, his white teeth flashing in the darkness. "But she didn't want to leave the baby. If you hadn't disappeared, you would be godmother to our son. Your maid Annie refused to leave Marseilles as long as you were missing. She would be here, too, but she married a Frenchman and is with child and couldn't face a sea voyage."

Nikolai had joined them, so Jean said, "I want you all to meet my husband, but first—Moses, you said that your teacher, Sekou, told you about African time magic. Do you have any of that particular talent?"

Startled, he said, "A little, and Sekou was most insistent that I learn to use it to the best of my ability even though I will never be one of the great time shamans. Why do you ask?"

"Because that ability is needed to send a friend home. There are several mages here on the island, but none of us has the time magic gift. Do you think you could perform a time ritual if we supplied you with enough raw magic?" Moses sucked in his breath. "I... I don't know. Perhaps. I can't guarantee it, since I've never led the ritual myself." After a long pause, he said, "I wonder if

Sekou was so insistent because he knew that I would need time magic someday?"

"The training you received might have been part of a great plan by the ancestors, because even without guarantees, you're Adia's best hope." Jean took his arm and led him to Adia. "We must talk."

IT WAS hard to wait for even three days, but Adia forced herself to do that. She had made friends on Santola, and when she left, it would be for good. Leaving Louise and her children was wrenching—Louise was like the sister Adia had left behind in Africa, and her children were like nieces and nephews.

Saying good-bye to Tano was hard in a different way.

When she called on him to say farewell, he inclined his head and wished her joy with sad, quiet eyes.

As she walked away, she knew that he would find another wife, but he would not forget Adia. As she would not forget him. A heart had room for many kinds of love.

Jean Macrae promised to take care of Bruiser. The fickle feline was already doting on the Scotswoman.

Guided by Moses, Adia and the other African priests had constructed a bead that contained threads from the garment she had worn on her journey through time. They had invested it with as much time magic as Moses could summon.

Along with the bead, Adia held the pathfinder stone that she and the wisewoman had created so many years and miles ago in the Carolinas. She had carried it ever since. Some of the patterns in blood had worn off, but no matter. The stone's energy was a connection between Daniel and her.

When the ritual was performed, every man, woman, and child on the island who had power participated. As Moses invoked the four winds, Adia called fire and prayed with every spark of power she possessed that the ritual would work. The familiar vortex formed, and Santola dissolved around her. With her last breath, Adia called her thanks to all who were helping to send her home.

Her second journey through time seemed endless. Awareness splintered into pain and terror as she fell endlessly, suffocating with the fear that she would be trapped forever in chaos. The time-magicked bead burned away. The pathfinder stone merely burned. She clutched it with all her strength, praying that if anything could lead her through other worlds to her true love, it was this stone.

Then the pieces of her soul reassembled, and she found herself lying on a hard surface, dizzy and disoriented. The darkness was absolute. She flexed her hands, and the pathfinder stone fell from her palm, its heat extinguished. Abruptly her mind cleared, and she realized with rushing joy that she was in the bedroom of her own small house.

As her eyes adjusted, she saw Daniel's long form sprawled on the bed. A warm, indulgent voice sounded in her mind. *Did you think we would abandon you before the end of your journey, child?*

Adia sensed that her grandmother would never speak to her so clearly again, and that was a bittersweet note in the heart of her happiness. Perhaps it made her joy even more profound. Clumsy with excitement, she stood and quietly undressed. Then she slipped into the bed beside Daniel wearing only her skin.

Her fatigue vanished in the desire to hold her husband flesh to flesh. She wrapped her arms around him, intoxicated by his dearly remembered scent and feel. Her hands slid around his ribs to the roughness of the scars inflicted after his first attempt to escape slavery. Her beloved, her husband, her Daniel. She breathed softly in his ear, whispering his name before tasting the salt of his skin.

His arms enfolded her sleepily as he murmured, "Dream woman, you are so like Adia..." His large hand slid down her naked back to cup her buttocks.

Desire scorched through her. "Not a dream." She nipped his ear, wanting to draw his blood and soul into herself.

He came awake with lightning speed. *"Adia!* Dear God, it's really you!"

"It is, indeed." She laughed with jubilation, glorying in his instant response to her presence. As she called a handful of fire to illuminate his strong, familiar face, she exclaimed, "And, oh, my beloved, do I have tales to tell!"

AUTHOR'S NOTE

THERE IS a lot about abolition that I was never taught in school. One of the biggest surprises was how the British offered freedom to American slaves during the Revolution. And how, much to their credit, they evacuated as many former slaves as possible to spare them from the slave catchers after the war ended.

Abolition contains amazing stories. Though I've taken some liberties, many of the incidents involving historical characters are real. Thomas Clarkson did discover his life's work while pondering beside the road as he traveled from Cambridge to London after winning the prestigious Latin essay prize, though he didn't need two passersby to persuade him.

Clarkson was also attacked by slave ship sailors on a pier in Liverpool during a gale, but it was his own strength and quickness that enabled him to fight his way free. In an era when few people could swim, he might easily have been drowned by the sailors, which would have made the history of the abolition movement very different.

Accounts were published by former slaves such as Olaudah Equiano (who had the slave name of Gustavus Vasa), and these helped Englishmen understand the nature of slavery. The story of an individual is always more powerful than abstract arguments.

As Clarkson was a brilliant and dedicated organizer, William Wilberforce was the much loved and respected politician who worked tirelessly to pass antislavery legislation, as well as other vital reforms. He was indeed struck down by illness just before the 1788 session of Parliament, where he had planned to introduce an anti-slave trade bill. Though he was sent to Bath to recover, I invented his collapse during a reception for supporters of abolition. He and his Evangelical friends, known as the Saints or the Clapham sect, spearheaded many wide-ranging social reforms.

Elizabeth Heyrick was a passionate, radical abolitionist whose belief that emancipation should take place *now* had a great effect on the mainstream abolitionist movement, especially in the 1820s. Women were generally more radical than men when it came to abolition, and all-female abolition groups were very influential.

It was pure invention on my part to place Elizabeth Heyrick in the House of Commons during the 1791 vote on Wilberforce's bill to end the slave trade, but the national sugar boycott did spring to life after the bill lost. Hundreds of thousands of people throughout Britain stopped buying sugar, though the word "boycott" didn't even come into the language until 1880.

Many of the tools of the modern social movement were first used by the abolitionists: protest groups, direct-mail advertising, logos and medallions, and boycotts. A small number of people set out to change the world, and succeeded.

However, while many abolitionists believed that banning the trade would swiftly bring about the end of chattel slavery by cutting off the supply of slaves, they were wrong. West Indies slaveholders might have treated slaves a little better because replacements were harder to come by, but slave traders still risked the British naval blockades and slaves still suffered and died. More than twenty-five years passed before Parliament passed an emancipation bill in 1833.

Emancipation became possible after the first of the nineteenth-century British political reform bills was passed in 1832, greatly increasing the number of men who could vote. There was still a very long way to go before there would be universal suffrage, but this first reform bill changed the makeup of Parliament enough to pass the emancipation act.

The conservative political establishment hated giving up power—doesn't everyone?—but there was increasing unrest in the general population, and political reform was preferable to revolution. Plus, bloody slave rebellions in the West Indies made it clear that slaves were willing to fight and die for their freedom—and that they fought very, very well.

The slave lobby, seeing that defeat was inevitable, campaigned successfully to get compensation for their "loss of property." No money was voted to compensate the slaves.

For those who wish to learn more about this amazing piece of history, I recommend Adam Hochschild's wonderful *Bury the Chains.* A nominee for the National Book Award in nonfiction, *Bury the Chains* has the clarity and page-turning excitement of a novel as he describes the people and politics who worked together to end one of mankind's greatest cruelties.

Simon Schama's *Rough Crossings: Britain, the Slaves, and the American Revolution* covers somewhat similar material to Hochschild's book, but from a more American perspective.

Other books of possible interest: *Epic Journeys of Freedom* by Cassandra Pybus tells the stories of slaves who escaped to freedom all over the world after the American Revolution. *Staying Power* by Peter Fryer is a history of blacks in Britain.

The world is an imperfect place, but through the courage and conviction of many people, it has become a lot better.

Thank you for taking the time to read *A Distant Magic.* I hope you've enjoyed it—and if so, please consider helping other readers find it by leaving a review of the novel at your favorite online bookstore or reader website.

If you enjoyed this series, you may want to try my romantic Young Adult trilogy, The Lackland Abbey

Chronicles, which starts with *Dark Mirror*, in which young British mages reach across time to help each other defeat Napoleon in the 19th century and Hitler in the 20th century.

Finally, if you would like me to let you know when my upcoming books are published, you can join my newsletter at MaryJoPutney.com.

Happy reading!

—Mary Jo Putney

ALSO BY MARY JO PUTNEY

The Bride Trilogy

The Wild Child, #1

The China Bride, #2

The Bartered Bride, #3

The Fallen Angels Series

Thunder & Roses, #1

Dancing on the Wind, #2

Petals in the Storm, #3

Angel Rogue, #4

Shattered Rainbows, #5

River of Fire, #6

One Perfect Rose, #7

The Silk Trilogy

Silk and Shadows, #1

Silk and Secrets, #2

Veils of Silk, #3

Other Historicals

Lady of Fortune

Dearly Beloved

Uncommon Vows

The Rake

The Bargain

The Marriage Spell (paranormal)

Putney Classics (Sweet Regency Romances)

Carousel of Hearts

The Diabolical Baron

The Lackland Abbey Chronicles

(Young Adult fiction, written as M. J. Putney)

Dark Mirror, #1 (includes a bonus Lackland short story)

Dark Passage, #2

Dark Destiny, #3

The Guardian Trilogy

A Kiss of Fate, #1

Stolen Magic, #2

A Distant Magic, #3

The Lost Lords Series

Loving A Lost Lord, #1

Never Less Than A Lady, #2

Nowhere Near Respectable, #3

No Longer A Gentleman, #4

Sometimes A Rogue, #5

Not Quite A Wife, #6

Not Always a Saint, #7

Rogues Redeemed Series (A Spin-Off of the Lost Lords)

Once A Soldier, #1

Once a Rebel, #2

Once A Scoundrel, #3

Once A Spy, #4

Once Dishonored, #5

Once A Laird, #6

The Circle of Friends Trilogy

The Burning Point, #1

The Spiral Path, #2

An Imperfect Process, #3

A Holiday Fling (novella, also published in Christmas Revels)

Shorter Works

Weddings of the Century: A Pair of Novellas

The Best Husband Money Can Buy (novella, also published in Christman Candles)

The Christmas Cuckoo (novella, also published in Christmas Revels)

The Black Beast of Belleterre (novella, also published in Christmas Revels)

Sunshine for Christmas (novella, also published in Christmas

Revels)

The Dragon and the Dark Knight (written as M.J. Putney)

Christmas Collections

Christmas Revels

Christmas Candles

Mischief and Mistletoe (contributor)

The Last Chance Christmas Ball (contributor)

Christmas Roses (contributor)

Seduction on a Snowy Night (contributor)

A Yuletide Kiss (contributor)

ABOUT THE AUTHOR

A *New York Times, Wall Street Journal,* and *USAToday* bestselling author, Mary Jo Putney (aka M.J. Putney) is also a recipient of RWA's Nora Roberts Lifetime Achievement Award. She was born in Upstate New York with a reading addiction, a condition for which there is no known cure. Her entire romance writing career is an accidental byproduct of buying a computer for other purposes.

Her novels are known for psychological depth and intensity and include historical and contemporary romance, fantasy, and young adult fantasy. Winner of numerous writing awards, including two RITAs and two *Romantic Times* Career Achievement awards, she's had a number of her books listed as top romances of the year by *Library Journal* and *Booklist,* the magazine of the American Library Association.

Her favorite reading is great stories, but in a pinch she'll settle for the backs of cereal boxes. She's delighted that e-publishing can now make available books that have been out of print.

CPSIA information can be obtained
at www.ICGtesting.com
Printed in the USA
LVHW111038061022
730091LV00002B/200

9 781948 880534